TARA JENKINSON CIGNARELLA

LILAC SAND

A NOVEL

By Tara Jenkinson Cignarella

Copyright © 2016 by Tara Jenkinson Cignarella

ISBN 978-0-9977311-0-1

Lilac Sand is a work of fiction. Names, characters, places, and incidents either are products of the author's imagination or are used fictitiously. Any resemblance to actual events, locales or persons, living or dead, is entirely coincidental.

Contact@TaraCignarella.com
Instagram: Author_TaraJenkinsonCignarella
Facebook: Tara Jenkinson Cignarella

For my children, may your lives be filled with everything you desire.

Chapter One

Lilacs

April 28, 1995

I WALK THROUGH THE heavy front door of the center hall colonial, and the noise from the party is deafening. "Only Wanna Be with You" is playing on the stereo. I adore this song so I convince myself to try to have fun tonight. Parties do not top my list of exciting ways to spend time, but Brooke begged me, so here I am.

I head into the kitchen where everyone is hanging out. I do not recognize anyone so I grab a bottle of water and take Brooke by the arm, forcing her into the other, less crowded room. We chat with a few people, but I am still restless. I will try to fit in, even if it is only for Brooke's sake.

"Be right back, Morgan," she yells over the music.

No, she will not. She found a boy worthy of her flirtation. After wandering around the house as if in a maze, running into one dull boy after another, I head out into the backyard to be alone. My cheeks feel cold instantly, like a strong wind hit them, but the air is very still, a creepy stillness that makes me sense a change is brewing. I shake the unsettling feeling and let the clean smell of lilacs bring me down to earth.

Only a few people have ventured outside, mostly the smokers. The backyard of this stranger's house is beautiful, large, with a covered pool and hot tub. Japanese flowering trees and several large lilacs line the back lawn near a wooden stockade fence. I am drawn to the trees. Each one stands strong, but they bend enough to form a canopy. They are so overgrown it almost looks like a cave. I walk to the back of the yard and under the large umbrella of branches and flowers. The ground is covered in pink, purple, and maroon petals. I sit against the trunk of a tree and a feeling of tranquility washes over me. I close my eyes and attempt to breathe in and out. This is me. This is what I enjoy. I feel relaxed and start to drift off to sleep.

"May I join you?" A deep melodic voice slightly startles me.

I say, "Yes," too quickly. When I open my eyes I meet two crystal clear blue ones. They are the saddest eyes I have ever seen. He closes them, cutting off the pain. As he sits beside me my breathing becomes erratic. His right hip touches my left. I have never felt anything move as crazy as my own heart is right now. Frederick Rhoades, lead singer of Cross-Rhoades, just sat down next to me. Inside my head I am making high pitched squealing sounds.

CrossRhoades is one of New Jersey's biggest rock bands. They have two albums under their belt, but in the past few months they have become a worldwide phenomenon. Their current song, "Wrong Love," is a chart topper, but the lyrics are blank to me now as I sit here wondering what to do.

I am glad it is dark; the new moon and bright lights from the house cast only a sliver of light toward the lilac trees. Something is wrong. Rick is heavy with sadness, literally the only thought in my head as we sit here. I want to reach out and grab his hand and comfort him, but I am way too nervous. We continue to sit in silence and I listen to the blurred noises from the party.

Calmly he says, "Party too boring for you?" His voice is so deep it grounds me to the dirt I am sitting on.

"Yes."

I cannot judge how much time has passed when I decide I should do something. I use every ounce of courage to bend my legs toward him and move my hip away from his so I can face him. I do not want to move away but I want to see him. He is beautiful. His hair is a chestnut brown and long enough to run my fingers through. The thought dries my mouth. He must have cut it recently. Music videos and magazine pictures show it longer. His jaw is defined. He is a rock star by all accounts. Those stunning eyes also expose his soul. CrossRhoades sells a lot of albums and makes a lot of girls do stupid things. Tonight, even with their sparkling beauty, those eyes are damaged. I face him for several seconds and stare at his striking face, finally finding the courage to ask, "What's wrong?"

He chuckles a little, tilts his chin down, taking his eyes completely away from me, and says, "Oh nothing you would be interested in."

"Try me," I say with the confidence I will myself to have for this conversation.

He lifts his head and stares into my eyes as if he can read my thoughts. I have never felt so drawn to someone. A desire to help and soothe him washes over me. He somehow gives me the power to be brave enough to at least attempt to steal his pain away.

Rick sighs and it seems to release some of his stress and pain; for some reason it makes me calmer too. I lean my head to the left onto the tree. The bark is surprisingly smooth and offers me support. I watch him, first his eyes close slowly, then his full lips part. Eventually, he says, "I guess life has me sad."

I close my eyes and absorb his words. I blindly move my hand forward a few inches and lay it on top of his. Such a simple touch, yet I fear it may alter my life forever. I wish I had some magic words to heal him. I do not know where to start and I clearly do not know what is wrong. How can this gorgeous and talented man be sad? I picture his life as being beyond perfect, but it appears money, talent, and fame do not provide all facets of happiness.

I do not move my hand from his, even though I want desperately to soothe him with my touch. Instead I remain as still as he is, my hand on his, my body not touching him but sensing everything it has to offer. I do not even know how to talk about his sadness, let alone help him. I choose to just sit and be with him so he does not have to be alone.

"Morgan!" Brooke screams from the back door, cracking the silence I was enjoying. I flinch and come out of a daze. Rick's eyes must have magical powers that put me in a time warp. Is it already time to leave?

"I will be right back." I push my palm into the back of his hand and stand up.

I feel disconnected from him, but I leave the lilac tree and walk to Brooke. "My sister is ready to leave, so we have to go."

"I have to use the bathroom first. I will meet you by the car." I lie. She walks away and I run back to Rick.

"My ride is leaving." I kneel facing him with my hands in the dirt.

"Okay." I fear leaving him alone is not the best idea.

"Hey, look at me!" I do not recognize my own voice. He looks up and some of the pain has left his eyes. "Will you be okay?" The pull to reach out to touch his face overwhelms me.

He stares hard at me. I should shake him and beg him for information, but even though I feel out of character tonight, I know I will never stray far from who I am. "Yes."

I believe him, but I am scared for him. I wish I had more time to talk. I spent too much time staring at him instead. I stand up and walk away. I am almost to the house when he shouts, "Thank you, Morgan."

I turn and yell back, "Wish I could stay and help." I walk out to the car as if I am floating on a cloud. It felt exhilarating to sit under a lilac tree with Frederick Rhoades.

* * *

Brooke sits in the front of the car with her sister Kelly. Brooke asks me what I was doing outside the second I climb in. I tell her I was just thinking. She buys it since I have no reason to lie to her. I am not ready to share what happened tonight. I will enjoy this simple pleasure in my own head for a little while at least. I am still in shock. I met one sad but hot rock star tonight. No big deal. Yet it feels like a big deal. Kelly pulls into my driveway. I am thankful no one wanted to talk on the way home. I say good night and head inside.

I cannot bring myself to change or brush my teeth. I throw myself down on top of my covers and stare at the ceiling. I should be tired yet I feel full of restless energy, so I put it to good use by writing two poems in my journal. Eventually I must have fallen asleep. I wake and sunlight fills my room and the peaceful sensation coursing through my veins leaves me truly content. Something about Rick Rhoades makes me feel alive and aware of myself.

My family lives in Madison, New Jersey. My parents both work boring office jobs, and I would call us upper middle class. I have many classmates wealthier than myself, but they might only appear to be. I am not trendy. I do not have the latest fashions or an expensive car. I consider myself to be a fairly simple person. I fit in fine at school yet would not classify myself as part of a group. I run track, but would not call myself an athlete. I love music but I am not in the band or choir. I have taken every art class I can fit into my schedule. I consider myself as uncategorized and that is how I like it.

Brooke is without a doubt my best friend and my only true confidante. She is the only person I share my secrets with. Strangely enough I also get along well with her older sister Kelly. I have wondered at times if Kelly and I were the same age would we be even better friends.

The first two weeks of May speed by. My spirits are high because most of my thoughts are overrun by images of Rick. I only spent an hour with him, yet he has invaded my brain like a plague. I have tons of schoolwork this month and track practice several days a week. Running grants me time to think or not think. I am a decent runner and have even won some races. I am average height for a female, but apparently I have very long legs.

I came home right after school today, glad not to have track. I want to listen to music and read, or maybe do nothing but sleep. I am desperate for a slice of time to myself. I walk into my room as the phone rings. Thankfully my brother answers it.

Ryan came home last night after finishing his sophomore year of college at Rutgers. We look alike, but our personalities are extremely different. Ryan is slightly over six feet and his hair and eyes are slightly darker than mine. Everyone clearly sees we are siblings. His outgoing and friendly natural ways with people are where the similarities stop. Ryan is always out and about and I seek more time to be alone.

I cannot believe how easily I got used to him being away. When he first left I was sad. It took only a short time for me to adjust to having the bathroom and phone all to myself. Ryan is a brain and a jock. He plays football and earns straight A's. At least we have a positive sibling friendship. We are close but we fight too. I enjoy our time together even more now that there is less of it.

Ryan opens his bedroom door and leans into the hallway. "Morgan, you home?"

I peek out my door slowly, trying to hide from the call. "Yes." I love my friends but I need time alone.

"Phone is for you." His voice is so odd I make a face before I answer him.

"Who is it?" I hope I can find a way out of it without seeming too introverted.

"Ahhh...Rick Rhoades?" His eyes are locked on me and bulging out of their sockets.

"Holy shit!" I sprint to the phone in my room.

Chapter Two

Love in the Dark

I RUSH TO THE edge of my bed and take a huge breath. I pick up the receiver and say, "Hello," as my brother hangs up his end. I am grateful I did not have to yell for him to do it.

"Was that your boyfriend?" Rick's sultry voice vibrates like warm jealous honey sliding off a spoon.

"No," I say confidently. I do wonder how in this situation he could sound jealous, and for a girl who talks too much I once again have so little to say. Why didn't I tell him it was my brother?

"Do you know how hard you are to track down, Morgan?" Rick says my name and it's like I have never heard it before.

"No, I don't! I have never tried to find myself," I fire back. A smile forms on my face as he laughs. I hope I broke the ice. "Where are you?" I ask as I glance at the caller I.D. and the number is not from New Jersey.

"L.A., doing some radio spots. We are also trying to start the new album." His words flow out naturally as he tells me all about his day. Finally, my body relaxes and I lie back on my bed. His voice is hypnotizing, the voice of a talented singer. With every word I can envision the brilliance of his blue eyes. In my imagination they sparkle with happiness. A soft moan escapes my mouth when I remember how it felt gazing into them. He talks in detail about what the band is doing and how recording works. I never knew I had an interest in record making, but somehow he has my full attention. This is by far the most interesting conversation I have ever had. His passion for music soars through the phone.

"Hey, how did you get my number by the way?" I ask.

"My cousin asked around for it. The party was at his parents' house, and someone named Grant finally knew a Morgan."

"That makes sense. Grant knows my brother well."

After two hours of talking I feel as if I have known him my whole life. I can honestly say the only other time I felt this was when Brooke moved to New Jersey in the middle of fifth grade. Some people have a chemistry together that can't be fully explained.

I can tell he does not want to hang up, but someone keeps yelling loudly for him to get off the phone. "Rick, I'll let you go now. You have work to do."

"It took me two weeks to hear your voice again." He pauses and I hear his breath hitch so I don't interrupt. "Morgan, I haven't had enough of it yet," he purrs into the phone, leaving my mind content in an out of control spiral.

"Call me later?" I whisper, full of hope.

"It will be late in Jersey by the time we finish out here," he says, almost as breathless as I am.

"I pick you over sleep," I say, feeling a deep connection build rapidly.

"Uh, talk to you later." He hangs up instantly, like ripping a Band-Aid off. The dial tone buzzes in my ear but I can't bring myself to hang up quite yet.

I lie on my queen-size bed, secured by half a dozen white pillows, yet my body is swirling unsecured, out of control. Never has another person had this effect on me, and I don't know quite what it means. Ryan knocks on my door, snapping me from my daydream. "Yeah?" I struggle to say.

Ryan opens my door. He has a look on his face I have never seen as he sits on my bed. He wants to say something but it seems he doesn't know what. When he left for college I had only been dating for a short time, but since then I have loved and lost and now a world famous rock star just called me.

"Was Rick Rhoades really on the phone?" he asks, lifting his brows in an extremely curious way.

"Yes," I say, hoping he leaves it at that, but no part of him seems to be moving. "I met him at a party in Edison a few weeks ago. He was sad and we talked." I sum it up, hoping to make short conversation of this.

"What the heck does he have to be sad about?" I realize that after hours of talking I never asked for any details on why life is making him sad, so I can't answer Ryan's question.

"I don't know. He was sad is all. I didn't ask why." I do long to know what made him sad but I fear it will make me sad too. He can tell me when he is ready, if he ever is. I will leave it up to Rick.

"Where did you come from? You never pry. How can't you be curious?" Ryan has never fully understood me; most people don't.

"I prefer to let people be, and they can tell me in their own time. You understand," I say. "I'm not nosey like you." I poke his shoulder because this conversation makes me uncomfortable.

"Morgan, you are the least selfish person I know. But why aren't you freaking out? Rick Rhoades called you, that's crazy shit." He releases a nervous laugh. I laugh back. Ryan gives me a big brother talk about staying smart and not getting hurt.

After his short monologue I tilt my head to the right and say, "Rick is calling later when he is done in the studio. Maybe you should turn your ringer off when you go to bed." Ryan and I share a phone number so we don't bother our parents. Ryan has received way more calls in the middle of the night than I have, so I am sure he understands.

"Fair enough." He gives me a warm hug and leaves. "Please be careful," he says from my doorway as he shuts it.

Alone with my thoughts, my mind is filled with only one; Rick Rhoades. That night I fell asleep again fully clothed on top of the covers.

The phone rings hours later as the warm sun begins to filter through the white sheers covering my bedroom windows. I jump but manage to answer it on the first ring.

"Hello, Morgan."

Coming from Rick's lips it's warmer than any blanket. "How was the studio?" I ask, wide awake.

"Fine, but all I did was think about getting back here to call you," he says, sounding chipper. He quickly adds, "Do you want to go back to sleep?"

"Hell, no," I say a little too fast. We talk for hours again. Conversation with him has become so easy so fast.

Brooke has been calling for over an hour, the call waiting beeps are getting annoying. It is ten a.m. and I realize Rick has been up all night when he starts to yawn. "Hey, you should sleep, and I must call Brooke back. I need an excuse why I didn't answer."

"Okay, I should sleep, and just tell her the truth."

Being honest I say, "I want to keep our conversation to myself for now."

"Well, I get the feeling you are a person who knows herself pretty well, so whatever you decide to do will be the right thing."

After another ten minutes we say our goodbyes and I call Brooke back. "Sorry, Ryan was on the phone." I lie to her, again.

Brooke is her typical bubbly self as she says, "I forgot he was home. Hey, there's a huge party tonight. Are you in?"

"Yeah, I should go out." I even shock myself.

* * *

Brooke has her sister's car when she arrives at six, even though we won't leave for the party until after eight. She insists on helping me get ready. I am not one to get all done up, but for some reason I agree to let her. Brooke spends a long time curling my long brown hair. She does my makeup and makes me look pretty, but I don't look like myself. My hazel, close to green eyes still shine under all the makeup she cakes on me. Brooke's strawberry blond hair always looks as if she just came from the hairdresser, and her makeup is always flawless. Kelly is similar to me; she has simple makeup and hair habits too, but she still has the same stunning strawberry blond hair that Brooke has.

Brooke drives and she tells me she isn't drinking tonight. I tell her I might and she is shocked. I rarely drink and have only been drunk once. Brooke and I were at the shore last summer when I had too much for the first time. It was not a fun time. Tonight, maybe I'll allow myself a drink or two.

We walk into a classmate's house, which we have both been to before. It's a large French Tudor that always smells like fresh fruit. Brooke has a way with people and starts conversations with ease. I am slow to warm up but the vodka will help.

After an hour, more people have arrived and I find myself playing pool with some super cute boys who do not attend school with us. I actually think the vodka is making them cute and they are average. As I lean over to strike the ball I see two haunting and familiar deep brown eyes, staring at me in disgust.

"Shit," comes flying out of my mouth. Brooke had to know Ben was going to be here. Ben Bailey is my ex-boyfriend. He was my first and only love. Our relationship started slowly during his senior year of high school. We both ran track so we knew each other, but when school started that year we ran into each other everywhere and suddenly we were inseparable. We dated just over a year and I know I am over him and have moved on, but I also haven't moved on with someone new.

Looking at him now makes me realize how much I used to love him. I put the cue stick down and walk toward him; my legs wobble even though I am not even tipsy yet. With the strength the vodka gives me, I reach up and wrap my arms around his neck and squeeze tight, giving him one heck of a hug. I don't feel any of the old sparks he used to ignite deep in my belly. I wonder if that is the vodka too, or am I completely over him?

"Can we talk?" he whispers in my ear. Even his hot breath stirs up nothing.

"Yeah," I say as we walk toward an empty room down the hall. We enter a large unfriendly and cold sitting room. There are three small couches covered in white fabric with pink and red roses all over them. The rest of the furniture is brown and nondescript. This room smells even more like fresh fruit.

I sit on the couch with my back to the door and Ben sits on the couch across from me. I can't remember a time ever when we sat apart. Even when we broke up we kept touching each other. "How are you?" he asks.

"I'm good, how are you?" I say, sounding robotic, so I smile a toothy fake smile.

"This is awkward. Would it be okay if I sit next to you?" he asks, sounding frightened.

"Of course," I say as he walks over, sits down, and takes my hand in his. There is comfort in his simple touch. I never thought his touch would stop feeling the way it used to. I was upset when I saw him in the doorway a few minutes ago, but now I realize I am completely over him.

"How much did you drink tonight?" he asks, sounding concerned.

"I didn't even finish one drink. You know I don't drink and when I do it works fast," I say, giggling because of the alcohol.

Ben squeezes my hand again and says, "Good, I was worried you started to party too hard. You look different but you are still…" he swallows painfully loud, "…just so you, I was a little confused." I do know the reason why Ben is questioning my attitude. I am more confident since we broke up.

"Ben, you know me better than that." We just stare at each other as we sit in silence. Silence often comforts me and I find myself leaning over and resting my head on his chest, because I sense it is what he needs. He leans back into the stiff couch and wraps his right arm around my back. He feels and smells familiar, but my feelings for him are drastically different.

We sit in silence more than we talk. He apologizes again for breaking up with me the way he did. I know he didn't do it because he was done loving me. He did it because he needed to be young and carefree. I understand how he feels and I will never blame him or tell him it was wrong. As difficult as being here with him has been tonight, I feel we have crossed a tricky bridge until he says, "I'm not sure I'm okay." I sit up and stare into the eyes I once loved very much. He leans in and kisses me. His kiss is soft. I unintentionally kiss him back. He kisses with too much force and too fast as his arms wrap around me. He is kissing me with a need I never felt from him before. His tongue is firm and curious in my mouth and I crave to answer him back with mine, but I don't because his kiss is not what I want anymore. I don't want him and my body is behaving well in letting me know.

"Ben, stop." I pull away, but I hold his hand. "I loved you. I loved you more than anything. You are the only man I ever loved. But it's over. I'm so sorry."

"Don't apologize. It was my fault. I ruined us." His fingers dig hard into my hip while he searches for air. It pains me to see him hurt. At my core I still have love for him. "We had something great, I just didn't know it."

"I'm sorry for us both, because losing a loved one hurts, but we are young. This is part of growing up."

He stares at me. He chuckles and says, "Nothing about you is young. I've met many new people and not a single person has the maturity you do. You are different, special, and incredible. I fear I will always regret let-ting you go."

I don't know what to say. Why couldn't he see that when we were together?

Ben and I sit for a few more minutes before I say, "Should we join the party?"

"Once we leave this room I will never hold you again. Just ten more minutes, please?" He sounds small and weak, causing a tear to run down my cheek. I don't say anything, I just let him hold me. I eventually get up and grab his hand to pull him off the couch. As we leave the sitting room and join the party, I find it quite fitting that a CrossRhoades song fills the house.

Brooke finds me a few minutes later and I can tell she is eager for information. I love her to death but we are quite different. Sometimes I wish she knew when to leave me be. I ask if we can talk later, and she says yes, even though her face tells me she wants to say no. I tell her that whenever she is ready to leave, so am I. An hour later we head out the door and she drives me home in silence. I keep telling her I will call her tomorrow every time she fires a question at me.

The house is quiet and cold when I get home. I find a note from Ryan by my phone. It says 'Rick called at ten-thirty, and he wants you to call him back.' I pick up the paper and stare at it in disbelief. I sit on my bed. How did I get here? I am holding a piece of paper with Rick Rhoades' hotel room number on it and he wants me to call him. I feel stuck in someone else's dream. For a few minutes I focus on the task of breathing. I know I will call; there is no other option I can live with.

Chapter Three
What's Your Name

RICK ANSWERS WITH the solitary word, "Hello."

It grants him my full attention. "Hello yourself," I say back.

His warm voice slices through my phone again. "Did you have fun at the party?"

"It was nice, but I spent too much time under lilac trees looking for hot rock stars," I say with a girlish giggle that is so unlike me.

"Good thing you didn't find one because I might have been jealous," he says, throwing me off for a second.

Rick tells me he is going in the other room and I wait for him to pick up again. "That's better." He sounds out of this world sexy, and it affects me right through the phone line.

"Are you lying on the bed?" I ask, needing to picture where he is.

"Yes," he says, sexier than any word I have ever heard. I ask him to describe the room and he does. I hang on every word out of his mouth even if it's only to tell me the color scheme of the room. Since he is in that room it has become interesting. He sounds breathless when he is done; I can't picture anything but his sexiness.

We talk for hours again and I turn off the massive flirting part on my end. Even if he tried he couldn't turn the sexy part of him off. My out of control mind is still stuck in a gutter. He told me he and the band were trying desperately to write new lyrics and nothing was happening. A dry spell he called it. The only thing on my mind, thanks to the vodka, is that I would love to be an inspiration.

We talk about nothing important yet the conversation has so

much value. Changing the subject, he says, "Hey, can I ask a rather strange favor?"

"You can ask, but I may not oblige," I say, smirking even though he can't see me.

"Well, if you are going to be like that, I won't ask," he says and I huff back into the phone, but he speaks again, "Would you mind calling me Fred instead of Rick?"

"Umm." I feel like I may stutter because I am thrown off by his question. "I can manage that…. Fred," I say. The word Fred sounds odd off my tongue. It sounds strange. Who is Fred? But he asked and I will try. "Why do you want me to call you Fred?"

"No one ever called me Rick until the band started. I sort of feel like I'm two people and I think of myself as Fred and I want you to think of me as Fred too. Can you do that for me?" He sounds young and needy. I have never heard him sound that way. How can someone so confident, so successful, so tall, sound small and weak?

"Yes, I can do that for you. I would be honored to call you Fred." He has blown my mind again.

"You still awake?" he whispers.

"Yeah, sorry. You just stunned me a little," I whisper back.

"This is a good place to say goodnight. It's almost morning there. Will you say goodnight to me?" His voice sounds so innocent and cute, certainly he is not nearly as innocent as he is cute.

"Goodnight, Fred." I pronounce each word as drawn out as I can while still trying to sound sexy and I hang up. I sigh and I try not to let my mind wander or try to overanalyze this. I think of him again as I fall asleep, once again on top of my covers fully clothed.

Over the next two weeks we talk almost every day. Between his schedule and mine sometimes we only get a few minutes and sometimes we get the whole night. I know I am sleep deprived and so is he. The beauty of it is that I don't feel tired and he sure doesn't sound tired.

We talked about everything and nothing, and both conveniently left out a few important issues. For one, I am way too young for him and even recently I read he was in a serious relationship. I can't help but wonder if these are the only major issues we have to contend with.

Chapter Four

Heart Starts

ALMOST EVERY YEAR since Brooke moved here, we have spent handfuls of summer days at her parents' house on Long Beach Island. Her father is an only child and when his parents passed away he inherited their shore house. This year we are going down on Thursday with Kelly and her boyfriend, John. On Friday Brooke's parents will come down. Unfortunately, we only get one parent-free night.

The huge house is half beige stone and half brown wood. It is all storage on the ground level. An outside shower, that always feels wonderful after a day in the sand, is near the carport. The second floor has four gorgeous bedrooms and two bathrooms. The top floor consists of the kitchen, living room, another bathroom, and a huge deck with an ocean view. The stairs on the deck lead to a roof deck. It is a stunning beach house that has given Brooke and me fantastic memories. We have both changed a lot since we were ten, but I feel fortunate to be growing up alongside my best friend.

Before we left I had a talk with my mom. I had to tell her that I made a few lengthy long distance calls and that I would pay for them when the bill arrives. I also had to tell her whom I had called. I can't lie to my parents. They are extremely understanding and treat me like an adult. I have always appreciated that, but until now it never truly mattered. Contemplating the possibility of a real friendship with an older famous man, how can they be okay with this?

After I tell her, she sits there with her mouth open, looking exactly as Ryan did when he found out. She doesn't say anything and that is scaring me. I start talking, telling her where and when we met and how we have been on the phone while he is in Los Angeles. She finally gets over her shock and all she says is that she trusts me. I'm not sure whether this is good or bad.

Kelly is driving us down the parkway while we listen to a tape her boyfriend made. Brooke and I are in the backseat and I feel ten again, but I also feel on the edge of grown-up changes unlike anything I have experienced before. We arrive at the house and the warm ocean breeze and salt air make me crazy ready for summertime.

John has been handed the chore of luggage duty, while Kelly, Brooke, and I head to the grocery store. I love food shopping at the beach; it gives me a true vacation feel, plus everyone around here is in a better mood than they are back home. We get as much as we can with the money Brooke's parents gave us and head back to the house.

It's too chilly to swim, so we all head to the beach for the sun. We pack some sandwiches, drinks and books and head out as fast as we can. The feel of the warm sand on my feet brings back memories of every childhood summer. If I had a kite I could pretend to be five again. There are a good number of people here but it isn't crowded. We spread our towels out and lie down. I pick up a copy of *Interview with a Vampire* and begin to read.

The book is interesting, but my mind keeps going back to Rick, I mean Fred. I'm still trying to get that straight.

Brooke snaps her fingers in front of my face. "Hey, what are you dreaming about?"

"Oh sorry, nothing," I say, but hell she knows it's something.

"You haven't turned a page in that book in thirty minutes. It must be something juicy." She raises her eyebrows and waits for details.

"I'm just tired," I say, as I roll over on my back and put the book over my face. I can't stop thinking about him. We have not spoken since Monday. I tried him a few times and the hotel phone went unanswered. He left a few messages on my machine when I was out but that wasn't enough for me to get my Fred fix. I know it's only been three days, but damn I desperately miss his masculine sexy voice.

Brooke shakes me out of my daydream and we head back to the house. After a long relaxing shower, I walk into the kitchen as the phone rings. I can tell by the way Brooke answers it that it's her 'LBI boyfriend.' She met him two summers ago and has a massive thing for him, but he lives too far away from home to make it anything but a summer fling.

"Mor, do you mind if I go see Jack tonight?" she asks.

"No, not at all, have fun." I would never interfere with her happiness.

She runs downstairs to get ready, and Kelly asks if I want to come play mini golf with John and her. It's a nice offer but I would rather stay in. I have a lot on my mind.

Pleasantly alone, I pick up my book, and realize I read only three pages at the beach. Oh no, I really have it bad for Fred. Just as I sit down the phone rings. Brooke's mother, Mrs. Byrne, tells me her mother, who lives in Scranton, fell today and she may have broken her hip. She and Mr. Byrne will be going to check on her for the weekend instead of coming to the shore. I tell her, sorry, and I will tell Kelly and Brooke when they get home.

I return to my book and the phone rings again. "Hello," I say. I wish this house had caller I.D. I got used to the luxury of knowing who is calling.

Hearing, "Oh, a sexy hello," from Fred's lips makes me hot all over.

"How did you know it was me?"

"Are you kidding? I would know your voice anywhere," he says confidently.

"Really, I never thought of my voice as distinct," I say, "but I like that you do. Wait, how did you know where I was?"

"I have my secrets," he says. "Actually, I called your house and your brother gave me the number."

I cringe, since no good can come from him calling my house, but I am excited he found me. We talk for a few minutes until he tells me he has to leave for the airport.

"Are you coming back to Jersey?" I ask, trying not to sound excited. Talking in the same time zone sounds ideal.

"Yep. I'm taking the red-eye. I can't wait to get home," he says and I wonder if he means because he wants to get back to his girlfriend. "Will you be at this number tomorrow?"

"Yes, all weekend. Call anytime, but I can't guarantee I will be answering the phone."

"Maybe we should use a code word," he says, laughing.

"No, just call. It's okay, you can't stay a secret forever." But I say it thinking maybe he can. "Have a safe flight, talk to you tomorrow."

"Tomorrow," he says slowly before he hangs up.

Fred leaves me with that feeling in my stomach again, the one that says he is beautiful trouble. What will tomorrow bring? I head back to the couch to read and this time I read a chunk of the book. Brooke, Kelly, and John all come back at the same time and I relay the news about their grandmother. It's late so we all head off to our separate rooms to sleep, almost as if we all wanted to be alone tonight.

The next morning the phone rings and Brooke is lightning fast answering it. I fear it is Fred. After a few words I can tell it's her mom. She gets off the phone and tells me her grandmother is bruised from the fall but nothing is broken. Her parents are going to stay with her the rest of the weekend. Brooke is ecstatic because it means more time with Jack.

There is rain in the forecast so we head to the beach as soon as we can that morning. We don't last long in the cool wind and overcast skies. Kelly and John leave to see *Brave Heart* and Brooke goes upstairs to shower when the phone rings. "Hello," I answer.

"Wow! Even sexier when I'm closer to you," Fred says, and all I can picture is his sharp blue eyes.

"Does it feel good to be back home?" I ask, feeling happiness in every part of my body. My grin is so big I feel like my voice isn't my own.

"Yes, Jersey will always be home, and I'm a homebody."

All I can focus on is the word 'body', and he has a mighty fine one.

He interrupts my daydreaming again. "Are you alone? Can you talk?"

"Brooke is still here but she is leaving soon."

He asks me to call him back when I can and he gives me his number. Twenty minutes later Brooke leaves, but it feels like twenty hours. I am addicted to a man whose eyes I have only looked into one night.

I call him back on the number he gave me. "What is all that noise?" I ask.

"Let me put the window up," he says. "Now tell me what direction to head in to get to you. What town are you in?"

My mouth is hanging open.

"Morgan, are you still there?"

"Wow! Sorry, I wasn't expecting that," I stammer. "Harvey Cedars. Where are you?"

"At exit sixty-seven."

Again I am silent.

"Can you give me a street name?"

I remain silent.

"I have never heard so few words come out of your mouth," he says with a slight chuckle.

"Sorry, I'm shocked that you are coming here and calling me from a car phone, too. Geez, you are probably driving some expensive sports car. You stunned me silent," I say before I realize I babbled all that aloud.

First laughter comes through the phone, then he says, "I'm glad you found your words again. I love all your words. I would miss them if you went silent," he says genuinely.

My cheeks are getting red hot. I need to compose myself before he gets here. I give him the address and he pulls up while we are still on the phone.

"Yep, expensive black sports car. You are so cliché and predictable," I say with a Cheshire grin plastered on my face.

"Hang up and get out here. I will show you how unpredictable I can be."

I hang up without saying another word, grab my purse, and run down the stairs. When I get to the door I pause. I take several deep breaths because I sense this is a pivotal moment. I can feel it in my bones. I open the door and the heavy rain has lessened to a gentle mist. I walk calmly to the car, open the door and slip in, trying to be cool, but cool and excited don't mix.

The car smells of warm leather and new car. The seats are black leather and feel warm and comforting against my body. Soon the smell of the car recedes because when I look into Fred's eyes the only thing my mind can handle is him. And I am not sure he can be handled.

"Damn, you are sight for sore eyes," he says. "You are even more beautiful in the light of day. Even a cloudy day like today. I can't wait to see you in the blazing sun."

Once again I become tongue-tied.

"Should we drive around? I can't go to many places anymore without causing commotion." He is talking a little too fast. He might be as nervous as I am.

"Yes." I pause, too stunned to speak. "Sorry, this is all a little surreal. I mean on the phone I know it is you, but seeing you here makes it so real. I'm just having a moment." I inhale, trying to take all the air inside the car into my lungs. "Okay, let's drive."

Fred puts the car in gear, releases the clutch and off we go. The road noise is a pleasant hum that helps me think. Or not think. I'm not sure which. Damn, he is even more smoking hot than I remember. His face is rugged and masculine.

We drive in silence before we start talking like we do on the phone. It takes me a few minutes to come back to the realization that he is a person first, celebrity second. He came to get me and he wants to spend time with me and oh boy do I want to spend time with him. I admire him from the safety of my side of the car while his eyes are on the road. I keep hoping he doesn't catch me watching him.

I tell him to turn around and head north up Long Beach Drive because there is less of everything that way. I crave to have his eyes on me instead of the road, so I am hoping we can park somewhere. Soon enough he pulls the car over where we can see the ocean out the front window. The waves are grey and angry. The day is dismal, but I am not. I love the way I feel in the presence of Frederick Rhoades. He brings me a new kind of contentment. One I have never felt before.

We relax in the car and turn toward each other at the same time. I want to reach over and touch his leg or grab his hand, but I am experiencing a different type of petrified than I ever have. We talk about California and the music video for a few minutes before the rain lets up.

"Should we to get out, walk on the beach a little before it rains again?" He doesn't sound sure it is what he wants to do.

I feel cozy and safe in the car and the clouds shelter us like a warm blanket. Still I say, "Okay, let's give it a shot." I open my door as he reaches under the seat to get his sweatshirt. The wind and rain have made it chilly for May. We walk a few feet and he grabs my hand to help steady us both over the dunes. It takes me a few seconds to register that he is holding my hand as we walk down the beach. I was afraid to touch him, yet he took my hand so naturally I didn't even realize it.

We walk down the beach in silence, holding hands until the rain picks up and the ocean spray is angry. We both start laughing and try to run back to the car but it is hopeless. We are drenched. We are soaking his fine leather seats and I should feel cold and uncomfortable but that isn't a feeling I can feel right now. He is easy and carefree and we find ourselves giggling. He starts the car. Heat in May has never felt so heavenly.

At least I think it feels heavenly until he takes my left hand and starts running his index finger with slow and rhythmic movements over my palm. This simple touch is hotter than the heat. At first I watch as his finger caresses my hand. I raise my eyes to meet his and they are full of passion. I can't bear to keep my eyes open, so I tilt my head back against the seat and stretch my hand out toward him, spreading my fingers as wide as I can. With the pad of his index finger he moves slowly up and down each finger. He has such control as he moves slower and slower as if he knows once he gets to my pinkie he will stop. That is exactly what he does, but the damage is done. He leaves me breathless and out of my mind. My clothes are beginning to dry and I am not sure if it is from the car heater or the heat burning from inside of me.

I hear him moving in his seat, restless, as I open my eyes. His eyes lock on mine and we say nothing; our eyes speak for both of us. We have never felt something so simple yet so extraordinary. He reaches across the space between us and takes my hand again, but this time he just holds it. We sit in the car holding hands in silence. Time passes but I can no longer tell how much. I am content but terrified of the hurdles we have before us.

"Will you come home with me tonight?" he whispers with his eyes shut. I keep staring at him. I just stare. This talented, famous, wealthy, sexy man has asked me to go home with him. I stare at him but he doesn't do or say anything. It is only minutes later, but it seems like an eternity when he opens his eyes and shifts his body toward me. He takes my hands in his and moves his right thumb against me as if he is nervous. I must say something but I don't know what to say. I squeeze his hands to get him to stop moving.

I am so glad he speaks because I can't. "I can't be without you. I don't know what it is but something about you makes me need more. You always know the perfect words or the perfect time to be quiet. And I can't fathom dropping you off at your friend's house and driving away. I need more time with you. I want to talk and laugh. I have become addicted to you." I watch his lips as he talks and I feel like pinching myself to see if this is real.

"Okay, I should go back to the house and tell everyone, then pack my bag." It just rolls off my tongue, because I too cannot fathom watching him drive away. As happy as he makes me, I am terrified of the sadness that awaits me. I want what we could have, but we can never have what we want. How can something that feels so thrilling have so many issues before it even starts? I must have a tough conversation with him soon. Very soon, but I decide I will wait until we get to his place.

Back at Brooke's I head inside and I am glad it is overcast. This weather makes me feel safe and hidden. Fred waits in the car. I find Kelly in the kitchen washing dishes and she tells me Brooke isn't back yet. I head downstairs to call home and tell them where I will be. I realize I should give my mom Fred's number so I walk back outside to get it. He puts the window down and says, "Change your mind?"

"Absolutely not. Can I have a number at your place in case anyone needs to reach me?" I hand him a slip of paper. He writes his number down, smiles, and hands it back to me. I needed that smile. It makes me feel strong and confident. I walk back inside and pick up the phone in the room I am staying in. My mother asks me how I am and I tell her I have a favor to ask.

"Well, I know you gave Ryan the number for Rick so you must be okay with me talking to him. Mom, he drove down and we spent some time together today and I enjoy his company. And well he asked me to go back up to his house in Mantoloking." I pause, knowing I have been running on and on. "I understand if you say no, but you know it's just a friendship and he needs a friend right now. I will give you the number there so you can call anytime. He will drive me home on Monday." I am done talking and I close my eyes waiting for her to say no because I know what I am asking for is crazy.

She sighs before she speaks, making me sense that she won't allow me this. "Honey, you know I trust you, and you could have gone without telling us and had Brooke cover for you. How can I say no when you are so mature? Just be careful and if anything is wrong call us right away and we will come get you. I know you will make the right choices. I love you."

"I love you too, Mom. Thanks." I hang up after giving her the phone number to Fred's house. She can trust me, but I also realize I am still calling him Rick to her, not Fred. Will I be able to stay honest and trustworthy through this? I pack up everything I brought and head back upstairs to tell Kelly. I tell her a friend came down and I am going to leave with him. I tell her my parents know and I give her the number also.

She doesn't ask anything else, but she tells me she will keep the number to herself and she will let Brooke know I left without any details. We know Brooke will think I left with Ben. I love it that Kelly understands me without words. She just gets me and I have never needed that more in all my life than I do right now. Out of the blue she gives me a hug and says, "Be careful, but have fun."

I have never seen how much she and I are alike until today.

"Morgan, wait! I have one question."

"Sure."

"Is he as hot as that car?" she asks with a huge smile.

I exhale dramatically. "No, way hotter."

I walk out of the house and the sun is peeking out just in time to set. I stand in front of the car so Fred can open the trunk. I throw my bag in, slam it shut, and get in the car. He is smiling even bigger at me, and with all my nervous energy that smile somehow puts me at ease.

"Damn you are so hot," he says with his eyes locked on me.

"You like the rain soaked, air dried look?" I ask with wonder.

"No, well yes, you look cute, but no, it's hot that you knew the engine was in the back."

"Oh, okay. I do have ears and can hear it."

"It's just you are not like others girls, are you?"

I am not sure if that is a question or a statement. I answer anyway. "I'm nothing like other girls."

He stares at me without making a comment and puts the car in drive.

We travel north up the parkway. His Porsche hugs the road like I desire to hug him. We talk casually and it has granted my mind relief. He pulls into the driveway and the house is as stunning as he is. It is dark grey and tall and has more glass than siding. It's a basic square home but the stone work and details make it unique. I picture the inside to be even grander. We sit in the car with the engine off for a few minutes and I hear him let out a long puff of air.

He opens his door and comes around to open mine. I don't know if I sat there waiting for him to do just that or if I was frozen and unable to do it myself. He takes my hand to help me out but releases it as I shut my door. He takes my bag out of the car and starts to walk to the side entrance of the house.

"Wait," I snap and he stops and turns toward me. He puts the bag down on the top step and comes back over and wraps his arms around me. Pure comfort. The sun has set and there is no moon. The only lights are those coming from the few houses around us and a few sporadically placed streetlights. The beach will be dark and I need the blanket of darkness to cover us for this conversation we have both been avoiding. "Can we sit on the beach and talk?" I whisper.

"Come." He takes my hand and I walk beside him. "I have something to tell you, but I don't want to." He sounds as upset as I am.

I release a nervous noise that isn't a laugh or a cry. "I have something I don't want to tell you too."

He leads me down a wooden walkway. Good thing he knows the way because it is pitch black. I am also glad we both have dry clothes on because the night is cool and the sand is cold and damp, but it is keeping my mind alert and I need that terribly. We walk a few feet and then we both sit cross-legged facing each other in the sand, my back to the ocean. The roar of the waves soothes me since it is more violent than my heart is right now.

He takes my hands in his and places them in his lap. I look into his face and it is almost too dark to see, but somehow his blue eyes still shine. I know I will never tire of looking into them.

"So who goes first?" I ask. He touches first and I talk first. Typical of men and women, I suppose.

"I can't imagine anything you have to say being as bad as what I have to say." He is clearly not ready for this conversation.

"I am certain what I have to say is worse. Besides, I might have figured out what you have to say."

We sit in silence holding hands, touching each other ever so slightly until he puts both hands on my face and lifts my chin to meet his eyes. He says nothing. After a deep inhale, I break the silence. "Will you kiss me just once before everything changes?" I know he doesn't understand me, but he kisses me without hesitation.

His lips are loving and gentle as he lightly brushes them against mine. Then he presses deeper into my mouth. I part my lips and I can't control my tongue as it slips into his mouth to find his. Hot and wet pleasure rains through my body. His left hand moves to the back of my neck as he pulls me forward, moving me into his body. I am sitting in his lap now with my legs wrapped around his hips. He is well over six feet and all lean muscle, but it surprises me how wide and muscular he feels against me. I press my body harder into his as his tongue enters my mouth again. My hands are all over his head and back and I know this instant that I will never get enough of this.

He places light kisses down my neck to the top of the zipper on my sweatshirt, then looks up at me as I open my eyes and look at him. He pulls his lips away from my skin and swallows loud enough for me to hear it. I would be shocked if he couldn't hear my heart pounding.

"Is Beth what you have to talk about? I'm guessing you are not dating anymore." I pause and move my hands down to his shoulders. "Are you engaged or married?"

"Unfortunately, I married her." He lowers his eyes in shame. "You really did know. Did you guess or did you read it somewhere?"

"I guessed. Nothing else came to mind to be troubling you. Plus, I knew it was something you couldn't talk to me about."

He starts talking and it's a relief to get more time before it's my turn. "Beth and I were in Vegas for the bachelorette and bachelor parties two days before her best friend's wedding. She was mad and upset it wasn't her getting married. I was drunk and asked her if she wanted to get married. She said yes. And we did. I felt hollow and empty afterward. I thought it would help the connection we had lost, but it didn't. We were married on the twenty-eighth and we came home that day. She spent that night with her friend getting ready for the wedding, and I went to my cousin's house and met this really cute and amazing woman."

My mouth drops open. Not sure if it is because he married her a month ago and I was thinking it was a long time ago or if it was because he called me cute and amazing. "Wow, that pain in your eyes the night we met was because you had married the woman you have been dating since high school? Marriage is not supposed to be painful, especially the day of the wedding." I realize too late that I sounded mean.

"It's not, but I asked her for the wrong reason. I wanted to fix us. Marriage fixes nothing."

I want to ask what he will do now. I also don't want to ask because if he doesn't tell me what I long to hear I know I will be devastated, but it doesn't matter because I can't have him anyway.

"Your turn," he says and I say nothing. A tear runs down my cheek and he wipes it away even though I am not sure he can see it. "Hey, it's okay. You can tell me anything."

I pause. I swallow hard. My throat is dry. My tongue feels swollen. A need to vomit makes me feel faint. I have to end my pain. "My birthday is next month." I feel stupid. What does that mean?

He looks happy but confused. "Are you a Gemini, because if you are then your problem is way bigger than mine." He laughs and I laugh too, only my laughs are from nerves.

"No, it's the twenty-third. I'm a Cancer." I feel a little more comfortable because of the laughter, but my heart is still out of control.

"How is that a problem?" The confusion in his voice is as crystal clear as his blue eyes.

"In a few weeks I will be seventeen." I spill it.

Silence.

Chapter Five

Kill the Lights

NO ONE MOVES. No one talks. Fred wraps his arms around me and squeezes me with life altering tightness to his chest, but having him push me away would have hurt so much more. "Can I show you around the house?" he asks. It's a welcome change of topic.

"Please." I stand up and mindlessly brush the sand off myself. I am unable to feel my legs beneath me. Fred supports me as we walk back to the house. My arm is around his waist and his across my shoulder, as if we have done this our whole lives. I don't know why we are closer when we should be further apart. It feels good to be connected to his body. The cold sand and the lateness of the night have left me exhausted.

He takes his arm off me to pick up my bag and opens the side door. He flips the switch on and the dining room light is intense. It blinds us both and he turns it back off.

"Wait here." I do as instructed but I admire his walk to turn on the stove light. I watch because everything he does is a show. "Sorry, I'm still not used to this house," he says.

I say nothing. I just take it all in. The kitchen is spacious and sparkling new. It does not look lived in. The black granite counter tops are shiny and cold. The cabinets are a warm white at least, so the way too blank kitchen has some appeal and warmth.

"Did you just buy it?" I ask, curious but truly wanting to know where his wife is.

"In January. I thought it would help fix the problems between me and Beth. She hated it and wrote it and me off. She was only here the day the realtor showed it to us. I bought it anyway. I should have known she and I weren't on the same page. I have lived here and she has lived in New Brunswick ever since." He answers my unasked questions.

I just stare at him. He takes me by the hand. "Let me give you a grand tour of what would be my bachelor pad, if I hadn't been so stupid."

"It wasn't stupid. You love her and you wanted to make it work. You picked the wrong way to fix it. Or maybe it isn't fixable. Only you and Beth can find the answers." He turns and looks at me with longing.

"Did you lie about being sixteen? You don't act sixteen at all," he says, not even blinking.

"I wish I were lying."

He leads me into the living room and puts a tabletop lamp on. We are holding hands and looking toward the dark beach. The main focal point is the stone fireplace, which is centered on the outside wall surrounded by floor to ceiling glass panels on either side. It must be exquisite in the light of day. The dining room is to the right of the fireplace. There is a large lonely glass table. The entire room appears unfinished. The living room though is a place I could call home. There are two plush white sofas on an off-white rug. All the tables are glass and wrought iron. The room is warm and embracing. The black baby grand piano makes the biggest statement of all, as if it won a prize and is on display. I walk over and sit down on the bench. Fred leans his elbows on the closed lid and stares into my eyes, making me blush.

I take a deep breath and play one of the few songs I remember from my childhood piano lessons, "*Für Elise*." Fred smiles and claps when I finish and, amazing myself, I didn't butcher it too much. I stand to bow and we both giggle. He takes me by the hand again and shows me the room off the kitchen he is going to make into a recording studio. For now, it has a treadmill and some free weights. The image of him hot and sweaty has invaded my already weak mind. Hand in hand we walk up a grand staircase to the top floor. Every floor has the same wall-to-wall off-white carpeting. It feels fresh and clean the way a shore house should. At the top of the stairs there are three large bedrooms, each with their own bath. Their windows overlook the houses between here and the bay. The rooms are sparse and lack character.

Fred hesitates at the next door, so I take his hand in mine. He looks at me again with desire, and even though I feel I know him well already I believe some pieces of the puzzle are missing. It will take some time for us to sort out what we are doing. Maybe it will take a whole year and I will be legal. I laugh aloud and Fred looks at me in confusion.

"Sorry, inside joke."

"Inside what?"

"Just inside my head," I say seriously. "When the time is right I will share. Please open door number four. The suspense is killing me." I try to make light of something apparently difficult for him.

He opens the door and switches on the lights. I step inside and catch myself forgetting to breathe. I have never seen anything this stunning. The same fireplace that is downstairs extends up here. The room is way too large and it makes the furniture look small, but the big king bed catches my eye. The bed is a chunky pale grey, a distressed sleigh bed, and if you lie on your left side you have a view of the Atlantic when you wake up. The bedside tables match the bed perfectly, and the lamps are made of what looks to be green and blue sea glass. There are several large vases filled with fresh lilacs and several more filled with the largest sunflowers I have ever seen. I touch one and a tear runs down my cheek.

Fred wipes it away. "Please don't cry." He leans down and brushes my lips with his thumb, then with sweet care he does the same with his soft full lips.

"This is a room I would pick for myself." I am not sure if I am asking or telling.

"I used to sleep in the other bedroom on the futon. I couldn't bring myself to use or decorate this room, but after I met you I felt I had a new reason to live, to live here. Talking to you all those nights, well it made me hopeful. I hired a decorator when I was away." He runs his thumb over the back of my hand again like he did in the car. "Didn't you find some of the questions I asked on the phone were a little weird?"

"No, I just thought you were weird. Honestly, I thought you were trying to get to know me. I thought maybe you wanted to buy me flowers. I never thought you needed help to decorate the master bedroom in your house." I put my other hand over his to stop his nervous movement. "You filled the room with my new favorite flower too. The lilac will always remind me of you." I close my eyes and smell them, attempting to etch it all into my mind for eternity.

"I can't explain what it is that you do to me. I feel this easy happiness when I talk with you. I want to do things for you," he says, holding my entire face in his extra-large warm hands.

"You make me feel cared for," I whisper, locked on his baby blues.

We are frozen. The number of times we leave each other breathless is becoming time consuming. At this rate we will never eat or sleep again. My eyes are locked on his, fearing someday soon they won't be mine to look at.

"Got a fancy bathroom or closet around here to show me?" I ask, even though I could stay right in this position for a lifetime. He drops his hands from my face and intertwines his fingers with mine. He takes me to the right side of the room to a bathroom as dark as the bedroom is light. The contrast is dramatic. Almost as dramatic as the situation we have brought upon ourselves.

The bathroom floor is made of dark grey and deep blue-grey slate tiles. The walls are also a deep dark cool grey. A grey claw-foot tub almost blends in. It is placed near the wall of windows at the back of the house. I can't stop my mind from wandering. I imagine being supported by Fred's body in that tub, the hot water relaxing us. I close my eyes and all I smell is the lilacs from the other room. All my senses have gone to heaven and they don't want to come down to reality. Fred squeezes my hand gently and I slowly come back from my dream. Reality isn't so bad either.

We walk to the other side of the bathroom past the double vanity to the shower. It is all glass and cool grey tile. The ocean would be visible from the shower in daylight, and maybe with a full moon too. I am hoping I can be here to witness both someday. In the corner is a small room with a door and a toilet. Thankfully, Fred doesn't take me in there; it would wake me from the fantasy this room radiates.

"I will get your bag and you can shower and change." He pulls me into his side with one arm and says, "We both need some rest."

"Okay."

I shower and find that he has an extra robe. I put it on and walk back to the bedroom to get clothes. Opening my bag, I realize I don't know what to wear. What does one wear to bed in this situation? I tell myself to stop analyzing everything and just be me. I take out a pair of men's XS flannel boxers and a plain black t-shirt, my typical pajamas. I convince myself that being myself is always the best option.

I am combing my wet hair at the bathroom mirror when he walks in through the open door. Our eyes meet in the mirror. Fred glides toward me without breaking eye contact and I stop moving. Only my heart is beating, as I see nothing but heat and lust coming from his eyes. From behind he leans down and kisses the top of my head. My heavy eyes shut and I feel weightless yet strong. My arms fall to my side, limp, as he runs the backside of his hands down them.

"When was the last time you ate?" he whispers but still startles me. As if my stomach is linked to him it rumbles with hunger. He laughs. "I will see what we have downstairs. Are you craving anything?"

I don't have the courage yet to tell him what I crave most. "It seems you know me so well. Let's test it and see if you pick something I like." I smirk into the mirror at him.

I sit cross-legged on the bed, trying to find bravery as he walks in with a tray of food. He looks so cute and domestic it makes my heart flutter. He tells me to close my eyes before he places the tray down. The bed dips as he sits, and I instantly smell peanut butter.

"Can you guess?"

"Peanut butter and jelly. I prefer it on white bread, not toasted, with ice cold milk."

"Wait, keep your eyes closed. Open your mouth," he says and I open wide for him. He puts the sandwich to my lips. I take a bite. Having someone know you so well never tasted so delicious. He puts his left hand under my chin and lifts the glass to my mouth. The milk is icy and smooth as it slides over my tongue and down my throat. I open my eyes and feel content looking at him with pride all over his face.

"How was my guess?"

"Absolutely perfect. Did you really guess or have you been stalking me?"

"Pure luck, plus there isn't much food in the house. Sort of how I lucked out on the randomness of meeting you." I have no words to follow up how grateful I feel that I met him under that lilac tree.

I eat my sandwich a little too fast. Fred removes the tray of dirty dishes and sits back on the bed. He is sitting with his knees touching mine and he rubs both hands up and down my thighs. It is arousing and comforting at the same time, but I can tell by the pressure he is using he is uncomfortable.

"Will you lie down with me until I fall asleep?" I ask, knowing his pain comes from not knowing if we should share a bed. So with the courage I know I have, I say, "I would prefer you held me all night in this bed." He stands up and grabs my hand and gently pulls me to stand beside him. We stand frozen watching one another until he bends to pull the covers down and climbs in. He lies on his side, supporting his head with his right arm, and I am grateful he has a shirt on or I might lose all control. He holds the covers up for me and I slip in beside him.

The sheets are crisp and new. They smell of fresh rain and feel like cotton spun into silk. They are smooth and warmer than I expected. I forget the sheets as I lay my head on the pillow and stare into two blue eyes brimming with passion. If only we could use our passion on each other. He lays his head on the pillow and we continue to watch one another. He takes his left hand and runs it through my hair, fanning it out on the pillow. I should lift my hand to touch him but I am certain I do not possess the control he does to stop.

"Roll over." His voice sounds wobbly. Perhaps he is also a big mess.

I roll over and slide up against him. His body is like a warm coal burning hot against my entire backside. The feeling takes my breath away in the most pleasant of ways. He wraps his arm around my waist loosely as his other hand moves through my hair again.

"Let's sleep, JB," he says.

"Huh?" I say sounding sleepy. "I don't want to guess, so good night, Fred." My body may never calm down enough to sleep, but apparently I don't know my body as well as I thought I did. I fall into a peaceful sleep rather fast.

I wake and the room is bathed in bright warm sunlight. The ocean is calm and glistening. The smell of the lilacs is stronger than it was last night. His room is even more beautiful in the daylight. I sit up and stretch. Nothing feels normal, yet I feel at home. I lift the pillow Fred slept on and bury my face in it. It smells of the strawberry shampoo in his shower, and earth after a hot rain, and lilacs. I smile and put the pillow back down as Fred walks through the open doorway. So glad I didn't get caught sniffing his pillow.

"I was coming to wake you, sleepyhead," he says, smiling and making the room even brighter. He has on a pair of loose shorts and no shirt.

I may be drooling when I say, "Good Morning."

He places the same tray as last night on the bed. This time it has food for only me. He has cut up pineapple and a bowl of cheerios for me. "Did you already eat?" I ask, as he sits down on the bed in front of me.

"Yes. It's almost noon. I even ran on the treadmill, and I need a shower," he says, getting up and heading to the bathroom after he flashes a smile that weakens every cell in my body. I watch every step he takes away from me. His body is glistening with sweat and it makes every muscle look even more delicious. I sit alone and eat, but there is nothing lonely about it. I finish eating and realize for the first time that there is a narrow deck attached to the bedroom, a perfect place to check out the day before it starts. I find the lock on the sliders and open the door and step outside. The air is cool compared to the bedroom, but it is still a warm beautiful spring day. The ocean's rhythm has me in a trance when Fred comes out and stands beside me. He covers my hand on the railing with his own. So simple, yet so full of meaning.

"Would you mind if I went for a run?" I ask a few minutes after we both just stare into space.

"Why would I mind?" he asks, still staring at the crashing waves.

"I don't know. I feel guilty that I can run down the street free and you have to watch over your shoulder all the time for someone to recognize you," I say, thinking he is similar to the vampires in the book I was reading yesterday. Even though yesterday seems like a lifetime ago. "You remind me of a vampire. You can only leave in the cover of darkness."

"I get out occasionally, but it is difficult for me. I would never stop you from doing what you want. I want you to feel that this is your home too. You don't have to ask to do anything," he says, sounding so comfortable yet tragically sad.

"Okay, I'm going to change and go." I rise up onto my toes to kiss his cheek. Not sure if I am ready to kiss his lips first yet. I change, grab my Walkman, and put *For the Love of Strange Medicine* in. Not the best running music, but I won't need help with speed today. I need help with clearing my head.

I head downstairs on my way out and find Fred looking lifeless at the piano. I sit beside him and this time I place my hand over his. "I have a lot to think about so I might be gone awhile." I get up and walk out the door without looking back, knowing he is watching me as I have watched him. I start walking and before I know it I am running and it feels exhilarating. I have such control of my own body when I run, I feel alive and strong and full of confidence. I also love the way Fred makes me feel. Keeping his company is natural. I simply get to be me with him.

I get back to the house and the door is unlocked and Fred is still at the piano. I have been gone two hours and it shocks me he has been there this long. He is playing a beautiful hauntingly sad piece. I have never heard it before and I hope he isn't playing it because I have made him sad. I leave him alone and head upstairs to shower.

When I come out of the bathroom I'm showered and dressed. I find him in front of the bedroom fireplace, looking excessively relaxed on the pale grey couch. He was waiting for me and now is watching my every move. I sit on the floor near his head so we are eye to eye. He takes a strand of my damp hair in his right hand and twists it around his finger.

"What should we do tonight?" he asks.

"What are my options?"

With a sad laugh he says, "Well we don't have that many." He crinkles his nose in a cute boyish way.

"Good thing it doesn't take much to make me happy. How about we have dinner, watch a movie or walk on the beach after sunset?"

"It all sounds perfect, perfect like you." It sounds so promising yet so heartbreaking as he says it. "Let's go to the store and get some food."

"Together?"

"That isn't a crime is it?" He stands up to help me off the floor.

"No, but what if someone sees us?"

"Well then, they see us." His smile makes everything seem normal. Even though for me this is still far from normal.

"Food shopping it is," I say and we walk downstairs together.

Chapter Six

I Could Get Used to This

HE OPENS THE detached three-car garage and we get in his black Jeep Wrangler. He is so super sexy in the Jeep; it makes my desire to touch him that much stronger. We drive a few minutes to a small grocery and meat market on the bay side. Fred opens the door for me and once I am in front of him his hand brushes against my lower back.

We walk up and down the aisles and I feel like everyone in the store must feel the magnetic pull between us. Our eyes or hands are on each other every chance we get. We both sneak little touches here and there as we browse, but we have been here ten minutes and the basket is still empty.

"Morgan, what can you cook? I don't think you should have any of my cooking." His words come out so sad he looks at the ground.

I shift his chin so his eyes are on me. "You have made me two meals and they were perfect. We can make something together. My mom loves to cook and she has taught me a lot," I say cheerfully. He smiles back, erasing those sad eyes. We decide to make risotto with shrimp and a salad. Once we have all the ingredients and some Ben and Jerry's Cherry Garcia I climb in the Jeep, euphoric.

Everything is new in his kitchen and sparkling clean as if it has never been used. The fridge is enormous and looks even bigger since it is virtually empty. The freezer now holds the ice cream we bought and vodka that was already there. Fred helps me find the pots and dishes; he doesn't know a thing about his own kitchen. We are silent as we make dinner. It amazes me how natural we are together. I love it that silence is as easy as conversation. I love that working together is as easy as being lazy. Everything we do together instantly becomes easy and natural.

While I cut the onion he puts some music on. Suddenly the onion is stinging my eyes worse than ever just as a beautiful classical piano song starts to play. I am torn between crying or laughing at how odd this moment is when Fred takes the knife from me and finishes the job. With the grace of a dancer he moves through the kitchen, working around me to cut all the vegetables for the salad. I break the silence by asking how he learned to cut so well, since he said he can't cook.

"My mother wouldn't let me help in the kitchen, but I would beg and beg and eventually she gave in. The first time I burnt something she was mad, so then I was only allowed to cut, not technically cook. And for some odd reason I find it sexual to cut vegetables and fruits, so maybe that helps me enjoy it."

I can't stop watching his hands and fingers. I stir more broth into the risotto and my mind continues to wander back to his hands and the fact that what he is doing makes him feel sexual. I need to feel those hands on my skin. On every part of my body. I force my eyes back to the risotto and my own hands make me fantasize about all the places I desire to touch him. Cooking has become way more erotic than it should be. As I put the shrimp in with the risotto I shake my head to try to turn off these arousing thoughts.

Fred finishes the salad as I put the dishes on the table. He comes up behind me and wraps his arms around my waist. At first he says nothing and his breath on my neck makes me close my eyes while still holding a plate midair.

"I have already crossed too many lines, but do you like champagne?" he whispers in my ear, sending another shiver down my already out of control body.

It takes me a minute to realize that was a question because he is heating me up, his body pressed against my backside. "Yes." He doesn't move. I don't move. I lower the plate to the table. "We should eat before it gets cold." The sexual tension in here could reheat the food in seconds.

Slowly he moves away from me and goes to get the champagne out of the wine fridge and brings it over to the table with two glasses. He puts the glasses down and I watch every move he makes as if I had hit the slow motion button. This moment already feels monumental. He opens the champagne cork with skill and grace and a pop. Fred pours champagne into each flute and sits down at the head of the table, his back to the ocean. As if still in slow motion he puts the bottle down on the table; all my physical and mental abilities have shut down.

We have the sliders to the deck open and the rhythmic roar of the ocean matches my heart pounding in my chest. This man has completely turned my brain to mush and set my body on fire. He lifts his glass to make a toast. I follow him and lift mine too; the smile on my face almost hurts because it feels so exciting to feel this elated.

He clears his throat as I smile bigger and he says, "To beautiful spring days at the shore, meals that smell delicious, and a woman who has made me happier than I have ever been. Thank you, Morgan. You are a gift I fear I don't deserve." We clink glasses and I sit still—stunned.

I clear my throat and say, "How do I follow that up?" I close and open my eyes very dramatically trying to find my voice. "To finely chopped vegetables, the constantly moving ocean, and a man who has filled my heart and mind with pure joy. Fred, I hope we always deserve each other." I smile and clink his glass. I take a sip of the champagne and it is just the right amount of smooth with a small bite. The taste is exquisite. That is also how I would describe how Fred might taste, and I laugh out loud.

"What is so funny?"

"Did I laugh out loud?" I place my glass down on the table. He nods as he takes my hand. What the hell, I have nothing to hide from him. "I was laughing because I was thinking that you and the champagne have a lot in common."

He chuckles and we both start to eat. "This is delicious," he says and I believe I have dodged a bullet. "So how am I like the champagne?" Nope I didn't and now I have to pick how honest I should be.

"Well, the champagne is smooth. It is also a little spicy. Its flavor is only second to the way you taste on my tongue. It's cool at first but becomes warm from the heat of my mouth and it could make me moan as it slides over my tongue and down my throat." I say this very seriously with my eyes locked on his.

No one blinks, we are both deadly silent when I hear him swallow. He gets up and comes to stand next to my chair as quick as lightning. I get up to kneel on the chair. My body is as close to his as it can be without touching when he puts his hands on my shoulders.

"Fuck," he says, breathless as his lips crash into mine. His hands squeeze my shoulders and he kisses me with a passion I didn't know existed. His lips are wet and hot. The champagne tastes even better inside his mouth. He releases his hands from my shoulders and runs his hands down the front of his shirt as he sits back down. I watch him, unable to move. He starts to eat again as I attempt to sit back in my chair.

I lift my champagne and swallow the entire glass in one gulp. Again he has left me wanting and needing more, so much more. I can't take my eyes off him, but I try to eat. He reaches over and grabs my hand. His skin is so hot it makes me crave any contact I can get.

"Sorry, I can only fight this desire so long. You leave me mindless and make me lose all control. Nothing about you is sixteen. The way you talk. The words you say. The way you move. The way you kiss. The way you cook. It's so confusing. I'm so attracted to you. Everything about you has me longing for more." He sighs as I squeeze his hand. "I can't live without you and I can't have you." The pain in his voice has caused yet another tear to slide down my cheek. This time he doesn't notice. His own eyes are wet and blurring his vision.

"When you can't take any more, tell me and I will walk away," I say because I don't know what to say. No one would ever choose to be in this horrible place. But there is nowhere else I want to be.

He lifts his head and wipes a tear from his eye. "Okay, but I will never want you gone." He takes another sip of champagne and starts to eat again. We eventually regain our ability to talk without going all philosophical on each other.

After dinner we clean up and I can't believe the sun is already beginning to set. If I spend too much time with Fred, I will be eighteen soon enough. While I am washing the dishes Fred comes and leans against the counter. "We have a dishwasher," he says with his arms crossed and a smile that makes women stupid. I do note to myself he said 'we' and I still haven't decided if I should be honored or scared.

"Yes, but the water is therapeutic, and after that kiss I need therapy," I say, giving him my winning smile.

"Okay, Dr. Frederick is prescribing a walk on the beach, right this second." He turns the water off and hands me a dishtowel. Firmly taking my left hand, he guides me outside and down the wooden path to the beach. I feel a little sick to my stomach with the memory of telling him I am sixteen, and just as I finish that thought he takes my face in his hands as if he knows I am hurting.

"Somehow we will survive this. Together. I just pray you stay as mature as you are today," he says, sounding as if he had mixed it up, but he got it right. I too hope I can stay mature through this. We hold hands and walk up and down the beach by the house. We pass two other couples as we walk. They don't appear to see us as anything out of the ordinary, even though we are extraordinary together.

Chapter Seven

Hold on to the Nights

WE WASH THE sand from our feet outside under the spigot near the deck. We take our cold wet feet and head inside holding hands. Fred leads me over to the sofa and leaves me standing there almost lost as he walks over to the large armoire and gets a blanket. I watch every step he takes. Eternity would not be enough to give me my fill of him. He lies on the couch and fans the blanket over his legs, then lifts it for me to join him. As I wiggle down between his body and the back of the couch I focus on the firmness of his muscles. The blanket hits my bare legs and I feel the soft luxury and warmth it offers. I have every feeling I could ever long for, right here, right now.

I rest my head on his chest and smell his musky soap and the salty ocean air that is trapped by the fibers of his shirt. The smell is intoxicating; it is both Fred and the ocean in one. I close my eyes as his fingertips run up and down my back slower than anything has ever moved across my skin. I feel so relaxed, I may be asleep when he whispers, "Hey, you tired?"

"Yes, or extremely relaxed. I can't tell the difference anymore," I mutter, trying to lift my head to look at him.

"Let's get some sleep and we can wake up early and watch the sunrise from the beach," he says as he wiggles beneath me to get up. We both get ready for bed in silence. He is ready before me and the sight of his tanned skin on the white sheets suddenly has me fully awake. I prolong my walk to the bed, wanting to remember how he looks in this moment for the rest of my life. I climb in beside him and there are a million thoughts going through my mind of the things I want to do to him. I peck his cheek and slip my head down to his chest. He kisses the top of my head, wraps his left arm tightly around me, and we both fall asleep.

The alarm is blaring and Fred moves his arm from around me to turn it off. I can't believe we stayed in the same position all night. It is five a.m. so maybe it wasn't all night. We both get up and put warmer clothes over our pajamas and head downstairs. Fred grabs two blankets and we head down to the beach.

He spreads out one blanket on the sand and we sit so he can put the other around us. I am sitting inside his legs with my head leaning back onto his left shoulder. His arms make me feel more secure than I knew I could feel. I caress his thighs in silence as he does the same to my arms. We remain in this trance as the earth moves to reveal a blazing orange sun. The reflection of the sun on the calm ocean is striking. My first sunrise with Fred is perfection.

When the sun is above the ocean, I turn to Fred. He looks content and I want to say something poignant but no words form as he takes my face in his masculine hands and lightly kisses my mouth. He stares into my eyes for a minute before he says, "There is only one thing fitting to say at this moment, but this is not the right time."

We gather the blankets and head back to the house side by side. I thought we had such poignant moments in the past few days but nothing for as long as I live could ever be as powerful as what I just experienced. His touch, his gaze, spoke to every cell in my body.

Once back inside, I feel closer to Fred than I ever imagined possible. We talk about breakfast and decide instead to take the Ben and Jerry's ice cream we didn't eat last night back to bed with us. We talk and laugh; it's amazing how comfortable we have become in such a short time. Even with our big bad problems always knocking on our minds.

"Will we always do things a little out of order?" I ask before he puts the spoon in my mouth again.

He laughs. "Maybe. And maybe it will be better that way. Dessert for breakfast is pretty awesome."

Fred puts the empty pint and spoon on his side of the bed and slips down under the covers as he pulls me into him. The room is bright and the lilacs still fragrant; bliss washes over my other emotions. I nap cradled in pure comfort.

I wake and sit up against the headboard. I thought Fred would wake with my movement but he doesn't. I sit and watch his chest rise and fall. With each breath he takes I become more and more intrigued by his body. On his right bicep he has a tattoo band around his entire arm. On the inside is a Chinese symbol. I crave to know what it means but more-so I crave to trace it with my fingers. He also has a tattoo of MCMXC above his ribs on his right side. That I know is 1990 and an educated guess tells me it reflects his first record deal. I want to wake him, but I think better of it and tiptoe downstairs instead.

I am not hungry and I do not want to run today, so I take a beach towel and head outside. I spread the towel out on the deck and do some stretches and moves that I remember from my favorite yoga videos. I fell in love with yoga last summer after my first class. I never thought I would get to a point in my life where I needed it. An hour later my mind feels clear and alert so I head inside to find Fred perched on the kitchen stool looking straight at me.

I walk over to him and step between his knees. I have never been the one to start kissing, but feeling empowered I contemplate doing it. I lift my head to meet his gaze. He closes his lids and I reach up and kiss him gently at first, but my desire for him boils to the surface fast. Within seconds my hands are in his hair and my tongue is in his mouth. He kisses me back, as if he finally woke up, and his tongue is curious and strong in my mouth. His hands find my ass as I push into him. I instantly feel that he is as aroused as I am. "Oh, Morgan," he moans. My ears have never heard anything so erotic as my own name.

This man has me joyfully frustrated and I can't stop. I kiss him like my life depends on it until I rip myself from his body, realizing this isn't fair to either of us. As I step away I ask, "How about leftovers for lunch?" I walk over to the fridge and take the food out. He says nothing so I turn back to look at him. "Cat got your tongue?" I'm trying to make this less uncomfortable.

"No. A hot little kid who just turned me on got it," he says, not missing a beat.

"Don't call me a kid!" I snap as I put the food in the microwave. Fred comes up behind me at the counter and engulfs me in his arms. His bare chest flush against my sweaty back sends a chill down my spine. I turn around inside his embrace to face him.

"What does this stand for?" I trace the Chinese word on his left arm.

"Determination," he says. "I went on my seventeenth birthday. I was nothing like you as a teenager. Looking back, I was very immature, but I wanted so much. Even if I wasn't rich or smart, I knew I had enough talent and determination to make it as a musician." He moves his right arm toward me and shows me another symbol on that bicep. The same tattoo band surrounds it. "This one means artistic creativity." He traces it himself.

I trace the Roman numeral and he shivers like he is ticklish. "Does that tickle?" I ask, looking up into his clear blue eyes.

"Maybe. I don't know. Your touch does things to me I don't understand," he says, making me close my eyes and still my hand. He wraps his arms around me again and squeezes tight. The microwave keeps beeping so he leans over and stops it. He eventually releases me and we take the food outside to eat.

After we eat, I put my bare sandy feet in his lap. He brushes the sand off and rubs my left foot with both hands. It feels magical to lay my head back, close my eyes, and feel my body connected to his.

"Wanna play a little game?" I ask, feeling more confident because my eyes are shut.

"Sure." His voice is higher pitched than normal.

"I will ask you a question, but I also have to answer it. If it's something you can't answer about yourself, you shouldn't ask it," I say. "And if someone doesn't answer, the other person gets a free question. I will start. What is your favorite food?

"Just one food?"

"Yes, one favorite food, and it has to be food. Please refrain from sexual innuendos. I can't handle that right now." My eyes are still shut, but I can sense he is watching me. It feels erotic but I don't let my mind go there. Well, I try not to let it, but I can't control my thoughts around him.

"Hamburger. Is that a food?"

"I will accept that. You are a typical male, aren't you? Mine is chocolate. Now it's your turn."

"What is your favorite color?

"Purple. Deep, dark, rich purple."

"Orange," he says. "It always was but after the sunrise today it always will be."

"Favorite TV Show?" I ask, wanting to comment on the sunrise answer.

"Don't laugh, but I don't watch much TV. I had time to see ER a few times and it was a great show."

"Do you think George Clooney is hot too? I remember him on the *Facts of Life*. I pick *Party of Five*." I talk way too fast and he just laughs.

"How many people have you slept with?" he asks, getting me to sit up and fling my eyes open like I was hit with a Taser.

"You're gonna answer that one yourself, Mr. Hot Rock Star." I'm talking too loud as I shake my confused head.

"I got the hang of this. Answer, Ms. Jailbait."

"Hot Rock Star is a much better nickname," I state. "One."

"Did you love him?"

"That is two questions," I snap, "but I might answer so I can avoid hearing you answer your own question."

"Three," he says, and I think at first he means three questions, but then I think he is having a stroke.

"You have only slept with three people?" I clarify.

"Yes. You sound shocked."

"Look at you! Shocked is too simple a word. You are so attractive, so accomplished. You must have a pool of girls to pick from, especially after a concert," I say. "Aren't you like twenty-seven or twenty-eight?" Strange how my age has become such a burden and I don't even know his.

"I will be twenty-eight on August seventeenth," he says. "I don't remember whose turn it is."

I take my feet off him, get up and slide my legs under the arms of the chair so I am in his lap facing him. I run my fingers through his hair over and over again. I stare at his face so long I could draw it from memory. His eyes are shut and even without them he is the most beautiful thing I have ever seen.

"I should try calling home again and then let's get some food. And more ice cream," I say as I get up and walk away. I called yesterday but no one answered so I head inside and pick up the phone in the kitchen. My mother answers on the first ring and we make small talk. I almost want her to ask something, but she doesn't and I am grateful for that because I don't want to lie. I tell her that Rick will drive me home tomorrow and she says okay, before adding she can't wait to meet him. It makes me smile.

I pop my head back outside and tell Fred I am going to shower and change. The shower feels cathartic. I have done so much talking and feeling the last three days. It is exhausting being in limbo. Saying goodbye to him would be way worse than never having met him. I tell myself to make the most of it, whatever 'it' is.

I head back downstairs and Fred is sitting on the kitchen stool, smiling. "Come here." I walk into his embrace and it heals all my doubts. "I'm so sorry this is difficult. I wish it could be different. Let's just do our best to get through whatever happens together." His arm securely around me somehow makes it okay. "Let's get some food," he says, as he kisses the top of my head and we release each other.

We come back with a pizza and ice cream. We eat almost the whole pie and share a beer. It might be one of the best meals of my life. "You will drive me home tomorrow, right?" I ask.

"Of course, why wouldn't I?

"I'm just making sure. A lot has changed since you picked me up Friday. It feels like it was a lifetime ago, yet the time with you has gone way too fast."

"Life is funny that way sometimes," he says. "Our last night, one more walk on the beach?"

I don't answer as I stand up and take his hand. We walk more than we talk, then he asks what time I want to leave tomorrow. I answer honestly. "Never or after dinner. Traffic will be lighter later."

"Glad you didn't say after breakfast," he says and squeezes my hand tighter.

It is almost pitch black as we stand on the beach in front of his house. We are staring at the house and it looks different from this viewpoint. A couple lights are on, and the house looks warm and inviting. I have been here forty-eight hours but I could call this home. I am not ready yet to spend my last night here.

As if Fred can sense my melancholy, he steps behind me, wraps his arms around me, and hugs me tight to his chest. He says nothing but I feel he is often on the verge of wanting to say something. We walk back to the house holding hands as if we have done this for years.

I get ready for bed while Fred is downstairs. I toss my clothes in my bag as he walks in the bedroom, stealing my breath away yet again. He takes the dirty clothes I wore to bed Friday night out of my bag and throws them in the hamper. I watch him, unable to speak.

"You can come back for them once they are washed," he says, as he goes into the bathroom. I am content on top of the covers when he comes back. I have so much I want and need to say to him, but I can't bring myself to say a thing. I assume it is from fear of not hearing what I long to hear. I just stare at the ceiling, hoping the answers will rain down on me.

I hear his steps get louder and next thing I know he is doing a belly flop onto the bed next to me. I can't help but laugh and he laughs too. I lean over and start to tickle him, glad he has a shirt on, because if I were touching his skin this would turn more sexual. We roll around the bed tickling each other and I feel sixteen for a change.

It feels euphoric to laugh and it feels even better to have my hands all over him and his all over me. We are both breathless when he leans over me. His face is inches above mine. His eyes are closed. I should be closing mine but I can't stop staring at his beautiful face. His head drops down and his lips touch mine, gently and lovingly. Exactly what I was craving. He rolls over and exhales as if it took every ounce of energy to move away from me.

We climb under the covers and lay facing each other. We talk most of the night about nothing important yet because he already means the world to me every word out of his mouth is etched in my mind. We are still talking when the sun comes up.

"I'm going to be so tired tomorrow, there is no way I will sleep without you here tonight." He sounds painfully sad.

"Hold me while we nap?" He wraps his strong arms around me. I reach my hand over him and lift the sleeve of his t-shirt to reveal his tattoo, the one that means artistic creativity. I trace it with my finger over and over again, longing to be artistically creative with his body. He shifts slightly from side to side in the bed. I know he is aroused, but I also hope I am relaxing him. I hope we both have determination to make something of our time together as I fall asleep.

I wake up hours later and roll over to see the eyes I was just dreaming about. Fred smiles a smile that is so sexy it makes me stupid. "Damn, Morgan, you are gorgeous," he says without breaking his stare. I don't know what to say so I get out of bed and walk away.

I am gone a few minutes but his mood has changed and he looks sad. "Sorry, I had to pee and I didn't know what to say either." Before he can speak I lie down flush against his body and kiss him. My kiss is desperate and full of need. A need to know this isn't the end. A need to know we can endure our problems. He flips me over and lays his weight on top of me.

We kiss each other longer than we ever have. We can't stop. My hands roam the span of his muscular back, as his mouth possesses mine. His kisses are nothing like anything I have felt before. We both needed a good make-out session. Nothing about us though makes me feel sixteen. I wish for my world to be surrounded by all things Frederick Rhoades.

I bring my hands to his face and move my mouth to kiss his nose, his eyes, his forehead and I shift his head down so he is resting on my chest. I desire to hold him as he has held me so many times. His weight is such a comfort to my soul. We lie still for a while and it's still not enough, but I know it is getting late.

"Do you want to meet my parents, or is that too creepy?" I continue to run my fingers through his hair.

"Yes, I would like to meet the people who are responsible for making the remarkable woman you are. Plus, I may never see you again if I can't gain their trust. Also I get more time with you tonight." He kisses me too fast, making my lips hungry for him.

"Okay," is all I can muster. "You can't touch me around them. They will pick up on it. Well, my mom will."

"I can't promise anything." He smirks. "I will do my best though."

We leave the bedroom and Fred carries my bag for me again. Once downstairs I stand frozen, staring out at the ocean. He comes over and turns me around to face him. "You will be back, so stop looking so sad," he assures me. "I will do whatever it takes to make this work. I'm as scared as you are. The one thing I know is that I can't live without you." He hugs me tight before we walk to the Porsche. I have never felt such happiness and sadness in the same moment for the same reason.

Chapter Eight

Home

THE RIDE HOME takes over three hours with the holiday shore traffic. I feel content and relaxed and I don't mind at all that it is taking longer than normal. We are nearing my house and I am not nervous but I feel odd, different, a feeling I am unsure of. As if Fred can sense this he asks to see my school. I tell him which roads to take and before I know it we are in the parking lot.

He gets out of the car and I follow him, looking around to make sure we are alone. We go down to the track and walk around. We walk up by the school and he softly pushes me against the rough brick wall. He puts his hands on the wall above my head, and without touching me with any other part of him, his lips find mine. His kiss is sexy but holds more than any kiss ever has. He takes my hand and we go back to the car. No one has spoken a word and somehow I feel braver and ready to take Fred home.

As we pull into the driveway he puts his hand on my knee, gives it a squeeze, and says, "It will be fine. I won't embarrass you."

"I never thought you would. I'm afraid someone will see right through me and know how I really feel about you."

"How do you really feel about me?" he asks, looking more like the boy who is still inside the man.

I get out of the car and walk around to his side and open his door. His eyes are locked on me. He gets my bag and carries it for me. I stop short before I open the door and he bumps into me. I don't even say sorry. I just say, "What do I call you?"

He laughs. "What are the options?"

"Stop. You know what I mean. I still call you Rick to my family."

"Do whatever you feel comfortable doing. Now open that door, JB, or make up a nickname for me."

We moved into this house when Ryan was three years old and I was three months. White clapboard siding with red shutters makes it appear cozy. To the left of the entry way is a formal living room that we rarely use and dining room used on holidays. To the right is one of two staircases that go upstairs. At the top of the stairs, at the front of the house is my room. Ryan's is at the back on the same side and the bathroom is between them. My parents' room takes up the other half of the upstairs. They have a master bathroom off their room. The other staircase is near their bedroom and leads to the kitchen. The kitchen takes up most of the back of the house. There is also a family room at the back where we spend most of our time. Off the family room are a guest room, guest bath, and a two-car garage.

We can hear plenty of chatter coming from the kitchen. It's now or never, I say to myself. I touch Fred's arm for strength, to attempt to pull myself together. As I walk towards the family room he places his hand on the small of my back. He runs his fingers under my shirt. It's a touch that lasts two seconds, but it is enough to make me stand tall and fill me with courage.

My mother, father, Ryan, and his girlfriend from college are sitting at the kitchen table. They are all drinking coffee and eating dessert when I walk in with Fred right behind me. Ryan and Faith started dating in March. I have never met her but I have seen her photo. I thought Faith Finley sounded famous and here I am meeting her with a famous person at my side.

My mom's eyes lock on Fred's and I think she is tongue-tied, but it is Faith who squeals. I want to laugh but that would be rude so I bite my lip instead. My mom gets up and walks over between Fred and me and introduces herself. "Hi, I'm Gwen," she says, poised as she reaches out her hand. She is only forty-three, same age as my dad. They were married at twenty-three when they found out they were having Ryan. I smile, trying to cover the fear that my feelings for Fred are written on my lips. She releases his hand and asks if he wants coffee. She is already headed to get it before he says yes.

"My dad, Scott. Ryan, my brother, and Faith, his girlfriend," I say, pointing to each of them. "This is Frederick Rhoades." I pull a chair out for Fred to sit beside Faith, but first he leans past me to shake my dad's hand and then my brother's. He leans down and hugs Faith and she turns pale. I sit between him and my father before my mother returns with the coffee.

"Holy shit," flies out of Faith's mouth. I am glad she was the first to say something. Everyone lets out a little laugh. "You said she met him at a party. I thought she got an autograph. Oh my, he is sitting next to me." She tries to whisper but it isn't working.

"We did meet at a party and Morgan didn't even get my autograph. But I got a new best friend," he says, so matter of fact. I feel tears well up in my eyes. My mother is watching us like a hawk but with that comment I see her relax. Fred has everyone in a spell and it makes me wonder if I too am in it. But I don't care because whatever he does to me I just crave more.

"So, did you just find him outside again somewhere?" Ryan asks with the attitude of a protective big brother.

"No, he picked me up at Brooke's. Mom knew. Didn't she say anything?" I turn to look at her.

"It wasn't my business to tell," she says to Ryan.

I never loved her more than I do in this moment. My mom also loves to feed everyone so she offers Fred a pastry. "Rick?" she says.

"My family calls me Fred. I would be honored if you would too." He takes the plate from her. Damn! In one sentence he has won her over and confirms what I feel for him too.

The conversation at the table becomes more relaxed. My mom gets up to clear the table and I help her. We are at the sink and she turns toward me and tucks my hair behind my right ear as she has done since I was a little girl. "I love you." She leaves it at that as she hugs me. I feel there is a hidden meaning in it but I don't know what it is.

We are all back at the table when I say, "I should get my bag ready for school tomorrow. Fred, can I show you the rest of the house first?" He gets up and follows me. I turn my bedroom light on and watch him take in my room.

"I'm glad I have a place to picture you in when we talk later." He turns and smiles at me. He makes my heart melt and my feet feel like Jell-O. I spent the weekend in his house, in his bed, but having him stand in my room is surreal. I was never the kind to hang posters of hot boys on my walls, which is a relief right now. It would suck if Fred saw he wasn't up there. My room decorations are simple. Items my mom picked out when I was thirteen after we stripped the horrid pink wallpaper off. Most of the room is off-white. The accents are purples, light purples, and now I prefer dark purple, but I still love my room. My books and notepads and my awesome stereo represent me well.

I show him the bathroom, Ryan's room, and my parent's room, then take him back down the front stairs so we can avoid everyone. We walk through the doorway off the family room and I point out the guest room where Faith has been sleeping. I take his hand and take him out the back door. We walk behind the shed at the corner of the yard. The darkness and cool air help me decompress. I have been holding my breath for hours.

"It feels refreshing out here." I lean against the shed and close my eyes as I reach for his hands.

"Anywhere you are feels good." He moves his head closer to me. I reach up and kiss him. My hands snake around his neck as I pull him closer to me. His tongue is sweet and gentle as he moves it everywhere inside my mouth. My body is burning with sensation, yet I feel calmer than I have felt all night. I kiss him faster and harder with my tongue searching for his constantly. I realize I could live my whole life locked away at the shore with him and never need anything else.

I pull my lips from his and place light kisses all the way across his chin to his ear. I lightly suck and bite his ear lobe, then whisper in his ear, "You are such a smooth talker. I never noticed. Was I oblivious to it and is that how I landed myself in this predicament?"

He moves to get his hands on my shoulder and he centers me in front of him. "I kind of enjoy being in this predicament with you. I do have a charm trait, but I never used it with you. With you I'm myself." He brings his mouth back to mine. I need him. All of him. He pulls away and stares at me. "How will I ever sleep without you tonight?"

"I wish I knew. I will be tossing all night. Will you call me when you get home?"

"Yes, and I could spend the whole night on the phone with you and not have enough. Now let's get back inside before we get caught and I never get to see you again." He releases my hand and we head back inside. Fred says his goodbyes to everyone with that new charm I saw for the first time tonight. He leaves everyone with silly grins on their faces as I walk him to his car.

We get to the driver's side of his car. "You know they are watching. Be good and don't touch me." I point dramatically to the way he should head and he laughs. I laugh back. He makes me feel light, carefree.

"You are the best friend I could ever ask for. Regardless of what else I feel I would still hug a friend before I left. I'm going to hug you and they can all go crazy when they see it," he says, not taking his eyes off me.

"Okay. But would I hug a friend with my arms at your waist or around your neck?"

He laughs. "Damn, why do you have to be so freakin' cute? You are killing me. Let's go with above the neck. I will lean down to hug you, short stuff, and you can reach up. That work for you?"

"Absolutely."

"Oh shit, we are gonna screw this up, aren't we?" Even his exhale is sexual as he reaches down to hug me. My arms snake up around his neck naturally and I squeeze his back as hard as I can. A planned desperate hug. I release him first and he stands before me. "Wow, you are strong."

"No, just desperate for contact with you. Now go before I get sappy," I say and he opens his door.

He climbs in and shuts the door and puts the window down. "Go inside before I drive away." I shoot him a look of confusion. "I'm going to watch your ass so I have something to dream about in bed later." I walk away and give him what he wants without another word. I hear the car pull out of the driveway as I close the front door.

Everyone has a question when I go back in. I can't understand anything they are saying. The phone rings upstairs and I run to get it, glad to get away from them.

I answer it and Fred says, "Did I save you from the firing squad?"

"Yes, thank you." I throw myself on my bed. "Sure has been a long but wonderful night."

"Yes. Wonderful," he says when the call waiting beeps.

"It's Brooke," I say, knowing I sound frustrated since he is the only one I want to talk to.

"Go talk to her. Talking to a friend will help even if she doesn't know why."

"Okay. Will you call me when you get home so I know you are safe?"

"Yes, I will," he says extra sexy, making me want to stay on with him instead.

"Hey, Brooke, how's it going?" I try to sound casual but I know I can't pull it off.

"Give me all the dirt. What have you been doing all weekend?"

"I'm not ready to talk about it yet," I tell her honestly. "It's been wonderful and difficult. I need some time to process everything first. Okay?"

"Sure. I know I can be nosy but I love you too much to push," she says, making me glad she is my friend.

"So tell me about Jack." And boy does she tell me about Jack.

We get off the phone. I finish getting everything ready for school before I climb into bed. My mom comes in and lies down with me. I put my book down to talk but we are both silent for a minute. "Thank you for trusting me," I tell her eventually.

"I will always trust you. I hope you trust me too, especially if you need to talk," she says, squeezing my hand. "I love you, enjoy yourself, but be safe. I won't interfere unless I have to. But, honey, he is one gorgeous man. And the way he looks at you says it all." She pauses, rendering me stunned. I thought we covered it well. "Your father is clueless by the way." We both giggle.

"We are just friends, Mom. He obviously knows I'm sixteen."

She changes the subject and asks what we did all weekend.

I tell her all the fun wonderful things but leave out the best parts. She kisses me goodnight just as the phone rings. Before she leaves she asks if it is Fred and I nod yes. She reaches out her hand, asking for the phone, and I tell Fred to hold on.

She takes the phone. "Fred, thank you for taking care of my baby." She pauses and smiles. "She is special and I'm putting a lot of trust in you. Morgan enjoys your company. I would never deprive her of that." She looks over at me. "I will let you talk to her now. Good night." She hands me the phone and leaves.

"You okay?" I ask.

"Shit, your mom is cool. If you ever get sick of me I could replace you with her."

"That is so gross." I sound my age for a change. Then seriously I say, "I better not be replaceable!"

"You aren't," he whispers in his super sexy rock star voice.

"I can't handle much more tonight. I know I won't sleep well but I will try. What are you doing tomorrow?" I ask because I am nowhere near ready to hang up.

"Nothing. Maybe I will try to write or work out. I don't know. I will be a little lost without you."

"I will be lost without you tomorrow too, but at least you are home and free. I will be stuck in school."

He whispers, "I couldn't imagine going to school again. Is it like that all the time for you? I mean do you always feel you don't fit in because you are different?"

"Well, I guess I usually make myself fit so it doesn't matter. But I do know I am different and it sucks, but I have no other options."

"Time to sleep. Will you call me as soon as you are done at school?"

"The second I walk in the door. About two-thirty."

"I will be waiting by the phone," he purrs, speaking to the parts of my body that tingle the most.

"Damn, you can't be that hot and sexy when I have to sleep alone."

"Sorry. I'll hang up now even though I don't want to. I miss you, Morgan. I'm hanging up now because your mom said I have to…" His heavy breath arouses me again before the evil sound of the phone clicks off. I hang up and lie in my bed, eyes wide open. I imagine the comfort of his strong warm arms around me before I fall asleep.

The alarm is blaring and the sun is shining and it takes me a few seconds to realize where I am. I can't believe after three days with Fred his home has made mine feel foreign. I get ready for school in slow motion.

My dad always drives me in on his way to work now that Ryan is away at school. My dad is never talkative and neither of us is talkative in the morning. I walk into school and head to my locker. I am also glad I won't see Brooke until fifth period physics, because lying is hard.

I walk into the class and Brooke isn't at our lab table yet. When she sits down I turn toward her and get crushed with a loving hug. "I missed you so much. You look good. What have you been doing all weekend?"

"Just relaxing, hanging out. Nothing much." I wonder if she can see a change in me. Life around me is the same even though I feel dramatically altered. I know I will never be the same. Fred has changed me on some level for eternity. Class starts so at least I don't have to explain more, yet.

While walking to lunch I keep thinking about Doug on *21 Jump Street*. I feel like a narc. I become worried everyone will notice I should not be here, but this is where I belong. The two sides of my life do not mix. I am relieved I have three weeks of school left; maybe then this lost feeling will vanish.

I get a ride home with Brooke and our friend Heather, who was given a brand new Mercedes for her seventeenth birthday. I should feel some jealousy, but she is the sweetest girl I know. They drop me off first, which is awesome since I never wanted to get home from school as bad as I do today. I head right to my room and grab the phone.

Fred answers on the first ring. "Hey, hot stuff." He is so sultry he could melt the phone.

"What if it wasn't me?" I say.

"Well, you and Gunner are the only ones with this number, unless you are giving my number out. Good thing it wasn't your mom, right?"

"Stop! She is so in love with Dad you don't have a chance in hell. Also I would never give your number to anyone."

"Should I put her love of your dad to a test?"

"Hell no! She is human. I could lose you both."

"Okay, no more mom jokes. Besides I only want you."

He makes me feel sexy and strong. "We make quite a pair. Damn, I want you so bad."

"Shit, babe, don't get all phone sex on me. I won't survive."

"Okay, PG-13. I promise. Even if I'm somewhere between R and XXX."

We talk until dinnertime, then I tell him I will do my homework, eat dinner, and call him back. He tells me he will write more, but he isn't getting anything to click. I want to help him make everything click.

* * *

We talk every day after school and every night that week. He says he wants to see me for the weekend. I want nothing more than to see him, but I have no idea how to make it work. On Thursday night he asks me to get my mom because he wants to talk to her. Against my wishes, I leave to get her.

She comes with me into my room and I hand her the phone. I leave the room for a few minutes because it's not easy to listen, but I return because I don't know what else to do with myself. Their conversation is interesting from this end but also upsetting. She seems tearful and she does not say a thing. She hands me back the phone and leaves, saying nothing to me.

"What did you say?" Fear and excitement fill my voice.

"I bought you some more time with me." I can tell he is smirking.

"What did you say? My mom looked teary."

"Well, I told her how helpful you were with writing and that you had great thoughts and a different outlook on life, unlike anyone I ever met. I told her you were inspiring. And I read her a poem I wrote about you."

"Can I hear it?"

"Not yet. When the time is right for you to hear the end you can hear it all. I only read her the beginning. When we are alone and together, soon, I will share it with you."

"Damn, you are always leaving me burning for you and spiraling out of control."

"Damn, JB, you do that to me too."

"Stop calling me that!"

"But you are so sweet and tiny like a jellybean."

"Oh really. What flavor am I?

"I don't know yet. I haven't tasted all of you."

"Shit, if I have to be PG-13 so do you. Wait, I heard her say something about a job?"

"I told her I have been thinking of hiring an assistant and that you are brilliant and creative and I would love to work with you. I want to write with you. You feel so much and we have to put it on paper. She said yes." He sounds as if he is holding his breath.

"Does your work place frown on inter-office romance?"

"Hell, no, it's highly regarded."

"Okay, then I want you to employ me."

"How can you make the word employ sound dirty?"

"I think everything might sound dirty to you." I need to change this topic. It is going too far too fast and we both know it. "Maybe we should both get some sleep so we can stay up all night tomorrow and I can get friendly with my new boss."

"Not boss. How about co-worker?"

"Okay, co-worker, I should rest up for my new job. I'll miss you dreadfully again tonight."

"I'll miss you too." I hear him sigh and I just hold the phone to my ear, enjoying his breathing. "Hey, you still there?"

"Yes," I whisper huskily.

"A small part of me wants to say you are a cherry jellybean, but then that isn't you at all, so I will pick cappuccino. You are hot and comforting, you feel great in my hands, and you give me energy to make every day count. Good night, Jellybean." He hangs up, leaving me missing him and falling fast.

Chapter Nine

Ice Cream

DAZED AT SCHOOL on Friday, I fear everyone can tell I am lost in my head. Fred floods my mind so much, a tidal wave of thoughts could wash out the entire town. Brooke is absent since her cousin is getting married in Connecticut. She is in the wedding party so the whole family left last night for the weekend. I miss her but also I am grateful that she is away so I don't have to lie. No one else at school knows me well enough to notice anything is off. I get through the day and Heather is driving me home when I realize that Fred could be in my driveway already and I start to panic.

She pulls up to my house and sure enough his Jeep is right in front of us. I become excited but stupid nervous too. Heather says have a good weekend and leaves. Crazy me, nervous for nothing. Fred is not in the Jeep so I wonder where he is. I unlock the front door and go inside. The house is quiet. I call his name and he answers me from upstairs. Damn, that man better not be on my bed. I walk upstairs and there he is. I have never wanted him as bad as I do here and now.

"How did you get in?" I ask with my eyes locked on him.

"I called your mom at work and she told me where the key was hidden. I thought she would enjoy hearing from me." He smiles and I swear his eyes twinkle.

"Stop it! How did you get her number?" I hit him with a pillow as I kneel on my bed next to him. He catches the pillow and pulls me into him.

"I asked her for it the other day." He rips the pillow out from between us and I fall happily on top of him. He smells even more yummy than I remember, like strawberries and licorice, but not strawberry licorice. He looks even better too. He is relaxed and happy. We are staring at one another and I swear I smell smoke from the fire burning inside him.

"Damn, Morgan." He leans up to kiss me. His hands are on my face as his lips move against my lips. His tongue slides across mine as he flips me over onto my back. His body presses hard into me; the weight of him is exquisite. His left hand works its way down my side before he caresses my breast through my shirt. As his thumb moves in slow circles over my nipple I arch my back into him, wanting more. I moan a little too loud as he works his kisses to my ear. His hot breath on my skin is making me squirm underneath him.

I need and want more, so much more. Then he moans in my ear, "Morgan, I missed you." I can't understand how he is able to form words. I crave his mouth, his body, anything, on me. I kiss him harder and deeper, with even more need than I thought a person could possess. He kisses me back and it's life altering and mind numbing, but I know we must stop. We could easily get caught.

"Let's go downstairs. I can't fuck this up," he says. He doesn't curse as much as a rock star usually does. He is unquestionably having a tough time stopping. I should say something but there is nothing to say. We get up and walk to the door.

"Wait," I say and I startle him. He turns to me like he often does because he reads me so well. He engulfs me in his large arms and lifts me off the floor. I wish I never had to be disconnected from his body. He lets me go, but I prolong my slide down his body. I reach my hands up to grab his face and pull it down to mine. I kiss him and say, "I am sorry this is so hard."

"It's worth every damn second. I will never get enough of you," he says, taking my hand as we walk downstairs.

We discuss dinner when he says we should stay at my house. He thinks spending time with my family might help our situation and I agree, but I can't help be nervous that we will slip up. I call my mother before she leaves work to tell her we are going to pick up some pizza. She is extra bubbly on the phone, which makes me think Fred has us all under his spell again.

I order the food and Fred drives us to pick it up. It is exciting doing something so mundane, yet I am nervous we will be caught. We are not doing anything wrong, but the more people who know we know each other the greater the chance is of this having to end. I run in with Fred's money and get the food and we head back home. At a red light he says, "Come over here." I lean toward him without question and he kisses me with a passion that holds such promise. His eyes are locked on mine and we are literally lost in each other until the person behind us starts beeping. "I hope that isn't your dad."

"I would punch you if you weren't driving," I say with a fake frustrated face.

"Were you ever wild and crazy?"

"Not really, but everything about you makes me wild and crazy." He takes his right hand off the wheel and reaches for my left. I love the way his hands feel tangled with mine.

We pull in the driveway and head inside. Fred just has to pinch my ass in the doorway and make me squeal. I tell him to stop but I certainly don't ever want him to stop. My mom is the only one in the kitchen when we walk in and she already has dishes out. My dad comes down a few minutes later and we are eating when Ryan comes home. Faith has gone back home for her new job, and I might prefer her not being here. I don't know if I feel that way because I don't like her and my brother together or if I prefer the smaller group of people. I don't want anyone to see what I truly feel for this man I claim is a friend.

We clean up and my mom takes me aside to ask how I am. It's weird because at first I don't know what to say. "I told Dad last night that Fred offered you a job in Mantoloking as an assistant and writer. He was shocked and I told him it is a great opportunity. He is skeptical of a man wanting to spend so much time with you and not have other motives. It took a lot to convince him to say yes. Have the time of your life, but please be safe and smart. If anything changes or becomes a problem, we are always a phone call away."

She is so accepting, it makes me feel lucky, but I wish I wasn't lying.

I don't know what I could say that is fitting, but I say, "Sorry, this is unusual. I love the way I feel when I am with him. It's a marvelous way to live, so creative and relaxing. I feel so full of life. Thank you for letting me have this."

"You have always been a smart mature child and I couldn't be more proud to have such a beautiful independent girl, woman. I have to let you go and grow. I know you can handle any obstacles you encounter, and I trust you to lean on me and your father if you need to."

I'm so glad I have her for a mom. I hug her tightly as Fred comes back into the room.

Fred and I walk up to my room to get my bag packed. All he does is fondle my underwear and informs me that I don't need much else. We are laughing and giggling when my dad sticks his head in the doorway.

"Just wanted a hug before you leave," he says. I get up and hug him. "I love you, Honey. Have a nice weekend. I will miss you."

"Thanks, Dad. Sunday isn't far away."

"I know, but time is going by too quickly. You will be grown and gone soon. I have to make a call for work. I will see you Sunday. Maybe you two can come back by dinner?" he asks, sounding a little sad.

"Absolutely, we will be back for dinner," I say before he leaves. My dad has never been a conversationalist and he doesn't show emotions often. It feels new and good to see him emotional.

Fred is watching me. We head downstairs and only my mom is around. We both say goodbye and walk to his Jeep. Fred grabs my hand and asks me to look at him. "Are you okay? Do you want to do this?"

"I want every second I can get with you. I have never wanted anything more than I want time with you. It is challenging for me to have to watch my parents witness me grow up so fast. They deserved to have a kid for longer, but I was never a kid. They accept me for who I am, and I am very lucky because of that." He lifts my hand and kisses it and I don't care who sees.

"You are damn special. I have taken you from them. They should be sad, but lucky me gets to enjoy your company. Thank you for giving me the honor." His words sound sexier than I have ever heard words spoken. I fall a little more.

"Shit, you are making me melt with that voice. We should drive now because I need to be alone with you." He starts the car and we head home. I have two homes now, but I could live anywhere because Frederick Rhoades is quickly becoming my home.

The ride takes a little over an hour without shore traffic. The sun is setting as we pull into the driveway. It is a beautiful night and even though I want badly to go inside and do crazy fun things to him, I suggest we walk on the beach first. He smirks, kisses me, and starts walking while holding my hand. The sand is warm today and it smells of summer. Clean fresh warm ocean air fills my nostrils and excites my mind.

"Why are you so happy?" Fred asks.

"I love the beach and I love summer. I can smell it, and it smells majestic."

"You are beautiful and way more majestic than summer, especially when you smile."

"You are pretty damn cute when you smile. And pretty damn hot when you are laughing." I start to tickle him before I run away. He catches me and grabs me around the waist.

"Damn, you run fast. Did you not want to be caught?" I turn inside his embrace to find the blue eyes that warm me to my core.

"I always want you to catch me. I have to put up a little fight sometimes, so I don't look desperate."

"Nothing about you is desperate." Fred's lips are on mine before I blink. His kiss is passionate and suddenly we are in the sand. I fell and didn't even attempt to catch myself. Fred is on top of me. The sand is supporting me on this ride to heaven. There has never been a moment more exciting. Last week was a dream. This time I know this is real. I am back and he wants me regardless of my age. I feel complete as I kiss him over and over again. We kiss like we are both teenagers. But I know nothing about our kisses or the way we feel is immature.

"Want to go to bed?" He pulls away from me, leaving me speechless. Several minutes later he asks, "Did I take your tongue by accident?"

"I'm in awe of you. You make me happy, alive, content and many things there are no words for. I have never wanted to just live in the moment like I do when we are together. Yes, I would love to go to bed with you," I say with pure conviction.

He sighs and says, "I love it when I leave you speechless, then suddenly you have so much to say so fast. It's so damn cute. I love how much you excite every nerve in my body too."

We walk hand in hand back to the house. He left the sliders to the deck open again. I ask him why he never locks the doors. "I will once you are inside because you are the only thing in here I couldn't live without," he says, stopping me, frozen right in the doorway. "Hey, you okay?"

"I know you aren't feeding me lines. Everything you say is genuine. I'm trying to absorb it all. It's a tad overwhelming."

"Morgan, I feel marvelous crazy things for you. You have flipped a switch on in me that I didn't know was off. I don't understand it but you have made me a different man. I'm excited to see what life brings me every day because of you."

We head upstairs and I realize my bag is still in the car. I don't leave to get it because Fred has my pajamas on the bed and a toothbrush in the bathroom. He is making me feel even more at home.

Fred is sitting on the sofa when I come out of the bathroom. He looks beyond yummy in a pair of black and grey pajama bottoms. I almost can't believe this man is waiting for me, but when I see the smile on his face I believe it. I sit down facing him. "So who washed my clothes?"

"Why do you ask?"

"Well, I know you would do anything for me, but I can't see you doing laundry, food shopping, cleaning. I know it's not your thing, and you have enough money to not do it."

"I have someone come twice a week. Her name is Nina, and she is sweet. You will have to meet her soon. She cleans, does laundry and my food shopping. I do hire people to do just about everything. Do you want more details or would you rather I kissed you?"

"Kiss me."

I climb into his lap as he shifts his hips to face me. I stay up on my knees wanting badly to lower myself on to him, but I don't and I don't lean in to kiss him either. I lock my eyes on his. I run my right hand through his hair and down to his shoulder and do the same with the other side. No one blinks. With both hands on his shoulders I gradually lower myself onto his lap. I move slowly – it seems an eternity before I touch him. It was worth the wait.

I move again slightly until his erection is pressed exactly where I crave it. I shift my hips again and still we don't close our eyes. He moves his hands to my hips and moves me slowly back and forth. The pleasure is too much for us both. I shut my eyes and he moans. I move my hands up to his cheeks and his stubble is arousing. I kiss his lips. They are soft, warm, and moist. I can't be gentle anymore. My tongue finds his as his hands dig into my hips. We are both frantic. I push my legs down deeper into the couch, trying anything I can to be closer to him.

There is only one way to be closer and we can't do that. Is this exciting because it is forbidden? He kisses me back and I know it would take almost nothing else to make me explode. Torn about whether I should push harder or let go, I realize he has to be strong for us both because his touch makes me weak. He moves his hand back to my face and his kisses trail down my throat. Then he pulls away and looks up at me.

"Morgan, this desire is controlling me." He kisses me again. "Not now. Not yet. Ice cream?" he says with a desperate need to make the sexual pain end.

"No, but it's best." I get up off him and the couch, shocked by how weak he makes my limbs. He reaches for my hand to support me. "Thanks."

"I hope I can always be the one to catch you."

"Me too."

We eat the ice cream in bed and once again time flies when we are together. I want it to move faster, so we can get to the future. I know I can't stay stuck in limbo much longer.

Chapter Ten

Sunday Morning

FRED'S ARM IS across my stomach when I wake warm and cozy in the bed of the man I am falling for. I don't want to move, but I have to get my bag out of the car. I am careful as I wiggle out from under him, trying not to wake him, but when I return he is sitting up in bed as if he was waiting for me.

"I would have gotten that for you," he says, yawning.

"It's okay. You are cute when you yawn, by the way," I say because it is so damn true.

I put my bag down and the need to run today hits me hard, but I don't want to be apart from him. I walk over to the bed and wiggle myself against the headboard behind him. I spread my legs and slide them down his and he leans back against me. I feel small trying to fit around his body. His skin against mine ignites every nerve in my body.

I start rubbing his shoulders. He has beautiful muscles that beg to be caressed. It shocks me how little my hands look as they glide over his body. Smooth tanned skin over defined hard muscles, I never want to stop touching him. I continue to rub his shoulder and arms as I attempt to absorb how overloaded my mind is on sex. Every other thought flies right out of my head; my mind only has room for Fred.

"I'm going to go for a run, then I will cook breakfast."

"Okay."

He turns around and I slide my body down under his. I just stare up at him as he supports himself above me. I lower my hands to his ass and push him down so he is flush against me. I feel him wanting me, as I want him.

"I'm going to get up now and get a drink of water, put a CrossRhoades tape in my Walkman and run and run until I burn off the ice cream from last night and the need that burns inside me for you." I kiss his forehead and he lets me up. I hear him sigh, and I turn around and lean back down next to him. I whisper in his ear, speaking soft and slow, "You should take a shower and imagine my hands all over you. Picture me touching you. When I get back you will be beyond relaxed." I walk away hoping he is watching my ass again. My entire run I imagine him in the shower and it makes time fly.

I come back and Fred is in the kitchen. Khaki shorts and a crisp white shirt never looked so good. He has pans out and looks confused but it's cute. Then again I can't imagine him not looking cute. I ask him what he wants to make. He turns to me and wraps his arms around me.

"Hey, you okay?" I pull my head off his firm chest to find his eyes.

"Yes, just so damn messed up."

"Sorry."

"It's a nice messed up. I am crazy about you. I can't even walk ten feet without you flooding my mind… and body. You have consumed me and I want so much more of you. Will you help me make breakfast to get my mind off what I can't have?"

"Fred, I don't want you to be frustrated. I know how difficult this is."

"You make me feel incredible, even if it's a little painful sometimes. I don't mean to sound negative. You wound me up big time. Next time I will go running with you."

"That would be fun. I've never felt this comfortable with someone. I know this is tough and not quite what we both want. We need to be able to say when we can't take anymore, okay?"

"Yes, it's all going to be okay," he says and his eyes reassure me more than his words.

"What do you want for breakfast?"

"Fuck, Morgan, I just want you," Fred mutters as he slams my back into the fridge, making it rattle. His hands are all over me making my body tingle to life. His kisses are desperate and I feel what he is feeling. I become desperate too. I push my body and mouth into him as roughly as

I can. We sink to the floor, then I push him against the cabinet opposite the fridge. I climb into his lap with only one goal. I reach down and grab the edge of his shirt and take it off him. It is necessary for my sanity to feel his skin this instant. I reach down and take my shirt off.

He lowers his head to kiss my neck and shoulder. Our hands don't leave each other. He pushes his hand under my sports bra and its unbearable to have his hand on my exposed flesh. My mind and body are in heated bliss. Then a loud noise makes me pull away from him.

The kitchen door slams and I hear unfamiliar voices. I stand up as fast as I can while making sure my bra is on right. *Holy shit!* rings through my head. I'm relieved I didn't say it out loud. I take one big deep breath, summon every confident cell in my body, and walk over to Fred's guests. Meeting two of Fred's band mates, unplanned while in this state, is not something I saw coming.

"Hello. You must be Alex and Zach. Nice to meet you both." I reach my hand out to shake theirs. I sound formal, better than sounding nervous, I guess. "I'm Morgan."

Alex Duval, rhythm guitar player, is the youngest member of the band, but I don't remember how old he is. I guess maybe twenty-three or twenty-four, but my brain is so jumbled looking at them I get flustered. Zach Thompson is the bass guitar player, and I realize I know nothing about him. Gunner Cross, the drummer, is not with them. Strangely I feel a marked disappointment.

They are all crazy good looking. Are all three of these men in the kitchen really that smoking hot or does their profession make them appear that way? Fred finally gets up from the floor and he's holding a frying pan. He tries to cover for us both, but I doubt his friends will buy it. I wish that Fred and I had spent some time talking about them. Especially about who I am supposed to be or how old. I walk back over to Fred and take the pan out of his hand. Then reluctantly I ask Alex and Zach if they want breakfast.

"Breakfast? It's almost noon," Alex says, making me think he is my least favorite of the group.

"What sort of a rock star are you? I thought late nights and sleeping mornings away was part of the job description," I say, trying to cover my hasty distaste for a person I just met.

"I don't know, maybe the kind who is wondering who the hell you are," Alex says, staring at me as I pick my shirt up off the floor and put it back on.

"I already introduced myself. Now raise your hand if you are hungry. You can decide for yourself whether to call it breakfast or lunch."

I make a large plate of scrambled eggs and bacon while Fred, Alex, and Zach head outside. Thankfully no one asks me any more annoying questions, and when we are done eating I make everyone clean up. I tell them I love cooking, but I don't clean up. All three of them look at me, say nothing, but they clean while I head upstairs.

The showerhead is large and the water pressure is perfection, but seeing the ocean while taking a shower is one of the most marvelous feelings on earth. The combination of fresh water and salt water heightens all my senses. As I turn the shower off and wrap a towel around myself, a sudden feeling of contentment, almost euphoria washes over me. I open my eyes and Fred is standing in the doorway, looking lustful.

"You don't knock anymore?"

"You don't lock the door anymore?"

"I don't think I have ever locked that door, have I?"

"I don't know. I never tried to open it while you were in here." He sounds youthful and carefree. "They left."

I say nothing. I just walk to him and stare up into his beautiful blue eyes. He stares back at me and wraps his arms around me. My towel is falling and I try to tighten it around me when I realize I would prefer it if it fell off.

I want to ask him what our story will be to those in his life. We have established what my family knows at least. I don't want to talk about it though. I wish I were eighteen so it wasn't an issue. Then I remember he is married. I walk back into the bedroom to find my suitcase is missing. "Hey, where are my clothes?"

"I put everything away."

"Thanks, you didn't have to do that." I walk back to him and lean my head on his chest. "Why is it so easy to be with you?"

"I don't know yet, but it will be fun figuring it out. I hope you will be here enough that you can leave these clothes and stop packing."

"Me too."

I take out shorts and a tank top once Fred shows me what drawers my things are in. Seeing my clothes in his dresser is enthralling. I head to the bathroom to change but I leave the door open. Nothing about being naked in front of him would bother me, but I would be torturing him and myself if I changed out there.

Somehow time is moving at an accelerated speed again. Fred and I have been in the hammock and I can tell hours have passed only because the sun is setting. I have never spent time like this. He is all consuming, satisfying all my needs. When we are together I don't feel hungry, tired, bored, or lonely. He fills in all the empty spaces. Fred gives me life with each breath he takes. He makes me feel everything and nothing. It's such a divine gift.

"Hungry?" I ask.

"A little. I can't move yet."

"Me either."

"I could hold you for eternity and it still would not be enough."

"Let's try."

His stomach growls and I laugh. "How about food, then eternity in the hammock?"

"Perfect," he says, but we both still don't move.

"What are you in the mood for?" I ask.

"Cappuccino jellybeans."

"You are very bad." He leans over and kisses me soft and sweet.

"Okay, let's get food."

We drive around for a while. The hum from the car and the salty breeze puts me in a daze. It feels damn good being with him. How could I ever live without him?

"Chinese take-out good for you?" he asks.

"Absolutely."

He parks the car and opens his door but I stop him. "Hey, you can tell me what you want and I'll get it."

"It's not a crime to be in a restaurant with you. It won't take long to get the food."

While we are waiting a few people stare at him and one man looks like he is going to say something but he doesn't. It's kind of fun watching the expressions on their faces. "Is it weird for you?" I ask.

"Is what weird?"

"Having people recognize you. Do they ever act like they know you?"

"It used to bother me a lot. That is why I don't go out much. I hate when they act like they know me personally. That happens a lot." He wraps his arms around me and pulls me too him, kissing my forehead. "You are not like that. You never pretended to know me."

"I would never have pretended to know you. Actually getting to know you is half the pleasure."

"You don't think like other people. I love that about you."

They call us for our food, but Fred has me staring at his hotness, leaving my mind empty. At least he has enough sense to respond. We get the food and head home. I love that we can be silent and not try to fill the air with words all the time.

It starts to drizzle when we pull in the driveway, and I can't wait to eat and get cozy with my hot singer. Fred takes the food and puts it on the coffee table. He gets us each a glass of water and sits down with the remote control. He turns the TV on and I realize we have never watched television together.

"What should be the first thing we watch together?" he asks.

"Damn, I just said to myself that we've never watched television together. I swear you get in my brain sometimes."

"There are other places I'd rather get into of yours." He says it so slow and sexy I have a burning desire to spread my legs for him. He pushes me back onto the couch, his eyes locked onto mine until his lips are on me. He kisses me slow and sultry, then his tongue is frantic in my mouth. He lowers his hips into mine and I moan with a need of frustration I have never known before.

"Damn, Fred, you are killing me."

"I'm killing myself too," he says as he gets up and opens the food cartons. I sit on the couch disheveled. I pick up the remote and scroll through the channels and find a replay of a French Open Tennis match from earlier in the day. It's almost over and Andre Agassi is winning.

Fred hands me chopsticks. "Really? You think I can eat with these?"

"I want to see how skilled your hands are."

"Damn, what happened to PG-13?"

"That doesn't work around you. You make me feel alive, as if every cell in my body is awake. I want to be me and I want you to be you. No rules."

"Okay." I lift my glass to toast. "To our new rule. No more rules." We clink classes and I take my chopsticks in my hand and try to get a piece of shrimp.

"We never eat out of the carton. My dad always puts it on plates."
"Really?"
"And we use forks. Guess he is a little uptight."
"Your dad is cool, but maybe he needs to live a little."
"I agree. It might take me all night though to eat with these chopsticks."

I struggle, but I get the hang of it when I notice Fred is watching me. He lifts his chopsticks to my mouth and feeds me. Moving my tongue over his chicken and locking my lips around the chopsticks has me all worked up again. His eyes watch everything I do with bated breath. He feeds me another bite and I become frustrated from the passion boiling inside me. He is the most erotic creature I have ever set eyes on, once again elevating my level of yearning.

I can't snap out of my trance watching him. He takes a gulp of water and turns back to me. He puts his chopsticks down and puts his hands on either side of my face. He holds my head and stares at me. I will never tire of looking at him. Leaning in he is almost touching my mouth, but hovers over me instead. I want to move to touch him but he mesmerizes me, and I want to see what he wants. He licks his lips in a slow suggestive way and I can hear him swallow when suddenly faster than a bolt of lightning, he has me flat on my back on the floor. His tongue dips deep inside my mouth.

His body grinds against mine, bringing me a pleasure that requires more pleasure. I push my hips into him and dig my nails into his muscular back. I pull him as close to me as I can. We are so wrapped up in each other that I never want to let go. He continues to kiss me with every ounce of passion he has. His body is firm and hot, consuming me with his touch. I continue to push myself into his leg, getting as much pressure as I can. My heart races and my body heats up like a volcano about to blow. His thigh is firm, his kisses erotic, and I feel close to coming right here on the floor fully clothed when he abruptly moves off me.

His eyes are locked on me and they are dark with lust. I stare back at him, wishing he didn't pull away when I want him more than ever. He gets up and sits with his back to the couch and looks at the TV, then back at me. He gives me his hand and pulls me up. I sit next to him for a few minutes, then turn to talk to him. He puts his finger over my mouth. I swear he knows what I will do next when I don't even know myself.

He turns his face back to the TV and stares blankly until he says, "Sorry, that was too much. I can't help how turned on you make me and I can't always control myself. I don't want to hurt you or make you come on the floor beside half-eaten Chinese food." He releases a nervous chuckle. "But if I did I bet tennis would always be your favorite sport." He laughs again and I laugh with him. I climb into his lap. My legs are spread around him.

I run my hands through his hair and whisper in his ear. "Okay." I stare at him before I speak again. "I understand and accept it. Stopping is not what I want. I want you to know I crave all of you from deep within my soul. I love how you can read me so well. You know me better than I know myself. There is no room for food or TV when you are in my head. Next time, don't worry about our surroundings because all of my senses are focused on you." I trail light kisses down his neck and back up. He moans and it has me melting all over again. "This is too much again. Should we sleep separately so it's not as difficult?"

He pushes my head up and stares at me. "Please sleep with me. I need to hold you. Always. I won't push you that far again."

"You never push me. I sit before you giving you all of me. I never want to stop." I speak breathlessly from the burning sensations of lust coursing through me from head to toe.

"Damn, Morgan, where the hell did you come from? Fuck, I need you so bad. Not yet. Not tonight. Let's go to bed. Let me hold you, even if all we do is talk and sleep. Next to you is the only place I want to be. Please trust me."

"I have never not trusted you." I stand up and take his hand. He stands up next to me and I bring as much of the food as I can carry and put it in the fridge. He turns the TV and lights off and follows me in silence into the kitchen. Only the light from the stove is on, as I put the water glasses in the sink. His arms hug me from behind.

He squeezes me so tight I can't turn around to face him. It feels safe having his strength wrapped around me. I lower my chin and he moves his left hand up and pushes my hair off the back of my neck as he leaves feather light kisses on my sensitive flesh. When I turn around to face him his eyes are on fire. They are the deepest blue I have ever seen and I want to drown in them. I reach up on tippy toes and kiss his lips, then pull away slightly to say, "Take me to bed. I need to have your arms around me so I can fall asleep."

My arms are around his neck when he reaches down and lifts me up from behind my knees. I squeal like a little kid, but I feel like a woman, as he carries me up to the bedroom. Fred walks to the couch and sits down while still holding me and drapes my body in his lap. I lay my head on his shoulder and inhale the intoxicating scent that has captivated me from day one.

"I can't wait until it gets cold and I can hold you with a fire blazing," he says, as we hold each other. "I wish it wasn't getting harder when it should be getting easier. I might be greedy, but I can't imagine not spending every second possible with you. Can you forgive me for needing you so bad?" He speaks with control that I know I do not possess right now.

"I will never forgive you. I am guilty too," I say. I kiss the top of his head and get up to grab my pajamas. I don't want to walk away and change in the bathroom, but I also don't want to torture him by changing in front of him. I walk over, standing between him and the fireplace. My eyes are locked on his as I wish for a fire because his gaze gives me chills.

I take my shorts off and put my bottoms on over my underwear. His eyes are glued to me and I have never felt sexier. I slowly take my t-shirt off and put my top on over my bra. I pull a *Flashdance* move and take my bra off. I drop it to the floor and walk over to get pajama bottoms for him. I come back and lean down to remove his shirt, his eyes never leaving mine. It's so damn hot it feels like there is a fire burning in the fireplace. He moves his back away from the couch and lifts his arms for me. I drop his shirt to the floor and grab his hand to pull him up. Fred stands before me, his stunning beauty leaving me speechless. I swallow, looking for air, as my hands start to unbutton his jeans. I slowly undo all five buttons and pause before I put my hands inside his pants and slide them down past his hips. He steps out of them and takes his pajama bottoms and slips them up over his boxers. He comes back to stand inches away from me. Changing clothes just became my new favorite hobby.

"Damn, you are sexy. I fear I would not survive having sex with you." He is very serious. I feel laughter building up but he is too serious so I don't laugh. We would both survive, but nothing will ever be the same after that night under the lilac tree. He kisses my lips and carries me to bed, then pulls the covers back before he lays me down. The sheets are cool and refreshing. Fred wraps his arm around me, and my head settles into his firm chest.

"You mesmerize me, but we should sleep. I can't even form words that make sense tonight." I say as he caresses my back and within seconds I drift off to sleep, engulfed in the safest place I have ever been.

I wake up lying on my right side and I open my eyes to a most beautiful sight. Fred is awake and watching me. His eyes are crystal clear, content, and super blue. He blinks and says, "Good morning." I stare at him. "It's raining. You up for breakfast in bed before we head back to your house?"

"Yeah," I mutter, still in awe of him.

"Still sleepy?"

I shake my head. "I have to get over the shock every time I wake up and see you. It is like having a recurring dream where fantasy keeps becoming reality."

"Would it feel real if I touched you?"

"Yes."

He uses the back of his hand to caress my shoulder. He runs it down my arm. I have goose bumps and my insides are boiling. What a contradiction. He takes his hand and cups it around my breast. His thumb rolls over my nipple until it is hard and wanting. I lick my lips and moan. My breasts feel heavy and my mind has gone blank again.

My eyes are still shut when he moves to get up. He is standing on the side of the bed when he finally speaks and I open my eyes. "Coffee? Bagel? Butter or cream cheese?" he asks and, damn, what the hell is a bagel? My mind is vacant.

It takes me a minute to say anything and he waits patiently. "Coffee, definitely. Bagel please with cream cheese. I will come help you."

"No, stay here." He leaves so I get up and use the bathroom and brush my teeth. He returns with the food to find me content against the headboard watching the rain. A shirtless Frederick Rhoades is bringing me breakfast in his bed. I take my hand and pinch myself.

"Whatcha doin'?" he says as if he is singing it.

"I was checking to see if this is real or a dream. You are so damn sexy and you are half naked and you made me breakfast. Did I win the hot man lottery?"

"No. I'm the winner. I have you and a rainy Sunday morning. I feel peaceful and relaxed. I never had anyone to enjoy this feeling with. I love that you can lie here with me and it's enough for you too. I love that you are so complex yet so simple."

"You leave me unable to form words too often." I want to ask why he hasn't shared lazy Sundays with Beth. I say nothing because I don't want to hear the answer and I can't utter her name. We eat in silence and I'm sure it's because Beth is on both our minds.

"Morgan, we are a lot alike. It is no effort to understand you – it comes naturally to me. You were a missing part of me and now that I have found you I feel complete. I know it sounds cliché. It's just that I don't have to think about what to do to make you happy. I get to spend the day being me and somehow that makes us both happy."

He always says such wonderful things. He is right though, so I back up what he is saying. "We can be silent and still seem to know what the other one needs. It's a priceless gift."

"You're priceless." He leans down and kisses me. We hold each other in bed and watch the rain hit the window. His hand is around my waist from behind. My fingers run over his arm repetitively, hypnotizing me. I don't want to go home and sleep without him again or study for finals. I hardly ever get bored, but it surprises me how much time I can be with him and do nothing and be completely content.

"Do you ever turn your mind off?" I ask.

"Huh? It might be off now," he whispers.

"Do you always think about writing, or lyrics and melodies? Is it easy to get them out or is it frustrating?"

"I guess both. Sometimes things come to me easily and sometimes I struggle. Music is easy, lyrics are difficult. Gunner is a lyric whiz. When I work with him it's a little easier."

"You make beautiful music with Gunner. That sounds very romantic."

He tickles me, making me laugh. I feel youthful and alive. He stops and we are still again until I say, "I sometimes feel trapped in my head. I have so many ideas and feelings. My own thoughts invade my mind. School and track help me through it but when I get overloaded sometimes I feel frantic. It's hard because I must process everything, but I don't have time or don't know how. Being with you for some reason takes the frustration away. I can't explain it. You override that part of my brain and give me relief. I have space in my head filled with errant thoughts and random ideas and now it's filled with you. It feels good, and complete."

He pulls my hip to roll me over and takes my face in his hands. "Oh, baby. It's frustrating being trapped inside your head, but when you get it out the release is freeing and you realize you wouldn't want it to be any other way. Do you write?"

"When I can find time. Just short stories and poetry."

"How did I not know that yet?"

"No one knows. Math and science come more naturally. That is what I told you even. That is what my grades show. Writing and art are my passion, well, until I met you." I don't let him comment. "Art is my greatest passion, but everyone says not to pursue it because you can't make a living at it. English and writing suck at school because I don't excel at them. My teachers and my parents deter me from it because I could do more with something that comes naturally. At least that is their advice. Being good at something doesn't mean I enjoy it. It is frustrating not fitting the mold everyone wants me in."

"I had no clue you were that frustrated. You seem fine with everything. Like nothing bothers you."

"I didn't realize it was a problem until I felt relief being with you. I write when I have free time. I'm fine, I'm not nuts or anything. There is such comfort in being with you. Nothing I do or say has any forethought. You are a drug erasing my mind and I have become very addicted to you. I have never felt this and it is making me see how I used to feel. I enjoy this way a whole lot more."

"I feel the same way about you. You make me complete. It's an amazing feeling to be with someone and not have to be conscious of your actions. But I fear, unlike you, that I'm nuts." He laughs.

"You are not nuts, but I bet you have some that would fit nicely in the palm of my hand," I say, biting my lip to be seductive.

"Shit, why do you do that? You will kill me with that mouth one day."

"I hope to do a lot to you with my mouth, and I can assure you it will not kill you, but you might see heaven."

He kisses me and rolls me over so he is on top of me. He lifts his head and stares at me. He is pure magic. Under his spell is a special place to be and I pray it never breaks. Chances are high one of us will hurt the other. I will try with every fiber of my being though to make this work. His kisses are comforting and even though they are becoming so familiar, they are very satisfying.

"We need to get up and get dressed soon," he says.

"I know, but I will never be done touching you."

"I need you so bad," he says, but he gets up and goes to the bathroom. I hear the shower start. I wish I had the guts to join him. Instead I sit on the bed thinking about everything Frederick Rhoades. He has invaded my mind and pushed the wandering thoughts away. He walks out in a towel and now my brain only has room for the image of his wet almost naked body.

"Hey, stop staring or I will drop the towel." He snaps his fingers trying to make me blink.

"Dare ya."

He walks over to the bed. "You think I won't do it?"

"I think you are chicken."

"Are you testing me?" He starts to drop the towel. I wait on the edge of a dream. He sits next to me on the bed. He places his hand on my thigh. "Soon, baby, soon. I don't want it to be quick and rushed. I want to give you all of me when the time is right. You are too special for me to mess this up."

I sit up on my legs and turn to him. "Thank you, but you said soon and I might have to hold you to that." I get up to shower, hoping it will calm my wild thoughts.

We are almost to my house when Fred takes my hand and asks, "What do you write about?"

"Stuff."

"Did you just say stuff? You finally sound like a teenager."

"Hey, don't pick on me. I said stuff."

"What kind of stuff?"

I don't answer.

"Do you not what to tell me?"

"No, I do, but I'm thinking about what to say before I can say it." I swallow and he squeezes my leg.

"It's okay, I won't push you."

"It's not that. I need to process this in my head. No one knows what I write. It's a big moment for me."

"I am truly honored."

"I know you are. That's what makes you special. The poetry is mostly love, friendship, and relationships. But the short stories are sci-fi. I know that doesn't fit me, but I have this fantasy world fantasy." I even chuckle.

"I wasn't expecting that, but I do know you have a vivid imagination. Someday, if you are ready, I would love to read something you've written."

"Soon. Or maybe we can try writing something together first."

"Yes. I want to write with you very badly."

He makes me feel complete by doing so little. We pull in my driveway, Fred turns the Jeep off, and takes my hand. We sit in silence. Neither of us is ready to leave our lie-free bubble. I drop his hand abruptly and get out of the car because my nerves are winning.

My mom is cooking when we walk inside. The smell of pasta sauce is unmistakable. The garlic and tomatoes flood my nose. I have never felt more at home, in my own home, bombarded with memories of childhood and staring at a man who has become my new home. I have a delightful moment of peace wash over me before I enter a room of lies.

We have a wonderful Sunday afternoon. It is only my parents and Ryan. The conversation is easy. The day is perfect. It's late when Fred leaves and I don't know how many goodbyes I can take. I know though that I will endure a lot to stay with him. I study and get ready for bed before I call him to say good night.

He answers the phone on the first ring. So I ask, "Were you sitting by the phone waiting for me?"

"Yes."

"Where are you?"

"At the piano."

"Were you playing?"

"Yes, I was."

"Can I hear it?" He plays a light but hearty song that makes me shut my eyes. All I can picture is the grace of his hands moving over the keys. My mouth is dry when he comes back to the phone.

"You there?"

"That was lovely. You leave me a mess, you know that?"

"I want to write some lyrics for this music soon. Can you come down this weekend?"

"I don't see why not, but I didn't ask yet."

"Should we invite your parents down?"

"I never thought of that. We should, but it scares me. I am afraid I will mess up."

"You won't. You are way too smart and competent for that."

"Damn, you have a lot of faith in me, don't you?"

"No, just being honest."

"Well, thank you. That was a lovely compliment."

"I mean it. You are many things to me and you should know that you are special."

"You have a wonderful way of showing me and telling me. I hope I have expressed my feelings for you too."

"Oh, Jellybean, you have shown me exactly how you feel."

"Thank you so much for spending the day here. It was a fun day."

"I would do it every day if I could. I want to be with you wherever you are. It's you that I want, not a place." We hesitate but eventually around three in the morning we finally say goodnight.

On Monday, Fred spoke to my mom at work again and invited her and my dad down for dinner on Friday night. I call him after school on Friday to make sure we have everything planned so we don't mess up.

"Did you move my clothes to the other bedroom?"

"No, they won't riffle through the drawers."

"We can't mess this up. Move my clothes. Please, you know how terrifying this is for me."

"Okay, bossy. I will move your clothes. But your pajamas stay with mine."

"Fine, I will say Nina messed up."

"Yeah, blame her. Also I put your things in the other bathroom and I put an alarm clock, tissues and your notebook in the bedroom to make it look lived in. Everything will be fine."

"I trust you. You know that, right? Even if I sound a little frantic."

"You are not frantic at all. This is an odd situation and you are handling it better than I could have expected. You handle everything beyond what a sixteen-year-old should, but, Morgan, this isn't a crime. Sixteen is the age of consent. It's all about what your parents let you do, and regardless of what they believe is happening between us, they trust you."

"I know, but you have the world watching you and that is a different story. We should be there by seven." I need to talk less about the things that upset me.

"Dinner will be ready by then, and I don't care what the world thinks. But I will stop talking because I know you don't want to talk about it. I ordered food so I don't kill your parents. Hey, should I offer them alcohol or skip it?"

"No, you can. My dad won't drink since he is driving, but my mom might. She gave you beer, after all. Don't mess up and pour me any. Or maybe I will ask her if I can have a glass of wine. She has let me before and it might help her feel she still has a say in my life."

"That sounds weird, but it's so true. This really is a simple thing turned complicated. Or is it a complicated thing turned simple."

"Wow, you got me. Once we make it through dinner I can have you all to myself, right?"

"Yes, you can, all to yourself. I can't wait either."

"Hey, my parents are having a small party for me next Friday for my birthday. Brooke is leaving for Spain for six weeks the next day so I will tell her about you. It will be Brooke, Kelly, their parents and my family, maybe Faith too. Will you come?"

"I wouldn't be anywhere else."

"Your voice sounds so sexy sometimes I fear the phone could melt and I wouldn't be able to talk to you anymore."

"You really are cute. Go study so I can spend a weekend with all five of my senses intoxicated on you."

I say goodnight and fantasize about him holding me tight as I fall asleep.

Chapter Eleven

Save the Best for Last

WE PULL INTO Fred's driveway a little before seven and I feel the most nervous excitement I have ever felt. I walk in ahead of my parents and again he hasn't locked the door. Fred is standing in the kitchen wearing the same button fly jeans I took off him Saturday night and a tight black t-shirt. I stare and fantasize about him becoming the most delicious meal I have ever had. I am starving and craving him bad.

He wraps his arms around my back and gives me a friendly hug. He does the same to my mom after she hands him a bottle of wine. He shakes my dad's hand. The tension in this kitchen is tighter than my ponytail.

"Let me show you the house," he says to my parents as he walks toward the stairs. It is such a relief to have them away from me so I can catch my breath. I use the bathroom off the kitchen and I stare in the mirror. Looking back at me is the same face I always see, yet the reflection is so different. I feel getting to know Fred is a route to getting to know myself. I never knew I wanted to change and now that he has made me question myself I prefer the new me that I see. I can't imagine what the future holds, but it is clear I am already forever changed. I hear voices outside the door and I know I need to return to the charade.

Once we are eating, things are easier. I have a small glass of wine with dinner, but I can't eat or drink much of anything. It becomes surreal, being at this table with my two worlds colliding. I am experiencing a full sensation of bliss, and I never want to forget this feeling. I have no idea when or why this bubble will burst, but I fear it will be soon.

My mom hugs me tight before she leaves, as if she knows less of me belongs to her now. With her arms around me, she says, "Honey, have fun, but please behave. This is a different world than what you are used too."

I hug her back then hug my dad good-bye. I never expected this to feel so bittersweet. I tell them I will be home Sunday night, but I can't hide the gloom in my voice. I watch the car drive away and I think my innocence just drove away too. I head back inside and Fred is leaning against the counter with his arms crossed. He looks super sexy and on some level he is all mine, for now. I walk over to him and wrap my arms around him. He hugs me back and I realize he makes me a kind of happy I have never been.

We walk upstairs and head to bed. We talk and hold each other until the sun is coming up. The last thing we talk about before falling asleep is writing together. I fall asleep with my mind full of thoughts, yet free enough to sleep peacefully.

We sleep until past noon on Saturday and I feel sluggish, so I decide to go for a run. I end up down at Jenkinson's Boardwalk and I head into a candy store, surprised to find cappuccino jellybeans. I buy a bag and head back home.

Showered and changed, I walk downstairs and Fred is sitting in silence at the piano. I find the prettiest glass bowl he has and I fill it with the jellybeans. I walk up behind him and tell him to close his eyes. I put the bowl down on the piano. I put one jellybean in his mouth and watch him eat it.

I whisper in his ear, "I'm going to sit in the kitchen and study physics. I want you to focus on that jellybean and the physics of our physical attraction, and write a song that is sexier than anything I have ever heard." I walk away and sit at the island with my physics book open, but I am not reading much. Fred begins to play the piano. He starts and stops often but it all sounds beautiful.

I tear a piece of paper out of my notebook and start to write ideas, lyrics, anything that comes in to my head. Fred finds a rhythm and he begins playing a melody that starts to take shape. I don't hear the door over the piano, but I look up just as it opens. Gunner is standing half in and half out of the doorway, staring at me. I should feel uncomfortable but instead

I stare back. He walks over and sits on the stool beside me. All the while Fred is still playing the same piece. There is no way Fred heard the door.

Gunner is stunning and I suddenly feel like a groupie as he continues to look at me. My eyes lock on his and without moving them I put a piece of paper and pencil in front of him as he sits beside me. I move my eyes back to my paper and try to focus my thoughts. I wish I could write but no more words form. The two hottest men I have ever seen are in the same house as I am.

Fred owns my heart, but damn I could stare at Gunner awhile too. He is maybe an inch taller than Fred, but his very light brown hair is spikey and that might be why he seems taller. His eyes are a yellow-green, unlike any I have ever seen. They seem to be translucent, but I need to see them again for a clear evaluation. I turn my head to look at him and he is writing feverishly, as the words come pouring out of him. His eyes are focused on the paper. I continue to look down but suddenly his hand is under my chin and he pulls my face gently towards him.

He drops his hand and points to my physics book as the piano stops. Seconds later Fred has his arms around my neck from behind and his mouth kisses my hair. He has never touched me or kissed me with another person around and I almost fear he didn't see Gunner when I realize that is not the case.

He releases me, but as he walks around the island he traces his hand down my arm. He draws it out like he is putting on a show. I watch his eyes as he does this and they are moving from mine to Gunner's and back. I feel like property that is being marked. I want to slam my book and storm upstairs, but it's also endearing that he feels that way.

Fred is just staring at me when he says, "Gunner this is Morgan and Morgan this is Gunner." He points dramatically at us. I twist my right arm to give him my hand to shake and he takes it and kisses the back of it. I pull my hand away before his lips touch my hand, then slam my book down and stack my papers.

As I stand up I look at Gunner first. "Nice to finally meet you." Too crazy pissed at Fred to say it like I mean it, so I stare at him with a scowl while I speak to Gunner. "I don't know why all that happened, but I will not be anyone's fire hydrant." I walk upstairs and fling my books on the bed and then myself.

Not even a minute later Fred is leaning in the bedroom doorway. He knocks on the door even though it's open. I turn my head to look at him and he comes in and lies down on top of me. I can't move under his weight and then he starts to tickle me and I want so bad to not laugh but damn, I can't control it. The laughter is euphoric even if my mood is still sour. He flips me onto his lap and starts kissing me in one swift movement.

I am mad at him, but too crazy for him to stay mad. "Why did you do that?" I ask.

"Honestly?"

"Yes. You made me feel so little, like property."

"I didn't even realize what I had done until you walked away. I guess I acted on instinct."

"Are you that protective of me?"

"Yes." He is breathless and hot. He kisses me on a level I never knew existed.

"Is Gunner still downstairs?" I ask reluctantly, pulling away from his mouth.

"Probably, should I get rid of him?"

"Yes, but then I would be rude like you, so, no. I should go back and apologize."

"I don't think that is necessary. You didn't do anything wrong, and he understands."

"Oh, did he say something?"

"Sort of."

"What did he say?"

Fred stares at me not answering.

"Was it something mean?"

"No, he just said, 'Damn, she is way too good for you, jackass.' Then he punched my shoulder."

"Maybe I like him after all."

"You can't like Gunner," he says, kissing me again and touching me frantically.

"Stop. Fred, I don't like him like you are insinuating, but why can't I be his friend? Did something happen between you and Gunner to make you act this way?"

He says nothing.

"I don't care, but leave me out of it."

I try to get up and he flips me on my back and pins me down. He kisses me and even though I am mad, damn he is so good at this, he paralyzes me.

He stops and looks down at me. "I'm sorry. Another day we can talk about Gunner. Let's go back downstairs and see if I can fix this."

We walk downstairs and he releases his painful grip on my hand. I walk up to Gunner, who is now outside on the hammock. I say his name as a whisper in case he is asleep. His eyes open. I stare at him more intensely than he is staring at me. I can't look away. I have never seen eyes like his, and they lure me in.

"Sorry I stormed off. I would appreciate a do-over." I reach my hand out again to shake his, and I say, "Hi, Morgan Evans, nice to finally meet you."

He doesn't put his hand out to shake it. Instead he stands up and hugs me tight, lifting me off the ground.

"We are past handshakes." He puts me down.

"Can you try to stop this shit, because I will be a part of your life and I don't do drama."

"No more shit from me. I can't speak for Rick," he says with his hands up as if he is surrendering.

"Whatever." I walk back inside and Fred is in the kitchen. He's watching me and eating the jellybeans. I wrap my arms around him tightly. I pull away and look up into those eyes that leave me weak and stupid every time. "I am going to study. I need a mental break. I will come back down and we can make dinner. There is enough food if Gunner wants to stay."

"Do you want him to stay?"

"No, but I want the three of us to get along. That won't happen instantly, but the sooner the better. Maybe you should sit outside, have a beer, and see who can spit farther or piss longer. Get this shit out of your system, so we can have a nice dinner with adult conversation." I pull him down to kiss and I kiss him with every cell in my soul. It doesn't feel bad marking one's territory. "I will be down in an hour. Now go play nice with your friend."

He laughs and pinches my ass as I walk away and I don't look back. I study for a while and I get some work done for a change. I head back downstairs and pause at the bottom step to admire Fred and Gunner on the deck. They are laughing like kids. They are drinking beer and for a second I forget they are famous rock stars. They appear to be two friends hanging out on a Saturday night, their fame erased. I walk over to Gunner and ask if he is staying for dinner.

"Yes, that would be nice."

"We were going to have hamburgers and salad. Is that okay with you?"

"Perfect." He has turned off the aggravate Morgan button and it is a lot more pleasant.

Fred stands up and we walk to the kitchen together but we don't touch. He comes up behind me and whispers in my ear. "What do you want me to do?"

"Is this a general question or something about dinner?"

"What do you want it to be about?" He vibrates me without touching me as he speaks.

"Well, if it is about dinner then I want you to turn on the grill. If it is a general question, I would have to say I want you to fuck me like there is no tomorrow right here on the kitchen floor."

He bites my ear lobe and groans painfully loud. "Fuck, I want you bad, Jellybean." He pushes himself into me as I attempt to support myself on the cool countertop. The heat coming from his body is making it tough for me to stand still. I don't know how much more of this game I can play. "I will start the grill, but it is not what I want to do!" he growls and walks away, leaving me, as always, wanting more.

I get my Walkman and put a Bush tape in and start to make the salad. I love feeling alone when I listen to music with headphones. I turn around to bring the salad out and Gunner is standing right in front of me. His arms are crossed and he is staring at me. "What?" I say, even though I can't hear myself and I can't hear him either. I walk past him, head outside, and put the salad down. I head back inside with anger in my step and take my Walkman off.

"You sing nice," he says.

"Thanks, sorry I snapped. You scared me."

"I scare all the girls, but you have a nice voice. Bush though, not CrossRhoades?" He smirks a bad boy smirk. It's different than Fred's smirk. Basically Gunner's smirk screams bad news.

"I don't listen to you here. I have the real voice, live, right in my ear."
I don't reveal that I bought their music for the first time last week.

"Okay, smart ass."

"It's not wise to pick a fight with me. Don't forget that."

"Cocky much?"

"Only when I have to be."

I walk outside and Gunner follows. We sit down and eat and some-how manage to make it a nice night. Maybe I will survive all this testos-terone. Gunner and Fred are cleaning up when Alex and Zach walk in. Watching from outside, the shock on their faces from seeing Fred and Gunner washing dishes is hysterical. They are genuinely confused.

"Hello again," Alex says.

"Wow, you were serious about them cleaning up, huh? I never thought in a million years I would see these two washing dishes," Zach says.

"But they look cute together, don't they? So domestic," I say.

Gunner and Fred finish cleaning up and I hop up on the counter near Fred. He comes over by me and stands between my legs. His hands are close to me but nothing of him is touching me. I lean up to whisper in his ear, "What are you doing?"

He leans down to whisper in my ear, "I don't know."

"How comfortable are you with them knowing?"

"I wish the world could know, but I also want to keep you to myself."

"I don't know if I want them to know too much yet. Tell them we were talking about making cupcakes and what flavor I should make. Then back up away from me and take them outside so I can bake for you. When they leave you can take me upstairs and we can lock ourselves high above the ocean, away from the bad parts of life."

"Fuck, Jellybean," he says softly, but it gives me chills. He moves away from me and I look over at the four men staring at me but trying not to make it look as if they are.

"Everyone outside." As they follow my direction and leave, I take out everything to make some cupcakes and I turn my Walkman back on. I love to cook and bake but I have a weird moment; it doesn't seem real being in this house baking. The whole band is here and one of them leaves me weak and strong all at the same time. Having my 'how the hell did I get here moment', eyes shut, Walkman on, I open my eyes and find

Gunner standing in front of me again. I take my headphones off my ears and say, "What?" with way too much attitude.

"You say that a lot around me. Do I leave you questioning things?"

"Geez, no, you leave me questioning Fred's judgment in friends." The timer dings and I check the cupcakes and take them out.

"They do smell yummy."

"Thanks, so now two nice things have come out of your mouth aimed at me. Maybe we have turned a corner."

"You're funny."

"I'm going outside while these cool," I say because I can't decide what I think of Gunner. He joins us with beer for everyone a few minutes later. I never touch mine, but Fred drinks it. I bring the iced cupcakes back outside and we all eat too much. It's well after midnight when Alex gets up and says he needs to get home.

"How are you getting home?" I ask, wondering because he is clearly drunk.

"My car."

"Hell, no. Give me your keys." He does and so does Gunner. "Now upstairs to bed, everyone!"

"There is no damn furniture up there," Gunner tells me.

"There is now. Go, I want to sleep." I point up the stairs.

They are too obedient and it's weird, but maybe drunken rock stars are the best kind. They head upstairs. Fred and I walk into his room and for the first time I lock the door behind us. He is drunk and he takes me in his arms as soon as the door is shut. "You have any idea how hot you are?"

"I'm going to get ready for bed," I say, walking away.

I come back out and he is sitting on the couch. "All yours," I say.

He gets up and walks over to me and picks me up. I wrap my legs around his hips and my hands around his neck and he stares at me until he slams me into the wall. "Yes, you are all mine," he says, breathless and overflowing with lust.

"I meant the bathroom."

"But I want you so bad."

"I know, but not tonight, not drunk."

"You didn't drink anything."

"I mean you."

"Oh, am I drunk?"

"You are a hair under trashed."

He walks us over to the bed and tosses me down. "I will behave." He walks to the bathroom. When he comes back he crawls into bed with to me. "Sorry I got drunk."

"You don't have to apologize. You didn't do anything wrong. It's okay to get drunk. It's fun to hear you be carefree and funny with everyone."

"Did I say anything bad?"

"No, Fred. You were a gentleman like you always are. Just a more carefree gentleman."

"Well, thank you for hanging with the guys and me. I never knew a girl like you. You are so feminine yet you are also one of the guys. You are the most beautiful and smartest woman I ever met. I can't believe I get to hold you." I don't have a response. "Hey, you fall asleep, Jellybean?"

"Nope, just speechless again. I'm the one honored, being held by you. In such a short time you have given me so much joy. Thank you for being you." I lean into him and kiss quick. I roll over so my back is flush with his side and once again fall into a peaceful sleep that is one better than the last.

I wake before everyone else and change for a run. I leave a note on my pillow for Fred. "Hope you aren't hung over. I went for a run. XOXO, Jellybean."

When I return only Gunner is around. Why Gunner? He is by far the most irritating of them all. But he made coffee and that might make me forgive him for being a bit of an ass.

Gunner goes outside with his coffee in silence. Clearly I prefer the quiet Gunner. Pouring myself coffee, Fred comes down the stairs, looking hot. His sleepy eyes and messy hair leave me gaping at him. He wraps his arms around me. "Morning, Jellybean."

"Morning to you too, hot stuff. How do you feel?"

"Great, now that I have you in my arms. I missed you this morning. I don't want to wake up without you and I have to do it all week again."

"I know. Sorry, it sucks. Want coffee?"

"Yes." I pour his coffee and hand it to him black, the way he prefers it. The sun is warm but the air is still cool as the three of us caffeinate in silence. Taking another sip, I consider trying harder to get along with Gunner. I also tell myself it is best that Alex and Zach are still asleep. When I am done drinking and thinking, I kiss Fred gently on the mouth, and tell him I am going to shower. It sounds like an invite. I quickly got over his friends knowing about us last night. It was way too difficult to keep my hands off him.

As much as I want him to join me in the shower, we have never seen each other fully undressed. If we did, control would be out the window and floating in the ocean. My entire shower I fantasize about how bad I want to see him walk through the door. He doesn't. I can't tell if I am relieved or sad.

I wrap a towel around myself and head to the bedroom to get my clothes. Fred is sitting on the sofa staring at me, his eyes brimming with lust. I walk over and sit on his lap. It's a miracle my towel doesn't fall off. I can't stop kissing him. He is the most magical thing I have ever felt. His hands are on my face again and he kisses me over and over and every second the sensation is elevated. We are both getting worked up and this game of start and stop can't continue on much longer. We have already crossed many lines we should have stood behind.

He starts kissing me down the side of my neck under my ear and down to my shoulder. Gentle feathery kisses that get me even hotter than the strong passionate ones. He looks up as I open my eyes to look at him. His eyes are sparkling with desire and it's hotter than any kiss ever could be. He shuts his eyes and places small feathery kisses down my neck. I wiggle in his lap with impending need. Watching him kiss me increases every desire beyond limits. It is more arousing to watch his mouth move across my body than to feel the actual kiss. I close my eyes as I tilt my head back to let him kiss up to my chin and back down. His head moves lower and lower as I shift my body to loosen my towel. He moves the towel off my right breast and the sensation is almost too stimulating. His hand brushes across my nipple as the towel falls to my waist.

Intent on watching his slow, gentle movements, I focus on him fully. He puckers his lips gently around my nipple. The moisture from his tongue makes my eyes fall shut for a second, but I open them again to see him looking up at me. With my eyes locked on him he sucks my nipple harder, drawing me into his mouth and past his teeth. I want to scream, moan, release this pressure, but I become lost in his eyes and this sensation that I can do nothing but watch and endure. He rolls my nipple out of his mouth and kisses my breasts and chest a million times until he finds my mouth again. If he didn't have such a hold on me this towel would be gone. He stops kissing me and pulls away, so I open my eyes to look at him. He stares longingly before he says, "I need you, but not yet. I can't have you, then take you home and leave you there. Don't be mad at me, please. I want you so bad. But not yet. Okay?"

"Yes, I mean no. Yes, it's okay. No it's not what I want." I am still on his lap, towel around my waist, and I understand his words but I want nothing more except his touch.

"You are so damn beautiful. I have no idea how I have any control."

"I don't either. I have close to none." I get up and let the towel drop to the floor as I get my clothes. I change with my back to him and I can feel the heat from his eyes across the room. Once dressed, I slink back to the couch and straddle his thighs. I stay up on my knees, looking down at him and I kiss him passionately. I slide my body back onto his lap so I can feel him hard through his jeans. "I want you." I get up and leave the bedroom.

The guys left a note on the counter saying goodbye. That was all. It shocks me for a second that they didn't come upstairs and knock on the door to say goodbye. My friends would have been banging the door down. Fred comes down and asks me what time we should leave. I say I don't think it matters.

He comes and stands in front of me. "Can you call your mom and ask if you can stay tonight? I will drive you right to school in the morning."

Looking into his eyes and feeling his hands on my hips makes me weak and mindless. "How could I say no to that?"

Fred is playing the piano when I call home. "Hi, Mom." I hope I don't sound unusual.

"Hey, sweetie, how is everything?"

"Good. I finally met Gunner last night and he is interesting but kind of annoying, and even better looking in person. It's quite intimidating."

"You can handle yourself fine with that smart mouth of yours."

"Yes, but that isn't a very nice thing to say."

"It's true though, honey. You are witty and wise. I know you can hold your own."

"Maybe you're right, like always. I was wondering if it would be okay for me to stay tonight and have Fred drive me right to school in the morning?"

"Okay, but you will be up very early."

"I know, but I want to be here as much as I can with them and it is going so well. I can handle it."

"I know you can. Be safe and I will see you for dinner tomorrow."

"See you tomorrow. I miss you."

"I miss you too." Her upbeat voice clashes with her sad words. Once I hang up I sit next to Fred at the piano. His music is so melodious, I could listen to it all day. I lay my head on his shoulder and close my eyes. He starts to sing a song I have never heard, and it's simply beautiful.

Closed off from the world, floating near the clouds
I watch her hair twirl, we never go near the crowds
Gusts of ocean air, warmth from sunlight everywhere
We are not just a pair, but a soul shared

In April, April, April
I caught a glimpse of hazel
In April, April, April
Her eyes were playful, graceful
All I see is hazel
It all changed in April

Hidden above the boardwalk, we share hours lost in talk
Ever since April
When her hazel eyes became a fable
Ever since April

She makes me stable
Since April, April, April
When April turned Hazel

Her smile like the ocean
When she puts it in motion
All the words, all the thoughts, all the kisses, more powerful than the waves
She floats my heart in her hand, I never want to come down on land
I am stable, never wanting to touch the sand

To stay afloat would be grand, with her holding my hand
My heart lost in April to the set of hazel
Our soul is shared, since April

He stops and we sit in silence. He takes my hand and holds it tight. "What did she say?" he whispers.

"She said I could stay." I am so riveted by his song I feel paralyzed.

"Good. I can't bear to be without you. When school is out can you stay longer?"

"I hope. What difference is a weekend or a few weeks, right?"

"I don't know how to live without you. How did this happen so fast?"

"I don't know, but I think we are pretty lucky."

"We sure are."

"When did you write that song?"

"Last week, when you were rude enough to leave me for school."

I poke him in the side. "Hey, that's mean. And that isn't what you read to my mother over the phone, I hope."

"No."

"When do I get to hear what you read to her?"

"Soon. Not yet. Soon. So what are we going to do all afternoon, Jellybean?"

"Not sure that should be up to me. I'm not as well behaved as you."

"Just wait, baby. I will show you bad behavior."

"Is that a promise?"

"Yes, so what do you enjoy doing the most?"

"You want me to answer that? Honestly, right now?"

"Yes."

"Well, in the state of mind you left me in, sex would have to be on the top of my list."

"So then what's second?"

"Oh Fred, you kill me. I guess coming in a far second would be talking to you. I love walking on the beach with you. I love to cook, and cooking for you is incredibly satisfying. I would love to write with you and I could take a nap and listen to you play this piano all day. But you can't tire your fingers out, since I am going to demand you place them all over my body." I lift his hand off my thigh and I kiss each finger pad, slowly and methodically. Then just as slowly I run my tongue up each finger from his palm to his fingertip. I take his middle finger in my mouth and suck it until my mouth and tongue are wrapped around him. I'm sucking my way back to the end when I hear the kitchen door open. "We should lock that," I say, after his finger makes a popping sound leaving my mouth.

Fred and I turn and look in unison to see Gunner staring at us. "I left my wallet here." He walks through the kitchen upstairs and quickly gets his wallet and comes back down. "Sorry," he shouts and leaves. Fred promptly locks the door.

Fred comes back to the piano but doesn't sit. He gazes into my eyes and leans down and kisses me. "Maybe leaving it unlocked could help us stop touching each other." We both laugh, knowing the sexual tension between us is growing too strong to continue sweeping it under the rug.

"What do you want for dinner? We both know I can't cook anything."

"Stop, you have fed me quite well several times."

"Oh, Jellybean." He closes his eyes as if he wants to say more but can't.

"What are you telling the guys about me?"

"Nothing. No one would ever believe you were sixteen. So why say anything? Is that okay with you?"

"Do I have a choice?"

"Yes, if you want them to know, we tell them. If you don't want to lie we don't have to. They won't say anything."

"Let's not say anything and if something changes we can discuss it then." I kiss him again because not touching him is harder than stopping. "How about steak and potatoes, a man's meal? I feel full of testosterone myself after hanging with you all last night."

"That sounds perfect. Come on, let's leave now because I can't be alone with you and stay in control."

We escape the supermarket unnoticed once again. We make dinner with piano music on the stereo. I never realized how much I love being surrounded by music. Or maybe Fred makes everything around me more beautiful. Dinner is much more enjoyable when you can see and hear the ocean and a man with a voice that sounds like pure sex all the time is the one you are making dinner conversation with.

The sun is setting when Fred says, "Hey, wanna see how cold the water is?"

"You serious?"

"Yes."

"Skinny dip or bathing suit?" I try to smirk as he often does, but I fail.

"How is it you always surprise me every time you open your mouth?"

"Fred, you haven't seen anything yet that I can do with my mouth."

"Okay, a bathing suit is required." He taps my ass and pushes me up the stairs.

Chapter Twelve

Dreams

WE WALK DOWN to the edge of the ocean hand in hand. I love the warm sand between my toes and cool air soothing my aroused skin. The air still smells hot and humid, one of my favorite scents. The sun has set, but I can see the beautiful man beside me, thanks to the bright moon.

"Together on three?" His face shines at me in the moonlight. "One, two, three." We both run into the freezing water. Fred keeps swimming out farther and I stay with him, but I can't stand. Thankfully the waves are not too strong. Within seconds he has me wrapped around his body. My hands snake around his neck as I kiss him. His hands are holding me under my ass and suddenly the water isn't cold anymore. We kiss and hold each other, moving in sync with every wave. It could have been hours or minutes that pass, I can't tell time when my body is all mixed up with his, when suddenly a huge wave takes us both by surprise and knocks us under.

I come back up halfway to shore and Fred is right next to me. We struggle but get ourselves back to the beach and grab our towels. "It is cold out here! Back in the water or back inside?" I ask.

"Inside, come on." He grabs my hand and we run back to the house. We get to the deck door and he opens it and lifts me up under my knees and carries me upstairs. He puts me down, opens the shower door, and turns the water on. When it is warm he reaches out for my hand and I step inside with him. Our locked eyes mixed with the hot water make my skin boil. I run my hand up and down his arms, and we are both silent

— wrapped up in each other. Fred reaches around to the back of my bikini top and undoes the hook. It is still hanging around my neck and covering me when he takes his right hand and cups my left breast. He is so gentle and sensual it has me in a trance.

He reaches behind my neck and unties my top and lets it drop to the floor. He never breaks his loving gaze. Leaning down he kisses me numb. I don't have the strength to kiss him back. He reaches for the shampoo and I watch him squirt some in his hand. He tells me to turn around and he lathers the shampoo in my hair. So loving and sensual, I know I can't take another second of it without finally finishing it. After he washes my hair I do the same to him. Having my hands in his hair and watching his face is almost as erotic as having him touch me—almost.

As I finish his hair he picks up the licorice soap and the scent brings back memories of rolling around in bed with him. Now I will have memories of this night as well. I cannot wait to feel the soap on his hands cleaning my body. I understand now what he meant about not surviving sex with me. I have arrived at that point myself. I close my eyes. The sounds of the running water, his shallow breathing and the smell of licorice have me adrift in an abyss. His soapy hands run up and down my right arm, then my left arm. He washes my back and my belly before finally thoroughly cleaning both of my breasts. I can't bear to open my eyes. This feeling is exquisite. His hands are masculine and strong on my soft skin. Yet his caress is so sweet and sensual. I want so much more of him.

He stops washing me and I open my eyes to see him staring passionately at me. I stand up on my toes to kiss him as I reach down to take the soap out of his hands. I lather my hands and nudge him to turn around. I put the soap back down and run both my hands up and down his muscular back. Cleaning him and massaging him. I will never tire of the way his skin feels, pulled tightly over his rock-hard muscles. I run my hands up and down his arms many times, but it is still not enough. I nudge him to turn back around and face me. I can see he is in the same state of mind I am.

I pick up the soap again and I wash his front as I did his back. Once the soap is all washed away, I lean down and kiss his chest from one side to the other. Glad he is broad, it takes many kisses to get across. I stop both times I reach a nipple and I kiss it gently and suck just enough to make him moan.

He takes my hands in his and intertwines our fingers. He kisses my forehead and I look up at him. I can see in his eyes he is about to tell me we have to stop. I cut him off. "I don't want to stop."

"Don't make this harder on me, please." His eyes almost make me want to listen to him.

"Sorry, but I want to keep going."

"Me too. I will never make it until you are eighteen, but not yet. I have never needed anything as bad as I need you. This isn't the right day."

I reluctantly say, "Okay." I kiss him with more passion, hoping to sway him.

"Close your eyes and keep your hands to yourself," he says and I laugh and do as instructed. I hear his shorts hit the floor and a minute later he opens the shower door and leaves. I open my eyes and watch him wrap a towel around himself. Damn, he has one fine ass.

I push my bikini bottoms down, shower the rest of the sand off, and join him in bed. He has no lights on but the moon has flooded the room romantically. I put my head on his chest and close my eyes. "What time do I have to set the alarm for?" he asks.

"Next June."

"Yeah, I wish."

"I have to be at school by seven-thirty, so we should leave by six. At least we don't have to shower in the morning." He sets the alarm and we fall asleep.

Before I know it the alarm is blaring and Fred is hitting it with a grumble. The warm sunlight has erased the cool moonlight. "Hey, how did you get so beautiful, Jellybean?" His kiss is the best way to start a day but then he runs his hands down my back and rests it on my butt. "You should always sleep naked."

"Wow, I didn't even realize I wasn't wearing anything. Guess maybe I'm a little too comfortable with you." To prove my point, I get up and walk across the room, get my clothes, but then head to the bathroom.

We manage to stay away from each other and leave on time. We have a few minutes before school starts so I tell Fred to pull behind a closed shopping center. "How will I ever make it through the day? School seems wrong now because I feel even more out of place."

"I don't know. You can dream of me all day, but you might flunk out."

"I will do it anyway. Now kiss me and drop me off at my prison."

He drops me off right at the edge of school so we are not seen together. I don't even make it to the front door before Brooke is in my face.

"Where the hell have you been? I left twenty messages. I almost called your parents' line last night."

"Sorry, I was working. Ryan is in Connecticut with Faith. You know my parents never answer our phone."

"Oh, working?" She is mad. I have never seen her this upset. Fortunately, the bell rings, saving me.

"We can talk later, not here, not now. Okay?"

"Sure," she says and I fear for the first time I might be hurting our friendship. I love her but I have no intention of changing my behavior. Fred has become my world, and I can't live in any other world but his.

I make it through the day somehow. Doodling sure does have its benefits. At lunch Brooke is behaving like the friend I know. She doesn't say anything out of the ordinary or quiz me, but she asks to come over after school.

We head home and at first all we do is study. Soon enough Brooke starts talking. "So, what is this job? Tell me about it." She raises her eyebrows and I know she means business.

I take a minute to try to figure out what to say. "Sorry, this is hard for me."

"Really? You never had trouble telling me anything before."

"I know. It's not you. It's everyone and everything else. It's overwhelming."

"Well, I guess a job that has you working all day and night would do that."

I giggle a little to ease the tension. "You know I write poems already and sometimes I write short stories too. I have a job writing with some talented people."

"With whom exactly?"

"Can you give me a few days to process it all and then I will tell you everything."

"Really? You are going to make me wait?"

"Yes." I feel as Fred must every time he pulls away from me. It's what has to be done but it hurts like hell. She tells me how excited she is for

Spain and we study a little more. As much as I love Brooke, I can't wait until she leaves so I can call Fred.

He answers on the first ring when I call, his voice close to frantic. "You okay?" I ask.

"Yes, just worried. It's after six."

"Damn, it's like having two fathers."

"That is sick."

"Yes, it is. Brooke came over after school. She has a million questions I can't answer."

"Why not? You are close to her, so you should tell her."

"I told her about writing with other people and I will tell her more soon. I can't tell her the whole truth yet. If I tell Brooke, I betray my mom, and telling my mom means I'm asking to never see you again. They must see a working partnership, okay?"

"Yes, Jellybean, that is more than okay. I wish you had someone to talk to. If you are ever overwhelmed or this is too much you must tell someone."

"You will never be too much. You have no idea how strong and determined I am."

"No, I see it and I see the nice, sweet, loving, and passionate side of you too. I see it all."

"I'm not nice around Gunner. He pisses me off."

"Really? I guess he is as strong and determined as you."

"You think I'm like Gunner?"

"Yes, you are very much alike. That is why I have such a wonderful friendship with both of you."

"That might be the meanest thing I ever heard. I am nothing like him. He is a smartass."

Fred clears his throat and leaves me thinking.

"Maybe if this gets too tough I can talk to Gunner about it then."

"Hell, no, I don't want you that close to him, but I will say he is as brilliant as you and he would probably give you great advice."

"Enough of this shit. What did you do all day?"

"You want the truth, right?"

"Yes."

"Well, I wrote some melodies. But I wanted to jerk off. I didn't though because the tension is keeping me alert."

"Holy shit. Really? Your balls must be killing you. How the heck can you do that?"

"I don't know."

"But you do that, right?" I smirk again even if he can't see me.

"Normally, hell yeah, but I want to wait until I have you."

"You leave me shocked and hot again. How long has it been?"

"Too long. The day before I picked you up at Brooke's."

"Fred! Have you checked to make sure they are okay? You might have shriveled black balls by now."

He laughs. "You are so fucking cute it hurts more not holding you than any ball pain. But you are so shocked it's a little unsettling. Should I ask the same questions of you?"

"Sure. You know I'm an open book when it comes to you."

"Good, but I will wait to ask. If I had to listen to your answer I might not last another second."

"Fair enough. Blacky. Wait, I might have a nickname."

"Shit, I don't like it, it sucks."

"I do too if you would let me."

"Oh, really?" he says and I moan into the phone. "What happened to PG-13?"

"Really, Blacky, hold my ass in the ocean and take my top off in the shower. Practice what you preach."

"Shit, that's Gunner calling. He never freakin' calls. It can't be good news. Can I call you back?"

"Give me thirty minutes so I can shower and eat something, okay?"

"Yep. Bye, Jellybean." He hangs up and I sit on my bed for a few minutes trying to absorb everything between us. I shower and eat like I am on a mission. Exactly thirty minutes later the phone rings.

"Dang you are punctual."

"Sorry, I am just pissed."

"See? Gunner is bad news."

"Ha-ha, he did bring bad news. We have to go back to California to do reshoots for the video. Not sure exactly when. He thinks Friday or

Saturday for three or four days. I will know more tomorrow. Oh, Morgan, how can I be without you?"

"We are so fucking hooked on each other, it's a little sick. I have never felt this, but it's a beautiful addiction."

"Hell yeah, more thrilling than my wildest dreams. I wish you could come with us."

"Next time maybe I can, but I have finals next week. It's actually perfect timing. I will spend the weekend with Brooke. And you can spend it with Gunner. Better to be me."

"You should study, and I bet Brooke is way better looking than Gunner."

"I don't know. Gunner might be irritating but he is hot."

"Really? Should I worry?"

"Hell, no, Blacky. I only have eyes and other body parts for you."

"Maybe we should try G ratings for a while."

"Not sure I have that in my DNA, but I will try for you."

"Hot Gunner just walked in. Call me tomorrow when you are done and I will tell you all our plans. Depending on when we fly maybe I will stay with you?"

"That would be nice. Faith won't be here. The guest room is all yours."

"I will take whatever I can get. Goodnight, Jellybean." He hangs up, leaving me with my wondering thoughts once again.

The next day his plans are set. They will be flying a private plane in and out of Morristown Airport. They are leaving Saturday morning at ten and landing Wednesday morning at ten. Now I just have to have the courage to ask if he can sleep at our house on Friday night.

Chapter Thirteen

Kiss Me Slowly

I SUMMON AS MUCH bravery as I can to ask my mom if Fred can stay here Friday night. Without hesitation she says yes. Once again I got all worked up for nothing. Getting through the school week is hard again but I remind myself daily he will he here when I get home Friday. I have one final that day so we have a whole afternoon alone, before he leaves to make music videos. Saying that in my head even sounds unreal.

Sean, one of Ben's friends, drives me home Friday, and he is the first person to comment on the Jeep in the driveway. I become nervous he is onto something, but he starts asking me what year and model it is and I remember how much he loves cars. I tell him what I know. I wanted to say it was Ryan's friend who was here, but I decide to say nothing about the owner.

I get out of Sean's car and say goodbye. Then he yells, "Morgan, wait." I turn back to him. "Sorry Ben broke up with you. We all miss you and he isn't the same without you. He fucked up."

I walk a few steps closer to him. "I miss you guys too, but it wasn't meant to be. And he did mess up. Take care of yourself. Stay in touch." I walk away and head inside.

Fred is standing at my window looking outside. "Hey, Blacky, the view is better this way."

He turns around and walks over to me. "It sure is. Who was that?"

"Jealous much?" I say, kissing him with my eyes open.

"No, who was that?"

"You hungry? I'm starving, I haven't eaten breakfast yet," I say, walking out my door.

"Yes, but really, who was that guy?" he asks, following right behind me.

"Fred, you have a wife somewhere. Don't give me shit about getting a ride home from school." I hurry down the stairs to the kitchen.

He comes up behind me and hugs me tight. He kisses my hair. "I am so sorry. I get very jealous. You clearly don't deserve to be treated that way."

"I already know that, now hopefully you do too. No more of that shit. His name is Sean. He is a friend of Ben's. And he did say Ben messed up breaking up with me, that was all."

"I am one hundred percent wrong. I apologize," he says softly but firmly.

"Apology accepted. Now learn from this."

"Learn what?"

"Don't mess up like Ben."

"I pray to every god that was ever imagined that I never fuck this up." He leans down and kisses me passionately, as if the gods are watching.

* * *

When everyone gets home my parents make us dinner. I watch them and for the first time I see that they move as if they are part of a choreographed dance. I realize that is how it is for me with Fred. It's a comforting thought that perhaps my parents are as content as I am.

Fred was going to drive himself to the airport and leave his Jeep there, but now he is asking Ryan if he can drive him. I am a little shocked, but also excited to have my brother meet the other guys. Fred and I clean up dinner, while my parent's head upstairs and Ryan heads out for the night. He invited us, but I gave him the look siblings understand means stop.

"Want to sit outside and talk?" I ask.

"That sounds perfect. My second favorite thing to do with you."

"Oh, what's the first?"

"An unmentionable."

"Really now," I say, hitting him with a dishtowel. "That is mean." We are still laughing when suddenly he stands tall and stiff. I look behind me and there is my mom.

"Geez, I'm not the fun police. Keep laughing. It's a pleasant sound." She gets her reading glasses off the counter.

"We are going to sit in the back for a while," I tell her.

"Okay, sweetheart, have a good night." She walks away, making it seem that this is normal. Nothing is normal to me anymore.

We head outside to sit down. Before his hot ass is down he says, "You have a pool?"

"Yes. It wasn't open for Memorial Day. My dad was lazy this year, I guess."

"Want to swim?"

"Why the hell not?"

"You never curse, and for some reason it gets me a little hot."

"Well then, I will fucking get changed now. Wait, do you have a suit?"

"No."

"Be right back." I skip upstairs and change, not acknowledging his bathing suit issue. I grab two towels and head back outside. Fred is already in the pool and I hope he left his underwear on. That isn't true, but my parents are not far away, which makes clothed rock stars the better option.

I dive in off the diving board and come up right in front of him, shocked I didn't crash into him. It is cloudy tonight and exceptionally dark. The clouds block the stars and moon. He says nothing as he wraps his arms around me and kisses the top of my head.

"You leave me breathless constantly. I'm not sure how much more I can endure before I stop breathing." He holds me and kisses me intently. I am too busy enjoying his body to talk.

"We are way too serious sometimes. I don't want to move my head because I love listening to your heartbeat. It's strong like you."

"Oh, baby, I am weak, you are the strong one."

I hope he is right about me being strong, but in this moment I feel weak. I move away from him and swim the length of the pool underwater. The silence and darkness attack me and all I want to do is cry. I come up for air and realize this man will break my heart. I know I should run now. I know I won't. I swim back to him.

"I want you no matter how bad you will hurt me someday," I say, returning to his embrace.

"I don't want to hurt you."

"I know you don't, but you will."

He kisses me and it's bittersweet. The tears flow and he kisses them away.

"This is way too deep. You are leaving in a few hours and I don't want this sour taste in my mouth anymore. Kiss me again. Just keep kissing me." He does and it is desperate and needy. Two things I have never been before I met him.

After a lot of kissing we get out of the pool and sit in silence on the deck. It is a warm night, so even wet I am not shivering, but it might be Fred's kisses that made me so hot. I want to put my feet in his lap or lay my head on his shoulder, but unfortunately I don't take risks often. Kissing him in the pool was enough of a risk for one day. We are just talking when Ryan comes home and joins us. We make small talk and all head to our respective bedrooms.

I lie in bed for two hours with sleep eluding me. I sneak downstairs and tap lightly on Fred's door. He opens it and I walk in. He has the light on low and a notepad on the bed. He returns to his notes as I sit and watch him. It is apparent that watching him write has become a major aphrodisiac.

He is wearing a shirt and pants and it has been awhile since he wore this much to bed. I pick up a paper and read it. The thoughts are scattered but are all sad, dark, and depressing. "I didn't mean to make you feel this way."

"It's not you, it's me. I will work through it. You are the best medicine in the world."

I look up and smile. "I don't want to make you sad. I want to make you happy, whole, and complete. In such a short time you have made me much more than I ever knew I could be. I want to make you more too." I take his hands and admire his perfect face before I speak again. "Can I make you more?" I drop one hand and run my hand up his shirt. I move my eyes to watch my hand move across his abdomen.

"Yes," he whispers and the sex meter rises. "Yes, you do make me more, so much more."

He kisses me and kisses me again and again. I love my blank mind and I dream of losing all of myself in him. I pull away and stop us this time. I even know the timing isn't right. It is almost four a.m. and we didn't get much written. I start to get up when there is a light tap on the open door. I look up and see my mom.

"Everything okay?" she asks, sounding sleepy.

"Yeah, we're good. I was just going upstairs to sleep."

"Okay, I'm going to the kitchen for water. You two need anything?"

"No, thanks," we say in unison.

"Goodnight."

I wait a few minutes to be sure she is gone and I lean in to kiss Fred. "Goodnight. I feel better, and hope you do too. See you in a few hours." I leave without letting him say anything.

I get to the front stairs and my mom is sitting on the top step waiting for me. I have a sudden moment of panic as I sit down next to her. She wraps her arm around me and squeezes me tight to her side, as she kisses my hair. "I love seeing you full of joy. Enjoy being young as long as you can."

"Thanks, Mom. I will try."

"Do you stay up late at his house too?"

"Yeah, why do you ask?"

"Just reminiscing, I guess. In college I dated your dad's roommate freshman year, and that is how I met your dad. Brian and I were both art students and we used to stay in the studio painting all night. I love your dad, I have zero regrets, but I did love that feeling of being so into something and someone. That time flew by and before I knew it the sun was up."

"It's pretty damn awesome to get wrapped up in what you are doing that you feel nothing, no hunger or tiredness. I guess I get this from you?"

"Morgan, you are so much like me and yet nothing like me. Follow your heart and do what makes you happy. I lost a part of my happiness when I changed my majors. Art was my first love. I love you. Now go to bed. You have to be up soon."

"I love you too. Night." Walking towards my room, I turn back and ask her, "What happened to Brian?"

"We can talk more another time, but basically he had to leave school because his parents couldn't afford it anymore. He sent me a letter the summer before sophomore year saying he wasn't coming back. I never heard from him after that." She shrugs her shoulders and walks away.

My alarm is going off way too soon. I wake up feeling sad that Fred is leaving, but Ryan's excitement on the ride to the airport is contagious. I am a little nervous about him meeting the other guys. I don't want anyone to say anything because I am certain my brother is already onto us.

We park the car and head inside the building. I have never been to a private airport before; it seems really small. Fred talks to the guy at the desk before we all walk outside toward the planes. We are standing at the bottom of the staircase when Fred asks if we want to see the plane. "Hell, yeah," Ryan says.

The inside is pure luxury. The smell of leather and the clean shine glistens off every surface. "How much does it cost to fly this thing?" I ask Fred.

"Today it's on our label. We make them enough money so they can do this for us," Fred says to me as Alex, Zach and Gunner board the plane.

They each give me a hug, including Gunner. It feels good to know they are welcoming me into their life. My brother is standing at the back of the plane looking a little star struck when I introduce him to everyone. When Alex shakes his hand he says, "Wait, I know you. Ryan Evans. You're the quarterback for Rutgers. You'll be starting in the fall, right?"

"Yes, guess you follow college football."

"Just a little." Alex chuckles. "You must get me some tickets next year."

"I can do that," Ryan says, still in shock.

We all get a little laugh and even though this is fun I want to get it over with soon. I fear someone will realize I am not of legal age. The guys take their seats and Ryan and I head to the doorway when Fred says he will come back outside with us. Ryan says he will meet me in the car and he walks away without looking back. "I will call you tonight, okay?" Fred whispers as he moves my hair behind my shoulder.

"Yes." One tear runs down my face, and he quickly leans down and kisses it away.

"I know none of this is easy, but it feels too good to quit. I will try harder."

"You haven't done anything wrong. Sometimes getting to know someone has a few bumps along the way."

"You are so damn perfect there are no bumps I can't handle for you. I need to be with you more than I need to breathe."

"Go get on that plane before Ryan comes back, or worse, Gunner comes out."

"Miss you already, Jellybean." He walks away and turns around to blow me a kiss. I walk back to the car numb. We drive home in silence and I walk inside and head right to my bed. Too sad and too tired to do anything else. How did I become the girl who misses the boy?

The phone rings not long after I fall asleep, and I snap at Ryan when he comes in to tell me it is Brooke. I pick up the phone anyway and try to sound normal.

"Hey, you okay?" she asks.

"Yeah, just tired."

"Want to go out tonight?"

"No, yes, I don't know. Maybe for a little while. I still have to study and tomorrow is Father's Day."

"Is your Dad taking you all golfing again?"

"Eight a.m. tee time. Yippee."

"How about you study now, go out for a little bit later and I promise to get you home early so you don't fall into a sand pit. Can I come get you at seven?"

"Sounds good. Thanks, Brooke. You are a great friend. I will miss you so much when you are in Spain."

"I can't talk about that yet, okay? Bye." I am interrupted by the phone again while I'm studying Spanish. I smile and my glum mood is erased by Fred's warm voice.

"Thought you said you would call tonight," I say.

"I can hang up if you prefer."

"No, that is not what I prefer."

"I had a few minutes and I missed your sexy voice too much to go another minute without hearing it."

"You are so damn sweet. I am a lucky girl."

"I miss you and it's a great feeling because it makes me feel alive. I love knowing I have something worth missing."

"Okay, stop. I can't take anymore and not be able to wrap myself around you."

"Understood. Gunner is here, so I have to leave anyway. Miss you, Jellybean. Have a good night. I will call again later. It might be very late though."

"That's okay, call anytime, I miss you so much, Blacky. Maybe try to fix that problem since you are far away."

"I might."

"Go before I combust. Good Night, Fred."

I study some but there are no brain cells left for history. They must all be filled with images of Fred. I want to make history with him. It seems minutes later Brooke is here. She is always so bubbly, it's contagious. I feel lighter after she is only here a few minutes. We drive to one of Kelly's friend's house for the party.

It's small and a little too intimate for what I want tonight. I realize why we are here though when I see Brooke talking to a handsome boy. I head into the TV room to see what is on. A living room full of men watching hockey and drinking beer. When did this become my comfort zone? I join them and even though I enjoy the conversation, I can't stop thinking of Fred. I am sitting on the couch, numb. He has become my defibrillator and I need a jump-start. I tilt my head back needing to close my eyes to try to absorb these strange new feelings I have. Next thing I know Kelly is yelling my name.

"Damn, you scared me!" I try to say it softly but I fail.

"Sorry, were you asleep?"

"I don't know, maybe."

"Come, let's get some fresh air." She leads me outside to a worn out patio set. It's humid as June usually is, but it's not hot. We make small talk, but something is off with us both tonight.

"Where is John?"

"That fucking bastard," she yells. Kelly never yells. "Want to drink or smoke with me?" she asks with a mean tone she normally doesn't possess. I get up and find someone who has cigarettes and return quickly.

I put one in my mouth and once it's lit I give it to her and take one for myself. We say nothing. Most of the first cigarette is done when Kelly starts to laugh. I laugh with her because it is contagious. Until she says, "I really want to cry."

"Kelly, what did he do?"

"He slept with Dawn."

"Damn. Yikes. Bastard."

"Biggest asshole, it's so over. I don't want to talk about it." We sit in silence and she lights up another cigarette. I sit lost in my head waiting for her to speak again. "What's up with you?" she whispers.

"Nothing," I say.

"C'mon, you know I don't buy that. At least tell me about the Porsche guy."

I take a second cigarette and light it. A few minutes later I tell her to hold it for me and I walk inside and get a shot glass full of vodka. The warm liquid gives me the courage to talk. "Well, he owns a Jeep too and it fits him way better than the Porsche."

"And how do you know what fits him so well?"

"Damn, Kelly, this is difficult." I feel like my emotions will make me burst.

"Wait, what is wrong?" She instantly brings me comfort when she squeezes my shoulder.

"Do you have your car? I don't want to be overheard."

"Yes, come."

Once in the car I feel safe and loved. I know Kelly is the best person for me to talk to, but I fear Brooke will never forgive me. Kelly squeezes my thigh. "Hey, it's me, no stressing. You want to talk, we talk. You don't, we don't."

"That is exactly why I should talk to you." I am painfully silent until my diarrhea of the mouth starts. "Well, Frederick Rhoades owns the Porsche. We met at that party you took us to in Edison back in April. He knows I am sixteen and he has met my parents and we are writing together. I have met the whole band and I have been spending weekends at his shore house. He is in L.A. and I can't breathe when he is away. My family calls him Fred because that is what his family calls him. We pretend to be friends, but we are more. We haven't had sex but it takes every bit of willpower we both have to stop."

"Holy shit," she says, drawing out each word.

"I know I say those words in my head a lot. He will be at my party Friday, as a friend. I have to tell Brooke, but I want everyone to think it is platonic. My mom isn't dumb but she has to be kept in the dark. It would be difficult if she knew. His friends know we are together but don't know my age."

"Damn, this is fucked up and awesome."

I laugh. "Yeah, it is. Really awesome."

"I'm so happy for you."

"Kelly, you are a great friend. I'm glad it's you who can see through me and make me spill my secrets." She asks me a lot of little questions about Fred and the band and it is a relief to make basic conversation about the last few weeks of my life.

We head back to the house. In the middle of the front lawn I stop her.

"What's wrong?" she asks.

"Nothing. I am in love with him. I haven't told him yet, but I want you to know now. It's the most amazing thing I have ever felt." She hugs me and it's the best hug I have ever received from a friend. Everything looks a little different now that someone in my world knows my truth.

At home I find my dad on the couch and walk over to him to say good night.

"Good night, honey. Eight a.m. tee time. We will leave a little after seven."

"Wouldn't miss it for the world. Who won the hockey game?"

"Devils. Great game."

"Glad they won, good night." I kiss his cheek and walk away.

"Good night, my sweet baby." How can a few words make me go from feeling like a mature adult to being his little girl again? Confused, I head to my room. Ryan left a note with a number to call Fred. It was only five weeks ago this happened for the first time, yet it seems I have known him my whole life.

I call Fred and much to my dismay Gunner answers. "Hello…"

"Gunner, are you drunk?"

"Maybe, are you hot stuff?"

"No. Get Fred. I don't want to talk to you."

"Oh, why not?" He says as if he is stomping his feet.

"Because I don't like you."

"That is your problem."

"Yes, it is. I will try because I love Fred more than I hate you. I will do anything for him. Now put him on the damn phone before I fly out there and cut your balls off for irritating me so much."

"What the hell did you say to him?" Fred says as he comes on the line.

"Don't worry about it. How are you?"

"I'm good, but you sound funny. Is Gunner getting to you or some-thing else?"

"Well, Gunner does bug me, but I'm assuming what you can read in my voice is that I told Kelly about us. I couldn't keep it in. She will be here Friday night and she can always see the truth when it comes to me, and I know she will know that you aren't just a friend. I feel guilty that I told her and not Brooke or my mom, but if they love me they have to accept what I choose. Brooke has a new boyfriend, the Devils won game one of the Stanley Cup, that will keep my dad in a good mood, and I smoked too much. But it was a good night." There is silence on his end for a few minutes. "Hey, did I lose you?"

"No, I'm trying to process all that."

"Sorry, smoking makes me hyper."

"Yes, it does. No more smoking for you."

"Fine, I don't like it anyway."

"Was it a relief to tell someone?

"Yes, but scary too. I am relieved because she would know for sure when she saw us together. With Brooke though we are still friends, okay?"

"Okay with me. Whatever works for you."

"Thank you, Fred. I love that you accept me. I need to get some sleep. We have a Father's Day tradition of golfing. This year we have an eight a.m. tee time. Brooke is worried I will fall in a sand pit."

Fred laughs. "I will come riding in on a horse to rescue you. You can save yourself just fine though. How about I grant you some naps on my chest when I get back home."

"That is perfect. I will fall asleep now dreaming of your chest."

I do exactly that.

* * *

After golf and lunch we head back home. I try to study a little but I fall asleep. Ryan comes in to tell me Fred is on the phone. I pick it up and a sleepy "Hello" comes out of my still tired mouth.

"Hey, sorry I woke you."

"It's okay. I have a lot to study. What's wrong? You don't sound right."

"I called home for Father's Day and my dad was rude and unpleasant as usual."

"I'm sorry, Fred. He should understand what your job entails by now."

"He should, but we don't have a family that fits together like yours."

"I don't think many people do."

"I don't want to talk about it anymore. I will let you study."

"If you want to talk about it later let me know. I will comfort you any way I can."

"Umm, I can come up with a few ways. But I'm hanging up. Bye, Jellybean."

I went back to studying, but it was difficult to concentrate, so I wrote a poem instead. Lucky for me most tests come easy to me, but if I fail my parents will certainly never let me see Fred.

After our last final of the year, Brooke and I go back to her house. She has been making a few phone calls looking for a party, so I go upstairs and lie down on her bed. I fall into a peaceful sleep with dreams of the ocean and Fred's piercing blue eyes locked on mine. I am in the middle of the dream when Brooke shakes me awake.

"Hey, you okay?" she asks once my eyes open.

"Yeah, sorry."

"It's okay. Did you study that much or is something else making you tired? You slept over two hours."

"I did? Wow, I'm sorry. Did you find a party?"

"Don't I always?"

* * *

"After the party you can sleep over and we can go to the airport in the morning. I have someone special to get and you will finally know why I'm so tired." Brooke opens her mouth but I stop her. "It's not like that. I will explain tomorrow."

"Damn, only for you could I be this patient."

"Thanks, Brooke."

The party is boring. We leave early and go back to my house. Brooke is in the bathroom when I call Fred. He says to come get him after the guys leave the airport. I hang up before Brooke gets back to my room. We lie in bed and talk and giggle like we have since we were kids. I cherish the pieces of childhood I still have left, but I'm also crazy excited about my adult future.

Chapter Fourteen

Edge of Seventeen

THE FIRST DAY of summer leaves me cheerful and carefree but also filled with nervousness about my new life. Perhaps because my life became interestingly odd overnight. Brooke and I leave my house to pick up Fred. She parks the car and we head toward the main building of the airport. Since Brooke's dad often has clients fly into Morristown Airport, she never once thought it odd to come here. I see Fred through the window and I wonder how this will all play out. Should I see if Brooke recognizes him first? This is becoming fun.

I open the door for her and she steps inside and turns back around so fast she crashes into me. "Oh my, holy…" she whispers, unable to complete a whole thought.

"What?" I say back, trying not to smile.

"Rick Rhoades is in there!"

"Are you afraid of him?"

"No, I'm just freaking out."

"Take a deep breath. Want to say hi?"

"Yes." She takes my hand and opens the door again, but I lead the way.

We are walking toward Fred when he gets up and comes over to us. He leans down and gives me a brief hug and says hello loudly, then whispers Jellybean in my ear. He looks at Brooke and says, "Nice to finally meet you, Brooke." He leans down to give her a quick hug as well. Nothing on her has moved. "Hey, Brooke, you okay?" he asks, holding her shoulders.

She turns to me and says, "I am going to kill you. You could have given me some warning."

"Sorry," I say, but I am not.

"Shit, it's okay. But. Like. Oh. My. God," she says in slow motion. "Is this for real?"

"Shall we leave?" Fred asks, raising his eyebrows.

"Brooke, give Fred the keys so you don't get us killed going home." She takes the keys out of her pocket and hands them to him. I climb in the backseat thinking it might be best for her to be in the front. We leave and Fred impresses me because he already knows his way around here. Brooke is mute. I ask Fred how his flight was, and he tells me they are done in L.A. for now, then we are all silent again.

Back home, Fred takes his bag with him and says he is going to shower and change. I grab Brooke by the arm and pull her to my room.

"Brooke, can you talk?"

"Holy shit, Morgan. Rick Rhoades drove my car and he is in your shower. What. Is. Happening?"

"Remember that party we went to with Kelly back in April?"

She just nods at me.

"Well, that is his cousin's house and we met that night, outside, under the lilac trees."

"Wow." She sounds like she has cotton stuck in her mouth. I tell her how I will be writing with him and assisting him and the band. I fill her in on some things we have done together, but I tell her none of the juicy details.

"Why do you call him Fred?"

"That's what his family called him before the band. So he asked us to."

"Us?"

"My family. He has been here quite a bit. And I have been at his house in Mantoloking most weekends since Memorial Day."

"Damn, I thought you left with Ben."

"No, definitely not Ben. This is quite different than my relationship with Ben." I'm not lying since it is extremely different.

"Does he know you are sixteen?"

"Yes. It's not like that, so it doesn't matter."

"How can you keep your hands off him? I want to touch every inch."

"He is gorgeous and the rest of the band is too, especially Gunner, but it's not like that with any of them."

"I would touch them all." She has her daydream face on.

"Why don't we go downstairs and get some lunch?"

"Okay." I can't believe how unsure and nervous she is. This isn't the Brooke I know.

"You will get used to it. He is the same as any other person." But he is nothing like any other person I know.

"Let's have lunch," she says, sounding more normal but still not like herself.

I leave Brooke in the kitchen and go to get Fred. He is in the guest room with the door open. I shut it behind me as I wrap my arms around his waist. I press my head into his back and I can feel the warm moisture from his shower through his shirt. He smells delicious and the last thing I want to do is leave this room.

He turns around to look at me, then back at the door, then back at me. His lips brush mine as his hands move up my neck to my face. Once he is holding my cheeks he slips his tongue in my mouth. He kisses me briefly before he takes my hand and opens the door. I do not want to leave him. He hesitates to release my hand as we walk into the living room and we join Brooke in the kitchen. She drinks some water and the color is back in her face.

"When can I meet the rest of the band?"

"Oh, Brooke, it's great to have you back," I say.

"You can meet them soon, but probably after Spain," Fred says.

"Damn, I don't want to go anymore."

"Brooke, your mom would kill you."

"I know, but this is much better."

"Some boy in Spain will make you think differently."

"I doubt it."

We eat and hang out and everything is way easier than I imagined. My two best friends are forming a friendship and that warms my heart. I just wish we weren't lying to Brooke. It's almost dinnertime when Brooke leaves, and she runs into my mother in the driveway. I watch them talking and I can tell by the smiles on their faces they are talking about Fred.

* * *

Friday is here before I know it. I feel delighted and nervous about my party. At eight am sharp my mom takes me to get my driver's license. She assures me I will pass and off I go. I do pass. After that I thought this nervous feeling would be erased, but it isn't.

We head back to the house and Fred is on the front step looking yummy and delicious. I can't understand why the neighbors haven't walked over and tried to take a bite. I walk over to him and take my license out of my wallet and hold it up. He wraps me in a big bear hug and lifts me up and I don't even care that my mom is watching. He whispers in my ear, "We can celebrate tomorrow." I want him more than I have ever wanted anything in my life. This need ignites every inch of my body and every cell in my mind.

Nothing I attempt to do gets done. Suddenly my mom says she is leaving to get lunch and she flies out the door. Wondering if she can tell I am out of sorts, it's odd for her to leave instead of talking to me. I realize maybe she knows the one I want comfort from is Fred. Perhaps moms do know everything.

Once she leaves I take Fred upstairs to my room and open the window so I can hear the driveway. He is standing at the foot of my bed. I walk to him and he lifts my chin and asks, "Are you okay?"

"No, and how can you guys tell?"

"You have a worried look in your eyes."

"I didn't realize."

"Should I leave, not come tonight, so you don't have to lie to everyone? I understand if that would be easier."

"No, I want you here. I feel out of sorts. This is harder than I thought it would be. Not telling your friends my age doesn't bother me at all. Does that bother you?"

"No. It's our business not theirs."

"You are right. What I do in private is not their concern."

I push Fred back on the bed. I sit on top of him and interlace my fingers with his. I close my eyes and tilt my head back, concentrating on feeling him grow hard underneath me. I bring my head back and circle my hips. He releases my hands and sits up, capturing my body in a firm embrace. His lips tear into mine. His passion is going to be my downfall. He is extremely firm and broad and I want to touch every inch of his body this instant. His kiss consumes me. I need his body, his soul, and his mind. I want this man, now.

He flips me over on my back and puts all his weight on me. It's too much to take in. I have missed him more than I realized was possible. It's been almost two weeks since we have been in his bed. How can a man I have not had sex with make my desires stay so elevated? I push every inch of my body into him, as his kisses get faster, certain he can't take this anymore than I can.

Out of control, I grind myself into him, and it makes me feel wild. I push myself harder and harder, needing the pressure to build, so it can be released. I dig my nails into his back just as I hear the car door slam in the driveway, but it's too late to stop. I bite his shoulder to muffle my moans as my body gets what it needs and I come fully clothed underneath him. My body is in a spasm of pure pleasure still as he moves off. His hand remains locked with mine. I attempt to stand next to him but it's of no use. I lie back down and say, "When you can walk, can you go tell my mom I'm lying down for a few minutes."

"Okay."

Lying with my eyes closed, I don't hear him leave, so I look up. He is still standing there. "Be right back," he says with longing.

He returns minutes later and sits on the edge of the bed, his firm ass hitting my hip. "I got Advil from your mom. I told her you had a headache."

I take the Advil from him. I open my nightstand drawer and toss them in. He puts the water down. "What?" I ask because he looks confused.

"Nothing."

"Really? Your face says otherwise."

"Damn, Jellybean. Did you just come?"

"I don't know. That was way better than any orgasm I had before," I say as I close my eyes. "I wish you could have been there with me. Sorry I want to say I feel greedy, but I feel too damn good to say anything else."

"Fuck, I need you," he says, squeezing my arm.

"Don't talk like that. You will get me all worked up again."

We sit on the bed in these same positions for quite some time. There is a knock on the door and my mom comes in. She walks over and touches my head. "How are you, honey?"

"Better. I am going to shower and get changed. Thank you both for taking care of me." I get up as my mom leaves. I wink at Fred and head to the shower. My skin feels different under the water. It feels alive yet relaxed. It's not him being here that is a problem; it's me not being alone with him that is.

My mother is excellent at putting a party together. I envy her for her extroverted ways. I wish sometimes I had some of them. Right now I would rather be locked away in my room writing. More so, locked away with Fred. But the party must go on. Faith arrives before Brooke's family. She is a little more natural around Fred now and it is helping me to feel comfortable too.

I told Brooke she could tell her family so they would be prepared, but Brooke's mother has her mouth hanging open as she shakes Fred's hand. He has a paralyzing effect on women. A party of ten people is usually my thing, but tonight it feels too small for comfort. I fear they can see right through me. After we eat I become more relaxed and I try harder to have fun.

Kelly, being her cool, confident self, comes up behind Fred and says, "Fred, let's sit outside and talk." She takes him by the hand and starts walking.

"Sure," he says as his eyes dance up to look into mine. I can see Kelly on the deck and after five minutes she waves to me to come out. I walk outside and the humid June air feels so wonderful that it warms me to the core. I hate central air, but my parents love it. Fred's house is never ice cold and I love that he has the windows open a lot, or perhaps it is the shore air that I love.

I start to sit next to Kelly, but she snaps at me, "No, sit next to him." I do as I am told and sit too close to Fred. "I wanted to see you next to each other. You too have avoided each other to the point now where it looks like you are trying."

"Oh damn, really?" I reach my hand behind his back and move my fingertip in circles on his back, under his t-shirt. I watch his face, as his eyes shut and his lips part. When he opens them he looks drugged and burning hot. Even Kelly is in danger of melting.

"Now I see why you can't be anywhere near each other. Shit, you are intense."

"Kelly, you have no idea how intense this is," Fred starts. "I wish everyone could know what this feels like. There is nothing so satisfying as being with a person who makes you feel more in one caress than every caress before it combined. Morgan has changed my life and there is no going back." He speaks with his eyes locked on me.

"I have no comeback for that. Just be careful. I want the best for Morgan."

We say thanks in unison and Brooke comes bounding out. She is clueless to the meaning of the looks on all our faces as she talks in length about leaving tomorrow. It's still early, but I am over my own party. We head back inside so I can open gifts. Brooke's family gave me a ton of clothes. Kelly gave me a leather journal. Brooke gave me some phone cards to use to call her. Fred gave me a guitar. All he says is I want to be your teacher. I melt into my mom's expensive Italian carpet with everyone I love watching. How can I hold myself together with all this attention on me?

The party is winding down, as Brooke and her family leave. Faith is going to sleep in Ryan's room and Ryan will be on the couch tonight. Mantoloking is calling for me to return, which is all I can think about as I get ready for bed.

My bedroom door opens just as I reach to turn my lamp off. Fred walks in, then I turn it off. He leans down and kisses me gently on the mouth, then leaves soft kisses up to my ear and says, "I hope you had a happy birthday." He nibbles on my ear. "Tomorrow I will give you your real present."

"What?"

"Shh, go to sleep. Tomorrow." I want him to stay, I want to scream for him to hold me, but I watch him walk out of my room. How does he have this much strength?

Saturday morning I wake up early, already having Mom's permission to take her car. I leave the house and drive alone for the first time. It is one heck of a power trip. I can do anything I want. If only I had money and was eighteen it might feel a lot more powerful, but for now it feels amazing. I drive over to see Brooke and she is trying to pack, but it looks like her entire bedroom is on the living room floor. She refuses help.

"Kelly, let's get out of here. Let's go to the mall," I say, walking toward the door. Kelly follows.

We arrive at The Mall at Short Hills, then walk and chat about nothing important. We are on the top floor and the smell from Illuminations is enticing. We walk around smelling every candle when Kelly says, "How is it that you haven't slept with him?"

"I don't know. I want to. He always stops us. I mean we have only kissed and touched over clothes or above the waist."

"Damn that must be tough." She scrunches up her nose.

"It is pure TORTURE." The sales lady looks up and we both giggle a little. "I can't last much longer. I don't think he can either."

"What is he waiting for? He looks at you with pure lust. He wants you, bad."

"I'm hoping he was waiting for me not to be sixteen, but not waiting for me to be eighteen." We are walking out of the store when I say, "Let's buy me some sexy underwear for tonight." She pulls me to the underwear section in Macy's. We laugh and talk. I am happy she is the person I confided in. My instincts were right on this. I decide on a pale lilac bra and matching thong.

When I drop Kelly back home, Brooke is still in a slight panic, but it is almost time for her to leave. She has to accept what she has packed and move on. She gives me a huge hug and says, "I want to stay. Hang out with CrossRhoades all summer."

"When you get home – if they are around – we will all have to get together. Now go break some hearts." We have never been apart for this long since we met. I will miss her, but I have a great distraction waiting for me.

I head back home and the house is full of laughter and loud garbled conversation. I run upstairs and put my bags in my closet and walk back downstairs. My parents, Ryan, Faith and Fred are playing UNO and it's a sight to behold. I become a little overwhelmed when I see Fred at ease with my family. I love that they are all accepting each other. I hope it never changes, but I have a fear it has to. A tear runs down my face as my mom comes to stand beside me. "Honey, it's okay. Brooke will be back soon enough and you'll have your own exciting adventures this summer."

I hug her and say thanks. I'm relieved she doesn't know what is actually making me emotional.

Dad deals me in on the next game, as Fred says, "I have four tickets to the Devil's game tonight. Would you like to join us?"

"Sure." I mean it, but I'm questioning it because I want to be back in his bed more than I want anything else.

Chapter Fifteen

No Ordinary Love

THE ENERGY IN the Brendan Byrne Arena is palpable. I have never been to a hockey game before and what a first game this is. Everyone is screaming because the underdogs are clearly going to win the Stanley Cup tonight. Their cheers make me feel hopeful for myself.

We took a car service to the arena and we are taking one back home. My dad and Ryan have thanked Fred a million times; he looks uncomfortable with their words of thanks. We are all loud on the way home perhaps due to my dad and Fred's drunken state. We get home late and we are still way too loud, but we make it to our respective sleeping areas.

I use the bathroom after Ryan is finished getting ready for bed, which tonight will be the couch in the living room. I am about to shut the bathroom door as it is pushed open. Fred sneaks in and locks the door. He grabs my shoulders and slams me into his body. I slink my arms around his neck as he gently caresses my lips with his. His tongue moves faster and more desperately with each passing second. I need this man right now and I don't even care that we are in the hall bathroom of my parents' house.

Fred pulls away. I don't want him to ever stop touching me. "I wanted to give you a proper birthday kiss yesterday. I thought we would be back home by now too, but hockey and my love for your family got in my way."

"You make me so emotional when you use words and even more when you use your body. Maybe you should make it two kisses."

"I want to, but," he pauses, killing me a little, "I will give you a million when we celebrate your birthday alone, at home, tomorrow. Be ready to leave for brunch by eleven. Your mom knows our plans. She bought you a new dress to wear too."

I stare up at him, my mouth hanging open, and if it weren't dry I would be drooling.

He peeks outside the bathroom and leaves. I am left breathless and wanting. As much as this feeling can be torture, it's also the best damn feeling ever. Every second of every day has sensation and meaning. It's mind altering to be so intoxicated by another human being and to find such a compatible match in the sea of people on this planet.

I try to sleep but I do not sleep well alone anymore. I want nothing more than to be back in Fred's bed. Hopefully not sleeping, but regardless I will still be in his bed. Before I know it it's nine in the morning and the alarm is blaring. I get up with a literal bounce in my step. I shower and head to my room in my robe. In the closet I find the long summery dress my Mother bought me. It is soft as silk and off-white with a modern floral print in pinks and lavenders. It reminds me of the lilacs I met Fred under. I know my mother has no idea, but somehow she has bought the most incredible dress at the most remarkable time. I am struggling with the zipper when there is a knock on the door.

My mom enters and helps me with the zipper. She doesn't say anything for the longest time. It makes me uncomfortable, which is a rare feeling for me around my mother. I just say, "Thank you, Mom."

She hugs me tight. "You're welcome. I love you, honey. You look lovely. I hope you have a great day. You have many wonderful adventures ahead of you."

"Thank you so much for allowing me to have this."

She kisses my cheek again and leaves. I pack up some things, not even knowing how long it will be before I come back home. It's weird how today has been discussed between Fred and my mom. I begin to wonder what else they talk about.

I carry my bag downstairs and it's too quiet in the house. I walk back to the guest room and find Fred packing. I stand in his doorway as he turns and locks his eyes on me. He walks over without saying a word. He stares at me long enough to make my blood hot; then again it doesn't take long so I guess one look is all it takes. "Damn, Jellybean, you look absolutely incredible and breathtakingly beautiful." I can see the reflection in his eyes of the joy he brings me. I feel more beautiful than I have ever felt, but I think he looks far better than me. His body is so sculpted and lean that anything and nothing look amazing on him. His white dress shirt and black pants make him look as if he jumped off the cover of GQ.

"Thank you. I wish I knew what all the fuss was about. My mom is emotional and you look sappy. Can I have a clue?"

"I don't know what your mom is emotional about, except for the fact that she has you for a daughter. Brunch and then a little birthday surprise. Okay?"

"Yes." Because I trust him implicitly.

We are on our way to brunch in a town car. I will follow his lead today and do as he pleases, because I know I am certain to be pleased.

We rarely do anything outside our homes except food shopping, so this is bound to be fun. We are sitting against each other holding hands, and my fingertips are caressing his palm rhythmically. This simple touch is all encompassing after having to refrain for so long. I see the sign for the Holland Tunnel. "Are we eating in the city?" I lift my head off his shoulder.

"Yes."

"Food in public. Do people do that?"

"Public, yes, but in a private room."

"Sounds pleasurable. It has been a long time since we have been together in private," I say, my voice cracking.

"Damn, you can't say that," he snaps, but he also laughs.

We arrive at a small restaurant in Manhattan where the hostess takes us to a back room. She eyes Fred up and down, and for the first time I get to see what an attractive woman does when they see him. I am shocked he doesn't look at her twice. His eyes are only on me and it makes me feel powerful. Even if I don't know what to do with my powers.

The back room is small, just a few tables, but we are the only ones here. The back wall is all glass and opens to a small garden of potted plants and stonework. It's small but it makes you forget you are in the middle of a huge city.

We sit at our table and before I can utter a word a waiter brings us each a mimosa. I am not nervous but excited to be with Fred, and the champagne calms me in one sip because it reminds me of his house.

"You okay?" he asks.

"Yeah, why?"

"You have a funny look in your eye like you are unsure of something."

"I do? I guess I'm unsure of how I got here, so to say. I mean how is it I am here with you? I still have a surreal feeling sometimes when I look at you."

He takes my hand and traces his thumb up and down my palm. The feeling is a cross between relaxed and aroused. "Oh, Jellybean, I want to take you home right now to show you how real this is."

I close my eyes and try to absorb the rush of feeling I get from his words. When I open them again, I say, "I want you to show me too, but I will enjoy being here with you first."

He smiles and reaches for my other hand. He squeezes them both and says, "Today we will celebrate your birthday, just us. Happy Birthday, Jellybean. I hope I can make you as happy as you make me."

I wish for more words but the waiter comes back asking if we are ready to order. I love when he lavishes me with his words. Especially when those words are about how he feels for me. Sometimes I feel emotional and too deep with Fred; it's almost too heavy. The easy conversation we have throughout our meal is welcoming. Regardless how lighthearted our brunch has become, every time I touch him I am on fire.

"Ready to head home?" He stands to take my hand.

"That has a nice sound to it. I am ready to go home, Fred." I squeeze my hand into his.

We ride mostly in silence back to Mantoloking. Sitting against him I rest my head on his shoulder. This has become my new favorite resting place. We pull in the driveway and Fred has a funny look on his face.

"What is that smile for?" I ask.

He gives nothing away. He thanks the driver. He doesn't pay him or tip him so I assume someone has arranged all of that for us already. It has to be odd living your life with others doing most of the grunt work. I am learning that going along for the ride is pretty enjoyable though.

Before I take a single step away from the car he covers my eyes and turns me around. I hear the car back out of the driveway and Fred still says nothing. He walks me forward with his hand still on my eyes. "What are we doing?" I feel impatient but blissful to the core.

"Patience." I can hear the smile on his face. With his hand still over my eyes he whispers in my ear, "Happy Birthday." He takes his hand away and my eyes adjust to the sun but not to the shiny new car right in front of me.

"Holy shit. No, you didn't, you bought me a car? Holy shit, it's a freaking Mustang. A cobra. Fred, are you serious?"

"I hope you like it."

"I love it!" I squeal.

He hands me the keys. My arms wrap around his neck. I can't stop kissing him, in the driveway, in the bright sunlight, I have become bold. Being in the real world is leaving me careless. I almost don't care.

"Okay. Take me for a ride, gorgeous," he says and his smile is bigger than mine.

I get in the car. The interior is black leather. This is one damn hot car. I look over at Fred and can't believe he bought me a new car, and that we are taking a ride in it. The car is fun to drive. The day is perfect, like the weather. More like spring than summer and the smell of new leather and sea air is making me feel extra carefree. The stick shift is a little too sexy for words. Having Fred sitting next to me while I drive gives me gutter brain. I turn around, needing to get home as soon as possible.

"Hey, joy ride over already?"

I clear my throat.

"What? Cat got your tongue? Say something," he says, squeezing my thigh.

"Nothing I have to say is rated G."

This time he clears his throat with a sexy exhale.

"I have gutter brain." He doesn't say anything so I continue. "First shifting the gears is doing things to me and you talk about enjoying the ride. Really, Fred, I can't take much more."

He squeezes my thigh again, a little too powerfully, but I know it means he can't take much more either. I don't speed but I want to get home fast. I pull in the driveway and we both sit frozen in the car. It's deadly silent and I feel without a doubt that I will never forget a second of this moment, of this day. Fred turns to look at me. He leans across the car and grabs my face and kisses me. He is a skilled kisser and if I weren't sitting I would crumple to the ground. He pulls away but keeps his forehead against mine.

With a sexual whisper he asks, "Are you ready?" He takes a deep breath, as his cool exhale hits my flaming flesh. "To go inside?"

"I've never been more ready. Fred, let's go inside. Now." My voice is low and sexy without meaning for it to be. I hold his mouth against mine. I never want to be disconnected from him.

"Stay in your seat," he tells me and he moves as if in slow motion out of the passenger side. He walks around to my door and opens it. He reaches out his hand to take mine. Once outside the car he shuts my door. His stare is hypnotizing. He gently pushes me back against the car and leans his body flush against mine.

"You are such a gentleman," I say, before he kisses me again. But it's too quick and he pulls away. He is staring at me again and his fingers are digging into my hips. He is still trying to stop himself, but I don't want him to ever stop again. I grab his head, running my fingers through his hair and pulling his mouth to mine. I need him. Now.

"Don't worry, the gentleman act won't last much longer." He lifts me up with one hand on my back and the other under my legs and carries me up the stairs and into the house. Good thing he doesn't lock the door.

He carries me upstairs to the bedroom. He puts me down in the middle of the room. Once again he shocks me. The duvet is new, purple, and flowery. There are several large vases with all purple flowers in them. Extra purple throw pillows are on the couch. I admire everything as he lights a few candles and makes a fire in the fireplace. I have taken to watching him move about the room until he comes back over to me. "I know it's June, but I have wanted the fire in here since the first night you slept here."

"I think it was cool enough back in May."

"It was, but I never would have kept my hands off you if there was a fire."

"But, you didn't really keep your hands off me." I raise my eyebrows and add a smile.

"True, but it would have been a whole lot more."

I am enjoying this anticipation. "So, tonight, with the fire, a whole lot more?" I run my hand up his back and back down again. He runs his hands up my arms, real slow, real light, real hypnotizing. My eyes are heavy but I can't take them off his bright shining irises.

"Yes," he says and I have almost forgotten my question. We kiss and the passion is overwhelming. I did not know I could feel this much for one person and feel it through a simple kiss. This is finally the moment I have been waiting to share with him. "First though, come here." I don't want to stop. He takes my hand and tells me to sit on the couch.

I sit and watch him walk to his nightstand and take out a piece of paper. He comes back and sits with me as he places a white torn out notebook page in his lap. He takes my hands in his. He rubs the back of my hands with his thumbs like he often does when he is trying to find the right words. I love the pause; it makes room for me to feel more for him.

"I want to read something I wrote first," he whispers. I lick my lips. "Damn." He leans over and kisses me harder and deeper. "Everything you do gets me worked up." He swallows hard. "This first part is what I read to your mom that night on the phone."

"Finally," I say before he starts to read it.

Under a lilac tree
I hid alone my heart in pain
My mind and body heavy in a black sea
Then I saw her and I felt light again

Morgan
She changed my world
She changed my heart
With just a touch she made it start
My life began again

I never felt a pull of this magnitude
It was like a magnet to my heart
She saw directly into me
She pulled me out of the sea

Eternal friendship is all I need
But is that too much greed?
She is my rescuer, she is my protector
Shielded by the lilac nectar, she takes my hand

The fog is being lifted
A light from within
She is lovely and gifted
Healing me with the touch of her skin

A friend forever
I will always endeavor
She is ingrained in me
I am chained to her

Morgan brought me light
She gave me back tonight
With just the touch of her hand
Life was again grand

Morgan
She changed my world
She changed my heart
With just a touch she made it start
My heartbeat began again

We are both silent. I can tell by the tone of his voice how much this means to him. I only hope he understands what he means to me without the extreme prose, since I don't have his writing skills. I open my mouth but he puts his finger over my lips. A lone tear drops from my left eye. He wipes it away with love. "The end I didn't read to your mother," he whispers and pauses. He takes both my hands in his, the paper scrolled in masculine print sits unused in his lap.

It took no time at all
For me to fall
The second our eyes locked
My heart was unlocked

You crawled inside
It was a powerful high tide

A moment to record
A feeling that can't be ignored

You stole my soul
Made me lose all control
I am no longer blue
Because Morgan, I love you

I squeeze his hands a little harder. The tears roll down my cheeks now. How can I be this lucky to have this amazing man love me? I climb in his lap. And it's quite ungraceful in this long dress. I drape my legs over his and I take his face in my hands. His stubble distracts me for a second. I desperately crave to caress every inch of him.

"Frederick Rhoades, I love you too."

Chapter Sixteen

Finally

THE BLUE EYES I have fallen so hard for watch me as I shift to straddle him. I pull my dress up so I can move better in his lap. My legs are bent and my knees are against his hips and every part of his touching me feels new and different this time. I lean down to kiss him, my hands still on his face. My lips touch his, sweet, loving, crazy with need. He kisses me back and the way he moves his mouth is unlike anything I have ever felt. It's hot and electric, but coated in love. His tongue is slow and strong as it passes over mine. I have never felt this many sensations in one kiss when he runs his hands up my legs, pushing my dress up as he covers every inch of my thighs.

I become breathless from the kissing and touching, yet I have never felt more alive than I do at this moment. He breathes life into me. His hands have made it up to my hips and he grabs them firmly, pushing me down and into him. "Oh Fred," I moan as I kiss him across his jawline to his ear. I repeat the same kisses on his left side as his hands release my hips and run up my back. He gets to my neck and pulls my head back to his mouth and with both hands he slowly unzips my dress. He runs his finger down my spine at the same time his tongue runs over every inch of my mouth. The pleasure has become too much. I can't even moan.

My hands are digging into his biceps, as he brings his hands up to cup my face. His mouth moves away from mine but he is so close we are almost touching. I open my eyes to stare into his. The passion is like a laser cutting through my body and soul. "Stand up," he says in a voice so deep I almost don't recognize him. I get up, glad he is keeping me steady.

He turns me so my back is to him. His hands move across my shoulder blades and push my dress forward and down my arms until it drops to the floor. I don't move. I stand still, eyes shut, mesmerized by his touch. He unhooks my bra and lets it fall with my dress. He steps closer, and his clothed body is brushing my bare back. His shirt needs to come off, but I am paralyzed by the kisses on my shoulders and neck. Each kiss is feather light but ignites my skin to a boil. His hands reach around and he takes my breasts in his hands. I push myself harder into his hands as I bring my arms up around his neck and lay my head back on his chest.

"Oh, Morgan, I need you," he says as he nips at my ear lobe. I turn around to face him. Since I have my heels on I can reach to kiss his chin. I kiss down his neck into the opening of his shirt. I open my eyes and look up at him. He stares down at me and I undo each button of his crisp white shirt, our eyes never leaving each other. Once I get to the last button I run my hands up his bare stomach, then his firm chest. I push the shirt slowly off his shoulders then down his arms. His shirt falls onto the couch. So much fanfare for one article of clothing, but I also wish it took longer to remove. Without pausing I move to unbutton his pants. As I lower the zipper painfully slowly, one click at a time, his eyes close and his head drops back in pure bliss. I am high on him. I love that I can make him feel what he makes me feel. It's a powerful feeling to bring pleasure to another person. Even more powerful to a person you love. A pure love.

His zipper is down when I pause to take in this visual heaven. I reach my hands around to his hips and push his pants down to his feet and take myself with them. Squatting in front of him, he looks down at me. I push him back by the thighs so he sits on the couch. I remove his pants, shoes and socks before I lean in between his legs. I watch his face as I run my hands up each leg. Slowly my fingertips glide under his loose boxers. My hands are more confident than ever before as I trace my fingertips up further until he shifts and grabs me by the shoulders and stands me up with him briskly.

"I'm losing myself in you too fast, Jellybean." He kisses me with passion vibrating from his tongue. He moves his mouth down to my nipple, and his tongue circles it until he sucks it into his mouth, making me drop my head back. When he moves to the other side I decide to follow intently with my eyes. My eyes lock with his as his tongue circles me. I look down so I can see each movement of his mouth. Seeing my nipple in his mouth and the gratification on his face is so erotic, I can't turn away. I could stare at him touching me for hours.

He opens his eyes to see me still watching him. Just when I thought we hit the ceiling on passion it's elevated again. Fred lifts me under my knees and carries me to the bed, laying me across it on top of the duvet. Euphoria courses through my veins. He lifts my right leg and takes my shoe off, running his thumbs across my foot where the shoe used to be, sending a shiver through my body. He does the same with my other foot and for the first time I find my feet sexual.

His hands have been up and down my legs several times, as I have been squirming almost frantically. He crawls on the bed and straddles me. I open my eyes to see his darker than ever, staring down at me. He keeps his eyes on me as he takes his fingers and grabs the elastic of my underwear. In a graceful fluid movement, he works them and himself back down to my feet. Finally, for the first time I am laid out before him, naked, and more than ready to be one with him.

He takes my hands and pulls me to a sitting position. I put my hands around him and pull him toward me so I can kiss his muscular stomach, running my tongue from his belly button to his hip as I push his boxers down. I do it as slowly as he removed my clothes. When I have him undressed he abruptly walks around to the other side of the bed. I stand to watch him as he pulls the sheets back and climbs in. He is tan, naked and looks like a work of art stretched out on the bed. He lifts the covers for me, an invitation I could never decline. I climb in beside him as he drapes the sheets over me and pulls me flush against his body. His kiss sets me on fire again. My hands are all over his body looking for more pleasure to pile on top of the extreme desire I already am feeling. His hands mirror mine and together we burn with desire. I roll on my back taking him with me. He kisses me once more before he opens the drawer for a condom.

"You certain you want to do this?" I know he is only asking because I am seventeen. I appreciate it but I hate the reminder.

"More than sure. I'm also sure I don't want to use this," I say, taking the condom and putting it down. He stares at me, confused and maybe upset too. "I'm on the pill."

"I had no idea. I guess I don't pay attention too well."

"You trust me? I trust you."

"I trust you, Morgan."

He leans down harder into me. His weight is glorious. His kiss is heavenly. My desire is escalating. "Fred, now, please," I pant. "I want to come with you inside me this time."

He moves and he is very close to giving me what I want. "Morgan, look at me." I open my eyes and stare up at him. He is more beautiful when my need is reflected in him. "Don't close your eyes. I want to watch you." Slow and tender, he enters me. His eyes are locked on mine.

When he moves his hips back again I can't take the amazing sensation anymore and I close my eyes. "Fred, it's too much," I moan to release air and because this is too intense. I move my hips to match his. His full lips find mine and we kiss through every movement. His hands wrap around me and mine around him. I am wrapped in a cocoon of pleasure. He moves a little faster and it's too much to hold back. I wish this moment didn't have to end but after a month of foreplay, I am going to explode. The sensation in my belly is so tight and the release washes over me fast, but it lasts excessively long. I can't even form words as I come around him.

The aftershocks are almost as intense as the initial release when Fred shifts again suddenly and I look up at his face. His eyes are tightly shut, his face full of pure joy, as he yells my name. He comes inside me so warm and strong and I cannot imagine ever feeling this level of sexual pleasure again. But I will certainly try to.

Fred's body stops trembling and I hold his head to my chest and run my fingers through his hair. It is a close call as to what is better, making love to him or just holding him afterward. He shifts off me and lies down by my right side. I roll over and we lie there apart, staring at each other.

I reach out and trace my hand over the tattoo on his right arm and his perfect muscles. I close my eyes, absorbing the many desires he stirs inside me. I no longer have to imagine what it is like to make love to him. I finally know and I want more.

He leans over and kisses me softly, but his tongue still slithers into my mouth. He pulls away. "There is so much I have to say but I can't think straight," he says.

"Then just lie here and hold me." I roll toward him as his arm drapes over my hip and I place my hand on top of his. I feel relaxed enough to fall asleep, but nothing about me is tired. I am blissfully satisfied. I must drift off to sleep because the next thing I feel is Fred's hands running through my hair when he starts kissing the back of my neck. Small delicate kisses that turn me into one large puddle of mush.

Kissing across my shoulder and down my arm, he makes me moan uncontrollably again. I roll on to my stomach as he continues kissing my back. His hand cups my ass as his kisses continue down my leg, then back up my other leg. The covers are pushed to the end of the bed as I push my hips into the bed needing to move, but Fred lies down on top of me and I can't move under his weight. I feel him hard against my back and become light headed from this intoxication.

"Lie on your back," I tell him. I climb on top of him and straddle him. My eyes lock with his as I move myself down onto him. I push him into me one pleasurable inch at a time with my eyes locked on his. He lifts his hips and pushes himself deeper into me and I close my eyes and roll my head back. "Oh, Fred," is all I can muster up as we move together, slow, all consuming. He reaches down between us and rolls his thumb over me. Such a simple movement coupled with the rest of him brings my orgasm crashing down.

I fall onto his chest, as the power of that orgasm takes all my energy. He flips me over to my back without losing contact. Fred moves slowly again and I match his movements. When I open my eyes he is watching me. This time without closing my eyes, I move my hips faster and faster until I come beneath him, eyes locked. How is it he can bring me such intense feelings so quickly? I am so blessed to be with a man who can do this to me, when he comes, yelling my name again, erasing all thoughts from my mind and filling me with nothing but bliss.

* * *

I wake with my head on his chest, his arm holding me tightly to him. The sun is setting and the room is aglow in orange. The fire is a little too warm but it feels enchanting. My hands move constantly on his skin. When my fingers run up and down the outside of his thigh, his breathing changes. "Sorry, didn't mean to wake you."

"If you are lying naked next to me, I want to be awake."

"Oh, why is that?" I ask playfully.

"Because I love you."

I lean up on his chest so I can look at his face. I kiss him lightly. "I love you too."

I put my head back down and he continues to hold me.

"Why is this so damn good?" I whisper. I'm not sure if I am asking him or myself. I long to know what is making this love, this sex, exceed my wildest fantasies.

"I guess because we love each other. I don't know. We trust each other. That night I saw you under the lilac tree, I instantly knew I needed you in my life. I was drawn to you. And I have felt that way ever since. You make me feel more than I have ever felt. You flipped a switch on in me and the world is a different place."

"I love listening to you talk, and I love all your words. Your words make me feel complete and perfect. I love that being with you gives my mind a break from all the jumbled thoughts. You erase all my errant thoughts."

"None of your thoughts are errant. I love everything you have in this pretty head," he says, looking deeply into me.

I move to kiss him again and he pulls me on top of him. "Fred?"

"Yeah?"

"I fell in love with you the night I met you. I thought it was infatuation. I don't think that anymore. It was some version of love."

He puts his hands on my cheeks and gives me a firm kiss. He pulls away and locks his eyes on me again. "I loved you that night too. When you held my hand it shot right through me to my heart. I was so scared to feel it, but thankfully I did so I could search for you. You are a part of me…" He kisses me, leaving me unsure if he means right now or in general.

"You hungry?" he asks.

"Only for you."

"Ohhhhhh, Morgan," he moans into my mouth. "Let's shower and eat." He moves from under me and off the bed. He reaches out his hand and helps me up.

The shower is warm and soothing. I have waited a lifetime to stand in this shower, naked, and physically loved by him. He washes every inch of me. His soapy hands run over my breasts and down my back. He reaches from around me and starts touching me in my favorite spot. His fingers move fast and rhythmically. "Fred, that feels incredible." He doesn't stop and a few minutes later I come again. The all body consuming sensation has weakened my legs. I am forever changed by this love and the heightened sexual awakening he provides me.

Without warning, he pulls his fingers out and pushes himself inside me. His thrusts are so demanding I'm getting all worked up again. I have never had orgasms this close together before; I know this will be my new normal. My orgasm builds too fast and I come around him hoping he still has enough strength to keep us both upright. His orgasm is so powerful it's a miracle we are both still on our feet. I turn to face him. He looks beautiful when he is pleasured.

"I'm hungry now," I say.

He laughs and pulls me to his chest. "Me too." He squeezes me tighter. "Morgan?"

"Yeah?"

"I love you. I really love you. Showing you that physically, finally, is so satisfying. Sorry I waited so long. I was scared."

"I know you did the right thing. Just so you know, I was never scared. Age is a number not a mental state. Everyone who knows me knows I can handle more than the average teen."

"I know that now. You handle things unlike anyone I know. You are more mature than me too. I'm thankful your parents see it too, or you would definitely not be here."

"We are very lucky. I'm still sorry we have to lie."

"I know, but it's not the worst thing to have to lie about. If you need out, or need me to stop, you have to tell me."

"I will never want out and I don't want you to ever stop. It's a feeling greater than love. It's a feeling I didn't know existed. I don't think there is a word for this."

He kisses me. "There isn't."

We hold each other under the hot shower spray. The night is pitch black now. Fred turns the water off and opens the door. He wraps me in a towel before himself. It's a nice show, watching him move about naked. I will never tire of looking at him.

"What do you want to eat?" he asks as he pulls on his pajama bottoms without boxers. I can't stop staring.

"You," I say, puckering up my lips.

He has a t-shirt in his hand as he walks over to me. He waves his hand in front of my eyes to get me to stop staring. Then he puts the t-shirt over my head. I slip my arms in and let my towel fall. "You have a gutter brain again, don't ya, Jellybean?" I nod. "Let's eat, then you can devour me."

We head to the kitchen and I find that he had Nina fully stock the fridge. We take the cold cuts out and make sandwiches. The humid air hits my just showered skin as I sit next to Fred to eat. I don't realize how hungry I am until I take a bite. We eat in silence except for the roar of the ocean filling the air. I climb in his lap to snuggle against him as soon as I finish eating.

"You make me feel crazy wonderful things," I whisper.

"You make me feel even more than that," he adds, kissing me so I can't one up him like he did me. He stands up and carries me back to bed.

* * *

The sun is up and I have no idea what time it is. We made love and slept on and off all night and all morning. We won't be very useful today, I fear, so I turn to watch Fred sleep. Watching him is fascinating. I am so in love with him, I wouldn't be able to see his faults if he even had them. I put his t-shirt back on and slip out of bed. I bounce downstairs and make coffee. I check to make sure the kitchen and deck doors are locked. I do not want drop-in visitors today. I am not ready to share Fred again. As I turn away from the door, Fred comes down the stairs.

"Looking for a way out?"

"No, making sure no one can get in."

"Wise girl. That would suck if one of the guys showed up."

"Can you send a signal saying stay away?"

"I should get a bat light or a sex light, but don't worry they don't even know we are back."

"Did you guys always drop in on each other?"

"Gunner and I always have, since high school. No one ever drops in on Alex. He is always screwing around. I don't even know where Zach lives."

"Really? Does he live nearby at least?"

"He must. Don't you drop in on your friends?"

"No, I just got my license four days ago. And we are together all day at school. That's enough for me. Plus, I never run around my house half naked sexing up massively hot rock stars. My world is a little different than this one."

He pushes me into the kitchen door. His tongue hot in my mouth. I could kiss him every second of every day for the rest of my life and I would still not have my fill. He lifts me up and I wrap my legs around his waist. His hands support my bare behind as he walks us over to the couch. He drops me down and makes me giggle, but once he takes his pajama bottoms off and lies on top of me the giggles cease. He kisses me again before he whispers seductively in my ear, "I want to fuck you very hard and very fast."

"Oh, yes." My hands push his ass harder into me. He pulls back and a second later he is deep inside me. He doesn't even breathe and before I know it he is fucking me senseless. Pushing everything out of my mind. With every thrust he turns my mind into an empty shell being filled with love. He owns me and I never thought I would like that in a relationship. I would give him anything. I can't hold back the physical bliss. I come around him, yelling a mess of words I know don't fit together. He comes and collapses on top of me. We are hot and sweaty and I have never felt more beautiful and wanted.

He has taken a girl who was brave and confident and transformed her into a woman who is brave and confident. I am changed for eternity by the simple love I have for him. We are a force to be reckoned with. Unfortunately, I feel certain there is a force out there. I don't know which demon it is that will force its way between us. I quickly squash my wayward thoughts as I hear my stomach growl. Fred hears it too and he gets off me and helps me up.

We eat breakfast outside. I have never eaten outside at the beach with nothing but a lover's t-shirt on. I feel sexy. I like how I feel with him. I never wanted another person to be my crutch to happiness. I wanted to be an island. Feeling the love we feel has more than doubled my happiness; unfortunately, it could more than double pain too.

It has been twenty-four hours since we traded the words, "I love you."

It feels like a lifetime ago, yet every minute is ticking by way too fast. It doesn't take long and we are back in bed. Afterglow has become permanent glow. The day is overcast, but this bedroom is full of sunny energy.

"I want to take a bath with you," I murmur, running my hands over his chest. He slides out of bed. He is a graceful man for someone so tall and broad. I lay there watching him. His muscles are lean and defined, and I stare at them like a groupie about to drool. Only I am not watching him perform for thousands on a stage. I am in his bedroom, and I am the main character of this performance.

Watching him move, naked, is out of this world erotic. I want to just relax in a bubbly warm bath with him, but he arouses me again. I say a silent prayer that this honeymoon phase never ends, but he has a new bride and her name isn't Morgan.

He gets into the tub as it fills and he reaches out for my hand. I give him my right hand because I want to face him. "I wanted to come in here to relax, soothe my worn muscles, but you make coming in here too much of a show," I say, my eyes locked on his as I kiss him. I straddle him and push him into me as fast as I can. I move my hips around, up and down, deliberately slowly. Then Fast. Slow. Fast. Slow. We move together and he grants us a rhythm fitting for a musician. He is lost in me and watching him groan with pleasure has me focused only on his needs.

I lean my chest against his, but keep moving, as I whisper in his ear, "Fred, I want you to come first. I want to watch you without being consumed by what you do to me."

"Fuck, Jellybean, really?" He pushes roughly into me. I move my head back to watch him. His hands are on my hips now, mine on his shoulders. He moves with a quick pounding rhythm. I almost can't control myself. I want to close my eyes and have him push me over the edge. I stay strong and I focus on him. His eyes close tight as he screams my name and pushes my hips down on top of him. He explodes inside me. I don't move. I am close to coming but I want to watch every second of his pleasure. He comes down from his orgasm and he looks young and peaceful. Knowing I can make him feel this is a major turn on. Even if he only feels half of what I feel it's still a high to know I can give him this. My mind, my body, me, making him come undone.

"Where the hell did you come from? Shit, you have me all fucked up," he says, confusing me.

"Huh?" I say.

"Turn around and lie against me." I do and his hand snakes around me. His fingers are between my legs in an instant. I reach up and wrap my arms around his neck as his other hand finds my breast above water.

"I shouldn't have come before you."

"Why?" I can't form thoughts anymore; his fingers own me now. This topic can't end here. "Fred. Please. Let me take care of you too. I enjoy making you come so much."

"I know, but it's greedy for me to put myself first."

"No, it's not. I get lost when you make me come. I wanted... oh damn that feels good...... to watch you without becoming mindless from what you do to me."

He doesn't respond to me; instead he stays focused on my body. "Fred, please. Don't stop." A few minutes later I come around his fingers. It's so strong and endless. I come and come and once again end up slumped against him in weakness, but stronger than ever.

I didn't know muscles could be this relaxed. "I'm so in love with you, it is making me crazy," he whispers in my ear. Tears escape instantly from my eyes. I am grateful he can't see me, and the room is darkening as the sun is setting. I know it hurts because of my age and because he has a wife. I don't know which one is causing more pain.

The water is getting cold and our skin is wrinkled when we get out. He hands me a robe. "Come lie in bed with me. I want my arms around you," he says, sounding sad. I never want to hear him sad. It breaks my heart.

Chapter Seventeen

Pillow Talk

WE LIE IN bed and I hold him a little closer to my heart this time. Fred squeezes me and pulls me over on top of him. He lifts my head and stares at me like he is afraid I will disappear. The light is dim, but I can see his eyes burn for me. Knowing he needs me as bad as I need him, helps my mood.

"Morgan. I need you." He kisses me. "I want you." He kisses me again. "I never felt this." He kisses me. "It's scary." He kisses me. "It's the most amazing thing I have ever felt." He kisses me twice. "I love you." He kisses me. "I am so fucking in love with you and I want to tell the world." He kisses me. "You are perfect. I love you." He kisses me. He rolls me over so he is on top of me.

I can't form a single word to match what he is saying. I answer him with my body and we make love. I felt our first time would go down as the most soul satisfying and emotional love making I have ever felt. This moment is surpassing it. The emotions I feel coupled with the erotic sensation of our bodies together are more powerful than anything this earth has shown me so far.

I wake in the middle of the night, feeling startled. Fred wakes with me. "Hey, what's wrong?"

"I just woke up and I felt disoriented. What time is it?"

He looks at the clock. "A little after three."

"I haven't called home. I haven't even told them about the car. I feel terrible."

"Hey, come here." I place my head down on his chest and it calms me. He makes me feel safe. I love that he has the power to alter my moods for the better, but I fear that means he also has the power to alter them for the worse. "Don't worry, you can call in the morning."

"I get worried they will know and they won't let me stay here."

"It will be fine."

"Why do you say that? They are giving me a lot letting me be here. I don't want to mess this up."

"I know, but your mom is cool. She isn't blind. I think she knows."

"You do? I do too."

He exhales and laughs a little.

"What is so funny?" I ask him as I tickle him a little for laughing regardless of me being upset.

"She might think you slept with me the first weekend you were here. Your mom thinks you are a little slutty."

"That is so mean. Damn if she thinks that I should have slept with you."

"You would have if I pushed you. I know I wanted to. I am glad we waited. Anticipation has its benefits."

"Oh, I should hold out on you, if you want anticipation so much."

"You can't. I bet you can't hold out even a few hours. You are way too into sex."

"Fred, I want to be mad and prove it to you, but I would rather be sitting on top of you right now." I run my hand down his belly without breaking eye contact. I fear I will never feel this way again for as long as I live. I may never find happiness even close to comparable to this. I am too young for this to be the climax of my love life, but I wouldn't change a damn thing. In this moment at this time he is everything. He is my every-thing and I want him and everything he can give me for as long as I am lucky enough to have it.

I get up on my knees and wiggle my way between his thighs. He is watching every move I make and that arouses me more. I lock my eyes on his and our bodies meet again. The pleasure is overwhelming. Our bodies are so wrapped up in one another, my mind is telling me that my heart is outside my chest and it is colliding with his. Thundering together they beat even stronger.

Our orgasms have left us both relaxed and lost in each other again.

My hands though are not relaxed and they are tracing every line on his body. He is so damn beautiful. This new intimacy makes him even more attractive. He takes a deep breath and I watch his body suck in the oxygen; he has become my oxygen. He breathes life into me now and without him I fear I will wither. Someday I know I will be without him. I know it for certain, as well as I knew I could love him the moment his eyes met mine under the lilac tree.

My crazy thoughts are erased because before I finish thinking he has me on my back. His mouth is hot as he kisses me from my shoulder down to my hip. Then across my belly. It takes a split second for me to surrender to him and find that beautiful place where my mind is blank. I only have room for Fred, my lover; he grants me relief in every form. His body turns my body into an inferno, content and relaxed, yet every nerve ending is feeling more than it has ever felt.

"Oh, Fred, oh Fred." I have no clue how many times I say it when I come without warning. My body melts into him. I come from the outside in and it's life altering. This orgasm will leave me a changed woman.

I am a jumbled mess of relaxed nerves when Fred comes up next to me and turns me so my back is to his stomach. As soon as I close my eyes I fall asleep. I wake to the daylight and the realization that I never want to leave this bed or this man. Lost in love and hoping to never be found.

I look over at the clock and see that it's a little after eight. I slip out on tip-toe so he can sleep, and I head downstairs for coffee.

My mother's office phone is ringing; with each ring my nerves elevate. I feel she will hear the change in my voice, because I am changed. Not because I had sex, finally, with Fred, but because of the mad crazy love I have for him. The phone rings a few times and she answers with her professional work voice. For a second she doesn't sound like the mom who loves me unconditionally and I flinch.

"Hey, Mom. Sorry I didn't call sooner."

"Honey, it's nice to hear your voice. We miss you, but it's okay. You don't have to call every day."

"I just feel bad."

She clears her throat, and I fear she knows my darkest secrets. "So, did you get your birthday present?" My face flames. She wouldn't be so easygoing if she knew all the ways I got it and how I enjoyed it.

"Yes, Fred gave me a car, a mustang. How did you keep it a secret?"

"It wasn't easy, I won't lie. Honey, I know how much Fred cares about you. He is a good man and I'm glad you have him. It's not easy on your dad, but we have accepted that you aren't an average seventeen-year-old and we are trusting you to grow and learn but also to be careful and safe."

"Mom, you make me want to cry. I don't know what to say. I guess I will just say thank you." I pace around the kitchen as I talk. Just as I say thank you to her for the millionth time, I get to the kitchen door and find Gunner sitting on the step.

Perhaps she can tell I am distracted. She says, "I have to get back to work. Call me at home later in the week and we can talk more then. I miss you." She hangs up as I open the kitchen door. Gunner flinches and I feel bad now having opened the door so fast because he may have been asleep.

He turns, looks up at me and smiles a strange smile that makes me uncomfortable. Gunner annoys me but uncomfortable is a new problem. I realize it's not him, it's me. I am wearing only Fred's t-shirt. Perhaps he can tell I have nothing on underneath it. I take a deep breath and muster up all my confidence. "You wanna stay out there or come in? I put coffee on." I turn and walk back into the kitchen and get two mugs out. He follows me and shuts the door behind him and I hear him lock it.

I know he is watching me and I might pick a fight with him, but that shit is old news. "How do you take your coffee?" I ask and turn to see him watching me. It's unnerving. But I will not falter and let him win this wordless battle.

"Cream, sugar, anything you have to make it sweet. I need sweet. My life is too bitter." He doesn't take his eyes off me. He needs a friend and I am torn between being there for him and just getting Fred. I don't know if I can be that for Gunner. There is something about him that leaves me angry. I don't understand why. If Fred and Gunner can be such strong friends and I can be so in love with Fred, why can't Gunner and I be friends? I fear he thinks I will be Fred's downfall. I don't know if it's a good guess, but if I accept my reasoning and tell myself that it's not so bad, then I can be a friend with Gunner. Before I can be a friend, it is best I wear underwear.

I stand tall and walk to the laundry room and find a pair of Fred's boxers in the dryer. I pull them on and take my hair tie out of my hair. I cinch the shirt and boxers together and gather them tightly into a knot. Dressed enough now to attempt to be a friend to Gunner, I walk back into the kitchen and fill both our mugs, making them both light and sweet. It hits me that I have something in common with him. It doesn't bring me peace though.

"Let's sit outside and talk," I say.

Gunner just stares at me like I have grown horns. How can I move from one extreme to another with him? I want to make this a normal friendship but he flips on a dime sometimes and it's confusing.

"What has you melancholy at eight a.m.?" I bluntly ask.

"A woman. What else would ever get a man up at this hour?"

"Well, a job would."

"True, but I'm blessed with amazing rhythm and I don't have to do that."

"Well, isn't that the best thing I ever heard out of your mouth. Damn, Gunner, will I ever understand you? I never met someone so confusing. I want to get along with you. You are Fred's best friend. And I love him more than words can express. I want all of us to be able to coalesce."

"Coalesce?" he pronounces with perfection.

"It was an SAT word. It means to form one whole."

"I can't even pronounce it. Where the hell did you come from? Don't answer that. I know he loves you too. I know I gave you a hard time, and I apologize. I am unfairly protective of him, and frankly seeing him this way is new. It scared me for many reasons."

I don't know what to say. He has stunned me again. The second the last word leaves Gunner's mouth, Fred walks outside. I look up and damn, he looks smoking hot, even when he's sleepy. He already has coffee when he joins us. We are all silent and it feels super awkward. I hope it doesn't always feel this way. I would rather deal with smart-ass Gunner than a Gunner who makes me uncomfortable.

"I'm going for a run. I'll leave you two alone." I get up and leave, not wanting to hear what either one of them has to say. I come back downstairs after I change and Fred is in the kitchen and Gunner is still outside. "Did you get a chance to call your mom?" he asks.

"I called her before Gunner showed up. All is well, so I feel a lot better."

"Good. Do you really want to go run? I could get rid of him, and we could go back upstairs." He smirks and it is mighty cute.

"No, I don't, but I'm going. As much as I would rather be in bed with you, we should have a few hours of normalcy in our day, right?"

"I don't know. Who says? I vote sex is normal." He laughs and it makes me wish we never had to leave our love bubble.

"Not the sex we have. But when I get back you can wash all the sweat off me and replace it with more from my workout with you." He is sexy as hell and if Gunner wasn't sitting outside I would screw him right here on the kitchen floor. Maybe I will do exactly that when I get back. I get myself out the door as soon as I can because if I think about this anymore, I will be screwing him somewhere.

I come back and the house is quiet. Gunner's truck is no longer in the driveway. I find Fred upstairs, lying in bed with a towel low on his hips. He is wet and, damn it, so am I now.

"Are you trying to seduce me?" I ask, contemplating whether I want a shower or him first.

"I am not sure I have to. You seem to be a constant willing participant."

"Oh well, seems I have been exposed for my true self. Yes, Fred, extremely willing, always." I walk over to the edge of the bed. "But I'm gross and sweaty."

"Nothing about you is gross." He lowers his towel, making me weaker and weaker by the second. "I like you sweaty."

"I am in the mood to make a deal," I say, trying to sound sexy.

"Oh, this sounds interesting."

"You want to make a deal?"

"Yes, but damn I just want to touch you."

"Nope, no touching, yet."

"Ugh."

"Okay, here is deal number one. Let me know if you accept it or want deal number two. And I have to warn you. If you don't take the first one there might not be a second because I haven't planned this out that far."

He laughs. "Okay, lay it on me."

"Did you take a class on being sexy before you signed that first record deal?"

"Stop changing the subject. This is me. All of me. Exposed to you because I trust and love you."

"Okay, then they gave you romance classes." I climb on top of him and straddle his legs, being sure to leave his towel covering what I desire most. If I see more bare flesh, I won't be able to talk. "Here's my deal." I inhale like I am going to sing a long high note in one breath, then stare into his telling eyes as I exhale. I take his hands and interlace my fingers with his. "I want you in my mouth again. I don't want to touch anything else on you and you can't touch me. Just my mouth. I never did quite what I did to you last night and I enjoyed it. Then I get to shower before you do anything to me, and if you let me have what I want I will let you have anything you want. Deal?"

He is silent. I am so freaking nervous. I never saw him this silent. He sit's up and kisses me. His tongue rolls with rough passion. "Yes."

"Yes?"

"Yes. I will let you have your way with me. Then I get what I want as long as I let you shower. Right?"

"Yes." My body has no more laughs. This is serious because the passion is now ruling me. I take his towel off. "Sit up against the headboard." I order him and he does. Now I wish I had left out that I needed a shower first. I want to sit on him and ride him until we are both falling apart at the seams. "Now, no touching me. Nothing. Only my mouth. If you fail, it won't be your choice what you do to me next."

"There is nothing I don't want to do to you. I can't lose, can I?"

"Stop. No talking." No more waiting, I am on my knees between his legs and without my hands I take him in my mouth. I take him down over my tongue to my throat, slow and at a steady pace. I know I won't be able to continue this pace. Soon I will be ravaged by lust. I use only my tongue around and around his tip and he is moaning. His hands are fisting in the sheets. I know he wants to put his hands on me but I will not allow it. I want this to last. We are always too hot to get to the finish line. I want to enjoy this slow run.

His flesh is smooth and warm in my mouth. I want to run my fingers over him, but that would be breaking my own rules. Instead I run my tongue back down him and then I run it over his balls. Slowly. Damn they feel good. They move like a large marble encased in a soft bag. He is moaning too much and I make him wiggle as he does to me. I know he needs more and needs it bad. I run my tongue back up him from base to tip, then I suck my way hard and fast so he is deep in my throat. I start a rhythm that I know won't last long. Minutes later he comes at the back of my throat and I feel victorious for getting exactly what I wanted, but now I crave sexual relief more than ever.

I get up off him without letting my hands touch him anywhere. I head for the shower, leaving my clothes on the ground as I go. I want him to follow me. I need him to follow me.

I turn the water on and step in. The water is soothing as it washes my run from me. The salt from the sea air goes down the drain with the licorice soap as Fred steps in and grabs my upper arms from behind.

His grip is tight, but it feels pleasant. He leans down and whispers in my ear with a grunt, "Give me the soap."

I reach up over my shoulder and he takes it. It seems to be hours before he takes his soapy hands and touches me. He starts with my neck and moves to my shoulders. He is moving so slowly it just makes me needier.

"I'm going to do all the touching I should have done in that bed just now but you wouldn't let me." He sounds tense, making me nervous that I upset him. I turn around in the shower to look at him.

"Hey, was that not good? I'm sorry. I didn't mean to do something you didn't want. This is all a bit new to me…"

He cuts me off. "Morgan, that was pure heaven. I need to touch you now. You have no idea what you do to me. Besides making love to you, which is the most amazing, all-encompassing feeling, what you did to me was so freakin' hot. You made me come with a force I didn't know existed and I was very satisfied, but I need you again already. It's confusing to come so hard and still need more. I don't get this. I want more. I need more. I need you."

He is all over me. Hands, tongue, everywhere. I feel dizzy. "Fred, don't let me fall." The soap is gone. My hair is not washed. He leans past me and turns the water off. "What are you…?"

"Shh, I need you in bed." I step out of the shower and he lifts me up in his arms. Soaking wet in more ways than one. He lays me on the bed. A chill runs up my spine. I don't know if it's from the shower or from him.

He lies on top of me and then his whole body becomes unnaturally still. He looks into my eyes and kisses me softly. As he lifts his head off me he looks deeply into my eyes. I hold his gaze and it is more telling than the words, I love you.

With one thrust he is hard again and deep inside me. I pause my body movement to take in this powerful sensation. I close my eyes and meet him thrust for thrust. I am drowning in his body, his mind, and his soul.

"Fred, damn, I can't take anymore," I moan.

"Morgan, I can't get enough of you. Fuck, baby, I am gonna come."

My body and mind are lost in an abyss of sensation. "Fred. You ..." I can't form words.

"Baby, come for me please. I can't control this." And I do. I start to come before him. But it's clear I finish after him. I missed his entire orgasm because of my own. He slides out of me and lies down on his back. We are both panting and I sigh louder than is normal.

"Morgan?"

"Yeah?"

He is silent.

Still silent.

I start to sit up and he quickly leans over to face me.

"I love you."

"I love you too."

"I really love you."

"I really love you too."

"I am questioning if I ever loved before. I am questioning everything I ever felt before. This is so much more. I didn't know these emotions existed. He leans down to kiss me. A sweet soft kiss that is so telling.

"Fred?" He is still staring intently at me.

"Yeah?"

"Nothing, I just enjoy saying your name."

"Enjoy saying it? Or screaming out in pleasure begging me to push you over the edge?" He snakes his fingers down between us.

"That isn't fair," I say, as his fingers slip inside me. His thumb rolls around outside me. I don't care about anything but how it feels to have his hands on me. Inside me.

"Oh, Morgan." He keeps a precise rhythm and it melts me.

"Fred, please. More."

I am about to come as he suddenly pulls his fingers out of me. I can't even complain before his mouth is on me. "Holy shit!" What he does to me has made me a cursing screaming mess.

His tongue is everywhere. Hot and wet and inside me. He puts both hands on my ass and pushes me into his face and it's my undoing. I come strong and fast and I swear I black out. Next thing I know my relaxed body is wrapped tightly around him and the sheets. I can't speak. I'm too numb from all the erotic sensation.

"Morgan, you okay?" he whispers in my ear.

"I don't know." Because I don't. This is more than okay. I am full of the type of emotions that change the way one views life. I am altered for eternity. I can't decide if it is for the better or worse.

I fall asleep from all the sensation and emotions coursing through my body. It's my mind's way of telling me this is too much to take on at one time. Fred falls asleep too. We have become gluttons to sex and sleep. How long can this last?

I wake up alone and it's a horrible feeling. Until I hear the piano from the great room downstairs. A light upbeat melody that makes me feel safe again. I lie alone under the covers – naked and content – but I want to be with him. I put on one of Fred's t-shirts and walk downstairs.

I sit next to him, happy he doesn't stop playing. I watch his fingers move over the keys. All I can imagine is that those fingers have been on every inch of my skin. They make beautiful music no matter what they are touching.

"I love you." It means so much. Yet it is too simple to describe what I feel for him. I watch the ocean glisten as he plays me into a daze. I get up and get a notebook and sit on the couch. He has inspired me to write. At first all my thoughts are on sex. I contemplate him reading it and I don't want him to think that is all I want from him. I reread what I wrote and even though it is laced with sex it's more about love.

Concentrating too deeply, I don't even hear him come over. He sits on the floor in front of the couch and leans his chin on my knee. I look down at him and I stare as if I am seeing him for the first time. His face is strong but I get weak every time I see it. We sit staring at each other. Normally this would make me uncomfortable, but with him, it is heaven.

"Hey, did you eat anything today?" he asks and I snap slightly out of my Fred daze.

"Um, I don't remember."

"Are you hungry?"

"Not really. Just hungry for you, but it's a permanent hunger."

He moans into my mouth as he kisses me. "Stay here. You look too comfortable to move."

I long to turn to watch him in the kitchen, but I know if I do I will not be able to stay sitting here. I will be all over him as I have been since Sunday. He comes back a few minutes later and hands me a bowl of Frosted Flakes. "This is perfect."

We sit and eat on the couch with our feet and legs intertwined. "Hey, are you really okay being stuck here with me?" I ask.

"Why would you ask that?" He truly looks upset.

"I don't mean stuck with me, I mean stuck inside. We can't go to the movies or walk down the boardwalk. We can't even go to a mall. Is this okay with you?"

"It is more than okay. I prefer it."

"I won't question it again. You really are okay being cooped up inside, away from people? I actually am quite introverted and this fits me perfectly. You are used to being in the public eye and on stage. How can this compare to that?"

"First, being with you compares to nothing. There isn't anything this exciting out there. My job is awesome; the live shows are not why I went all out to be a musician. Performing gives me a high, a rush, but it is temporary and very lonely. I'm lucky to do what I love every day and make a lot of money doing it. But for the first time I am glad it's not an everyday job. I used to hate downtime. It made me overthink everything. I have you now to occupy my mind. My body. I am more than happy with how this is." He runs his hands up and down my legs. It is relaxing but he is igniting me again.

I moan and try to talk. "Fred, will it always be this intense?"

"I will pray for it to be, and I'm not religious." He takes my bowl and puts it on the table with his. He lies down on top of me. There is a blanket separating our bodies. He kisses me. I kiss him back. His heart is pounding as out of control as mine. Time suddenly moves in slow motion and up until now all our lovemaking seemed more panicked and rushed. This is different; his kisses are extra slow, with depth, almost planned. He moves himself under the blanket with me. More kissing. I could kiss him all day and not get tired. He moves up and grabs the bottom of my shirt and quickly removes it. I am lying naked once again underneath him. He wiggles out of his pants in lightning speed.

I close my eyes, reveling in the feel of his naked body stretched out on top of mine. My hands move around his back and I slowly move them up and down. His muscles are taut and strong under my small hands. He is a beautiful man and I get to touch him whenever I want.

We make love on the couch. Every movement of his stirs emotion in me. Every movement of mine empowers me to love him more. Lovemaking has never had so many emotions tied to it for me. I am a bundle of sexual nerves needing release and a bundle of love needing to be held tighter. We move so slowly, so rhythmically. He has such control of his body, and I continue to learn how to control mine.

"I love you so damn much. I pray I never hurt you. I'm scared I will," he whispers.

"Please don't hurt me." There are too many emotions and no matter how slow we move I can't hold back. I come with my body wrapped tightly around him. I can only muster up his name over my lips as my spasms subside and his escalate. I watch his face twist in pleasure and then relax more than I have ever seen it relax before. He collapses on top of me, his weight the warmest blanket there is.

Chapter Eighteen

Epiphany

WE FALL ASLEEP on the couch wrapped in one another. I am not sure if we need each other this bad or if we are both afraid of letting go. Fred shifts on top of me. He looks down at me. "Damn, Jellybean, I will die never having enough of you." He sit's up, naked, and looks at me again like he has a question. "Can I read what you have been writing?"

"Sure." I reach over and pick my papers up and he pinches my ass. "Hey, that wasn't nice." I slap his hand away as I hand him my papers. "You can't make love to me then pinch me. I will get all worked up again." He just smirks.

I have been lying on the couch while he reads my notes, and it feels like minutes pass, but the light in the room has changed. Another day wrapped up in Fred has flown right by me. "Does time move faster now for you too?" I ask, interrupting him.

"Huh?" he mumbles.

I sit up and look at him. "Does the time we spend together go by faster than it does at other times?" He looks out the window because the sunlight is almost gone.

"Time with you is set by a different clock." I move to lie next to him, my head on his chest. He sets the papers down on the floor and hugs me tight.

"I don't want to lose the feeling that makes time tick by so fast, but I don't want it to fly by and suddenly it's just over," I whisper like a prayer, because I don't want this to ever be over.

He squeezes me tight. It hurts, but it's a hurt that heals. This super human feeling he gives me is bound to get me in trouble. He let's go and shifts himself down so we are lying face to face on our sides with no space between us. "I don't want this to be over, ever."

"I know, but Fred, there are bumps ahead in our road. With time I will turn eighteen, but we can't overcome the fact that you have a wife. Do you even talk to her?"

"No. I have no desire to share a single word."

"Does she have the number here? Does she know where you are? Should I worry she will walk in the door one day?"

"She won't come here. She doesn't have the number. She has the car number and has called once since Vegas. I couldn't take the yelling so I hung up on her and didn't answer when she called back. She has Gunner's house number. She has left some messages for me there. I will ignore it for now." He stops but I don't say anything. He watches me. "Is that okay with you?"

"It has nothing to do with me. Unfortunately, it's a choice you have to make alone."

"I choose nothing when it comes to her."

"You have to let me know if you want to be free to be with her. I would set you free. Please always be honest. Don't string me along."

"Yeah." He laughs.

"Are you laughing at me? That's mean."

"I'm laughing at the irony. This is forbidden because of your age, yet you are the most mature level-headed person I know."

"I can't change the way I am. But back to Beth calling Gunner's house. Does he know you two are married?"

"Yes, he is the only one I told."

We lie still, staring at each other. I have never felt so comfortable looking at another person. He makes it seem that it is normal to lie around this way. Never needing to know what is coming next. He is teaching me to live in the moment. To be present. I don't even know if he knows he is doing it. For the first time in my life I am not looking to the future and not trying to get to the next step. I am just here. Here with him. That's enough for now.

As a child, I wished to be older. As a teen, I wish to be an adult. I never fit in and I am always looking for the next phase of life, hoping it will finally feel right. And in an instant, nothing changed, time didn't pass, I didn't age, but I found Fred. With him I fit in somewhere. He may never grasp this gift he has given me. I am in my someday and it feels exquisite.

"Hey. You okay?" he asks, snapping me out of my daydream.

"Yeah, I'm really good. Sometimes all of this is a lot to absorb."

"Yes, it is. Want to go for a walk?"

We go upstairs in silence and change. I watch him put his clothes on and it is as sexy as watching them come off. I am so infatuated with him it's ridiculous. Somehow we manage to leave the house without stopping to have sex again. We are walking down the beach barefoot, fingers interlaced. It's a lovely night, cool, but humid. The slight breeze off the ocean smells salty and warm. I walk slowly like I am numb. We turn back to the house, but I don't snap out of my trance.

"You okay in that beautiful head of yours?" he asks, stopping and knocking on my skull.

"Yeah, just thinking."

"Nothing too serious I hope."

"I was thinking about life, us, love, sex. That sort of stuff."

"What about love and sex were you thinking about?" His smile is infectious.

"You really want to know?" I want to feed off his smile instead of my pain.

"Yeah, I want to know everything you think about. This is going to sound unromantic…" I stare up at him and he says, "I find learning all the things that come out of this beautiful head to be sexy and fascinating. Your mind turns me on, Jellybean." He kisses me. One of those kisses I will never forget. June 28, 1995, approximately ten p.m., this kiss will go down in my history book. My heart never felt so full, my mouth never moved so gracefully, it is the kiss to judge all other kisses against.

He pulls away. "So?"

"So what? I don't remember. Where were we?" Damn, I sound stupid drunk.

"Shit, baby, I have no idea." He sits in the cool sand and pulls me down with him. All parts of me are deadly still, my mind totally blank.

"Oh, I know." We both start laughing. I lie back on the sand, the contagious laughter taking over my body. Laughing out of control, he puts his entire leg over mine and shifts his head right above mine, but then he is not touching me. He hovers over my body instead. I pause and look up, trying to see his eyes, and I stop laughing. "I was thinking how we went upstairs and put clothes on and it was the first time we didn't stop doing something to have sex. It made me fearful the honeymoon phase was over already. Then I was mad for letting the word honeymoon into my head. You should be in that phase with someone. It isn't me that you should be in it with. I freaked out more about the fact that you have a wife. Suddenly the fact that we didn't have sex seems trivial."

He is looking at me and for the first time ever I am scared about what will happen next.

"I love you." Words uttered all the time between lovers but tonight it means more than ever. He kisses me, a passion, a love, coming from a different level. I don't question him further. He has had enough of his own demons eating away at him. I can't bring myself to make it worse.

Right there in the sand, between the ocean and his house, he tends to my body the way a lover should. I feel like liquid gold in his hands. Precious and shiny. We make love and I miss half of it in a smoky haze. I come underneath him, with a quick jolt. He comes right after me and he lies on top of me. He is still inside me when he opens his eyes. "You okay?"

I don't answer because I don't know. Once again he can tell when I am not okay. I didn't even realize I wasn't okay yet. He pulls out of me and while on his knees he pulls his pants up. I shift to pull my dress down. I feel catatonic and I want to snap out of it so he doesn't worry, but I can't. My brain is screaming, "HOLY SHIT, WAKE UP!" over and over again.

Fred shakes my shoulder. My vision is clear again, but I say nothing as we walk back to the house. I go all the way upstairs with him behind me; our pain leaves us both silent. When I get to the bathroom door I turn around and say, "Come shower with me." It's a command and a question. He follows me into the shower. We are naked, not touching, the water pressure trying to wash my pain away.

Fred hugs me tight, my body pressed against him, and then ugly tears ravage my body. He holds me as we sink onto the cool tile of the shower. The water is warm, the floor and I are cold. I am breaking. I didn't know

I could break. He is married to a woman named Beth, whom I have never met, and suddenly I want to see what I am up against. This is so unlike me. Normally I find it easy to be controlled, precise, and not emotional. Here and now, sobbing and completely lost, I try to snap out of it.

Time is moving slowly now, but I get a hold of myself and look deeply into Fred's eyes. He is pained by my pain and it makes me see that he does truly love me. He is holding me naked and wet in the shower and he looks small and scared. I have a seventeen-year-old girl epiphany. He isn't using me. He loves me. He is just a man with a past. He is a man who made mistakes and who will continue to make them. I kiss him deeper than I have ever kissed him before. He is confused but he follows along, like a man.

"Fred?"

He doesn't answer me but his eyes open and lock on mine. I stand and turn the water off. He follows me out of the shower and I grab a towel to dry him off. I am too numb to care how wet I am. He takes the towel from me and dries my hair and body. We both move too fast, but that means we will be warm and safe in bed soon. I lie next to him, watching him watch me. He is afraid of me and that is breaking my heart more than if he just up and ended this.

"I love you. I'm sorry. I don't mean to be so sad, and I don't know how to feel sometimes. I know now what it feels like to love someone I can't have." I haven't finished and his mouth is on mine, his tongue in me, raw and needy.

He pulls away from me and holds my shoulders. "Look at me," he shouts and I almost start to cry again, but I look up at him. "I love you. Only you. I fucked up. I can't take you this way. It's like you are dying right in front of me. Damn it, I love you. Morgan, please never leave me, physically or mentally."

His kisses are all consuming as I snap out of my weakened mental state and kiss him back. I don't know if we should talk or make love. The way his hands are moving all over me says he is picking the physical means to help sew this hole back up. His body is heating me up, as he lies flush on top of me. He is slow and delicate with me and it's comforting because it feels loving. With every gentle touch I feel more and more loved. I think I do know that he loves me. Perhaps more than he has ever loved. I also know I will lose this battle. Even if the fight hasn't even started. I vow to myself to live in the moment, enjoy this ride, and to always be honest with myself as I surrender to him, body, mind, and soul.

When I let go of the demons in my head, I feel my body respond as it should to his. I wrap my arms and legs around him and make love to him with every ounce of love I have in my veins.

* * *

I wake up alone again. I hate being without him. I have never slept with someone night after night like this and it amazes me how natural it is. I only spent the entire night with Ben once when we lied to his parents and mine were away visiting my aunt.

I hear the shower turn off. I sit up in bed hoping he comes out wearing very little. It seems to be hours before he emerges. He looks sad and it makes me sad. He softly says, "Good morning. I hope I didn't wake you up."

"No, you didn't."

He walks to get clothes and starts getting dressed.

"Hey, will you come over here?" I ask, needing reassurance. Hoping I didn't fuck this up last night with my irrational, wait rational, fear.

He walks over slowly, still holding his shirt. He sits on the edge of the bed a little too far away. I move toward him and he grabs me and pulls me onto his lap. He kisses me gently. I look into his eyes, glad the connection is still intact. "Sorry I was so emotional last night."

"No apologizing. I feel better seeing that side of you. I might have thought you didn't care enough about me to get upset. From day one you have accepted everything I have done, everything I am, you just let me be and it's awesome that you are never jealous. I love that about you. But it did feel good in a way to see those emotions from you. That was long winded. You are rubbing off on me." I raise my eyebrow and want so bad to make a comment on the word rubbing. I tell myself I do think like a seventeen-year-old sometimes.

"I need to go downstairs and call the lawyer to set up a time for him to come here."

Whoa, what are we talking about? I didn't want a change of subject. I like the other one better. "Huh, why?"

"I already talked to your mom. You both have to sign paperwork so you can get paid for any songs you write that we record. She said she has next week off from work, so she would love to come down. Is that good with you?"

"Yeah, it is. I wish you had told me. It's odd that you are having conversations with her about me. It makes me feel seventeen."

"I'm sorry, I forgot. Probably because of all this brain cell killing sex."

"That is enough of an apology for me."

"I also want her to trust me. If she doesn't, you could be ripped away from me in an instant."

"I doubt she would ever not trust you." I hug him and stand up because I need to be alone for a few minutes to process all the unusual events that have become my usual, so I head to the bathroom.

Chapter Nineteen
What About Now

M Y FOOT HITS the bottom step as Fred is hanging up the phone. "Hey," he says, turning to look at me. He acts normal again, so perhaps I haven't damaged him too much. "Your mom and the lawyer will be here Monday morning."

He hugs me but I pull away. "You called my mom just now?"

"Yeah, is that okay?"

"I guess. You talk to her as much as I do."

"She is easy to talk to."

"Okay." I try to end this conversation because I really hate the reminder of what we should not be.

"One more thing we have to talk about," he says in a voice a little louder than normal.

"This doesn't sound good."

"Let's sit outside. The sun looks warm and bright."

We sit down and I can tell my cold stare is getting to him. "It's not that bad," he says.

"I don't believe you."

"In order to have you on a contract, we have to get one of the guys to sign when you do. I already told them we are writing together and I told them I did the legal parts, but you must pick one of them to be here."

"Really?" I sit there across from him, my mind blank. "Well, you are closest to Gunner, and he knows you married Beth, so it has to be him. Unless you don't want him to know how old I am. He scares me a little, but if you trust him I will."

"I would pick Gunner, but I know you don't see him the way I do."

"Well, maybe trusting him is what I have to do to see him the way you do. Will he be mad at you for being with someone underage?"

"He probably will, but he knows you, so he will be less judgmental."

"Should you tell him or should I?"

"I assumed I would, but do you want to?"

"I don't know. If I tell him he might trust me more and hate you less. When should we tell him?"

"We should tell him before Monday. I wouldn't want to spring it on him when your mom is here."

"I agree."

Coming up from the beach toward the house is Gunner. What are the freakin' chances? Probably high, I suppose, since he is here all the time. He sees us when we see him and he waves. He comes up and sits down at the table next to me.

"Did you need a walk?" I ask.

"No, your door was locked and I wasn't up to being home alone."

"You could have rung the bell," Fred says.

"I didn't think of that. I didn't want to bug you guys either, and I don't want to be a third wheel."

"Gunner, please don't feel that way, I don't want to change your friendship with Fred." I stand up and they both watch me, creeping me out, so I ask, "Anyone need a drink?"

"Sure, just water. That sun is hot," Gunner says. "And Morgan, thanks."

I come back with three waters. I am happy to hear them talking casually. We sit outside for a while. I feel a little bit better, until Fred gets up. He leans over and whispers in my ear, "You should tell him." Then he just walks away. What the hell? Does he mean now? Why me? Why not us together? I am not ready.

"You okay?" Gunner snaps his fingers in front of my eyes.

"Yeah, just a lot on my mind."

"Really, you are always happy and relaxed like you don't have a care in the world."

"That is how you see me?"

"Yes."

"Is that why you pick on me? You think everything is perfect for me. Do you want to make it hard for the sake of making it hard?"

"I don't know. I didn't put that much thought into it. You just seemed easy to toy with."

"Well, that is a pretty mean thing to do to someone you don't even know." I find my confidence and speak again before he can. "I have something I have to tell you, and you must promise me you won't tell anyone else."

"Okay." He draws the word out like he is from the deep south.

"You know the lawyer is coming here to sign papers so I can be paid for anything I write that is recorded?"

"I do. When exactly is he coming?"

"Monday morning at ten."

"No problem. Do you think I have a problem with you getting money for your work?"

"No, I never thought that."

"What is wrong? You seem very uncomfortable."

"I need you to promise me again you won't tell anyone what I am going to tell you."

"I promise. I won't utter a word." He takes a sip of his water and I watch him while I look for courage. "Wait, is it something I have to keep from Fred?"

"No. He knows."

"Okay, then talk to me."

"I am trusting you, and Fred is trusting you. I know he can trust you," I say, moving my mouth, trying to hint that I know he knows a secret.

"He can and so can you."

"My mom will be here when we sign the papers and you can't say anything about me and Fred around her. She doesn't know we are together."

"Why have her here? Why not just tell her?"

"Well, she has to be here, and I can't just tell her, even though I am certain she knows."

"I don't get this." He shakes his head but isn't annoyed.

"Gunner, she is my legal guardian, and she has to sign the papers."

"Huh?" He looks blank.

"Gunner, you aren't stupid."

"No, but it doesn't make sense. Are you mentally incompetent?"

"That is priceless. No, I am underage, as in not eighteen."

And there it is, the blank look I was expecting.

"Holy shit, no way." He sits up tall in his chair. "You have got to be kidding me. Damn, I don't know what to say."

"Sorry, but please, you can't say anything. It is too serious and could lead to problems for Fred and the band – a big mess."

"It sure could. I promise your secret is safe with me. I might have to have a word or two with Fred, but I will never tell anyone. I never would have guessed you were seventeen. You don't act or look that young."

"Gunner, I know you can keep a secret too," I say, hinting at the fact he knows Fred is married to Beth. Unfortunately, I change the subject from a bad one to another bad one.

"Oh, you do, do you?"

"I do," I say, realizing those words were said by Fred to Beth.

"What kind of a secret?"

I tilt my head and blink my eyes.

"Do you really know?" he says.

"Yes," I say, still surprised I have allowed myself to love a married man.

"Dumbest thing he ever did."

"We agree on that. That was the day I met him. What a wonderful and horrible day. Sorry to put you in this position, but when my mom is here don't say anything or if possible don't push my buttons and aggravate me."

"I aggravate you?" He sounds surprised.

"Well, you did. You got under my skin at first, but we have come a long way, don't you think?"

"We have. Wait, did you just graduate from high school?"

"No, I will be a senior in the fall. I turned seventeen on Friday."

"Damn, you were sixteen when this started. Shit, I must have a word with him."

"He didn't know until the end of May."

"He was already in love with you then."

"I was in love with him too."

We sit in silence. I reach over and take his hand in mine. I just hold it. "Thanks, Gunner, it means a lot to be able to trust you. I hope you always take care of Fred. You two need each other." I need to run to help kill this restless lost feeling, so I drop his hand like a hot coal and head inside to change.

* * *

Fred and I spend the rest of the weekend wrapped in our love cocoon. It's days and days of nothing but hot sex, long naps, and me watching his creative mind and body at work. We write and write and it is almost as fun as the hot sex. Fred has been trying to teach me to play guitar for three days, but we never get too far. Watching his fingers strum the strings makes me need them to strum me. I can play a few chords, but my lessons are moving too slowly. My love for Fred, though, is growing by the minute.

Sunday after dinner, I start to get nervous again about the meeting with the lawyer. I even move my things into the other room. Fred says I'm crazy for being this worried, but I don't want a stupid little thing to blow this for us.

We are in the kitchen, his arms wrapped around me, when a knock at the door makes us both jump. Gunner comes in and even though we had a rough start, I am glad he is comfortable here. He walks over to the piano and is checking out the songs Fred left there. I head outside and lie down in the hammock. Watching the stars should help relax me.

"Penny for your thoughts?" Gunner snaps me out of my daze.

"They are worth a lot more than that, and you'll be signing papers tomorrow saying so."

"Ha, good one. Scoot over."

I slide over as much as one can in a hammock and he lies down next to me. He hands me his beer. If there was a night to drink it might be tonight. I take a sip and hand it back to him. We lie there peacefully watching the night sky. Gunner isn't who I thought he was at first; I am shocked that I am glad he is the one who knows the truth.

"Thanks again for being understanding."

"No thanks necessary. It's a cruel twist of fate that you and Fred didn't ask for. I like him with you. He is different. And not meaning to sound too freaky, but you two do write some great sexy music together. I'm excited to see what else you create with him."

I take another sip of his beer. This conversation is heavy. "Hey, I didn't see you drink once during the past few weeks. This is really stressing you, isn't it?"

"Yep."

"What about it is stressing you?"

"I guess having my mom here again."

"She's been here?"

"My parents came for dinner the day before I met you. I don't feel strange at my house with Fred there, but here I felt like I was outside looking in. Maybe because I don't sleep with him there. This is our safe place. Having her come here is risky."

"If she didn't trust you she wouldn't let you be here. Being with Fred is not going to damage you more than any other relationship would."

"True, but so sad. I don't want to end up damaged. You have a way of seeing things that helps me deal with them. Things are changing between us, Gunner.

"See, I'm not that bad."

"I never said you were bad. You just got under my skin."

He is silent and it's making me feel uncomfortable. Then he says, "Morgan, I will never be able to get under your skin, and you don't know how bad I want to."

Shit, now I wish he had stayed silent. Did he really just freakin' say that? I try to tell myself the beer is making me not hear right, but instead I store those words far away in the basement filing cabinet.

Fred is inside playing the piano and with the windows and sliders open it flows out into the night. Next thing I know Fred is carrying me to bed. He undresses me and tucks me in. "Damn, I am tired. Did Gunner drug me?"

"No, Jellybean, you are stressed. Let's sleep. I have the alarm set so no worries."

"Okay, I love you." I go right back to sleep.

I wake up before the alarm, slightly nervous but better for some reason. Maybe because I have both Fred and Gunner in my corner now. I head downstairs to leave for a run, startled to find Gunner sitting on the couch reading my papers.

"Hey, did you sleep here or just get here?" I ask him.

"I slept on the hammock for a while but I couldn't get back to sleep. I did some light reading instead."

"Oh." I don't know what to say. I never know what to make of Gunner.

"You have some great ideas here. I hope you don't mind that I read it."

"I don't mind." I sit down on the other end of the couch with him. "A few weeks ago I might have been irritated with you, but my feelings toward you have changed. So now it doesn't bother me."

"Good. It kept me busy most of the night. Thanks, and maybe tonight, after the lawyer and your mom leave, we can all work some of the ideas around."

"That sounds nice, I would love to. We can make the contract worth all the fuss."

"Exactly." He watches me. I sit and stare into space until Gunner snaps his fingers. "Hey, penny for your thoughts?"

"Not that again. I must stare into space too much. And come on, up the ante. You are loaded."

"That I am."

"I was wondering to myself how I got here. I mean sometimes it is like a dream. I have a beautiful man upstairs who loves me. I might be able to be friends with you. I look over at you and you are so damn attractive and talented. I was wondering how I got so lucky to hang with and work with such talented men. It is surreal. It feels good to feel good. I don't ever want to not feel this way. But how do I top this? Anyway, I should be back from my run before they get here. If not, let everyone know I will be back soon." He nods. "Thanks." I get up and leave before he can comment on my rambling words.

I get back and my mother's car is in the driveway. I take a deep breath. I walk in and she is sitting at the island next to Gunner and Fred is standing facing them. They are all talking and laughing and boy, it's weird seeing her here with them. She gets up and hugs me tight. "I miss you so much, honey."

"I miss you too." I should say I will come home soon, but I don't want to ever go home. My heart's home is here with Fred.

I jump when the lawyer knocks on the door, but I am glad he is here because talking to my mom with Gunner and Fred watching is a little awkward. We all sit at the dining room table and he goes over everything with us. I stand to make a damn boatload of money if even one song I co-write with them is recorded and released. If they have another number one hit with a song I write I might never have to get a job.

The paperwork is signed and sealed and the lawyer leaves abruptly. My nerves elevate now that this is so much more real. I don't have time to think about that because I hear Fred asking her what her plans are for the rest of the day. Huh? What? I can't hang with them together here. What is he doing to me? Does he have that much faith in me being able to keep my hands off him? I hear her say she has no plans and I start to hyperventilate.

"How about we all take the boat out and have a nice lunch on the water?"

"What? You have a boat?" I sound loud and snippy like I am having a mini heart attack.

"It's new," he says. I want his eyes to tell me he is sorry for this surprise but they don't. My mother and Fred are looking at me like I am insane, and frankly I am starting to feel that way. I excuse myself to take a shower. I have to remember to shower in the guest room and it's adding to me being on the outside of this day.

I head downstairs to find her packing lunch with Gunner. It's a sight I never thought I would see. I want to see this day as normal but it's not. She loves CrossRhoades music, so I imagine this is a bit of a thrill for her too.

Fred leads us up to a sparkling new and quite large boat that sits at least twenty people. It's hot and awesome like its owner. I could punch Fred for never telling me he had a boat. We could have gotten lost at sea for days with each other, but it was beneficial that my mom saw how shocked I was. At least she doesn't think we are screwing around on a boat all day.

"This boat is sparkling brand new. When did you buy it?" I ask.

"Recently." He is being so weird. It's annoying. "Would you help me drive?" he asks with a super sexy deep voice like big engines turn him on too.

"Hell, yeah!"

My mom knows I am excited because of how much I love things

like this. She doesn't have to think it has anything to do with the man beside me.

"Why didn't you tell me you had a boat?"

"I just bought it and it was delivered when we were back at your house last week. When we got back I was too damn busy falling into you." My mouth hangs open. I wish I could kiss him now, but even though no one is looking I can't find the guts to do it.

"Let's get out in the open water." He explains everything he is doing. I realize now that one of his many talents is being a teacher. He has been teaching me many things and I know there is a lot for me to learn from him. I can't wait for all of it to happen, but I fear the end and don't want to speed anything along.

We are out in the Atlantic when Gunner and my mom come to talk with us. The pleasure Fred brings me must be written all over my face, so I get up and ask Gunner if he wants to sit at the back of the boat with me as we ride the waves. He says yes without hesitation, which surprises me.

We are both lying down on bench seats with the tops of our heads almost touching. The sun and breeze feel exquisite. Gunner breaks the silence. I should be mad at him for interrupting my quiet time, but I am learning that I love conversation with Gunner. "What do you think they are up to all this time?" He laughs a sinister chuckle that makes me mad.

"That is a horrible thing to say. Stop." I lift my arm up, trying to smack him but I can't reach.

He puts his hands up to surrender and rolls over on his stomach to look at me. "Sorry, but your mom is hot, and not much older than Rick. Just saying."

I roll over so I can see his face. "Stop saying that. It's not something I want in my head. They get along really well, and that's nice."

"Subject dropped. How old was she when she had you anyway? She seems young."

"Twenty-six. She is forty-three now. Don't tell her I told you because she would be really mad."

"Okay, lips sealed. Does she work?"

"She is an accountant. She wanted to be an artist. Even took a ton of art classes in college, but she ended up taking the safe road."

"Maybe that is why she is letting you be here, so you don't miss an opportunity or take the safe road like she did."

"Wow, Gunner, you might be right. You have a way of seeing things rather quickly, don't ya?" I lift my head to look at him. "You know, first impressions aren't everything. You are very different than who I thought you were."

"The way I saw you the second I met you is exactly who you are. What about your dad? What does he do?"

I want to ask more about his first impression of me, but I also want to never talk about how he sees me, so I say nothing and move on to talk about my dad. "He owns his own firm that does actuarial services. It fits him better than my mom's job fits her."

"Where did they meet?"

"Wow, lots of questions about my parents, huh? They went to college together. She dated my dad's roommate first."

"Everyone's life has its stories, doesn't it? Where did they go to school?"

"University of California, Berkley. My mom grew up in Arizona, and my dad in New York City. He was moving to New Jersey for a job when she found out she was pregnant with my brother. They came here together and never left."

"I know very little about my parents," Gunner says. The sadness washes over his face, making me want to hug him.

"Gunner, I know they are gone, but why don't you know anything about them? You were my age when they died, right?"

"I was sixteen when they died. I was bad and extremely tough on them. I never asked much, never paid much attention to them. I guess it was a combo of everything. Then one day they were gone, and I was left wishing I had the time back to ask questions."

"Gunner, I'm so sorry." I touch his cheek and he puts his hand over mine.

"Is there anyone you can ask?" I move my hand away.

"No, my family has a tragic history of dying young. My parent's family were all dead or estranged when my parents were married. My father's sister was the only one left when they died. That is why I had to move here."

"Gunner?" I stop but sound as if I had more to say.

"What?" He responds softly; it's quite soothing.

"Can you tell me about your parents and your childhood? I only know what I have read in magazines and you know how often those stories are exaggerated. I want to hear it from you. If you are up for it."

He starts to talk and I am surprised he is up for it. "My parents both grew up in Sydney. My mom's family was elite, so to say, and my dad's was like trailer trash. Maybe not that bad, but it caused a lot of problems for her. I don't know how or when they met, but I know my grandfather was against her being with my dad. He was a bitter lonely old man. When my mom was a one-year-old, my grandmother died in childbirth, and the baby girl died too. So only my mom and grandfather were left – well, them and a full staff of servants and nannies.

He was going to disown her for dating my dad, but then he died of a heart attack. He never changed the will, so she inherited his money. My parents moved to New Zealand right away. They didn't work for money. They worked because they loved music. They were composers of classical music. I grew up playing violin, cello, everything I didn't like, and all I wanted was a drum set. They put the music in me, but a different kind than they wanted. I always felt I was a disappointment to them."

"Gunner, nothing about you would ever disappointment them."

"They wanted to go to Sydney for a vacation, and I didn't want to. They called when they were away, and they sounded like they were having a good time. I don't remember what I even said to them, but it was the last time I would talk to them. Their plane crashed on landing coming into Auckland, and they died instantly." I hear him make an odd noise as if he is looking for air. I know the feeling, since I tend to hold my breath when he talks.

I open my eyes to see him watching me as he continues to talk. "I left that week to come live here with my aunt. I was a moody bastard. I told her I wanted to attend public school and I didn't want any special treatment or their money. She gave me everything I asked for. It was such a new experience. She even bought me my first drum set. She finished raising me, and as much as I loved my parents, she understood me naturally. Nothing feels as good as having someone who loves you also understand you."

"That is so true, Gunner. Is your aunt gone too?"

"Unfortunately."

I reach my hand out to him and he gives me his. I squeeze it a little too tight, but if I feel this much pain what is he feeling? He is still growing up. "Well, you have Fred for family now. I would love to be your family too. You can even borrow my hot mom."

He laughs. "Watch what you permit me to do. I am a bad boy."

"No, Gunner, you are not. You are a good person. I'm sorry your parents died and sorry you didn't get along with them, but I'm not sorry I'm getting to know you. Those are the events of your story, and you can't alter the past. It's a bit twisted when you start thinking of the things that had to happen to get us to this point. If my mom kept dating my dad's roommate, or your parents didn't die, we wouldn't be here. We wouldn't be the people we are today. Hey, wait, why don't you have an accent?"

He makes a very un-Gunner-like noise. With a slight accent, he says, "I still have it. I cover it."

"Why? Accents are so hot. It's part of you."

"Not anymore. I wanted to be completely different here. I am nothing like myself as a teen. It's why I got the tattoos too. It was my escape."

"You have not finished your escape. The original Gunner is still in there." I tap his chest over his heart and I see Fred come over by us.

"Hey, what's up?" I say, snapping both Gunner and myself out of this deep conversation.

"Nothing. Why don't we head back? Your mom has to drive home still," he says.

I give Fred my hand to help me up and I shake a little at his touch. I miss his touch. Gunner gets up too as my mom comes over. She and I sit together as Fred drives us back to the marina.

Turning to look at me she says, "You okay, honey? You look sad."

"I am sad. Gunner was telling me about his family. It is a painful story and I only heard a Cliff Notes version. I'm not sure I can handle it all. I am lucky to have you." I hug her and she hugs me tight.

"It is wonderful he has you, Morgan. You are an easy person to talk to. Just be a friend and it will be what he needs. This was a wonderful day."

"It was."

When she leaves I hug her and say my goodbyes. Gunner comes inside with Fred and me. I can't tell if he wants to be with us or if he wants to help me cover this illicit love affair I am so wrapped up in.

"Dinner?" I ask.

"Let's order pizza. That sun has me exhausted," Fred says. He hugs me tight, then orders the food. We sit outside and eat. I might be glowing, but I'm tired from the boat and the sun and the weight of the day.

"I'm tired, guys. Write me a lullaby and let me hear it tomorrow." I walk over to Fred and kiss him gently on the mouth. Gunner watches me, so I walk over and kiss him on the top of his head, and I say goodnight to them both.

Chapter Twenty

Firework

I LAY WATCHING HIM. I could watch Fred for hours and be completely content. He starts to stir in his sleep. When he opens his eyes they hint at a part of his soul nothing else could ever touch. It's magic. "Good morning," he mumbles and I crumble.

"So why didn't you tell me about the boat or the name of it?" I ask with an edge to my voice.

"Oh, you noticed?" He smirks and now that I know him better, his smile is his most beautiful feature.

"Not until we were leaving and you were not around, so I couldn't even give you a look. It was difficult to contain myself."

"Okay."

"That's it? 'Okay' is all you have to say?"

"Yep. I love you. I put your nickname on a boat. No biggie."

"To a seventeen-year-old, sometimes still star-struck girl, it's HUGE!"

"You are not a girl, and star-struck is cute on you. I love you, and I can't show it all the traditional ways, so I named a boat after you."

"I can think of one traditional way to show me you love me."

"Oh, can you?"

"Yeah, divorce your wife. What are you gonna do when she sees that boat?"

I am mad! I never get mad like this. But it hurts. It's hurts to have him say he loves me when I know it will never be a hundred percent. I get up and head to the shower. He leaves me alone. I don't know if I want him to leave me alone or want him to come with me. This is very confusing. I will do my best to look past it because being snippy with each other is getting us nowhere.

* * *

I creep downstairs and Fred is playing his guitar on the couch. "Will you teach me more?" He hands me the guitar as he moves closer to me. I learn some basic chords again, and then I sit there mindlessly listening to him and the guitar. He is the off switch for my worn out mind.

"So, it's the fourth. Are you up for a party?"

"Whose party?"

"Gunner's. It won't be too many people. There is nothing to worry about. A couple friends from high school and some guys Gunner knows from – I don't know where from."

"Sounds like an interesting group of people – especially the I don't know where they come from crowd. Let's go."

"Ya sure?"

"Yeah."

After dinner I get dressed and put makeup on for a change. When Fred comes in the bathroom, he hands me a small box. "I wanted to give these to you yesterday when we signed the contract, sort of as a celebration, but the day got away from me. Now I want to also say I'm sorry for this morning. You already know I can be a weak man, and I don't want to hurt you. But I did, and I imagine I will again. But I love you, Morgan. More than words can express."

"I love you too. I feel second sometimes, and although I am accepting, I won't always be. I wasn't this morning. I was mean, and I'm sorry."

"If that was your mean side, I'm one hell of a lucky guy."

"Well, as of now that is my mean side. Don't make me change."

"I hope I don't." He hands me the box.

I open it to find two large diamond studs. "Fred, this is too much!"

"No, it's not enough. I thought I would start with diamonds, because we met in April. I got a little behind in gift giving. I have been so lost in you that I forget to be romantic."

"Fred, you are extremely loving and romantic. Geez, you already bought me a car and signed my name as a writer with your record label. You have done more than you should. The bedroom, the lilacs, oh, Fred.

The way you make love to me, the way you look at me, you are the most romantic man." I take each earring out of the box, fearful I will drop one down the drain, but I somehow manage to get them in my ears safely. I have never owned anything worth this much. It still doesn't feel real to be in love with a man who has so much wealth.

"I fear I will never do enough." Our eyes lock in the mirror and I know what he means, but I can't talk about the day we are done and he is back with Beth.

We get to Gunner's house in Spring Lake and a party staff is setting up food and drinks. At first, the amount of work he put into this party surprises me, so I forget to take in his house. Gunner comes down the stairs and shakes Fred's hand and kisses me on the cheek. I don't know this Gunner.

"Let me show you around, Morgan." He takes my hand and off we go. Enormous isn't a big enough word to describe this home. I thought Fred's house was large. This is a mansion, a modern mansion. The interior fits Gunner's personality, but the place as a whole doesn't. It is sleek and modern, and mostly black. Color is almost nonexistent. The only other color besides black is dark brown.

Gunner still holds my hand as we walk around looking at one over-sized room after another. It's at least 10,000 square feet – gorgeous but overwhelming. The party will be over before I see it all. Upstairs each room is impeccably furnished and immaculate. "Why do you stay with Fred and hang out there when you have all of this?" I lift my left arm up to the ceiling.

"I get lonely here."

"I bet you can find many willing women to fix that, and why don't the guys come here?"

"Fred used to come over a lot, just to get away from Beth. Then, after he bought the beach house, I saw less of him, and now with you here, well, he's with you. Seeing him the way he is with you means I have to let him go a little. And the women, yes, this house could get me any woman I want, I suppose. But I don't want any random woman. They want the money or the fame. It's not easy to find someone I can trust."

"Sorry, I bet it is hard. There isn't much I can do to help you. I can't exactly set you up with any of my friends." We walk down the hall to his room. That is when he releases my hand gently as if it is fine china that he doesn't want to break even though he dropped it. I try not to think why he did that. Gunner confuses me. His room is a bachelor pad to the max. "Really, Gunner, come on! I am sure there has been a parade of women up here. You can't be that lonely."

"No parade. I only ever told one girl I loved her and I only ever loved one girl. The funny thing is they are different girls. I slept with others, but never anyone here. I don't want that hollow empty feeling. You can be with someone and be lonely, and you can be apart from the one you love and not be lonely. It's about having the right person. I want someone special, someone worth it. Do you know what I mean?"

"Yes, Gunner, I do."

We walk back downstairs and Gunner greets his guests as if he is high society royalty. I find Fred, hoping he can bring me back down to earth. Fred grounds me; he is the right dirt for the type of growth I am looking for. Gunner has once again made my head spin, but as Fred's fingers are tracing circles on my back, he is erasing my mind.

"Hey, Jellybean, you want a drink?"

"Maybe I will have one. Champagne, please. It's fitting in this mansion."

"It's one hell of a house, isn't it?"

I nod in agreement.

The party ends up being fun. There are only twenty people here, enough to make it a party but not so many that it's overwhelming. I get to know one of Fred and Gunner's friends from high school. He is a nice man. His wife is here and she is quite normal as well. She is the only person I hear mention Beth's name. When she asks Fred where she is, his answer is: "I don't know and I don't care." He didn't know I could hear them. Sad but comforting.

Alex and Zach came too. Alex is all over the women, even the married ones. Something is off with him; he is different tonight than he is one-on-one. Fred comes back with my drink and we sit on a sofa that is bigger than any sofa I have ever seen.

"So, tell me more about Alex. He is a hard one to read."

"Yeah, I don't know much about him. We met him one night right after he graduated from high school. We were chatting and he said he played guitar and wanted to get a band together. Everyone else Gunner and I had worked with just didn't click. Alex was a good call and then he found Zach. I know even less about Zach. I don't ask many questions, Jellybean. I'm not like you. They both play guitar well and women think they are hot, so they landed the job."

"Do I ask too many questions?" I ask when asking another one.

"No, I love all your questions. You have a brilliant mind and it stimulates and intrigues me." He gets up and brings me more champagne without saying anything else. He tends to run off after saying heartfelt words. I fear I may do the same thing. Why do we both run away instead of together?

"Are you trying to get me drunk? You know I am a sure thing, right?"

"I have never been more sure about anything, but you are way too grown up, so maybe drunk you will let loose. I want to see."

"Challenge accepted. You could get in a lot more trouble than me for this. The alcohol, the hot sex, damn, you should be locked up."

"Only if I can be locked up with you. Far away from the real world. I could spend a lifetime locked away with you." He kisses me. Hot and unguarded, like he is the drunk one. No one pays us any mind though. As I'm pulling away from Fred, I see Gunner coming toward us.

"Let's all stand outside where we can see the fireworks." We all quickly head outside.

"Gunner, this yard is as lovely as the house. That is an awesome pool and a huge hot tub. I am impressed!" I try to whisper to him, but the alcohol makes me loud.

"It's all yours, anytime you want." He smiles at me and his eyes glow with the reflection of the fireworks.

Fred comes up behind me and wraps his arms around me. "I love you," he whispers in my ear. Having him hold me at a party, watching the fireworks, seems normal. Yet I continue to fight with my brain that always reminds me this isn't normal.

The rest of the party is a bit of a blur because I clearly drank too much. I remember playing pool, which is tough enough as it is, but I really struggle after too much champagne. Most everyone is still here when I tell Fred I want to leave. He is more than accommodating. We say quick goodbyes to those nearby and head to the car. I didn't realize

Gunner followed until I am sitting in the car. Fred puts my window down and Gunner leans in. "Goodnight," he whispers.

"Thanks for a great party, Gunner. I had a little too much fun. Your house is beautiful and I don't want to leave, but I must lie down. The world is spinning." My slur is so embarrassing that I wish I were drunk enough to not care.

"Glad you don't drink much, Morgan. I prefer sober Morgan. Thanks for being here. See you guys tomorrow. Be safe and good night." He taps the top of the car before he turns and walks back to the house. I watch him in the side mirror, with his head hung low, sad and lonely, and I don't know why, but I hurt for him.

Chapter Twenty-One

Love Walks In

MANY PEOPLE MIGHT see our lives as dull. We sleep, eat, talk, write, listen to music, and lose ourselves in each other for hours at a time. I run often to be out in the world. Fred rarely leaves. I never would have thought he was the type of person who could enjoy this lifestyle, but now that I know him so well I can see that it fits him perfectly. He is as introverted as they come. I wonder how he can turn it on when the band is on tour. I have never been to one of his concerts, but from his MTV videos, I can see that he is a natural.

I try to call my parents twice a week. It still shocks me how understanding they have been. I doubt I would let my child do this. My aunt is flying in from Arizona for a visit the same day Brooke gets back. I will be home for part of the week and I feel totally unsure if I will be able to handle it. Fred tells me I will be fine, but he won't. I love him for his strange ways of trying to comfort me. He says he will spend some time that week hiring a contractor to get the studio started and maybe he will join the band in California. I am excited for the studio, but I don't want to be apart from him any more than I have to. Still, when school starts in September I won't have a choice.

We haven't seen any other people in several days. Gunner came over a few times, but we haven't seen Alex and Zach since Gunner's party. I am lying in the hammock enjoying another lovely summer day when Fred joins me, making me even happier. "I want to take you out tonight," Fred says and his smile is as cute as a kid getting a huge gift.

I smile back. "Okay, where?" I take in his joy before speaking again. "Dang, you are cute when you are happy."

"Cute? I thought you said I was sexy."

"The sexy is an innate quality. The cute only comes out from time to time."

"Which do you prefer?"

"Oh geez. The sexy is better, but it's there all the time, so I guess the cute, since it's rare." He kisses me and like every time before, I am so stunned I become forgetful. "Wait, you still didn't tell me where we are going." He pulls away and locks his crystal blue eyes on mine.

He kisses me softly and says, "I can't decide if I should tell you or make it a surprise."

"I vote for tell me."

"Then I won't tell you."

"Stop, that is so mean."

"Oh, you want to see mean."

He starts to tickle me in the hammock and damn, he is strong. I start to lose quickly and my giggling gets so loud, I must end this, so I start kissing and touching him. It works fast, changing his tickle assault. Wrapped up in his body and panting, I am startled by a loud knock on the deck railing.

Fred gets up off the hammock, leaving me swinging wildly, but then my head is swinging even more out of control when I look over and see Fred shaking hands with Seth Heather, from Know More.

I get up and try to ground myself, but I know I can't do that. *Holy shit!* fills my head from ear to ear. I muster up some unexpected but welcome confidence, march right over to them, and introduce myself.

"Wow! Pleasure to meet you. I'm Morgan Evans." I put my hand out to shake his. "What are you doing here? Damn, that sounded rude. I meant, what brings you to Jersey?"

"We are playing at the Arts Center, and it should be me apologizing to you for my poor timing."

"Can I get you a drink?"

"Just water, thanks."

"And your timing wouldn't have mattered. You would have caught us in a compromising situation, regardless of when you showed up. Be right back." I take my time getting the water, and I try to find composure, but that isn't located in a kitchen. I assume since Mr. Heather knows where Fred lives that they are friends or acquaintances. I also bet he is wondering where the hell Beth is. Being the other woman is something I never thought I would be. It's a damn hard place to be, because guilt is not enjoyable. The problem is that nothing will stop me from loving Fred.

I walk back outside and put everyone's water down. They are chatting and for two attractive, talented men, they sure have some boring conversation. All technical equipment talk, but I guess to them it isn't boring.

I sit between them and put my foot on Fred's lap. He idly runs his fingers over my foot and leg. If we were alone my body would succumb to him instantly. "You want to go to the Know More concert tonight?" Fred asks, as he squeezes my calf.

"Absolutely." I pause and smile. "How long have you known each other?"

Fred answers, "A few years now."

"How long are you in Jersey for?" I ask Seth.

"Just the two shows, then off to Ohio."

"Is it hard, touring?"

"Yes, but it is also the best part of the job," he says.

I don't respond and get lost in the thought that Fred probably doesn't feel the same way.

"You want some lunch?" Fred asks us both.

We eat outside and talk like it's a normal thing to do. I guess eating with famous people has become my normal thing to do. People are people no matter what they do for a living. The day is once again flying by. We are going to leave in a few hours so I have time before I have to get ready, but Fred went inside to make some calls, so maybe I should go shower now so I don't have to make small talk with Seth.

"How do you know Rick?" he asks, before I can escape.

"How do I know him or how did I meet him?"

"Is there a difference?"

"Yes, if you asked me how I know him, I would say quite intimately, if you asked me where I met him I would say under a lilac tree at his cousin's house."

"Difference noted. Under a tree? When you were kids?"

"No, back in April when we were both trying to get away from other people."

"Rick isn't a large group of people guy, is he?"

"No, he isn't."

"What do you do, Morgan?"

"Well right now I'm sitting on a deck at the shore, making idol chit-chat with a musician, who's music frequently gets me to move my ass."

He laughs. "Damn, you can't just answer a simple question, can you?"

"Ask the right question if you are looking to get a particular answer."

"Are you a damn lawyer or something?"

"Hell, no."

"Are you from New Jersey?"

"Born and raised. See? I give you a straight answer when you word it right."

"Yeah, but I already knew you would say yes. Only people from New Jersey call this the shore. Everywhere else it's a beach."

"Good observation."

"What do you do for a living?"

"Much better and more direct. For the moment I am employed by CrossRhoades as a writer."

"Really? Cool."

"It is the coolest thing ever."

Relieved Fred has returned, I breathe more easily in his presence, because I feel like I have an underage stamp on my forehead. Plus, I never asked Fred if I should call him Rick around other people. We have too many other messy rules to contend with.

"I am going to get ready," I say as I head inside.

I turn off the shower just as Fred comes in. "Do you want to make me dirty again now that I'm all clean?" I ask him through the closed door.

"Boy do I ever," he says. I watch him strip and join me.

His hands are all over me, his tongue everywhere. I am weak to him.

"Turn around." His fingers are between my legs before I finish moving. "I need you so fucking bad, Morgan."

"Damn, Fred." His fingers are fast and talented.

A second later he is deep inside me, fucking me hard and fast and damn it's fantastic. He is powerful and all his mental and physical qualities have me constantly aroused. His fingers are digging into my hips as I come way too soon and he follows right behind me. I catch my breath and turn back around.

"What got into you?" I ask.

"Sorry."

"Don't be sorry. That felt great, just different."

We are standing still with the water pounding on my back. His face is relaxed; his eyes glisten with joy. "I don't know what came over me. I feel this animal need to claim you when we are around other people. I see how you are, so friendly, witty, and sexy. It is just who you are that turns me on so much. When I see how others react the same way to you, it makes me grateful that it's me who you want to be with."

"Oh, Fred, you are without a doubt the only man I want to be with."

"Is it wrong that I see how other men look at you, and I love that you only look at me?"

"No, it's always nice to feel wanted."

"You are so beautiful, carefree, smart, and different. I don't know how to explain it. Maybe it's confidence. You never falter or feel fear even. I can't explain it, you are a total joy to be with."

"Wow, those are some beautiful things to say. Thank you. I am just me. This is me. Whatever I am is what you get, so I hope you like it."

"I love it, and you hit the nail on the head, Jellybean. You know yourself so well, and it shows in everything you do. You are the most comfortable person I have ever met who is just happy being who they were meant to be."

"Damn, you sure have a way with words. You are clearly in the right profession." I kiss him, as passion and love flood my body. "We better get out of here and get ready. It's getting late."

He shuts the water off and we force ourselves to get dressed. Fred was ready before me so I head downstairs to find him. "Hey, should I call you Fred or Rick when we are with other people? Seth called you Rick all day. I didn't say your name because I didn't know which to pick."

"I can't handle hearing Rick out of your mouth. It would sound foreign."

"Then Fred it is, Fred. I didn't want to make this situation any stranger than it already is."

"There is nothing strange about how much I love you."

"No, that part is not strange. It's the rest that gets to me sometimes."

"I will drive there. Will you drive home?"

"Okay, but what is that smirk for?"

"Come with me."

I follow him outside and he opens the garage door. We don't go out much, but we have taken my car everywhere since the Jeep is still at my parents' house. Behind door number three is a black, Lamborghini Diablo, and it might be sexier than Fred. My mouth is hanging open. "I get to drive that home?"

He nods and smiles.

"Has this been here the whole time?"

"Come on, let's go. Maybe I need to give you a list of the cars I own."

We get in the car, and if I could be attracted to a car this is the one I would marry. We are heading down the street and slow is really tough to do in this car. "Fred?"

"Yeah?"

"I thought you were the sexiest thing I had ever seen, but this car might have you beat."

"Oh, really, then we take it out only for special occasions. I don't want you leaving my bed to sleep in the car."

"Good idea. Now I have to stay composed around everyone when all I want to do is get back in here to drive you home tonight. Damn, every other word in my head is stuck on sex. I want to drive you home in more ways than one. Shit, how can a car turn my brain to mush?"

Fred giggles and speeds up a little. We pull into a back parking lot of the Garden State Arts Center. The concert doesn't start for a few more hours so it's not buzzing with people yet. Fred parks the car far away, and I know it is because he wants to protect it, but I wish it was because he wants to do dirty things to me in it.

Fred knows his way around, so quickly we are in a hallway near the stage and we run into the rest of Know More. I am less star-struck than I have been in the past, but still this is a lot to handle. Fred introduces me to everyone and the nerves disappear as the excitement builds. I haven't been to many concerts and here I am backstage hanging with one band and loving the singer of another.

Seth takes us to a room with couches and drinks and food. He tells us to make ourselves at home. "I need to go out front to double-check everything, but you can come check it out with me if you would rather," he says, looking me in the eyes.

"Yes, I would," I don't hesitate to answer. Fred wraps his arms around me as we watch from the side. I lean my head back into his chest. Then he takes me down to the empty seats to sit. Fred's hands have been attached to some part of me all night. I like jealous Fred a little more than I should. It has its benefits. Seth comes down and sits with us.

"Go play us something," he says to Fred.

"No."

"C'mon, I wanna hear ya. Go." I nudge him.

He stands up and then pulls me up. "Only if you come with me."

"No!" I say loudly.

"See, you don't want to either."

"Well, I don't sing for a living. It's another day at the office for you. Go. I've never seen you sing on a stage." My eyes are locked on his, saying no.

"No, I can't leave you down here with him." He looks past me at Seth. "Come." If I weren't madly in love, I would have kicked him in the balls instead of letting myself get dragged up on stage.

"I don't want to do this," I say, ready to start begging.

"Me either, but only Seth is here. Let's do this for us." He kisses me. How could I say no to that? We are not hooked up to the amplifiers and have no microphone so only Seth can hear us. There is a white baby grand on the stage for the opening act. Fred sits at the bench, then taps it for me to sit with him. I sit and suddenly realize how weak my legs are.

"Same as at home," he whispers. "You ready, my beautiful Jellybean?" His eyes shine for me.

"Only because I have you with me."

He begins to play the melody. Our work blends as well as we do. It is surreal sitting on a stage with him. I never sang in public before and I never wanted to. Even though this is quite intimate, I am nervous. I block everything out but Fred, and we sing.

(Fred)
Meeting you made history
Finding you a mystery
My mind full on you
I didn't know
You were taboo

(Morgan)
Wrong from the start I gave you my heart
I don't belong to you since I am Taboo
She is not here but she belongs to you
I didn't know
You were taboo

(Both)
We are taboo
But I love you

We are taboo
But I love you

We are taboo
But I love you

(Fred)
One touch, I was changed
My heart dodging bullets
I was at the range
No matter the year
I only see you
Even now that I know
You are taboo

(Morgan)
Fighting love always fails
I pray we prevail

Wanting to be one with you
Even now that I know
You are taboo

(Both)
We are Taboo
But I love you

We are taboo
But I love you

We are taboo
But I love you

We are Taboo
Fighting against right
We hold each other tight

We can't fight the taboo
Love outruns the rules
Love outruns the rules

Even the Taboo ones

We make it through the entire song and our eyes are locked on one another. He takes my face in his hands. "Oh, Jellybean, that was so damn beautiful." He kisses me and I feel we are the only two people in the world. We stop kissing and stand up. I see Seth sitting down still looking speechless.

He comes back up on stage and goes over to Fred. "That was hot, sad too, but I can feel the passion between you two. You should record it together."

I say, "It should be recorded, but I won't be singing."

"You should. You have a beautiful sexy voice, and you and Fred have a chemistry that shows up even more when you sing together."

"You flatter me, Seth, but that is not something I want to do. I don't want the attention."

"Really, it's the best part." He laughs but he stops bugging me. "It's almost show time, so this place will be filling up soon. Let's head backstage."

We all walk in silence. Seth's hand is on the doorknob, but before he opens the door he turns and looks back at us both. We are holding hands, mesmerized by one another. "Wait, I have a question."

"Yeah?" I say.

"Is that song about what I think it is about?" He looks at me, not Fred. Damn, what do I say? I have a terrible poker face.

"I don't know. What do you think it is about?"

"Shit, that isn't an answer. I don't want to know. I will erase these thoughts, because it can't be what it's about." He drops the subject and opens the door.

I have enjoyed this night immensely. I forgot how much fun it can be to be around other people. Hanging out with both bands, I watched them perform from the side of the stage. And I did it all with Fred. What a special and thrilling night this has been.

The concert is over and we are saying our goodbyes. Fred is slightly drunk and he is much more talkative. I sort of like it. We get to the car and I nearly forget that I get to drive the sexy hunk of metal home. I will be super horny by the time we get to the house.

"You ready to drive me home, sexy?" He sounds cute when he is drunk.

"Very ready. Hang on." I back the car up slowly and head out to the parkway. The ride home is way too short. I want more time with my hands wrapped around the leather wheel, and I love the feeling of the gear shift in my palm. But all this hard fast driving has me needing Fred painfully bad.

He goes to open the door when I pull in the driveway. "Wait, don't get out yet," I say, tugging him back.

Chapter Twenty-Two

Ride

I GAZE INTO THE eyes that have captivated me since day one. In such a short time he has become a crucial part of my life, and right now it is crucial that I have sex with him in this car. I lean down and kiss him. Drunken Fred kisses are sexy as hell. I unbutton his jeans and lower his zipper. He takes his hands from my head and quickly pushes his jeans and boxers down around his ankles.

"Fred, I need you." I wrap my left hand around his pulsating hard erection and slip my underwear to the side with my right hand and I push myself down on him. I fear hurting one of us because of my extreme excitement. My breath catches from the sheer emotion physically and mentally of being with him like this. This night, this car, this man, have left me wanting and needing. His hands move to my hips and he moves wildly.

I stop and lift myself off him and I can hear him about to protest, but I turn around quick enough. Fred pushes himself back inside me. I don't even have time to think. He sits up a little more and wraps his arms around my stomach to hold me tight against his body. It only takes a few minutes before he is fucking me so hard and fast I can't even find the strength to moan. I support myself on the dashboard as my orgasm spirals out of control. Pleasure runs through every nerve ending in my body. I collapse back onto Fred's chest as he comes and bites by shoulder.

We are both still trying to regain our strength. He is still inside me and I can feel him getting soft. I know I love him growing hard, but

satisfying him and feeling him soften is arousing in a completely different way. I reach my hand up behind me to stroke his cheek and he kisses
my palm.

"I don't want to move but I'm tired and drunk and happily fucked. I
need a bed," he mumbles. Fred rarely leans on me or falters. I enjoy being
the strong one, if not just the sober one. I am glad alcohol is not a big part
of our lives.

* * *

I was asleep until Fred nudges me with a once again very erect penis.
"Damn, is that thing ever soft?"

He doesn't answer me. He flips me over and gets on top of me. I close
my eyes and accept this assault of love and lust combined to perfection.
This weekend has been nothing but fast, hard, erotic sex, and damn it is
so fucking amazing. So good, I have started cursing a little too much.

Once again, lying in my favorite place, Fred's strong embrace, I feel
philosophical. Then he says, "Damn, Morgan, I didn't know I could fall in
love with someone I was already in love with, but I fell all over again. You
surprise me every day, I love you so much."

"Fred?" I ask, and he answers me with a kiss. How do I top that? Sex
is amazing, every fun or kinky thing we have done is mind blowing, but
at the end of every day, it's his kiss that means the most. Fred has become
my home and my soul; he is a part of me that I can no longer live without. I only ever read about a love that is so strong it changes the person
you are or the person you are meant to become. On this Monday morning, July 17, 1995, I know with absolute certainty, that I have been forever changed by my extraordinary love for Frederick Rhoades.

The thought of heading back home has left me sad and mellow. I
have never been the clingy kind. Never. Not with my parents, friends,
or boyfriend. Unfortunately, the end of July becomes a blur. It's mostly
sex and music, the two things in the world that I love the most. The
impending end of summer has left a sour taste in my mouth. I wish I
could drop out of school. I even mention the idea to Fred, and we have a
heated discussion.

"I can learn more and earn more here," I say with a little too much
anger. I rarely have this heightened emotion and Fred looks like he doesn't

recognize me. "I am just so sad. School doesn't start for seven weeks and still it is messing with me. Sorry to be so I annoying. I am mad at this whole situation."

He wraps his strong arms around my tired weak body. "Don't drop out. We will make it work. I will come to your house. You can come here every weekend. We will be fine. Never leave school. I can't live with that. It's bad enough I have sex with a seventeen-year-old."

"I know, I am messed up, I love you. I can't live without you, and the thought of a week apart has me a stupid clingy mess. How will I handle week after week without you?"

"You are strong and brave. I know you can pretend to be fine if you have to. Soon enough it will be over and done. We can move on. I will be at your side every minute. And if it gets easier as you get older maybe your family can know. I never imagined I would be in this position, but I wouldn't be anywhere else." I wish it could be true. Only then would I tell my family, but I know them finding out he is married would be harder on me than my age.

He kisses my tears and fears away, as he has done the last few months. He makes me safe and sound and it's a feeling no one else has ever provided to me. "I love you," is all I can muster out of my mouth before he makes love to me. We have touched and loved each other so many times by now it should have become old, or ordinary, but it is the exact opposite. The more I know him, the more thrilling it becomes.

I am taking Fred to Newark Airport since he is flying commercial to meet the guys in L.A. Even with my sadness I still find driving my Cobra thrilling. I never slept last night, nor did Fred. We talked and made love all night. I honestly don't know how I will manage not seeing him until Thursday. I never thought I would be the girl who missed a guy. Then again I didn't know Fred when I thought that way.

I park my car and sit in my driveway for way too long. I have not been back home since the morning we went into the city for brunch. I have not been here since I got this car, or the giant diamonds in my ears. I have not been here since I first had sex with Fred. I love my family, but I don't fit in anymore. Seeing Fred's Jeep in the driveway makes me sad. I didn't know I could miss another human as much as I miss him. I plummet further into sadness.

I muster up the energy to head inside. Ryan, my parents. and aunt and uncle are all in the kitchen. I head inside and turn back partially into the person they know, even though all I want is a nap wrapped up in Fred. Damn, I have it bad. I haven't seen Aunt Stacy in two years. She hugs me and says, "Morgan, you are so grown up."

"Did you drive your car here?" Ryan interrupts.

"Yes, come," I say after saying hello to everyone. We walk to the car and I hand him the keys. "I am going to sleep. Have fun.

"You serious?"

"Yes." I yawn. "Brooke and Kelly are coming over. The mustang is old news. I drove a Lamborghini a few weeks ago. Hottest damn thing." I yawn again.

"What the hell? Did you sleep at all last night?"

"No."

"I don't want to know. Are you sure I can take the car?"

"Go, enjoy. And I will never tell what I did all night." I smirk at him. I don't imagine I would ever tell Ryan the truth, but I would trust him with it. He puts the window up, looking curious like he wants to talk, but he drives off without another word.

I walk right to my room and fall on top of my covers and sleep. A sad, much needed sleep. I wake up and the house is silent. I can't remember the last time I was alone. I used to love being alone, but when I'm sad and missing Fred, being alone isn't the same.

I walk around the house in a daze. Food is unappealing, the TV is boring. I have changed so much in the last few months that my own mind hasn't been able to keep up with it. The doorbell finally rings; I am beyond happy for the company.

Brooke and Kelly come bounding in and I can't help but smile. Seeing friends has never felt so therapeutic. I hug them both and realize for the first time how much I have missed them.

"Hey, you okay?" Brooke asks.

I must look tearful. "I didn't realize how much I missed you until now. Let's sit outside and you can tell me all about Spain."

Brooke gives me a super short summary of her trip. "Now, your turn," she says to me.

"My turn?" I mask my fear the best I can.

"Yes, how are those hot rock stars?"

"Still hot, and still in L.A." I hope I can make it seem like I don't see them very much.

"When do they come back?"

"Brooke, leave her alone, she doesn't want to talk about them. She wants to talk about you," Kelly says, trying to save me.

We talk some more outside, and now that the sun has set the night is pleasant. Brooke heads inside to get some water and use the bathroom. "Are you okay?" Kelly asks kindly. "You seem sad, and I know it's not because Brooke was gone."

"I'm fine but sad too. I miss him so much. I've never missed someone like this. It is so good, so intense. I guess being apart is just as intense, only in a bad way."

"So, did you finally have sex with him?"

I laugh aloud. "Finally."

"Yeah, finally," she cheers, lifting her hands over her head like she is holding pom-poms.

"Kelly, you are the best. We should spend more time together."

"Yes, we should. How much time do you spend at his house?"

"Every minute. I left the Sunday after my birthday and I came home this morning."

"Damn, no wonder you are out of it. What are you going to tell Brooke?"

"I don't know. I didn't plan that far ahead, but I can't be with him and with her the rest of the summer."

"Let me know if I can help."

"Thanks. If I think of something I will tell you," I say as Brooke gets back.

"Have you written anything?" Brooke asks as she gets back.

"Yes, but I am not ready to share."

"Morgan, you are upsetting me. You are a closed book, and we share everything."

"Sorry, Brooke, this is so big, so real, so awesome, so everything, and it's a lot for me to handle at times. I am not ready to share my work yet. Fred is having the work on the recording studio start soon, and when the songs are more polished and recordable, I will share."

"Okay, you better. Can I come down one day too?"

"Yeah, I can make some time for you," I say, hitting her on the head with my flip-flop. "And maybe Kelly can come too. Maybe I can set her up with one of the guys."

"Huh? Why her and not me?"

"Because you are seventeen."

"Who cares about that?'

I laugh. I feel the same way, and she is my best friend, yet I still can't tell her my truths. We talk late into the night, and even though I miss Fred, it has been nice to be with female friends. I walk them to the front door when they are leaving. I didn't realize Ryan had come home and my car is back in the driveway.

"Did Ryan get a new car?" Brooke asks, stopping in her tracks and staring at me. I can tell she already knows that the Cobra isn't his.

"No, it's mine. He was borrowing it."

"Damn, Morgan, who got you that?" She asks me with a glare.

"Fred did, for my birthday."

"Holy shit! That is awesome."

"It is all awesome. Now go home before your mom gets mad. I will see you tomorrow."

I spend my days counting the minutes until we are together again, literally. I have been doing the math to count the precise minutes in my journal. I have more math than words written down. I cover most of this funk well enough. At least none of my family asks what is wrong with me. Only Kelly notices. I'm not sure if it's because she knows the truth or if it's just that she can read me well. I talk to Fred every night before bed. This time the time difference is helpful. Only five nights apart, but I act like it has been five years.

"What are our plans for tomorrow?" he asks me on the phone and his voice has switched back to all sex again.

"I think I crave your sexy, needy voice the most," I say, almost whispering.

"Oh, do you now? Maybe we should be apart more often so I can sound desperate for you once in a while."

"No, this is enough time apart, and school will separate us. I do miss talking on the phone. I like your phone voice."

"When school starts we will have to talk a lot on the phone."

"Yes, but no more talking about that. I want to go back to your being sexy and needy."

"Should I tell you how much I miss you? How much I want to touch you? Want to know how bad I need to get lost in your body?"

"Yes." I have no breath left to form more words.

"Oh, Morgan, I need you now. It hurts not touching you."

"You can touch yourself."

"I did, but it doesn't compare."

"Damn, it doesn't take much to get me all worked up and that is too much to handle. I miss you. I'm not sure I can make it until tomorrow."

"I know that feeling. What are our plans tomorrow?" His voice is soft and breathless. Damn what we do to each other is so good it might be crazy.

"You are my only plan. What time will you be here?"

"Plane lands a little before five."

"You should be here a little after six then. I will be up to let you in. We can spend some of the day with my aunt and uncle. They are excited to meet you. My parents are taking them into the city for dinner and to see *Phantom of the Opera*. So we can head out in the afternoon and go back home for dinner."

"Morgan, I love you."

"I love you too, Fred."

"I know I say it a lot. This is too intense sometimes and saying I love you releases a little pressure. I could explode from this feeling. I love everything about you. And everything I am when I am with you. Being apart has shown me even more what you mean to me."

I have tears running down my cheeks and all I can muster up is another, "I love you, Fred."

"Don't cry. I don't want you to cry."

"It's good tears. I have never missed another person even close to how I miss you."

"Oh, Jellybean, the plane is boarding and I'm running out of change. I will see you in a few hours. I love you."

"I love you too." The phone disconnects.

I have not slept well, so I am exhausted when the alarm goes off. I brush my teeth and head downstairs. I open the front door and walk outside to wait on the front steps. I feel like a crazy groupie stalker; the only difference is he is coming to me by choice.

The sun is almost fully up and the day already hot. Seeing Fred step out of the limo in his tight jeans and black tee melts me. I want to run into his arms but I am paranoid someone is in my house watching. He comes over to the steps and puts his bag down beside me. The limo backs up and drives down the street and he stares at me as if he is seeing me for the first time. If looks could unravel a person this would be the look that would get me.

He glances at the shut front door before he slams me into the siding. His kiss is comfort, it is hot and needy, and his erection is tight in his jeans and hard on me. I am weak and perhaps even more needy than he is. He slowly pulls his tongue out of my mouth but takes mine with his lips. He is sucking my tongue into his mouth and I didn't know he could get hotter. Without warning he pulls his whole body off me, picks up his bag and walks it over to the mustang. He comes back to me, takes my hand, and opens the front door. We stand inside, neither of us knowing what we should do next. I feel exposed and it's got me all worked up.

"You hungry, thirsty?" I ask.

"Yes. But not for food or water." I watch his face as the lust builds between us. "Let's sit outside in the back yard."

"Sounds safe." It better be because I want to take him right in the foyer of my parents' house.

We walk to the deck and sit on the bench. "Lie down and give me your feet," he says. "I can see if anyone is coming from here."

He rubs my feet until I fall back to sleep. I don't know how much time passes, but I wake up feeling like I have finally slept for the first time in days. When I wake, my aunt is casually talking to Fred.

"Hey, morning again, sleepyhead," he says to me as I look at my aunt.

"Sorry, guess I was tired. Aunt Stacey, I guess you met Fred." This is all very strange.

"Yes, honey, we have been talking, having a lovely conversation."

"Anyone else up?" I ask her.

"Not yet."

"I am going to shower and get changed."

"Okay," they both say.

"Fred, if you are hungry help yourself." I walk away. I shower and can think of nothing but being back in Fred's bed tonight.

I come downstairs and the house is full of noise. I don't even get in the kitchen and my aunt is at my side. "So, when can we hear some music from you two?" She points to Fred with crazy hand movements.

"Oh, geez, I don't know if I am ready for that." I look at Fred to save me.

"You are more than ready. You did awesome at the Arts Center," he says, clearly not saving me.

"No one was there, that's different."

"Wait, what were you doing on a stage?" Ryan chimes in first.

"We were with Seth Heather before the concert. I was terrified. I don't know if I can handle singing here." I sound so unlike myself.

"Come here." Fred takes my hand and walks me out the back door. "Stop freaking out. It's so not you. We won't sing that song. We can sing another. We have enough. Come on, you are amazing and they should get to see it. Everyone in that room loves you unconditionally. Let them see all your work. It will make it seem like we couldn't possibly have time for all the sex we have." He laughs, and I laugh with him.

"Two songs, that's it. I will get my guitar for you, and let's get this over with quickly."

I come back downstairs and everyone is in the living room and Fred is on the piano bench, waiting for me. This moment is surreal, and it's creeping me out how much he is fitting in, yet how much he is standing out. I hand him the guitar and sit next to him.

"Start with Summer Breeze?" he asks and I nod. He plays the guitar and I sing the song. I don't look at my family, because seeing them will make me lose the ability to sing.

The dark clouds pulled in the sun
Your laugh was fun
Kissing your hair
Running without a care

The air was alive

Your smile could not hide
Touching your cheek
It only took a peek

The strong breeze blew over the dune
As you sang an upbeat tune
Shining light your soul was on fire
Being happy our only desire

Summer breeze made me love
Summer breeze made me love
Summer breeze made me love

Light and airy, warm and lovely
The breeze blew the sun away
Orange and lilac sunset glow
Making your heart beat faster I know

The cool blanket of nightfall
Made my feet stall
Holding your smooth hand as
We fell in the sand

Summer breeze made me love
Summer breeze made me love
Summer breeze made me love

Your head on my shoulder
As the starry night grew colder
We still felt the warm summer breeze
As it blew the love in

Summer breeze made me love
Summer breeze made me love
Summer breeze made me love

We finish the song to applause. Even though it's my family I am still uncomfortable. The other songs we have are not upbeat. What could he pick next?

"Turn around," he says, staring into my eyes with so much heat, certainly everyone can tell what we mean to each other. He puts the guitar down and sits facing the piano with me. "This song is new and unfinished, so please excuse any mistakes we make."

"You sure?" I ask, knowing exactly which song he wants to sing. We wrote it last week in bed. It's sultry and hot. "You play. I'm too nervous," I whisper. He starts playing the piano. I am glad no one can see my face. It must show every secret I ever had.

Arms reach around me
Leaning into you
You are all I see

Desire, desire, desire

Legs tangled together
Wrapped up in you
You are all I feel

Desire, desire, desire

Tongues intertwined
Lost in your soul
You are all I taste

Desire, desire, desire

Bodies become one
Wanting more
You are all I am

My love, my lust, my desire
You take me higher

All of you the soul of my desire
All of me needing to take this higher
All of us, we feel the lust
When the desire takes us higher

Desire, desire, desire

"Wow, honey, that was beautiful." My mom comes over to me like she wants to save me.

"Thanks," I say, thinking I could shake I am so uncomfortable.

Everyone tells me how much they liked the songs and I still wish I never did it. At least I know something I am not meant to do. I will never sing for a living.

We are hanging around the house. Everyone has gone off to start his or her day and I sit here not knowing what to do next. Fred and I are sitting in the kitchen when my mother comes in. Fred gets up and leaves and I don't know why. I hate that he did.

"Why don't you head back to Mantoloking? We are leaving soon anyway," my mom says.

"No, it's fine. We can wait until later."

"Morgan, it's okay. Just say good-bye to Stacey and Mark first."

"I will. Thanks for understanding. That was really tough singing for you guys. I know I will never sing for a living, but they are going to record my songs."

"Morgan, you have a beautiful voice, but if you don't want to perform then don't. Follow your heart and trust yourself." She hugs me and I turn to walk outside to get Fred.

"Are you ready to leave? My mom thinks we are both uncomfortable here and she is shipping us off."

He laughs. "Yes, more than ready to get you home."

Chapter Twenty-Three
Endless Summer Nights

A S STRANGE AS it felt to return to my parents' house last week, returning to Fred's house feels completely natural. Fred slept the entire way. He often goes without sleep yet he is never tired. I am glad he rested, because he will need lots of energy for what I want to do to him.

I stop the car but leave it running, and sit absorbing the silence and the beauty of his face. He stretches and slowly wakes up. I have reclined my seat to enjoy the view, waiting for his lids to lift, to expose the eyes that burn through me.

As his eyes meet mine he says, "Whatcha doin'?"

"Watching the man I love sleep and enjoying it a little too much." He leans over and kisses me, soft and loving, but desire makes me numb yet full of sensation. I melt with each movement. He pulls away and lies back down, stretching and exposing his muscular stomach. I reach down and run my fingers across his flesh.

"Let's go inside." He gets out, comes around and opens my door in lightning speed.

He lifts me up and carries me inside. I want to giggle, but this is intensely serious. This is real. This isn't a young girl crushing on an idol. It's a love people would die for. We are both lucky to get to feel this, and even luckier that we know now, while we still have it, how lucky we are.

He carefully puts me down in the bedroom and kisses me from my neck to my mouth. He stops abruptly after gently kissing me once more and walks away again. My eyes are glued on his every movement. It only takes a few of his large steps to reach the stereo. Taking his shirt off as he walks back to me, "I'm on Fire" starts to fill the air. The fire inside me gets hotter now that Fred is topless. Full of lust he takes my shirt off. Having him stare at me has never felt so hot. His eyes are burning with passion and it's going directly to every nerve in my body.

My hands are all over his body, but somehow I have the ability to control them. I run them slowly and patiently over his chest, down his arms and across his back. Urgency is lost; time is in control. For the first time I feel like I am not losing him. We were apart and now we're together. He wants me as much as I want him. I lose my mind to his gentle kisses in a whole new way.

He reaches around to undo my bra and I look up into his eyes. I lower my hands and let it drop to the floor as his fingers make their way to my nipple. He is slow and gentle – it's barely a touch – yet it affects me deeper than ever before. I love this slow drawn-out pace, but I am getting needy. I slowly unbutton each button of his tight sexy jeans and now I have him losing control.

It has been less than six days, but it seems a lifetime ago that I was last in this bed. I missed him so much, I was broken. I become slightly grateful for our time apart, as it has led to a new level of love and trust. Our lovemaking has taken another giant emotional leap. I am committed to him, his mind, his body, and his soul. I feel eternally connected, deeper even than when his body is part of mine.

The sheets are a tangled mess, I have wild thoroughly fucked hair, and my skin is aglow with sweat. I can't form words or move. My fingers are waking up, but only because they have something enjoyable to touch, Fred's chest. He is perfect. Big, toned, tanned, sexy, there is nothing lacking. I could watch my fingers move over his skin for hours.

* * *

It's a hot humid August night, but the ocean breeze makes it bearable, as we lie together in the hammock. It still amazes me how distinctive conversation can be with Fred. I always enjoy talking to my friends and family but lying around and talking to him is so fulfilling. I wonder if it's because we are good at it, because we are lovers, or because I trust him with every minute of my time.

In seventeen years of a wonderful life, I fear this snapshot of time will be the climax of my love life. No longer possessing this alive feeling haunts me, but the thought of losing Fred? That kills me.

"Hey, you okay?" Fred whispers, breaking my train of thought.

"I was thinking about how much I love you," I answer.

"You look scared or stressed though. Does loving me worry you that much?"

"No, you erase my mind and make me free, yet when I think about the future, it fills me with such pain and horror, I can't breathe."

"Morgan, I will never intentionally hurt you. You know that, right?"

"I know it won't be intentional, but I fear you will hurt me."

He squeezes me so tightly it almost hurts. We both stop talking. There is nothing to be said to fix this.

"When is the construction starting?"

"The day you go back to school."

"Oh."

"I didn't want to lose a single day alone here with you."

"When are the guys back?"

"Miss them?"

"Not really. Gunner a little, maybe. I want to work more on that song he and I were writing."

"You enjoy writing with Gunner?" he asks, shocked.

"Tremendously. It's different than with you. My brain isn't cluttered with personal emotions and lust with him. Plus, he is certainly talented."

"I might be a little jealous, but Gunner is gifted musically. I love writing with him too. Gunner should be back next week. He doesn't last long in California. He has this perfect house in Malibu, but he never goes there, so we usually stay in a hotel. The ride back and forth to L.A. can get long, but it's a gorgeous house. He has been my best friend for over ten years. He is my right arm, yet there has always been a missing link. Or maybe it boils down to the fact that he doesn't share much of himself with me."

"Have you ever asked him any questions?"

"No, if he wanted to tell me he would."

"That is the job of a true friend, to wait, and another reason for me to love you."

"Come, I want to go to bed with you." I go more than willingly.

* * *

The phone is ringing in the kitchen, and Fred and I look at one another like we have turned into aliens. The phone just doesn't ring here. I call my parents but they never call here. Gunner comes over instead, and thankfully Beth doesn't have the number.

"Hello. Yeah, Kelly, hold on." He hands me the phone.

"Kelly? Everything okay?"

"Brooke keeps calling Ryan, asking for your number. I didn't want her to start prying. I wanted to let you know so you can try to figure something out."

"Thanks, sorry to put you in this position. I will call her. I haven't been a good friend."

"You didn't do anything wrong. You're busy and she is working evenings up here so there wouldn't be much time to see each other even if you squeezed her in. We are going down to the shore house with my parents this weekend. After that her weekends are free, so she might want to come down."

"Maybe I will have you bring everyone down and make it a party. You up for it?"

"Who would say no to that?"

Gunner walks into the house. I haven't seen him in two weeks and I have an urge to hug him tight. "Kelly, I have to go, I will call you later."

"Okay, miss you. Talk to you later."

"Miss you too." I hang up and walk over to Gunner.

"I missed you too, Gunner. Welcome back." I reach up on my tippy toes and hug him tight. I never thought a day that I missed Gunner would exist, but here it is.

"What got into you?" he asks, hugging me back.

I let go of him and say, "Absence makes the heart grow fonder. I get it now why Fred loves you so much."

"Love is a little too strong."

"You can't deny your relationship with Fred is a special one."

"No, I won't deny that. I can think of some other things to deny though. Where is he anyway?"

"I don't know. My friend called and he disappeared while I was on the phone."

"Having friends call you here now, eh? Finally getting the courage to tell people?"

"Just one friend. Actually, she's the older sister to my best friend. She is the only one who knows the truth."

"You told your best friend's sister? Ouch!"

"I know, but if you met them you would understand. They will be down soon so you can meet them if you want."

"I want." He smiles and it warms my heart in a place he used to make it mad. "Sounds fun."

Fred comes down the stairs. "Everything good with Kelly?" he asks me.

"She was warning me that Brooke is getting ants in her pants to come down here. Maybe next weekend I will invite her down. And Kelly and Ryan too."

"Sure, Jellybean, whatever you want."

"It's not a want, it's a necessity."

It takes the next few days but Gunner and I finish the song we have been working on. He also starts to teach me how to play the guitar. Learning from another right-handed person is light years easier. I didn't realize how Fred being a lefty made it more of a challenge. In a week's time I can play the song we wrote on the guitar and it's a glorious feeling.

Eventually I speak to everyone back home, and they are coming down for an overnight stay next week. Certainly this is going to be very hard for me. It is just Ryan, Faith, Kelly and Brooke, but I am a nervous wreck. Fred says Alex and Zach are coming too. My nerves can't decide if that will help or hurt.

Fred and I have talked at length about how we will get through it. "It is only one night apart," he says.

"I can't handle even one. There will be too many in my future."

"I will sneak over to be with you in the guest room. Ryan and Faith can have one room and Brooke and Kelly the other."

I laugh. "You always make me feel better. You know you cure me, right?"

"No, but I'm starting to see it. A little."

Chapter Twenty-Four

House Party

KELLY, BROOKE, RYAN and Faith are coming down today, leaving my heart screaming code blue. I wake as the sun starts to rise, so I dress for a run. On my way to the door, I am shocked to see Gunner, fast asleep. His face never looked so beautiful or at peace.

When I return he is up and the aroma of fresh brewed coffee wakes me more than my run, but I still feel dazed. "Hey, Morgan, you okay?"

"No."

"What's wrong?"

"I am nervous," I say, grabbing a mug.

He comes up behind me and turns me around to face him. His eyes are just three inches away from mine. His cat eyes leave me frozen. "What is the worst thing that can happen?"

"They find out!" I say with too much force.

"Would the world end if they did?"

"If they tell my parents or their parents, my world could end. I hate being this invested in another person but I also think it is a rare feeling."

"Relax, they aren't the right friends if they would tell, and I am sure you have picked trustworthy friends. Do you trust your brother?"

"Yes, I think he and my mom have been onto us from the beginning."

"Go sit outside. I will bring you coffee in that mug. Drinking air isn't going to help."

I am feeling a slight wave of peace as we sit and drink. When did Gunner start giving me peace? Fred joins us and I feel even calmer. Being with them has become a new favorite hobby.

After sitting in silence thinking about Gunner and Fred, I head inside to get changed for what I know is going to be a tough day. Back outside I am rattled knowing they could be here any minute. Gunner asks if I want to play some music with him. I say yes, concentrating on the guitar should help my funk. I get up to head inside. "You need fresh air," he says, tapping my legs so I'll sit back down.

He is sitting in the corner of the new outdoor sofa that Fred bought last week. Pretty sure Fred had someone buy it for him, because he makes phone calls and new stuff shows up. It's large, white wicker, with solid deep dark blue cushions. Gunner sits with his left leg stretched along the back of the sofa and his right foot still on the ground. He pats the cushion between his legs for me to move over. I do it regardless of my apprehension, because all my previous lessons we faced each other.

He puts the guitar in my hands and moves my fingers with his own to adjust them. Even though it's Gunner this is still too sensual. The physical contact, his low soft voice, what the hell, I don't want these thoughts in my head. He strums the guitar and I feel his breath on my neck. I want to run because my thoughts betray me. I let the inappropriate thoughts out of my head as I tell myself Gunner would never make me uncomfortable. I am sure he did it since it is easier to teach me this way.

I do find it easier to learn this way. Gunner always knows what he is doing. I never heard the front door, so I am shocked to see my brother and Brooke here. I realize Gunner knew what he was doing. Not only did he distract me, but he also took them off the scent of Fred and me and put it on us. A scent that has no trail. I will have to remember to thank him.

I stand up and place the guitar on the table. Gunner stands beside me and reaches his hand out to shake my brother's hand. "Good to see you again, Ryan. And you must be Brooke." She jumps into him and hugs him with her entire body. Poor Gunner.

Faith, Kelly and Fred join us outside. I observe everyone and it's so awkward. I feel strange and out of place, and like she can tell, Kelly comes to stand beside me. "How are you?"

"Good, but this is odd."

"I imagine it is."

Our plans are to go to the beach today and then out on the boat tomorrow. I can't wait to get this moving, then my mind-reading lover says, "So how about a tour of the house, then you can all head to the beach?" It is wonderful both he and Gunner understand me so well.

Fred takes everyone upstairs, leaving me alone with Gunner. I pack the drinks and snacks before I speak. "Thank you. I didn't realize what you were doing until Ryan and Brooke were staring at us. I appreciate it. You are a smart and perceptive man, Mr. Cross." I wink and walk away.

It was a great day hanging with everyone at the beach. The sun was hot, the water warm, the conversation pleasant. I caught up with Brooke and felt much better about abandoning her. Fred and Gunner stayed back since it was very crowded here, but they came down a few minutes each, at different times. I missed them but I had a great day.

"I'm going to get showered and start on dinner," I tell everyone as I pack up to leave the beach. I get back to the house and Fred is alone at the piano. "Did Gunner leave?"

"Yes, he will be back in a little while," he says, his eyes still on his music.

"Okay. I'm going to shower before I start dinner." He looks up at me and his eyes melt me. "Come with me?"

I lock the bathroom door this time. Without uttering a word, he takes my bikini off then turns the water on. I watch him take his shirt and shorts off. The water is a gentle caress I need almost as much as I need his. The sunscreen and sand slide down the drain, and my need for Fred rises up.

When he kisses me I melt into him. He lifts my leg over his hip as he pushes me against the cool tile on the back wall. His hands tease my nipples. He starts to push himself into me, and his slow movements are driving me mad. He is filling me one inch at a time, exciting me further. He lifts my other leg and I wrap my hands around his neck as he moves in and out of me with the perfect rhythm. The pleasure is simple – I crave it unlike anything else in life – but before long I am looking for a mind blowing release. He shifts his hips a little and in a split second he is deeper and harder inside me and I bite his shoulder hard as my orgasm grips my whole body.

My thighs are still clenched around his waist as he comes with a deep groan. I lower my feet to the shower floor but I can't quite stand on my own yet. I lean into Fred's chest, he is my rock, my shelter. "I love you so much." There is nothing else to say when one feels this good.

"Oh, Jellybean, I love you so damn much too. I missed you today. Being apart is going to be a lot harder than I thought it would."

We are frozen but warm under the spray of the shower. We hold onto one another for way too long. I don't want to move and in this moment I don't care if we get caught. Then I force myself to say, "We should get back downstairs." The water starts to run cold before we get out; I have never used up all the hot water before.

We manage to get out of his room and downstairs without anyone noticing. Everyone is still on the beach. So far only Gunner has returned. "You two look a lot happier than you did earlier," Gunner says, smirking at me. Why me?

"Thanks for noticing," I say and hit him with a dishtowel.

"Need any help?" he asks.

"Sure. Set the table." He gets right up and takes the dishes out, shocking me. Gunner does not fit my first impression of him anymore.

"Anything else?"

"Not right now, but thanks," I say, glancing at the table that looks like it was set with a right angle.

"You make him happy, you know?"

"I know, but sometimes I second guess it."

"Trust it, but I bet part of it is just sex. Ugh, I don't want to know about that," he says, shaking his head with his eyes shut.

"A big part of it is sex, but nothing is ordinary about this. An extraordinary love will come with heart-stopping pain at the end. I hope the end is the part I have wrong." I look up at him and stop chopping the lettuce. "Gunner, he is going to destroy me one day." I could cry, but it's one of those moments too sad even for tears.

"Oh, Morgan," he says as he crushes me to his chest. Now I feel the tears, and of course everyone comes back when we are wrapped in another hug.

I pull away from him. "At least you didn't plan this one. Give me that onion." He hands it to me and we both giggle. They either saw nothing or are too afraid to say anything since no one speaks before heading upstairs.

Dinner is almost ready, since Fred and I always work quickly and naturally together. It still baffles me that I have that same ability with Gunner; he used to infuriate me. Lucky for me, Kelly comes down before everyone else. "So what's up with you and the sexy, super tattooed drummer boy?"

I laugh so hard I spit my drink out. "Kelly!"

"Just kidding, but Brooke noticed."

"Well, earlier he did it on purpose to throw them off. Just now though that was Gunner being a friend."

"He isn't what I imagined. I thought he would be tough and all bad boy. He is less lion and more kitten."

"I would spit my drink again if I had any in my mouth. Kelly, you are too much. Gunner is a good guy. Lost and sad, but good. Alex and Zach are coming over tonight. They know Brooke is seventeen. Gunner led them to believe I am your age. I don't want them hitting on her. You are free game though."

"Oh my, you are mean. I don't know what I want. They are hot guys, that's for sure. I'm still not over John. I know he isn't worth this energy but I loved him like I never loved before."

"I understand that. Help me get the food on the table." A few minutes later everyone else has come downstairs for dinner. No one asks me any horrifying questions and I am enjoying the company of friends.

After everything is cleaned up, we hang out like people our age should. Alex and Zach eventually join us and everyone is drinking way too much alcohol, except Fred, Gunner, and me. I don't know what I make of that.

The night is filled with laughter, music, and great conversation. Gunner comes over to me and Kelly and says, "I'm gonna get these drunk fools back to my house to sleep." He pushes Alex and Zach out the door.

"I will help you," I say.

"I'm goin' to crash," Kelly slurs as she gets Brooke and heads upstairs.

I walk to the door with Gunner, but he has everything under control. Ryan and Faith are still on the deck and Fred is in the kitchen doing nothing and it seems he doesn't want to do anything either. Then Gunner runs back up to me instead of getting into the car. "Which room are you sleeping in?"

"I'm sleeping in the room at the far end of the hall." I answer him even though I don't want to.

"No, you aren't. See ya later." He runs off. I close the door.

"Guess I will head to bed. Tomorrow night can't come soon enough," I whisper to Fred, even though everyone is too drunk to even know where their ears are.

"I know. I miss you already. Let's walk up together. At least I can hug you before you go to sleep."

We walk so slow it's pathetic. We get to my door and he scoops me up for a tight hug and a big kiss. "They are too drunk to notice." He puts me down and I turn toward the guest room. I get ready for bed, I am tired, and hope sleep takes me soon. I toss and turn before the light from the hall hits me right in the eye.

"Gunner?" I say as he takes his pants and shirt off and gets under the covers on the other side of the bed. "What are you doing?"

"Go. Go sleep with Fred."

"No, we can't get caught."

"Then get caught with me. Your choice."

"Damn, it's like old times with you irritating me again." I get up. "But, thanks."

"Sorry, but it's best when the two of you are happy, and you need each other. He needs you and I do love him enough to make sure he always has you."

I sneak over to Fred's room, our room. The lights are on low and he is sitting in bed writing. I lock the door and climb in next to him. He lifts his arms for me to lie on his firm chest. It blows me away that this is the only place I want to be.

"What are you doing?" he whispers.

"Well, Gunner showed up and climbed into bed with me and said I had to pick you or him to sleep with. So here I am."

"Seriously, Gunner is in the other bed?"

"Yep, he said he wanted us to not be apart."

We share no more words that night. He turns off the light and makes long, slow, quiet, and satisfying love to me. Content again, we sleep until the sun comes up. We are both downstairs with Gunner when everyone else trickles down.

"Why are you okay, and we are all messed up?" Ryan asks.

"We didn't drink our weight in vodka last night," I say and give him a look between siblings.

"Are we still going on the boat?" Kelly asks. She is in a little better shape than everyone else.

"Whatever you guys want," Fred tells her.

"Let's do it," she says.

It is lunchtime before we get the boat off the dock. Not a cloud in the sky. Everyone is doing better physically now, and we enjoy another nice day. I have been in the sun way too long and I am getting tired since I was up most of the night.

I wake up and see Fred tying the boat to the dock. Gunner is sitting alone so I head over and sit next to him. "You trying to make them think we have something going on now too?" he asks.

I chuckle. "No, I picked you because I like you."

"You're too sweet, way too sweet for Fred. Did you have a nice nap?"

"Yes, how long was I asleep?"

"About an hour."

"Sorry."

"Don't be sorry."

"Well, I left you to entertain my friends."

"Honestly, did you not get any sleep last night? You still can't stop yawning."

"Gunner, you are terrible to ask that. I slept very little last night." I sigh.

"What's that like, to love someone so much you can't get enough?"

"It's the most amazing thing I have ever felt, but the scariest too."

"Morgan, I hope he sees what he has in you. I have never been lucky enough to have that with anyone."

"Me either, until now." We are still sitting lost in our own thoughts as everyone else gets off the boat. Fred comes over and gives me a look I can't read.

"You spending the night here or coming with us?" he asks us both.

"Sorry," I answer as I reach my hand up for him to help me up, even though I just want to touch him. His touch is different than anything else I have ever felt. "We were talking about how amazing it is to love the way I love you." I drop his hand and walk away.

I turn back before I walk down the stairs and they are both staring at me. In such a short time I have learned to love them both, in very different ways.

Chapter Twenty-Five

Beth

WE WAKE AT noon on August 14th and all I can think about is how this summer flew by. The day is overcast; it might even be drizzling. Fred and are glued to each other like we have been apart for months. We lay silent. My hands can't stop touching him. I start to fall back to sleep when the phone rings and we both jump.

"Hello," Fred says, then moves the phone to his left ear. "I will ask." He winks at me. "No, I will do it. I will call you back in a few." He hangs up the phone and squeezes me tight.

"Is something wrong?" I ask.

"No. Stay here. I will be right back. Do not move!" He puts on his pajama bottoms and leaves.

"You know I don't do what I'm told," I yell.

"I know," he yells back.

"Ugh." I flop back on the bed and close my eyes. Fred knows I hate not knowing what is going on. Why is he torturing me? I lie there naked in bed, waiting for him.

He comes back with a huge Cheshire grin on his face. "That was Gunner. He asked if we want to go to one of his other houses, the one in Hawaii. We can celebrate my birthday there." I start to talk and he covers my lips with his fingers. "Wait, I called Kelly, and she said she's done with her internship and doesn't have classes until the twenty-eighth."

"What?" I say before he covers my mouth with his whole hand for a second.

"Stop, let me finish. I called your mom and she said yes."

"Really?" I'm shocked. "This is gonna be fun. What will I do about Brooke?"

"Kelly said she can't get off work, and their mom would kill her if she didn't work because she spent a lot of money in Spain. We can make it so Brooke doesn't find out."

"You talk to my friends and family more than I do," I say, scrunching my face.

"I like them and they like me. I have those powers to make people do what I want, remember?" He starts to tickle me. He is bending over me now and staring at me when he says, "I would do anything for you."

"I would do anything for you too. I am weak and under your spell, Fred."

"No, you are strong." I hope he is right, because now that I have loved Fred, I will need strength for the rest of my life.

Fred calls Gunner, I call my mom and Kelly, and after too much chit chat, everything is set. We are flying on a private jet out of Morristown Airport Wednesday morning and will make a pit stop in Vegas. Even though we will not get out of the plane there, it pains me to think that just four months ago he was in Vegas getting married. We will celebrate Fred's birthday on Thursday, then enjoy a handful of lazy days by a different ocean.

I am putting our clothes and toiletries in a suitcase when Gunner comes up to the bedroom. It's weird seeing him in here and I am dumb enough to say, "Gunner, you never come up here."

"Well, that's a good thing since I'm guessing you are always naked up here."

"Oh, damn, Gunner."

"Ignore me if you want. I would never ask Fred this, but do you really have sex all the time, because it seems you two can't stay apart?"

"All the time, no. Who could do that? It's a lot of talking, just being together, but a lot of sex too. We do sleep a lot. I don't know, I never had this before. It's everything, and there are no missing pieces. You know there isn't space to think. I never want more or less of something. There is no room to think about what could be different. I get to be me and feel good about it."

I look up at him when I finish talking, and neither one of us knows what to say. A few minutes later though, in typical Gunner fashion, he asks, "So you weren't a virgin?"

"Gunner, really? That is what you say after I pour my heart out? No, I wasn't. Bad enough Fred had to fall in love with a sixteen-year-old. Should I ask you about your virginity?"

"Nope."

"You two getting along up here?" Fred asks from the doorway.

"We are," I say, as Fred comes up behind me and kisses the top of my head. He hasn't been as territorial as he used to be but he still has to claim me around Gunner.

"Dinner is here," Fred says, taking my hand in his.

We are outside eating, when Gunner asks if I have ever been to Hawaii. I actually roll my eyes at him dramatically, letting him know I have not.

"Jersey will always be home because it's where I found my soul. But the Pacific is so much more…" Gunner says as he looks up, trying to find the right word. We both do that when we are writing. "…splendid. I am looking forward to seeing what you can write out there. I want to see if it inspires you," he says, as I stare at him and take in every word.

"I'm sure it will. Just being with you guys inspires me," I say, as Fred takes my hand.

Gunner drives Fred and me in a humongous SUV to the airport. Fred sent a car service to get Kelly at her apartment. She is in the lounge when we arrive and her smile is contagious. She jumps up and down like a kid who got a new bike when I walk in. "I'm so excited… thank you, thank you, thank you," she says as she hugs all three of us. This is so un-Kelly-like, but her joy makes me want to jump up and down too.

We board a plane even more luxurious than the one they took last time. Kelly and Gunner are each holding a glass of champagne and Fred and I are holding each other. "Who paid for this plane?" I ask Fred.

"Gunner."

"Okay." I want to ask more but not now.

With the ease of private jets and different time zones, we arrive in Hawaii well before sunset. Gunner has a car service pick us up right on the runway and take us to his house. I quickly realize I could get used to this life style.

"Another mansion, Gunner?"

"He has more than one?" Kelly asks.

"His house in Spring Lake is huge."

"It's a big house, but what does it matter? Let's go inside." Gunner is always avoiding talk about what he owns. He should embrace it, but I love that he is humble even when this house screams MONEY.

My eyes take in the Pacific, which is light years different than the Atlantic. On paper I would say without a doubt that the Pacific wins, but the Atlantic is my preferred body of water. It might be the darker grey, somewhat tired looking ocean, but I love the swings the east has. I long for the pulsating thunderstorms in the heat of summer, and the piles of snow we get in the winter. I crave the extremes. I don't like stagnant, even if it's beautiful.

There are even more windows in this house than in Fred's. Gunner gives us a brief tour. There are so many rooms that I imagine I could forget where I am sleeping. There is a modest pool, hot tub, and past that nothing but sand and surf. Gunner tells us to sleep anywhere, and then he introduces us to a stocky older woman, Kathy, who cares for the house year-round. She has stocked the house with an abundance of food. Gunner has a lot of money; way more than Fred does.

We sit by the pool and eat dinner, even though my body knows it is bedtime. Gunner has a huge party planned for Fred tomorrow, but I am unsure if I should be excited or nervous. For the rest of the day I read, relax, and enjoy watching Fred swim in a bathing suit that I wish were a lot smaller.

"You were born in New York City, right?" I ask Fred with a bad girl smirk, which perhaps Hawaii has taught me to do right.

"Yes, why?" His rugged face makes every part of me tingle.

"Well, it's after midnight there, so Happy Birthday."

"Oh, you wanna celebrate now?" Before I can answer he has me thrown over his shoulder.

"Goodnight," I yell to Gunner and Kelly.

"For you it will be," she yells back.

I spend hours devouring his magnificent body. It is a life altering feeling to have something so simple bring such joy, so at midnight, Hawaii time, I have to suggest we start our celebration all over again.

We are awake in bed the next morning, staring at each other like we do so often. "Happy Birthday, sexy," I say to him, still mastering the bad girl smirk. "I didn't buy you anything big and fancy because I haven't had much time to do any shopping. You keep a girl busy."

"I only want you happy. A happy Morgan is all I could ask for."

"Well, giving myself to you happily is easy to do. I wrote something for you though. I wrote it out in calligraphy and I painted the pictures too. I don't think I have the strength to read it, but I will."

Twenty-Eight Years
Twenty-Eight Things I Love

Your EYES
    The way they penetrate my soul
    The way they see the music
    The way they light up when we are together
Your MOUTH
    The way it moves when you kiss me
    The way it sings
    The way your lips part ever so slightly
Your HANDS
    The way they touch my skin
    The way they move across the piano
    The way they support me when I crave it most
Your BODY
    The way it moves in tight jeans and a black tee
    The way it shines undressed
    The way it fits perfectly with mine
Your MIND
    The way it thinks outside the box
    The way it sees me
    The way it goes blank and I think for you
Your HEART
    The way it pounds for me
    The way it skips beats for us
    The way it feels more than other hearts

Your SOUL
> The way it is light and dark
> The way it glows
> The way it loves me

I will love all of you for all the years to come.

Each bold word had a small image I painted. It was easy to paint his eyes, mouth, hands, and body. For his mind I painted a lilac branch, for his head I painted a heart with the beach in it, and for his soul I painted the word soul in Chinese, like his tattoos I love so much to trace.

I lean the frame against the nightstand and seconds later I'm tucked inside his embrace, and he makes slow sweet love to me again. Making love is more fitting than words. Afterwards we shower and head downstairs. Kelly and Gunner are finishing breakfast and they look nice together. Still, I am trying to decide if I could handle them being together. I love them both and would want that, but for some reason it isn't right. These thoughts fly out the back of my head when Kelly asks me if I am ready to leave.

"Yes," I say.

"Where are you going?" Fred snaps. "Want to eat first?"

"No, and we're not telling. We will be back later. Miss you." I kiss him and turn to leave.

"How can you miss him? You have been in bed with him for fourteen hours," Gunner says. He realized too late he was speaking out loud.

"I hope you get to feel this someday, Gunner. It compares to nothing. Take care of him while I'm out." I kiss Gunner on the cheek before we leave.

I already told Kelly and Gunner what I wanted to do today. They have both been very accommodating. Kelly and I are in a tripped out Porsche, since Gunner let her pick what she wanted to drive. We have the most expensive car for sure. I know that Gunner has at least eight cars between these two properties. I will start asking some questions, maybe start with how much money he inherited.

"You sure you want to do this?" she asks me as she parks the car.

"Very very sure." I sound as confident as my words because I want this deep down in my soul.

We are in the waiting area in the front when I ask her, "You and Gunner are getting along well?"

"We get along quite well. He is a good person, a friend."

"Oh, no sparks?"

"I don't think so. He is so attractive it's sort of intimidating. I thought maybe something would happen, but he is preoccupied with something. I don't want a fling. If I have a fling it can't be someone you are close to."

"Thanks, Kelly. You're too awesome," I say, tapping her leg as they call me to come back.

We return to the house later than expected because Kelly was having too much fun in the Porsche. Back at the house there is a driveway full of cars. Gunner sees us walk in the front door, and he rushes over. "Sorry, when your friends don't have a day job they tend to come by early."

"No explaining needed, Gunner. It's your house, and we are just guests."

"Morgan?" he says a little too harshly.

"Yeah?" I say, scrunching my nose.

"You know you are way more than a guest, right?"

"Oh, maybe. Thanks, Gunner."

"Fred went upstairs to change. How did everything go today?" he asks, changing the subject and I don't object.

"Good, and thanks again." I turn to go upstairs to change. I bought a skimpy dress and super high heels with Kelly's help for tonight. They will ensure I don't consider drinking.

"Hey, I missed ya," Fred says as he puts his guitar down and comes over to me. Apparently getting ready for his party meant making music to him. Thankfully he puts his hands on my shoulders when he kisses me. It's only been a few hours and we are kissing like it's been weeks.

"I'm gonna change. There are a lot of people here already."

"Yes, Gunner knows a lot of people."

"Yeah, and he seems so anti-social sometimes," I say, because I don't get Gunner sometimes.

"He prefers anti-social, but he does social like a socialite."

"Someday maybe we will figure him out."

"I doubt it."

I am second-guessing this dress. Kelly helped me get ready and she said I looked sexy, but my hair feels too fluffy and my make-up is way too heavy, but I feel safe behind the mask. I stand tall, wedge each foot into a heel, and walk out of the bathroom.

Fred is staring and I don't know if I should be turned on or mortified. "Wow, Morgan." He keeps his eyes wide open. "I can't take my eyes off you. Damn, you look so hot. So old. I dream of you being older, but I am not sure I actually want it."

"I can change."

"Hell, no. I plan on enjoying every minute of you all dressed up. Then enjoy it even more, and real slow, when I take it off you." He kisses me and I take his hand that is firmly planted on my ass and I cover it with mine. I push it down to my thigh. He runs it up my leg and under my dress, exactly what I wanted. When he realizes I don't have underwear on I pull away and walk to the door.

I start to open it, but stop and look back at him. "Hey, anything I should worry about tonight? Anyone who shouldn't know about us? Any chance Beth will show up?"

"First, no, nothing to worry about, but she is in Hawaii. A friend of Gunner's hangs out with her so Gunner asked. Gunner has security at the gate. She won't get in if she tries. Relax if you can." I would prefer staying locked in the bedroom all night. I want to take this dress off, wipe this make-up off, and hide in here with him. So I open the door and walk out.

I head downstairs looking for Kelly and Gunner. I sense I am standing out and I never enjoy being noticed. I see Kelly, all smiles, talking to an attractive man. I see chemistry between them, and her eyes are alive with joy. Perhaps this is what she sees between Fred and me.

"Hey, how's it going?" I say, squeezing her arm.

"Awesome! Morgan this is Steven Zemel." She introduces me to CrossRhoades' manager.

"Nice to meet you," I say, as I shake his thin but strong hand.

"You see Gunner around anywhere?" I ask Kelly.

"He was outside by the pool a few minutes ago."

"Thanks, I will leave you to what appeared to be a much more interesting conversation before I interrupted."

I turn to walk away, but Kelly grabs my wrist. "You okay?"

I shake my head and walk away. I can't say anything because I could end up crying. I can't cry in all this makeup. It would be a bigger mess than my heart is right now.

I find Gunner talking to an attractive woman. I almost don't want to interrupt them, but Gunner looks at me and doesn't turn back to her. He waves his hand to call me over. I pick up my pace, not sure why I am running to Gunner.

"Damn, you look beautiful, Morgan." He hugs me gently and kisses my cheek. "This is Sandra Storm. She sang "Don't Turn Around" with Fred on the last album."

"I knew you looked familiar. Pleasure to meet you." I reach my hand out to hers.

"Morgan has been writing some amazing pieces with us this summer."

"Thanks, but I don't know if I would say amazing." I see Fred walk outside and I am distracted by my attraction to him.

He is standing beside me when Sandra says, "Hello and Happy Birthday," with a warm friendly hug. I wish I could feel jealousy so I could feel something besides washed out and sad.

I have no idea how he can read me so well. It's a little unnerving, but wonderful at the same time. Gunner takes me by the elbow and says, "Morgan, I need your help. Can you come with me a minute?" I nod as he walks me through the nearest door and we are in a gaming room that I don't remember seeing yesterday. I lean against the wall for support. I might be hyperventilating for the first time in my life.

"Hey, you okay?" He holds my shoulders. He moves to lift my face by the chin.

"No, I can't breathe. I need to be outside. The ocean. Walk me to the water." I challenge myself to push out each word.

"Come, this way." He takes my hand and pulls me through a dark room and in less than a minute we are at the edge of the crashing waves. I take my shoes off and walk a few feet closer to the water. I collapse in the sand with Gunner at my side.

We sit next to each other, not touching, yet the comfort is as if Fred were holding me. I never would have believed I would find comfort in the form of Gunner Cross. I love that he can have no idea what is wrong, yet have the patience to wait until I am ready to talk.

"Let's go back. It's Fred's party, and I don't want to ruin it for him."

"If you aren't okay the party won't matter to him. All he wants is for you to be happy. He would send everyone packing in a second for you if that is what you wanted."

"Gunner, it scares me a little how well you know us."

We sit in silence another minute or two. I get up first. When we get back he instinctively holds my elbow so I can put these killer heels back on.

"I don't like you tall. Shorter is much more your thing."

I laugh and it feels healthy. "I needed that laugh, thanks again. Will they stop Beth from coming tonight?"

"Yes, Morgan. Security knows who she is. Go be with Fred. You have nothing to worry about. Trust me. He loves you. He needs you."

"Thank you again, Gunner. You have a way of caring for me unlike anything I have ever known."

"Morgan?" He stops talking but moves his mouth as if he has more to say.

"Yeah?"

"I would do anything for you. I mean it. You are the most amazing, strongest person I have ever met. You awe me. You have more maturity than anyone I know. You have taught me that age is just a number."

I hug him. There are no words to follow that up with. We get back and Fred is talking to more people I don't know. He looks painfully sad, and now I regret stepping away from him.

I walk up to him and put my hand on his lower back. He reaches his arm around to my side and I wince, but the relief in his expression makes me forget my own pain. He kisses my cheek and whispers in my ear, "I missed you, Jellybean. Are you okay?"

"I am now that I have your arm around me."

Soon enough I feel comfortable and the party is enjoyable. Being around people for a change isn't so bad. Hours later, there are still many people here when I find myself alone in the kitchen with him. "You have enough yet?" he whispers seductively in my ear.

"Enough of you, never, enough of the party, some time ago."

"Let's go to bed."

"You want to leave everyone? That seems a little rude."

"It's my party, and rock stars are rude, right? Come."

"Fred?" I pull him back.

"I need you, I can't stop thinking about the fact that you have nothing on under that dress, and about why you flinch every time I touch your side. You know my hand always ends up there. Let me fix this?"

I take my shoes off as we make a mad dash for the bedroom. Quickly we are safe and alone behind the locked door. His mouth is on mine when he pins me against the door. What a kiss. He has never needed me so bad. I realize he felt we were in jeopardy and he is scared. "I don't like you scared. I was upset. Beth freaked me out. I was hyperventilating and Gunner walked me to the water. You have one hell of a great best friend." I kiss him again. "Happy Birthday. I hope it wasn't too bad a day."

"It was the best, even with the bad stuff, because it started and ended with you. With you naked."

I smile bigger than I have all day. "What makes you so certain I will take my clothes off for you?"

He laughs at me.

"Am I really that easy?"

"No, Morgan, you are not easy. You simply know what you want and aren't afraid to get it. Why aren't you letting me touch your side? It's making me feel like you are pushing me away."

I have big tears welling in my eyes. This day has been long and emotional. "Sit on the bed." He does. I cross my arms and grab the hem of my dress and quickly take it off over my head. I have nothing on. He goes to touch me and I stop him.

"Did you get hurt?" He looks genuinely worried.

"It's your last birthday present." I turn to show him and he reaches out to touch me.

"What did you do?" he whispers, almost upset.

"It's the coordinates of Mantoloking and a lilac branch with today's date on it. I was torn about adding the words, but I wanted them. 'No regrets' is fitting. And now I got my first tattoo on your birthday just like you did." He is speechless and I know that feeling well. "Because you mean more to me than anything ever has and possibly ever will. I will never regret the tattoo or you, even if this ends, because I will always have this amazing love, one I fear will be the greatest of my life. I know you are going to break me and I have accepted it already."

He leans forward and kisses my belly, then his hands wrap around the small of my back. He looks up and his eyes are heavy, sadness and lust, an odd combo. I continue talking, "Sorry, to be a downer, but I have many emotions I don't know how to process. I love you. I love you like I didn't know a person could love another person. I was fine alone, but now I am afraid I will never be happy unless I have you." I inhale deeply, desperate for extra oxygen to deal with these emotions.

"Morgan, I want to make you happy…always." He kisses a trail of feather light kisses to my hip. "I never want to hurt you."

"I know. I never thought I would depend on someone else for my ability to breathe. And giving that responsibility to you means I give you me, all of me, but it means also I give you the ability to destroy me. Destroy all of me." He has nothing left to say; I don't either. I slowly undress him and we make love.

It is incredibly late when I finally feel like myself again. Fred and I haven't slept yet. "You want to sleep, Jellybean?"

"No. I'm afraid to wake up and be sad again."

"Let's stay up all night. Come shower with me."

The water is warm and it's making me sleepy. But Fred knows where to put his tongue and fingers to ensure I am very much awake. After we are both physically satisfied once again, we stand under the water staring at each other. I turn away so I don't get my tattoo too wet, because I want to preserve it as long as I can.

"I really love you with all my heart."

"I know, Jellybean. I love you more than you know. Do other people love like this or have sex like this?" He smirks and it warms my heart.

"No one I know does, but maybe someone out there does."

I yawn, and Fred says, "Come, let's sleep. It's the middle of the day back home. You will never get back on schedule for school."

"Oh, shut up. Don't remind me. It makes me feel five."

"You must have been so cute when you were five."

"Ask my mom. She will take the pictures out."

"I will definitely ask her. Sorry I hurt you. I know I can be more for you. I have to try harder."

I don't know what to say. I let him squeeze me tight and I fall asleep. My heart is so wrapped up in him, it will be completely destroyed when I have to separate it from his.

We wake up and staying up all night is almost as bad as drinking. We get up with silent slow movements and creep downstairs to find Gunner and Kelly laughing in the kitchen.

"Welcome back to the real world," Gunner says to us both.

"Nothing about this place or you are the real world," I say to him. "I feel hung over."

"Here, eat. You didn't eat last night, and now it's two in the afternoon. You are going to waste away. All that sex and no food can kill a person." Gunner laughs.

"Gunner, that's enough," I say, freaked out he knows I didn't eat. I know he is well aware of the sex I partake in.

Kelly says Steve is coming by any minute, so she is pacing near the main entrance. I am feeling lazy, so I tell her I am going to lie down outside. I see Gunner at the far end of the pool in a lounge chair, and I decide to sit as far away as I can. I prefer being closer to Gunner rather than irritated by him, but it also scares me because I know he is the one person who can set me straight if I need it. I hope I never do because it will be ugly.

I can't concentrate on my book, so I close my eyes. All I can see with my eyelids shut is images of Fred. He is ingrained in my memory like something I have taken a great deal of time to study. Kelly and Steve come sit by me and snap me out of my daydream. The three of us talk for a while and I can see why Kelly has taken such an interest in him.

They are talking about dinner tonight and all is well until Steve asks me, "Would you and Fred like to join us?"

"That is so nice of you, but you should go alone."

"Okay." He is surprised. Making me feel bad.

"Morgan doesn't feel comfortable being with Fred when he is recognized. Maybe if we are ever all in Jersey we can do something together." Kelly says, making me love her even more.

"I understand," he says to me.

I was going to close my eyes to erase some of the pressure I have felt this week, when I see something I hoped I would never see. "Holy shit." I might have said it a little too loud. Kelly and Steve are looking at me as if I have two heads. Gunner doesn't flinch; his headphones must be on super high.

"What's wrong?" Kelly says as she looks back towards the house. "Who is that?"

"Beth," I answer.

"His ex-girlfriend Beth?" she asks.

"No."

"But it looks like her."

"It is her, but she is his wife now," I tell her, trying to keep the putrid emotion I feel out of my voice.

Kelly and Steve's mouths are hanging open as Beth and Fred come out of the house. They are walking toward us so I get up and walk towards Gunner, pretending I didn't see them. The song "Insensitive" is blasting from the speakers. It should stop me because I am about to be very insensitive. I fear nothing can stop me now that I have my mind set on evil.

I lie down over Gunner, one knee between his legs, and one leg still on the ground. I take one ear bud out of his ear and lean down to whisper, "Don't move, don't talk." He looks up at me with a slight fear coupled with a desire to laugh. "Beth is at the other side of the pool with Fred. I'm taking a page out of your playbook and sending her on the wrong trail. Make her think it's you and me, but really I want to piss Fred off." I never knew I could be vindictive. He stares at me and I can't read him. "Gunner, I am going to lie down on top of you now. Stay still."

I lower my body until it is flush against his, but I put as much weight on my arms as I can. "I'm going to push the lever so this chair reclines. Once you are flat, I'll lean down and kiss you. It will be the hottest most sensual kiss you have ever felt. I want them to want to turn away, but they won't be able to. When my tongue slips between your lips, I want you to push my ass down into you. Then I will get up, dive in the pool, swim to the other side and introduce myself to Beth as if she means nothing to me. I will say I am sorry now, because I'm not sure you will ever talk to me again after this stunt."

He says nothing. I can't tell if he is terrified or excited, or both. I push the button on the chair and my mouth crashes into his at the same time. His lips are full and soft, and he parts them for my tongue to explore his. As instructed his hands cover my white bikini bottom, each on their own ass cheek as he pulls me down against him. He is hard, so fucking hard and big, I shouldn't be thinking about it because this is wrong. I am enjoying it a little too much, but not enough to forget how wrong it is that Fred's wife is on the other side of the pool. I kiss him longer than I intended. I thought I would find it repulsive, but Gunner sure can kiss.

I open my eyes and look at a man who by all means did not hate what I did. I get up and turn around. Good thing I dive into the pool and not the pavement, since my legs are weak. I swim to the shallow end of the pool, walk up the stairs, like a six-foot-tall Victoria's Secret Model. I stand taller than ever before as I walk right up to Beth. Extending my hand to her I say, "Nice to finally meet you, Beth. I'm Morgan."

"Hi." She appears tongue-tied as she shakes my hand and I taste bile in my mouth.

"Sorry, I can't stay and chat, but I have somewhere to be." I can't look at him because I don't want to see his eyes. They would destroy me instantly.

Thankfully they don't ask where, because my story isn't planned out. I run upstairs and into the bathroom, lock the door behind me and slide to the ground in a ball of tears. Way too much just happened. Twenty minutes later, still in tears, I hear the knob jiggle. Then a knock. And another knock. I get up and turn the shower on. I am determined to be alone. I want nothing but to be alone. This time in the shower I don't take any care to keep my tattoo dry. I don't care what shape it's in because my heart is a mess.

It's around seven when I have enough strength to leave the bathroom. I walk into a cold empty bedroom and grab my pajamas. I take my sorry ass to the empty kitchen. I don't know what I am looking for until I find the wine. I grab a bottle of red. I open it and head downstairs.

I sit down in the sand as the sun is setting. Drinking half the bottle of wine on an empty stomach has done nothing to help. I watch the sun disappear into the ocean, just as I watched it appear over the Atlantic three months ago with Fred, the day orange became his favorite color again. But this time I am alone. Drunk and about to fall over into the sand and cry myself silly, I feel warm strong hands on my head. I wish they belonged to Fred. Gunner sits down next to me and lifts the bottle of wine up to the light that is still glowing from the horizon.

"You must be feeling a little better." He laughs, but it's a laugh that sounds more like he wants to cry with me. He wraps his arm around me and squeezes me to him. We sit for some time, not moving. I am so sad, but I feel a glimmer of relief coming to the surface because Gunner isn't livid with me for kissing him.

"Let's take a ride along the coast in one of your convertibles. You up for it?" I hope he wants to be with me because I need some distance and now I can't drive myself. I haven't even asked him if Fred is really with her. I know I don't have to. If he wasn't he would have been waiting for me on our bed when I finally came out of the bathroom.

Gunner stands and takes my hand. He carries the empty wine bottle for me. He leaves it downstairs before we head out to the garage. Still numb, I climb into his silver Jaguar convertible. He backs the car out of the garage and puts the roof down. Either he is skilled at this or I am very drunk because he has such finesse tonight. Whether it's the wine, the ocean air, the view, or the fact that even after what I did today, Gunner is still my friend, something is helping. I put my feet up on the dash and close my eyes, relaxing a little.

"I am going to do everything I can to not let him break me."

Gunner doesn't respond but he is humming.

"I want him to know he can't string us both along. I am worth more than that. It would kill me to leave him, but if he can't leave her I will do it. But then I think what would be worse. My options are having half of him or none of him. Gunner, I don't know, maybe I should kick him in the balls to get the frustration out. But I love his balls – I don't want to hurt them."

Gunner stops the car and reaches into the glove box. He takes out a pen and paper; a writer is always ready I suppose. "Come." He gets out of the car, leaving the headlights on so we have some light. It's rockier here than at his house and it's even more desolate. "I want to see what an angry, frustrated, broken Morgan can write."

"Oh, Gunner, I don't know."

"Please? I will never mention what happened this afternoon again, and I will never hold it against you if you just try. Just me and you, the waves and sand, your broken heart and your creative mind."

"Geez, Gunner, you are poetic without even trying. Why don't you write something? You must have some pain you can channel from somewhere."

"I have a lot of pain, but let me hear yours. It will help you through it."

"I am too drunk. Write for me."

We sit in between the big rocks. I throw out a ton of ideas at Gunner, but I can't piece anything together with a rhythm. "Keep going," he tells me.

"But, Gunner, none of this makes sense."

"It all makes sense, it's perfect, and I can work with this. Give me more." I give him what little I have left in my head and collapse back on the sand.

"I am drunk."

"I know. I am going to write a song out of this. Thank you. Consider us even?"

"Yes. Can we stay out here forever? I'm afraid to go back."

"What are you afraid of?"

"That he will tell me he is going back to her, that we are done. Instantly done. One minute together, one minute apart." I lean my head back and stare at the stars, looking for answers. Gunner just sits patiently, waiting for me to finish. "I am not done yet with him, I never want to be done."

"Oh, Morgan, he won't go back to her. He is just calming her down. She is not levelheaded like you. But if you leave him, he will run back to her because he is weak with her. It's paralyzing to watch. He is controlled by her, yet she makes him out of control."

"This is too much for my drunk seventeen-year-old brain to take. Let's go back so I can face my fate." Gunner drives home a lot slower than he drove up. He stops outside the garage and kills the engine. He moves my face again with his fingertips on my chin, forcing me to look at him.

"If you need anything, anything at all, I'll always be here for you. We had a weird start, but Morgan, you are one of the most remarkable people I know. You are a true friend and I hope you can say that about me too. Fred loves you more than I have ever seen another person love someone.

Be strong and confident, give a little, and go easy on him. He isn't as strong as you. Anytime, anywhere you need anything. I want you guys to always be together."

"I want to cry, but every ounce of me is exhausted. I am ready to go inside." We are near the door when I stop Gunner from moving any farther. "What if he isn't back? What do I do if he is still with her?"

"He is back. The car he took is here, and the light in your room is on."

"Oh," I say. Even my voice sounds numb to me.

"Good luck, Morgan." He kisses the top of my head and walks away. He hangs his head again the way he did the night of the Fourth of July party and once again it breaks me in a way I can't handle.

I get to the bedroom door. I pause and inhale deeply, wishing I still felt drunk, instead of stone cold sober. I turn the handle and Fred is sitting in the chair across the room, looking beat and worn to shreds. He stands up as I walk in and he is wrapping his arms around me in seconds. For the first time I had forgotten how good it feels to be in his embrace, this hug feels new but also so familiar.

"Where were you?" he asks. "I was so worried."

"Where was I? Don't you think I should be the one asking that?" I snap. His smile teeters on the edge of laughter, but nothing about this night is laughable. "So, where were you?" I ask, shocked at how bitchy I sound.

"I fought with her at her friend's house the whole time. It was hell. I wouldn't have gone but she said she knew what I was doing and I had to make sure she didn't know anything about you. So I went. Which was stupid of me because she knows nothing about you, or your age. And what you did with Gunner made it super clear that you were by no means with me. She doesn't have any idea it's you."

There is too much going through my head. I feel drunk again. Drunk on confusing love. He grabs my face and kisses me forcefully enough to get me hot fast. Fighting the desire, I say, "I just need some sleep. I'm beyond exhausted." He lifts me behind the knees, carries me to bed, and we slide into the cold sheets together.

"Do you want to sleep in your pajamas?"

"Just tonight. It will help me keep my hands to myself. Just tonight.

Tomorrow I will try to be me again. At least I hope I will be me again. I like the me I used to be, not the me I am right now."

"I like you no matter who you are."

"Even the me who kissed Gunner today?"

"No, I hated that. It was creepy and wrong. I wanted to be jealous and angry, but watching you kiss him was a fine line between hot and sick. You are the sexiest damn thing in the world and seeing you kiss my best friend should have repulsed me, but I pretended it was me. I freaked out for a minute thinking maybe you two did have a thing going. But when I saw your eyes when you came up to me and Beth, I realized you did it to throw her off and it had the benefit of getting to me too."

"You know me so well."

"And now Gunner knows you a little better than I wish he did."

"Gunner is fine. He isn't even pissed."

"No guy on this earth would ever be pissed being kissed like that, even if it was for show."

"I don't get men. Gunner and I talked tonight. I gave him some song ideas when I didn't want to, and he agreed to never talk about today again."

"Let's never talk about it again either."

"Will you kiss me again? It might take a lot of kisses to erase the one I gave Gunner." I smile up at Fred as I tickle his ribs. He starts to laugh but finds the strength to tickle me. Feeling seventeen is exactly what I need. Once his hands move up my shirt and his thumb grazes my nipple I stop laughing because I am weak to his touch. "Please make love to me. That should help erase the day."

"You sure? I don't want to hurt you more than I already have."

"I'm sure. Wash the hurt away. Please. Make me forget."

That is exactly what he does with his body. He fixes most of me in one night. But I fear a part of me will always be unfixable and if I end up feeling this way over and over, eventually I will have nothing left to damage.

Chapter Twenty-Six

Come September

THE REST OF the trip is uneventful. Exactly what I needed. The sunshine is warm, the breeze is cool, and Beth isn't mentioned. I leave Fred in the shower and head downstairs alone the day after all the Beth drama. I find Kelly and Gunner in the kitchen talking casually over lunch. I don't have a clue where to begin to try to explain this to her.

"Hey, wanna take a walk?' I ask her.

"Yes, let's. Someone needs to tell me why you two were kissing yesterday."

"Kissed. It was just one," I say, correcting her as we walk outside.

"Who cares? It was hot and got me really bothered."

We walk past the pool to the beach. "Sorry, I didn't tell you everything. I hope you still trust me."

"I trust you, but the everything – do you mean the wife or the kiss?"

"The wife. The kiss was fake, a distraction for the wife."

"Damn, this is as fucked up as a rock star lifestyle should be, I suppose. The wife is real and Morgan, that kiss was real too."

"No, it wasn't. What did Gunner tell you?"

"He told me what you told me, but it was way too hot to be faked. I mean damn, you made that boy melt into that chair."

"I thought he would never forgive me, but he did. I'm lucky I have both of you."

"And we are lucky to have you, but watch yourself with Gunner. I think he feels differently than you do. What are you doing about the wife, and when did you know?"

"From the beginning. I met him the day they married. I found out the first time I stayed at his house."

"Ouch! Do you think it is better you knew from the start?"

"I don't know. How do I get mad at him when he loves me so much, but also he can't love me on some level because I'm seventeen. All of this is one giant fuck-up, but it's so damn perfect, nothing could get me to stop."

"Morgan, I understand. I hope you keep your head above water, and I will always be here for you."

"Thanks." I hug her tight. "How is Steve?"

"Oh. My. Awesome. I don't know, it's different. He is easy to talk to. Easy to kiss. I am ready to move to be closer to him."

"You serious?"

"Yes, I have one year of school left, but if this lasts, I will move for him. He is coming to Jersey for Labor Day weekend."

"Kelly, I am so happy for you, but we lied to Brooke."

"It's gonna be okay. We will make it all okay."

We sit and watch the ocean for a while, both of us stuck in our own heads, before going inside. As much as everything is sort of back in place, I am not sure I will ever return to Hawaii.

* * *

By the end of August, Fred and I are back to our typical behavior. We get into the groove of sex, napping, and writing again. Almost, as if Beth never made that appearance, but now my fear of her is greater than my fear of returning to school. One afternoon while Gunner and I are outside talking he tells me he is having a party on Saturday.

"So, Morgan, invite anyone. The party will be huge so you can get lost in the crowd."

I laugh, as I lie in the hammock, and he pushes me out of frustration from my laughing.

"Why are you laughing?" Now I really can't stop.

He pulls the hammock to a screeching stop and I fear flying out of it, but instead he lies down next to me. I stop laughing and look up at him. I can't help it – I start laughing again.

"Morgan, I am not sure if I like it or not when you finally act your age. What is so funny?"

I just laugh even harder, but I stop suddenly and look dead on into his iridescent cat colored eyes. "Oh, Gunner, sometimes I act younger than my real age. I needed a comic relief moment."

"Why?"

"Because you said huge and I have suppressed everything about that day in Hawaii."

"Oh my, Morgan, are you drunk?"

"No."

"High?"

"No, but I will try it someday."

"You have never had pot?"

"Nope. How did this switch from talking about the word huge to pot?"

"I don't know, but all aspects of this conversation should end."

"Okay, I guess I will invite Brooke and Ryan. Kelly has Steve coming to visit, but I will ask her too."

"Really, he is coming to see her?"

"He is."

"That is cool. I like them together."

"Me too. I kept thinking she should be with you, but that isn't right, and I don't know why. And I don't know what bothers me more; that I don't want that or that I don't know why I don't like the idea of you two together."

He leans over and stares at me, a stare I have never seen from Gunner, and for the first time in a long time he makes me slightly uncomfortable. "We need to write more, just you and me. I wrote a song from your ideas, and it's amazing. I want to pull more out of you."

"I never want to hear that song. And maybe get me high next time, to see what comes out of this mouth."

"Maybe. When you are eighteen."

Chapter Twenty-Seven
High by the Beach

I HAVE THE USUAL nerves in my stomach that I get every time I have to lie to people in my life. It is only my brother, Faith, and Brooke. What is wrong with me that I don't tell them? Telling Kelly was a relief; even having her know about Beth was helpful. I can't take it further and tell Ryan and Brooke.

I change into a simple, short, green sundress I bought when I was shopping with Kelly. Fred walks in the bathroom so I turn the hair dryer off and put it on the counter without losing eye contact with him in the mirror. He looks extra sexy today. His hair has lightened a lot from the sun and his eyes seem like they are full of that same sunlight.

He reaches around me to hand me a large jewelry box, unwrapped, but with a fancy green bow. "The bow matches my dress," I say, taking the box.

"What is inside does too. I love how in sync we always are." I open the box to find a bracelet –probably platinum – and it holds green gemstones all the way around. It's simple but magnificent.

"It's peridot, my birthstone, and there are seventeen stones linked together. I want you to think about nothing but me every time you see your wrist."

"Fred, it's stunning, but I don't need any reminders to think about you, and only you. You do know that, right?"

"I do, but I am human, and you are just too good for me."

"No, I'm not and I promise to think about you always, whether it is on my wrist or not. Now let's get out of here so we can get home. I'd much rather be tangled up in bed with you than at a party."

"Let's stay home."

"Don't say that. You know I will."

"Okay, let's go. We can make it an early night."

"Yes, please."

Gunner's house is packed with at least 200 people. He wasn't kidding when he said I could get lost in the crowd. Fred is holding my hand when we make our way toward the kitchen and find Gunner, Kelly, and Steve talking. Kelly comes over and hugs me tight. She tells me Brooke, Ryan, and Faith arrived a while ago and she has no idea where they went off to. We both laugh because in our world this party is not normal. Someday this may become my normal.

Fred takes my hand and leads me outside. "How do you always know what I need?"

"I don't, it's natural. I don't even think, I just do. Want a drink?" he asks as he rubs his hand on the small of my back.

"Water. It's all I can handle right now."

We sit relaxed in the backyard talking. There are still a lot of people around, but it's much less confining than inside. Brooke comes outside, runs over and flings herself at me.

"I missed you so much this summer! I can't wait for school so I get to see my best friend again." I cringe and hope no one heard her. I do miss her, but I will miss Fred way worse.

Fred comes back with two waters and sits next to Brooke. "Water?" she says. "Let's get drunk."

"Maybe later, but you go ahead and get trashed," I say, not sure what I plan on doing.

"I am totally getting smashed. Gunner said we could stay here. He must have fifty bedrooms."

"More like eight, but this a sickly huge house, isn't it?"

"Yeah, like yeah. I need another drink. You want anything?" she asks us.

"No," we say in unison.

She leaves and I realize I have been holding my breath. This is stupid. I am not a fan of lying, or maybe dishonesty is a better term. "Should we head inside and mingle?" I ask Fred.

"Not unless you want to."

"It's the last thing I want."

"Want a drink yet?"

"No, I want to smoke."

"A cigarette? Really?"

"No, a joint."

"Seriously? I never expected that from you."

"I know."

"Be right back." He returns minutes later, taking a joint and lighter out of his pocket. Fred takes a hit and passes it to me. I start to laugh before it even hit's my lips. "It's supposed to be funny after you smoke it, not before."

"Oh, Fred, everything since April has been funny in its own twisted way."

It takes longer to affect me than I expected, but before I know it, my green dress is glowing, I can't stop laughing, and my feet are in Fred's lap. I even let him trace circles with his fingers over my bare legs. Kelly and Steve find us in a fit of laughter when they sit down on the ground near the wicker couch we are on.

"What is so funny? You are acting weird," she says to me, squinting her eyes.

"She is just laughing," Steve says, sounding a little irritated with Kelly.

"Steve, she knows I don't touch Fred when her sister and my brother are around."

"Morgan, did you drink something?" she asks.

"Why don't you touch him when they are around?" Steve asks.

"Too many questions. Because they don't know we are together, and I'm really fucking high." I laugh again. Even the word high sounds funny.

"Oh, because he is married?" Steve whispers.

"No, not that. Can I tell you another secret?"

"Do I want another one?"

I lean over and whisper in his ear. "Kelly has kept too many secrets. She shouldn't have to keep any from you. I am seventeen, so they can't know."

"Holy shit." He turns to Kelly. "You are still twenty-one, right?"

"Yes."

I keep laughing and somehow end up in Fred's lap. I don't remember anything else of my conversation with Steve and the next thing I know, it's Ryan and Faith sitting with us. I am not sure I could ever get used to this, but not caring about anything is freeing.

Ryan is bombed, but after some time he does say to Fred, "What are you doing with my sister in your lap?" Fred doesn't answer him and I don't think he even cares.

"Has anyone checked on Brooke?" I ask, unsure whom I ask. The house is a little emptier now at least. "Fred, I have to sleep. Help me find a place to sleep, please?" I don't know why I say please; it sounds desperate.

"Goodnight," he says to them as I take his hand and pull him inside. I can't believe my own behavior. They are too drunk to even notice. We get in the house and Brooke is still playing some drinking game. She waves to us and doesn't care that my hand is wrapped in Fred's. I finally get to the landing and I stop when I see Gunner. He is sitting alone on the floor at the end of the hall, near his bedroom.

I whisper in Fred's ear, "Which room are we sleeping in?" He points to the door to his right. "I will be right back, I have to tell Gunner something." I let go of Fred's hand.

I crouch down by Gunner and say, "Getting me high would not be very beneficial for writing unless you want to write some stand-up comedy. Goodnight, Gunner, and thanks for a great party." I walk away and he says nothing. He has that sad look in his eyes that kills me a little every time I see it. It seems marijuana makes me funny and bold. I turn around and walk back to Gunner. I lift his chin with my index finger like he does to me. "I want you to find your joy, I hurt when you hurt, and I have no clue whatsoever what would make you happy. Give me a clue. I want to be the friend you are to me."

"Go to bed, Morgan. When I can tell you, I will, but please sleep off your high. It's freaking me out." He gets up and walks me to the bedroom door and nudges me inside.

The room we are in could fit ten of my bedrooms in it. Fred is only wearing a smile when I find him on the bed. I double-check that I locked the door, lift my dress off over my head, and slide my underwear off before I get to the bed. I never wore a bra today, and I have no idea when I took my shoes off, but I love being instantly naked. I quickly climb into bed with Fred.

His body is extra hot. I don't know if I am coming down from my high, or if this is just not funny, because I have completely stopped laughing. My heart is beating extra fast, and for the first time ever, making love to Fred slows it down. High or not, being with Fred, in bed, any bed, compares to nothing else.

I wake the next morning, and the sun is pouring in the bedroom. It takes me a few minutes to realize I am not in Fred's bed. I have a sudden urge to get out of this room before anyone else wakes up, but Fred has a firm grip on my right boob.

"Why is it always the boobs?" I ask, having no intention of moving his hands off my boob.

He laughs. "Why not the boobs? How are you feeling?"

"Fine, you?"

"Great, I have a boob in my hand. No, really, do you feel okay?"

"I'm fine, but I know I did and said things I shouldn't have. I hope everyone was too drunk to remember."

"They were, except Steve, but it's best he knows. They look perfect together and they should not have lies between them."

"I agree. She said when she is done with school she will move to California for him. At first I thought that was sudden, but I fell for you that fast, so who am I to judge?"

"Let's get dressed and get some food." He changes the subject quickly. We start to put our clothes back on from last night. I don't know what will be worse, wearing the same dress or having someone realize I didn't sleep in it.

"I forgot getting high makes you hungry. I wasn't that hungry last night, maybe I was hungry for only you?"

"Oh, Morgan, every time I get my clothes on you make me want to take them off again." He moans and kisses me gently. "Come downstairs before I rip that dress off you this time and you have to wear Gunner's clothes home."

"Now that would not shock anyone."

"Let's eat and head home so I can have my way with you again. I don't want to talk about what they think you and Gunner have going on."

Only Gunner is in the kitchen when we get downstairs. "Do you ever sleep?" I ask him, really wondering.

"Of course I do, but I wake up early no matter what. I nap more than you know too. Hungry?" he asks us both.

"I will cook. This kitchen is so hot I need to get my hands all over it."

The three of us eat in silence. I have never felt more at home. Such a strange combination of people, but for now, for me, it's the only way I want it to be. We finish eating before anyone wakes up, so Fred drives us back to his house to change. As usual, it takes a lot longer than planned to shower and change since our naked bodies always require so much attention.

We make it back to Gunner's and only Kelly and Steve are up. The silence is becoming uncomfortable. "Steve, sorry about last night. I hope you understand," I finally spit out.

"Don't apologize. If I hadn't gotten to know you first, I might have been appalled, but nothing about you is immature. Well, maybe the way you laugh when you are high is." He laughs a little and I don't laugh at all, to get him to laugh again.

"Thanks," I say as Ryan joins us. "Hey, you survived the night?" I turn to ask him.

"Yes, it's the day I'm worried about. Faith is a mess."

"Yikes, let me know if I can help. Anyone see Brooke?"

"She is on the floor still in the bathroom upstairs."

"You guys all drank too much. No more parties at Gunner's," I say, mostly because I can't handle having them here.

"Well, I am going for a run," I say to break the silence, and I walk out the front door.

When I get back everyone is lying around. I change and join Fred and Gunner in the pool. "Is it weird that it's always me and you and Gunner together? It's starting to look as if we are all together," I say to Fred, wishing I had the courage to kiss him.

"That is a horrible thought. I still have flashbacks of you kissing him that destroy me."

"Why? Because I pretended your best friend was my boyfriend, or because I did it with your wife watching?"

"Damn, Morgan, you say things that should piss me off. Then I realize how smart you are and all I want is to fuck you senseless."

"Well, you know you can do that anytime you wish."

"Oh, yeah. Dare me and I will take you over my shoulder and upstairs."

"You know I want to. I had enough pubic displays of affection for my comfort this weekend. In a few hours we will be alone. I have seventy-two hours before I go back to my parents. I want every second of it, alone with you. I don't even want to write,or eat. Just you and me because I love you so damn much. Fred, it hurts just to think about being apart." He turns to me and hugs me tight. I need this hug so bad I don't care who sees it or what they think. Once he let's go, I swim to Gunner and knock him off his raft.

* * *

As planned, I spend every second naked and rolling around in bed with Fred before going back to school. How am I am supposed to go from his bed to a high school classroom?

We get back to my parents' house after dinner on Wednesday. My parents are easy to be with and have accepted whatever it is they think is going on between Fred and me. I wish Ryan were here. We have become a lot closer since I met Fred.

"So, Morgan, you ready for school?" Dad asks me, and I don't know how to answer.

"No," is all I say.

"Honey, it will be fine. It's always tough to go back after summer break," Mom says, trying to comfort me.

"Yes, but this one is even harder." I want to say more but with Dad here I can't do it.

Like always, Fred sleeps in the guest room, and I don't know how I bring myself to not sneak down. We drove up in my Mustang on Wednesday since his Jeep has been at my parents' house all summer. We plan on leaving after school Friday in two vehicles. It's only two nights apart but it feels like an eternity. I go downstairs Thursday morning, and my parents and Fred are already in the kitchen. This situation is still odd for me.

"Good morning," bursts loudly from my mouth. "I am going to pick up Brooke. I will see you all later." I turn and walk away, not knowing what else to freakin' do.

I get to Brooke's house and feel like she has enough upbeat energy for us both. I wish school did that to me still. I can't even believe how much I have moved past my own years. Once at school, there are a few too many people interested in my car. Damn, I hate attention. I say thanks since

I can't find it in me to lie any more than I already have. Lucky for me, Brooke fully intends to keep my secrets.

* * *

I walk in the house after school and it is too quiet. I want to yell his name, but it will be more fun to find him on my own.

He is lying in my bed, naked, at least for all the parts I can see. He looks even hotter in my bed than he does in his. "What are you doing?" I say, but I still walk over toward him as I take my shirt off.

"I never came in your bed."

"Six words are all it takes to make me melt."

"Damn, you count fast."

"Bet I can come faster."

"Oh, no, I want you slow."

He climbs out of the bed naked. He stares me in the eye as he undoes the zipper on my white jeans. They fall to the floor in one movement. My hands are running through his hair when he removes my underwear and leads me back to the bed. The door is locked, the window open, we can hear if a car pulls in, and I am still paranoid, but not paranoid enough to stop.

I climb on top of him and kiss him silly before I line my body up with his. He sinks slowly and sensually deep into me. No matter what bed we are in, we are the same, but damn if it's not a little dirtier in here.

Unfortunately, I have had sex in this bed with Ben, but fortunately, it is a whole lot better with Fred. A whole lot better. I am constantly listening for a car, but it doesn't take long for Fred to make me forget. All I feel is his body, his skin, his relentless pounding of my body, thrust after thrust. Almost without warning, I spiral out of control around him. My body succumbs to his, my toes curling, and my ears hearing nothing but the beat of my heart and the moans of his pleasure. I am eternally drowning in an abyss of his flesh.

Chapter Twenty-Eight
Broken

PURE BLISS TAKES over every cell in my body as we head back to Fred's house on Friday. We didn't even wait for my parents to get home from work. I see studio trucks in the street and suddenly want a place to hide. I am a little nervous about strangers working on the recording studio seeing me here. I head upstairs immediately to get my homework done.

I sit on the couch by the fireplace in the bedroom to finish my history. Gunner startles me when he speaks from the doorway. "So, did you survive school?"

"Physically, yes, mentally, not even close."

"What are you working on?" he says, walking over to sit with me.

"I have a little calculus left. If I don't do it now I will probably be trying to do it on the ride back."

"You are really smart, aren't you?"

"I don't know about that. I'm decent at many things but not great at any one thing. I hope college and life can teach me something."

"What do you like to learn about?"

"Music and writing. Being with you and Fred is the best education I could ask for."

"Real world knowledge!" He smiles that smirk that makes everyone assume he is the worst of the bad boys.

"Sort of, I guess. To me this still isn't the real world."

"You going to college?" he asks, not commenting on the fact that I still find hanging out with him to be surreal.

"Yeah, I am."

"Where?"

"I don't know. I always imagined I would go to California, like my parents, but right now I don't know. I wish I could settle on Rutgers, so I can be here in Jersey, but that is a year away. Who knows how my life will change in the next year. It sure has changed a lot from a year ago."

"I know you will make the decision that works best for you. You are smart, and you know yourself very well."

"Thanks, Gunner, you always have the nicest words, but I fear now my judgments may be clouded by love."

Fred comes up and joins us a second after I stop talking. "You two hungry?" he asks, and I can tell he didn't hear what I just said.

"Yes," we both say as I close my book.

I am elated here at the shore. I haven't thought about school and I have my lover to lose time with. Fred and I have a wonderful weekend alone, well mostly alone. Gunner left Friday night after we ate and he has returned now to watch football.

We are watching the Jets play the Colts, and as much as I love football, I find myself stuck inside my own head. A moment of confusion comes over me. How the hell did I get here? I have watched hundreds of football games and somehow on this Sunday, I am with two hot men, who happen to be in a highly successful band. I consider pinching myself, but I have already been caught doing that.

Fred and I are planning on leaving after the game ends, but I wish a rogue wave would wash his road out and I could be stuck here for a few days. He is going to drive home with me tonight and Gunner is going to come get him on Tuesday morning, since they have a meeting in the city for the new album.

Next week I will try to get my parents to let me leave here early on Monday mornings instead of heading home on Sunday nights. I am already so lucky, I don't want to push my luck, but I know I will because I need all I can get of Fred. It is a feeling of needing every second possible before the bomb goes off. He has done nothing, besides not divorcing his wife, to make me feel this way. It's my instincts getting one up on my heart. Hopefully, I will find a way to make this work one way or another.

"So, Gunner, I wouldn't have thought you were an American Football fan," I say.

"Why not?" he asks.

"Well, the rest of the world watches soccer and in New Zealand, Sunday afternoon football would be on TV Monday morning."

"It's no fun hanging with a wise ass. I never watched American Football until I moved here. I have little understanding of how the game is played or who the teams are." He is laughing, but he might be pissed.

"Sorry. Didn't mean to out ya. You are somewhat of a mystery to me. Just trying to understand you. I can teach you all about football. My dad and Ryan made sure I understood it at a young age."

We watch the rest of the game and Fred says nothing about Gunner's admission to not knowing much about football. I am curious why he hasn't added to our conversation, but I don't say any more. The Jets lose in overtime but it means I was able to stay a little longer today.

Fred drives so I can finish my homework in the car. I hope my grades don't suffer. I will have a tough time with my parents if they do. Having Fred at my house is becoming more natural and easy for me. Staying away from him while he is in a different bed is not any easier though, but I still do it.

Week after week we fall into the same pattern. My parents have allowed me to leave Fred's on Mondays and I head back down on Friday's. It is still hard to live a double life, so to say, but I have become used to it. I don't think much about it anymore.

Everyone at school understands that I have a job, and that is why I am no longer hanging out with them. My generic answer is that I help at my dad's office because I want to take it over one day. It's a huge lie, but I have become comfortable with it, which scares me a little too. I have to do what I have to do to get what I want. I wonder who the hell I am. When did lying become my new normal?

* * *

The weather turns cool quickly as October slides in. Fall is supposed to be cool, but it seems extra cold. I don't need an excuse to stay wrapped up in Fred, but I still use it. On the last Friday of October, we are sitting on the

couch, only the fire is lit, no TV, no lights, and no moon. I love the darkness when I am not alone.

A feeling of peace and calm washes over me. It's an odd sensation,
and I don't know what to make of it. I crawl across to Fred and lie against
him, between him and the couch. He is comfort. I fall asleep and the next
thing I know the sun is hitting me right in the eyes.

I wake, my movement wakes Fred too, but he never minds when I wake
him. "Good morning, Jellybean. I guess we were tired last night, huh?"

"Yeah, I feel weird. I don't remember sleeping."

"I can make you forget a lot of things," he says.

"You sure can." I kiss his beautiful mouth. "I feel off, something isn't
right, or it's too right. I don't know – I feel something I can't explain."

"Hey, come here." He slides me over so I am flush against him. "Want
to talk? Did you have a bad dream?"

"No, I felt this way when we fell asleep. It was odd. I felt so peaceful,
but I felt that it wasn't a good thing. It was conflicting. Then we fell asleep
and now the feeling of something unknown is weighing on me." He hugs
me tight.

"What should we do to make you feel better?"

"I don't know."

"Eat, run, walk, talk, shower, call Kelly, call home, yoga, read, do
homework. Our lives are boring. Lucky for us we have great sex."
He laughs.

I laugh back. "I want to laugh."

He doesn't miss a beat. He is tickling me out of control and has
flipped me underneath him on the couch; I cannot escape. I don't want to
either. His hands on me, no matter what they are doing, can fix anything.
As always, laughter and touching lead to kissing and labored breathing.
Passion is so intense with Fred, and even the most daunting of moods can
be erased. At least while we are in the moment they can. While lying on
top of him, satisfied, I am awash again in a sensation of dread.

I don't want to say anything more about it though. I am hoping I can
will it away. We shower and eat and bundle up for a walk on the beach.
This time of year Fred and I can head outside a lot more since there are far
fewer people around.

"I hope we have a super snowy winter and every Sunday night I can't leave. I want to be snowed in with you." I squeeze his hand tighter. He squeezes back and stops walking.

"Damn, I love you so much. You are fun, sexy and smart. I didn't know I could love anyone this way." He kisses me, softly but with passion. "Every day with you goes by so fast, yet it feels like an eternity until you will be eighteen."

"I want to call home when I get back to the house." He looks down at me with a strange expression. "No, I'm not going to tell her. I haven't missed a day of school so I am going to ask if I can skip Monday. I feel off and I don't want to be apart from you. Is that okay?"

"You don't have to ask if that is okay. I want every second of your time I can get." He kisses me again like young lovers do.

I call and lie again, by telling Mom we are deep into a new song. It makes me sad that she trusts me and says yes to me skipping school. Maybe this weekend will lead to a new hit song and I will have a good enough reason to not let it bother me as much. I write a lot with Fred and Gunner. Even though we have a lot of down time I also have a book full of ideas, and lots of actual songs. Some lyrics, some melodies. I have amazed myself at what I have learned from them in such a short time.

The recording studio is almost done. We are going to record some songs as a test so they can decide what they are putting on the new album. Fred said after the New Year he will have to spend some time in California. They will record in New York part of the time too. I accept it, but I wish we never had to be apart.

Still feeling out of it, we take a ride in the Lamborghini to cheer me up. Fred sure knows how to make me feel amazing. We go out to eat in the middle of nowhere in South Jersey. Not only are we not caught, we aren't even seen. The restaurant is empty. We will have to go back. It was nice being away from the house.

Seeing Gunner for some football lessons on Sunday granted the more normal feeling I was craving, but my mind and I are still fighting with this weird feeling I have. I still feel odd emotions late on Sunday. Maybe it is because I am playing hooky tomorrow.

I call my mom Monday morning before she leaves for work to remind her to call me out sick. She tells me she already did, and I thank her.

Gunner walks in the kitchen as I hang up the phone. "What are you doing here still?"

"Skipping school. Such a rebel, ya know, even called my mom to make sure she calls me out sick today."

"Don't be a rebel, it doesn't suit you. What are you doing with your day off, besides Fred?" he says without missing a beat.

"I missed you picking on me – it's been a long time."

"I missed it too. Where is he anyway?"

"Asleep."

"You going back to bed?"

"No."

He stares at me, and his eyes turn blank. I never saw life leave a person. If he weren't breathing heavily, I would have thought he died right in front of me. I grab his hand. I squeeze tight. He looks right at me. It's chilling. Whatever is wrong with Gunner might be the reason I have been feeling so off. I never anticipated that.

I start walking to the back door, grab my coat, and take him with me. He doesn't hesitate to follow. We walk for quite some time on the beach, silent, hands grasped. It crosses my mind once that I shouldn't be holding another man's hand, while my heart is asleep with Fred, but with Gunner something is different. He is amazing. He is probably the best looking man I have ever seen. He could be someone I could love, and he is someone I love. It's a different kind of love. That does not explain why I am able to be so close to him and have it not mean the same thing it means with Fred. I am certain I will never understand what it means.

We walk for quite some time before we get back to the house. I pause and look up at him. Tears pool in his eyes but he won't let them fall. I lift my hand to his face and he closes his eyes so I can wipe my thumb across them to push the tears away. I take my time to make sure his eyes and face are dry, and I return my hand to his.

He opens his eyes and looks back at me. Life is coming back to him and I feel better seeing him slowly becoming Gunner again. "Gunner, whenever you are ready, I will listen like you have done for me."

"I know that. Boy do I know that. When I'm ready, Morgan, it will be you I tell. I'm not ready."

We walk in silence before we head back inside. When we see Fred in the kitchen, Gunner gracefully drops my hand. Their friendship has been around long before I arrived and it will be around long after I am gone. I try to focus less on what they think of my friendship with Gunner.

I walk to Fred in the kitchen, very surprised when he says to me, "Everything okay?" It sounds odd coming from his mouth, but I see the clock on the microwave and we have been gone over three hours, so I realize he has a reason to sound strange.

We all eat lunch together like we often do when Gunner asks if I want to help him with a song. I sense he needs a friend still, even if his mood is improving. We write a lot of different ideas out and I even get my homework done. The day has been long but still I find everything we do together pure joy.

Walking down the stairs after a long relaxing shower, I see Gunner outside on the deck. It is too cold for him to be out there in a tee shirt. My head snaps toward the front entrance when I hear Fred screaming. He is on the phone and going ballistic. I walk around to see him yelling into the phone. I have never heard him raise his voice. I try to get his attention, but he won't even look at me. It hurts more than I thought it could that he is brushing me off and shooing me away. To be closed off from him slices like an ice-cold knife to my soul. I would rather be yelled at than shunned.

I walk away, grab my coat, and flee into the cold with Gunner. He doesn't say anything. I don't say anything. I lay my head down on his shoulder and cry silently and he pulls me into the side of his hard body. Sometime later Fred comes out, still not calmed down, but not yelling. He says sorry to both Gunner and me. We are all silent still when Gunner gets up and leaves.

I hear his car start and back out of the driveway before Fred says anything. There is so much that needs to be said, and I don't know how or if I even want to say it all. Time is moving in slow motion. Eventually Fred comes and sits next to me. I keep thinking – should I or shouldn't I touch him? I need to feel his warmth, but I need not to be confused by it.

"Come inside with me?" He doesn't stand up, almost as if he is expecting me to say no. I say nothing. I head inside and take my coat off, then I sit on the sofa as if I suddenly became a robot. We are both moving in slow motion, and it gives my mind the time to fill in the gaps. I know

now that pit in my stomach was because this was coming. The demon that is my lover's wife was going to interfere, and who am I to complain. I am the seventeen-year-old mistress, and I have no rights. This isn't my battle; it's their battle. I am the outsider, the intruder, the marriage wrecker.

Fred takes my hands in his and puts them in his lap as he sits with me. I want to pull them back and keep them for myself but I can't, I can't move. I never knew his touch could leave me paralyzed. I even have to concentrate on breathing. This is much harder than I expected it to be.

"Sorry." The only word he seems to be able to say. He is killing me slowly. Is he sorry for what he did or what he is going to do? I can't believe how weak I feel, but this agony has to end. One way or another, no matter what he has to say, I have to move forward.

"Sorry for what exactly?" I finally ask in a whisper.

"Yelling, hurting you, involving you, not being strong enough to be the man you deserve, for being weak, and for being a worthless jerk." He pulls his hands from mine and in a flash his head is bowed into them. I can't tell if he is crying or hiding. Then in another super human quick move he pulls me to his chest. I don't even get to glance at his face as he holds me tight to him. His heart is pounding wildly, moving both of us like an earthquake. "I have to leave. I will be back later. We can talk then. I want to get this over with."

"What, do what, and you aren't worthless." He still has a tight grip on my body. "Fred, what are you doing? Say something."

It feels like a lifetime before he speaks. "I have to go see Beth."

"Well, I can't stop you. She is your wife, and I am just an underage idiot who knew my heart would eventually be ripped to shreds. I knew I felt off all weekend because something was going to happen. I will have my mom come get me, and I will leave the car here. I don't want it if I can't have you."

Holding my shoulder firmly in his large hands he stares at me like I have grown a tail out of my head. "Morgan, please don't leave me. I need you. I want you. I love you." He grabs my face and pulls my mouth to his, but I can't kiss him back.

"You are running to her and you want me to wait here? That's a little twisted. You can't have us both. I'm better than that. I might be seventeen, but I don't deserve to be pushed aside and told to wait."

"No, Morgan, you don't. You want to leave? You want this to be over?" he says, harsher than he has ever said anything to me before.

"No. No," I say out loud and over and over in my head as he gently kisses me. I still don't kiss him back.

"Stay, please. I need to fix her furnace. I know it's a ploy for her to get me over there. Will we be okay if I go up there and help her? Will you wait for me? I don't want her coming down here, but I will stay if you say you want me to."

"I want you to stay, but I am not the kind of person who controls people. I knew exactly what this was from the start. I accepted it. It hurts far more than I thought it could, so I have to take some time to adjust and think about it. We have a lot against us, yet we have found so much love in the chaos. Do what you must, just please don't ever yell at me like you yelled at her."

"I will never yell at you, Morgan. I love you, and you mean so much to me." He gets up and goes upstairs, taking the cordless phone with him. I sit frozen on the couch, confused by my life. I tell myself to fight for him. He is worth the stress and pain as long as I get him in the end. I will just do my best to stay whole as this unexpected life of mine unfolds.

"I will be back as soon as I can. She didn't start heading down here, so I can stop this. I am so sorry." When he kisses my lips, I kiss him back this time. He says he loves me, but either my ears have changed or his attitude has because he doesn't feel the same or sound the same. I don't say I love you back as he runs out the door.

I haven't moved in some time, frozen with fear of the unknown. I don't know if I can do this anymore. I have to decide what I can handle. Feeling this empty pit of shame and being second, but still having Fred to love, or leave it all behind. I don't have to decide tonight. I tell myself that over and over but I know it is an excuse to ignore my problems.

I have no idea how long I have been sitting here. It's been dark outside for some time, but with the time change this weekend, and my weakened emotional state, I am lost to time. The door opens and I don't get excited because I know Fred isn't back. I don't want Gunner to think I am disappointed he came in that door instead of Fred, but damn I feel my chest cave in. I sob. Gunner has opened the door to my emotions and the river is now raging.

He sits down where Fred just was, or was that hours ago? Gunner leans in and grabs me tight to him. It's not helping my mood, but it's helping my tears, perhaps because it's so tight I can't breathe to cry any longer. He holds me at arm's length then quickly let's go to wipe the tears from my soaked face.

"Did you eat?" he whispers.

"No," I say, wondering why it matters.

"You should eat."

"I don't want to."

"It's late. You should eat something. How about ice cream for dinner or chips? What is your favorite junk food?"

"Chocolate." I smile as I speak because his smile makes me able to feel again. He gets up and gets my sneakers. He kneels before me, and I let him put my shoes on and tie the laces. "You will make a great dad someday."

He hands me my jacket but lets me put it on myself. Then he opens the car door for me, but this is more like a gentleman than a dad.

We buy thirty candy bars at the gas station, since it is late, and nothing else is open. I am laughing like a kid who actually needs help tying her shoes as we get back in the truck, because all of this suddenly seems so silly. We are silent inside the cab of the truck when Gunner hesitates to start the engine. I sit and stare at him.

"Thanks for making me feel better."

"Anytime. It's not too hard, Morgan. You are easy to please and easy to spend time with too."

"Thanks. Are we hanging here to eat or are you taking me somewhere fancy to eat this gourmet meal?"

"I was thinking."

"Oh, I will be quiet."

"You don't need to be quiet. Do you want to go back to Fred's now or later?"

"Later."

He starts the truck and we get on the parkway. I lean back and close my eyes. Fifteen minutes later we come to a stop. Gunner turns the truck off and leans back to grab blankets off the back seat. He slinks like a cat and comes over to open my door. It is so dark I can barely see him in front of me.

"Is this some twisted candy murder plot?" I pause but he doesn't speak. "You could be the serial candy killer," I say, as I take his hand and let him help me down from his way too far off the ground pickup.

He chuckles. "I would kill Fred before I'd kill you."

"I would kill him before I killed myself too."

He opens the tailgate and lifts me up before he joins me. Gunner slides up backwards to lean against the cab; I follow. We are deadly silent as he takes the blankets and puts them around us. We sit side by side as he reaches into the bag and takes out two candy bars.

"So candy surprise dinner. Let's feel each bar up and try to guess what it is before we eat it," he says.

"Sounds fun. Is that why we are here, to molest candy bars?" I ask.

"No, but chocolate is sexy, right?"

"Yeah. Maybe. It could be."

"Okay, first bar." He hands me a chocolate bar.

I feel it up with both hands. It makes me miss Fred a little. I laugh.

"No laughing, chocolate is a serious business," he says.

"Going with Three Musketeers because it isn't lumpy. Guess yours now."

Gunner starts to laugh. "I think I have a Twix," he says and he sounds youthful. Gunner rarely sounds that way. I note to myself that I like it. "Don't open yours yet." He gets more comfortable and says, "Come here." I lie against him with my head on his shoulder. "Look up. See the stars are brighter out here, especially without a moon. It's darker than I expected, but we can see more stars that way. Not a cloud in the sky. Open your candy bar and give me a bite. I want to see if you got it right."

I try to take in all his words. They came at me at different speeds so they are sinking into my head slowly.

I open the candy bar and the chocolate smell hits my hungry stomach quickly. I slowly lift it to his mouth and he takes a bite. "Oh, it is a Mounds," he says, moaning a little with a mouth full of chocolate.

"My turn. Give me a bite of yours." He rips the candy open and I take a bite.

"So what is it?" he asks.

"I forgot we were playing games. I was hungry and it was delicious. Give me another bite." I thought he would be more playful but we might be taking this a little too far. I am way to comfortable with Gunner. This looks wrong but it's not. He always seems to fix me. I wish down to the bottom of my soul that I could help fix him. "You were right. It was a Twix. I didn't want to lose this game to you. Have you played before?"

He laughs. "I have never done anything like this before." I am not sure he means the part with the candy bars or the part with me. I can't think about it anymore. My life is a big enough mess as it is.

We lie back in silence. After I eat three whole candy bars, my belly is on chocolate overload. Gunner feels warm and comforts me in a way no one else ever has. His body feels different suddenly, hard and cold. I fear I am losing the connection I always have with him. "Are the stars easier to see in New Zealand?" I ask gently.

His whole body shakes as if he is cold. "Shit, Morgan, you read minds. Is that what makes you so interesting?" He instantly relaxes under my head as he continues to talk. "There were fewer lights where we lived, so yes. This is the other side of the world so it all looks different. I used to watch the stars and dream about what I could never have. I loved to lie in the yard watching the sky. As a kid I thought my parents didn't get me and didn't want to give me what I wanted. I never realized how much they gave me without trying. They never stopped me from lying in the yard until the middle of the night. They were night owls too.

"I loved watching the sky move. So did they. We had several telescopes even. As a teen I didn't see how alike we were like I do now. The more time passes, and I grow up, I realize the only thing they said no to was the drum set. I guess that was enough to make me feel they were keeping the whole world from me." He spoke so fast his words took his breath away. "Watching the sky is the only thing I still do that I did there. I changed my life myself. I guess I rebelled. But I never stopped watching the stars." He finishes and I lie still against him, absorbing this person I would sell my soul for even though I am just starting to see the man he truly is.

"Thank you for sharing with me. You are an amazing person, Gunner. I'm sad I can't meet the people who made such a wonderful man, but I'm glad you finally have your drum set."

He squeezes me to him. He is a complex man. I have only scratched the surface on understanding him. He holds me tight but it's getting cold and I shiver. "Come. Let's head home." He sits up and gathers the blankets and the candy bag. I sit frozen. "Hey, you okay?" he asks.

"I don't know where home is anymore."

"Oh, Morgan. Let's go see Fred. You will find your home in him again." We drive back in silence. Pulling into Fred's driveway I see his car is not here. It is after two in the morning, and my heart dies again as Gunner takes my hand.

"What do you want to do? Stay here? Come to my house? I can drive you home to your family. Whatever you want. Hotel? Drive around more? Go to Beth's house and punch the shit out of her stupid face?"

I laugh. "Gunner, you make me feel safe. Like you will always be there for me. Let's just head inside. I need to be where he has been, so I don't forget how much I love him and I don't kill him when he gets back."

"Morgan?" He pauses and turns his face away from me. "Do me a favor?"

"Anything," I say, because I honestly would do anything for him.

"Don't tell the guys about tonight, the stars, me, I mean, my family. I'm not ready for that. I never talk about it, any of it. But I can't stop myself around you. You pull it out of me without even trying. I don't want you to keep secrets from Fred, but if you could not tell him, it would mean a lot to me."

"Gunner, I would never tell anyone. Even Fred. It's not me lying because it's just between us. And if he didn't want conversation between us he shouldn't have left me alone to be with his wife." He lets me catch my breath before I continue. "Gunner, everything between us is only between us. Always. I love our friendship. It's different in a way I don't understand. It's different than anything I ever shared with anyone. You are special to me." I pause, afraid to say what I want to say, but tonight is about courage. "I need to say something, but don't respond please. Let me say it and then let's go inside." He nods and I see a glimmer of emotion in his eyes. I just don't know what it means. "I will love Fred for eternity, but I have this gut feeling that I met him as a means to get to you. In the end, he and I will never last, but you and I will be friends until we die. You already are the most amazing friend I have ever had, and I don't think you and I have even come close to sharing all we will share together in this world. You are a part of my soul that can't be detached. Fred will be ripped out one day, and you will be there forever. He will hurt me – you never will."

Tears are pouring down my cheeks. Neither of us moves, then suddenly, as if he has to move fast, Gunner climbs out of the truck. He leaves his door open and puts his hand out to me. I slide across his black leather seats and take his warm, strong hand in mine. He guides me.

He shuts the door to Fred's house behind us, then he takes both our coats off. I walk with him to the couch, my hand in his. Holding a blanket in his hands, he lies on the couch. He pulls me down on top of him and I land heavily but he doesn't care. I kick my shoes off as he covers us in the warm fuzzy blanket. He kisses my forehead as he squeezes me tight to his body.

"Morgan?"

I can't find the strength to talk so I squeeze his body in response.

"You have been a permanent part of my soul since June tenth, at exactly six-ten when your eyes met mine for the first time." He stops talking even though he doesn't seem finished. I am glad he isn't saying more though.

"Wow, Gunner, what a messy pair of friends we are. Let's sleep. I can't handle much more tonight."

"Me either."

"Thank you for getting me through a really bad day."

"At least we get to do that for each other." I don't know what I did for him or why his day was bad. I want to ask, but I don't have an ounce of energy left in me.

Chapter Twenty-Nine
Bottom of the Sea

GUNNER IS NUDGING me awake. It takes me a minute to realize we are on Fred's couch. Then it hits me like a ton of bricks that Fred never came home. "What time is it?" I ask.

"You have a few minutes to get ready if you are going to school."

"I hate school."

"No, you hate being tired and hurt by the man you love."

"Yeah, that too. Be right back. I need to brush my teeth."

I get back downstairs in less than ten minutes because I am too tired to change my clothes. Gunner is waiting at the door with my coat and backpack all packed up. "Thanks, you are quite the gentleman these days."

"I try. Come," he says, taking my hand. "I will drive so you can sleep some more."

"Gunner, you don't have to do that."

"I want to." We get in his truck and as he drives me away from Fred's house, I can't drive the sadness out of my heart.

"I won't have my car the rest of the week. Go back and I will drive myself," I snap.

"We can come back later and get it. That way you'll have a chance to see Fred."

"Okay." We drive in silence. I try to sleep but I can't. I feel trapped waiting for something to happen, but I can't do anything but go through the motions until something does happen. Even if I talk to Fred tonight, we can't even begin to patch this in one evening.

We pull in the lot. "Are you going back home or do you want to go to my house?"

"I guess I can go to your house. I didn't think this through. I was only thinking I didn't want you to drive alone."

"That was nice of you, thanks." I hand him my keys and tell him how to get there. "No one will be home."

"What time should I come get you?"

"Two-twenty. I will call my mom at lunch, tell her you are at the house, and that I have to go back and get my car. I will tell her I had a headache this morning. If she asks about Fred, I guess we can say he had a meeting in the city. That work for you?"

"Yes, Morgan, anything. You are getting skilled at lying, huh?"

"Sure am, and I hate every second of it." The bell rings. "I gotta go. I will call you at lunchtime. Answer the phone in my room."

"Okay."

"Bye," I yell and run, but I pause to watch Gunner's truck pull out of the lot and I wish I were going with him. I don't have the strength to face other people today. It works out well that I was out sick yesterday because I look sick today.

I can't will myself to get past lunch, so I call my mom from the nurse's office to tell her I am going home. I call Gunner second, and he answers my phone sounding scared. "Hey, it's just me. Can you come to the school and get me now?"

"Be right there."

I stand outside and wait for him. I climb in his truck, my mood already improving. "You okay?" he asks, squeezing my leg.

"Yes, tired and sad, but okay. I figured since I missed yesterday it wouldn't seem off to leave sick. My mom knows I left, but I didn't tell her you were here yet. Let's drive back to my house and I will call her."

I call my mom and lie again. I tell her I left because of a headache. Which isn't a total lie, I suppose. I plan on doing my homework and Gunner will drive us back to get my car. And for once I do exactly as I said I would. We get back to Fred's before three and his Jeep is in the driveway. I have a sudden feeling I could vomit. "You okay? Want me to come in with you?"

"No. Wait, yes. Please." I rattle off words I don't remember saying.

We get out of the truck and I stop at the door. I stop to try to get control of my liquid limbs. "You don't have to stay long, just until I get myself to feel more normal. This feels foreign and I need it to feel familiar."

"Morgan, anything, always, anything you need just let me know."

"I will. I will tell you to leave when I am ready to be alone with him." I swallow and open the door. I whisper to Gunner, "Thank you for anything, it is the most comforting word you ever said to me."

Fred is pacing the living room, but he turns sharply when he sees us. He is in front of me so fast, and within a second he has me crushed against him. "Where were you?"

"Do you think you have a right to ask that?" I mumble into his chest. "We have been in this situation before. Please stop making me feel like I did something wrong."

"No, I don't and you are right, but your car is here, and I was so worried. I was wrong, very wrong to leave you last night, but you knew where I was."

"Sorry, I should have left a note. We rushed out of here and Gunner drove me to school. I didn't think how it would look to you, my car still being here. I should have called."

"I'm sorry, so sorry, for all this. It shouldn't be this way."

"No, it shouldn't." I pull away from him. I look up into his eyes. "But it is." The pain in his eyes is worse than the night we met. I just don't know if I have the strength this time to help erase it. I want to try. I tell myself one more time. Hoping, but doubting I can keep this promise to myself. One more time. One more time. One more time. I chant in my head.

"Gunner, can I talk to you outside for a minute?" I say, already heading to the door. I walk him to his truck. I hug him with all the power I have left in my body. He gives me courage. "I am going to be okay. I need to talk to him more, and it's going to take a while, but I have to start now. I can't even begin to thank you for all you have done for me. Go home and get some rest. Can I make you dinner Friday night?" I babble way too fast.

"Yes, Morgan, that would be nice. I will bring something for dessert. We all might need some sugar by then. Drive safe tonight," he says, as quickly as I did, leading me to believe he doesn't want to leave me with Fred.

"I will. Thank you again. Gunner, you care for me, you love me, in a way no one ever has. I am glad I have what I have with you." I hug him so he doesn't see me cry.

"You can't hide your tears. I don't need to see them to know they are rolling down your face. I feel everything you feel, Morgan. Just be yourself with me, always, please."

"Okay." I pull back and stare at him, amazed at how he makes me feel. I never knew a person like him. "I am going back inside. Start to chip away at the block of ice in that house. See ya Friday." I turn and slowly walk back inside.

I feel alone without Gunner at my side. I walk in and sit with Fred on the couch. I don't know what I want this to be anymore, but I take his hand in mine. He pulls me into his lap and hugs me and even though it's not what I want, it's what I need.

We hold each other for some time before I pull away and look into the eyes that have stolen my heart from day one. "Where do we start?" I whisper.

"You are the smart one. You tell me."

"If I was smart I wouldn't be here. I would never have come back. That is what a smart woman would have done. But love trumps smart."

"You still love me?"

"Oh, Fred, yes, I love you. One bad night can't stop this love."

He kisses me through his own tears. "I'm sorry. I should never have gone. She lied about the furnace. She wanted to talk. I thought that was fair so I sat with her and I tried. I tried to talk to her like I talk to you. To be an adult, open and honest and normal. Minutes later she was a crazy woman, yelling, throwing shit even, kicking the walls, she is a total nut job. She was threatening to follow me back here. I wanted her to calm down so I could leave in peace." He breathes deep and it makes me realize I was holding my breath too.

He continues in a much softer voice. "It took her hours to calm down, and it took me hours to realize why. It wasn't that she and I can't talk like you and I do. It was that she wasn't hearing what she wanted to hear me say. I realized I could either lie to her or pretend I loved her or I could stay trapped there until she calmed down. I was stuck there all night since I couldn't tell her I loved her. I fell asleep against the front door. When I woke up she was calm enough to let me leave."

"Well, I am glad you picked what you picked out of what you saw as your options. But I wish you saw ending the marriage as an option too. I don't understand what you have with her. I guess it isn't my business to. It's getting dark out so I should head home."

"Will you let me drive you home? Please."

"No, I need some time alone."

He walks me outside to my car. I turn to kiss him goodbye and his mouth is moving desperately fast. He has never kissed me with fear. I don't like it. "I will call you when I get home. Also I invited Gunner for dinner Friday. You need to thank him for trying to glue me back together. We are both lucky to have him."

I kiss him quickly and get in the car. The ride home is therapeutic. It is relaxing to be alone in my head. Both times a CrossRhoades song came on, I turned it off. At home my parents are cleaning up dinner when my mom asks me if I am hungry. I tell her no. It feels good not to lie to her for once, but I realize if she asked if I ate, then I would have lied.

I shower and change for bed. I call Fred so he won't have to worry. He answers and I can honestly say I have never heard such sadness in a single word. He didn't even say hello, he just said my name. Maybe I will be his downfall too. Why are we together if we will only hurt one another? I suppose that is a question only time can answer.

"You okay?" I ask, feeling the amount I worry about him elevate because he is emotionally fragile.

"No, but I'm better now that you called."

"Fred, I love you. I miss you, but this hurts so much and scares me too. Let's slow down a little bit."

"I love you too. I don't know what to say. I miss you. Will you stay Friday night?"

"Yes."

"Get some rest. I can tell how exhausted you are. Will you call me tomorrow after school?"

"Yes. Goodnight, Fred. I love you." I hang up before he can say he loves me back. I feel bad but I can't hear it again.

I drive down to Fred's right after school on Friday. I should have talked to my mom or Kelly about my state of mind, but I normally keep all my troubles inside. Driving down the parkway it hits me that I do tell someone all my feelings. It's something I never did before, but Gunner gets me to open up. He gets me to expose my inner thoughts. I should have called him to talk it out, but we never talk on the phone.

I pull into Fred's driveway and anticipation is all I have left to feel. He comes outside before I even get the door open. It seems he was watching for me; I don't know if I should be happy or sad about that. I step out of the car and he engulfs my entire body against his. He kisses me and thankfully it feels just as amazing as it always has. I feel him mumble against my mouth that he loves me.

"Let's go inside," I say, not sure if it is because I don't want anyone to see us in the driveway or because I am not ready to be physical with him. I love the physical part, but it's not the same when the emotional part is in jeopardy.

The piano and living room are littered with papers. I walk over to see what Fred has been writing. I have never seen him this torn and sad, dark, and jumbled. This is different, even the work is a mess. I read over a few of his notes that are on top.

Controlled by the noises
Ruled by the world
She calmed the sounds
She soothed my soul

Then she was gone
I push the good away
Keep the dark
Without a spark
It's very dark

I might cry but I continue reading.

I
Need

Morgan

She
Brightens
Everything

We
Are
Amazing

Us
Must
Endure

This is the happiest one I come across. Everything else is depressing and heartbreaking. I pick up one more and tell myself I have to stop.

Dead
My heart is gone
When she isn't around
I can't breathe
Every time she leaves

I can't finish reading because I need to hold him before I crumble. I walk to him in the kitchen and hug him tight. "I don't want to hurt you," I mumble. He leans down and lifts me by the hips, then sets me down on the kitchen counter.

"You don't hurt me, I hurt me." He kisses me and all the passion we shared in the past returns to my body. Damn, I missed him so much. His touch. His mouth. His body. "I wish I didn't hurt you, Morgan."

"I know you don't hurt me on purpose. I wish you made me happy on purpose." I trace my thumb over his bottom lip as I stare, mesmerized by his captivating eyes. The kitchen door slams shut. I look over at Gunner. He looks fine. I don't know why he slammed the door. No one says anything. I push myself away from Fred, get off the counter, and take my books upstairs. I need a breather from these moody artistic men. Sometimes they are worse than the girls at school.

Eventually, I head back downstairs and in typical male fashion they are both perfectly normal. I wish I could be a fly on the wall to see what they do when I am not around. It would give me incredible insight into the parts of them I don't understand.

Fred has his papers all cleaned up, Gunner is half asleep on the couch, so I start dinner. Sometimes it's just easier to be silent. At least we don't scream and yell at each other. Gunner comes over after a little while. "Morgan, can I help?" He touches my back as if he is protecting me. I always feel protected by him, but I never noticed him doing it to this extent.

"I'm fine, thanks. Actually you could get me a glass of wine."

"Really, you hardly drink. Red or White?"

"Red. Then sit with me and talk, will you?"

"I would never say no to that." He smiles at me, a smile loaded with a mix of contentment and sadness.

Gunner owns a part of me I didn't know existed; he makes me feel feelings I didn't know one could feel. I wish now he could be truly happy so he did not have to keep breaking my heart with that look on his face. More so, I want him to be happy just for the sake of being happy.

Once we are all a drink in and dinner is starting to smell delicious, the conversation becomes normal. Well, our normal. I imagine very few people are in my position in life. It still gets me every time that my normal days are filled with world famous rock stars. Gunner leaves shortly after we eat. I enjoy his company tremendously, but with the wine making my brain fuzzy, I have been thinking of nothing but being alone with Fred. We don't say anything at all after the door shuts. I pick up my wine glass, lock the door and walk upstairs. Fred follows me with the bottle.

He sets it down on the nightstand before he takes my glass from me. We have been staring at each other, neither of us knowing what the other one wants. With sheer conviction and love, I kiss him. Only my lips meet his, my hands remain at my sides, afraid to touch too fast. Fred's tongue has just one question. He doesn't touch me, so I will myself to move my arms. I grab his biceps and turn him so his legs hit the bed and I push him down. He falls easily, at my mercy.

I climb on top of him, straddling his body. I rest my chest against his before I lift myself up and stare deep into the eyes that I will never say no to. I close my eyes extra tight and lean my head down to his ear. "I will always belong to you, you will never belong to me, but I am going to pretend you do for as long as I possibly can."

I move so I can start stripping the barrier of our clothes. He opens his mouth to speak and I place my fingers over his lips and shake my head. I don't want to talk anymore. I want to feel. Feel him. Feel the love we share. I need it to be as physical as my shattered heart will allow.

I slowly unbutton his jeans and pull the zipper down. I slide them off with his boxers in one swift movement as I climb off the bed. I stand before him and undress myself as his eyes fill with lust. I climb back on top of him and grab the edge of his shirt. He sit's up so I can take it off him. He lies back down and I gasp as if seeing him for the first time. He is exquisite, so perfect it's hard to stop admiring him. He is strong and sexy, smart and creative. He is my everything, but I may never be his. I make love to him as if we are each other's everything. I convince my mind at least for now that I am.

Chapter Thirty
I'm on Fire

GUNNER AND FRED spend Thanksgiving with me at my parents' house. We watch the parade and football, and my mom and I do the cooking. But we don't do any of the cleaning. The four guys were pretty much forced, but it was worth it because they were so cute.

Beth's name has not been mentioned since that horrible night. I wonder where she will be for Christmas a million times a day though. I wish I could spend the holiday with Fred, but I am not counting on it.

Fred's family was visiting his relatives in Ohio for Thanksgiving. He told them he had to work, but he told me he didn't want to go. It was an informative conversation. It took months but he is opening up to me about his family. He has never divulged this much to me before. He shares more about his feelings for me than anything else. As flattering as that is, I crave more on the other parts of his life. Fred's mother is supportive of him, his dad a little less, but he loves them unconditionally. He claims he is the black sheep of his family. If I ever meet them I can make all those judgments for myself. He isn't close to his sisters because of the age gap, but he adores them. Jacqueline and Victoria are fraternal twins, fifteen years younger than Fred. He moved out and lived with Gunner right after graduation when the twins were just three. "Basically, I don't know them," he said.

My view of the world has changed since I met Fred; Madison is in black and white and Mantoloking is in color. We weren't together the first time it snowed this winter, but we spent hours on the phone talking that night. Every time we get off the phone it always shocks me how much we talk about, but I get no info from his past. He talks music, the band, philosophy, weather, my life, but not his life. I don't know if he doesn't want to share it or if he is afraid it will involve too much talk about Beth. Maybe if she was the past I would be able to handle it. I fear she will always be past and present.

It is the week before Christmas and life has been blissfully drama free. I hope it can stay this way. We never fight, but we hurt each other. Fred shuts me out and I shut down, but we have been opening up a lot more. I was afraid to bring up Christmas and so was he, but he started the conversation late one night, when it was looking like I would not be in school the next day due to a snowstorm.

When Fred starts the conversation I can tell he is very nervous. A nervous Fred is not something I am accustomed too. His voice shakes with every word. "My parents always have family over on Christmas Eve, so I should go there for a little while. You can come if you want. After that can we drive up to your parents' house? I can stay in the guest room, if they would have me. I don't want to intrude on your family's Christmas morning. Gunner does whatever I do." He speaks fast, then pauses while I process everything. "Hey, you still there?"

"Sorry, I know how you feel when I talk fast and say a lot."

"Now I know how you feel when you have a lot to say and you are nervous."

"Fred, I want to spend any part of the holiday I can with you."

"You do?"

"Yes. Did you think I would say no?"

"I didn't know. Everything has been great, but I'm waiting for you to explode."

"I won't explode. You hurt me, so I think I am reserved at times now, but I won't go postal on you. I can promise you that much. We have a lot to work out. I will accept that we don't have to figure it out right now."

"I miss you so much. I miss the summer and I miss that carefree feeling I felt then. I am scared I can't be strong enough for you, but I won't stop trying. I wish I could hold you, and I wish you lived here."

Later that night I dream of Fred's arms holding me. I wake with the sunrise and the snow falling. I turn on the radio and hear that school is closed. I feel some youthful joy; my days without him just don't have the magic that my days with him have.

* * *

On Friday, December twenty-second, I drive down to be with Fred until we go to our families' homes on Christmas Eve. Everything is perfect for the holiday except one thing—Beth. He is going to see her before we leave for his parents' house. I was upset but what can I say about it? I did exactly that, I said nothing. He was upset with me that I had nothing to say, but I just couldn't form the words. He said he was doing it to keep her away, to keep her quiet. I understand that, I do, but I fear he is doing it because she told him he had to. I am starting to see that he is easy to control, to manipulate. The problem is that I don't find it easy to manipulate or control him. When I say that to myself I realize for the first time that maybe we aren't made for each other. Maybe he needs someone to control him.

On Christmas Eve morning, our limbs are wrapped around each other, a little tighter than normal. "What's wrong, Jellybean?" he asks, caressing my back in the most soothing of ways.

"I want to be friends today. At your house, just friends, can we do that?"

"Yeah, anything you want. What's wrong? Why are you saying that?"

"I don't want them to know me as your girlfriend and not know my real age, and I don't want them to find out you married Beth and I knew about it. I don't want to be that girl. I want to be a girl they would want their son to be with."

"Okay," he says, rocking me. "Hey, no tears on Christmas. You are the girl they would want me to be with, but I understand why you don't want to say anything."

I wipe my tears away. "I will tell Gunner not to say anything when I see him."

"Damn, this sucks."

"Yes, Fred, our reality sucks. It always has, but loving you is worth it."

"You are the most positive person I know." He gets up to shower. I want to follow him, but I don't have the energy.

Sitting on a kitchen stool in red dress pants and a white silk top, I see

Fred slink down the stairs, making my heart leap out of my chest. There is just too much lust. He pulls off dressy to perfection. There is nothing fancy about black dress pants and a hunter green dress shirt, but with the amazing body they are covering he appears delicious. "Damn, you look hot. I wish I were unwrapping you tonight."

He strides over to me. "You can't say stuff like that and expect us to get out of here on time."

I should say sorry but my mouth is occupied with his.

"Can you walk? Let's get this done so I can get you back into our bed," he says.

"I can walk, silly. Do you think your kisses make my knees weak?"

"No, I know they do," he purrs, so I smirk at him to let him know how right he is.

When we get to my car he hands me a wrapped box. "Open it," he says, exuding sex from every pore. "If I gave it to you inside I would have wanted to see you wear it. Naked." Inside the box is a simple but large blue gem stone on a chain. A teardrop. Fred grazes the skin on my neck as he fastens it.

"Fred, it's beautiful," I say, touching the warm stone against my chest.

"It's a tear drop, because when I'm not with you my blue eyes are nothing but tears." He leans down and kisses me. "Now go. It's freezing out here."

I get in the car and pause, since I can't get enough air to fill my lungs. I hate the times when I have space to think, because my thoughts are never positive. I need him to fill in the space, so I run up to his Jeep. He puts the window down. "I'm having a moment. Please block my thoughts, tell me something positive and kiss me."

"You make me want to be the strongest man I can be, for you, because I love you." He kisses me. I run back to the car and drive to Gunner's while singing along to "Breakfast at Tiffany's". Music helps and music hurts. Ever since October thirtieth, when he spent the night with Beth and I spent it with Gunner, I have been battling the spaces that aren't filled anymore by Fred. The spaces leave my mind too much time to over-think. I haven't explained this dilemma to Fred, but every time I ask for his help he has been accommodating like he was in the driveway.

I miss that feeling he gave me, the one where I felt nothing except the positive parts of love. I liked how he was my mind's eraser for all my wandering thoughts. Perhaps it was just innocence. Now I am stuck with thoughts that wander more than ever.

I plan on giving Gunner his Christmas present now since it is way too personal to give in front of my family. I ring his doorbell, carrying a large wrapped canvas, and I shiver, feeling out of place. I have never rung his bell and I have never been to his house alone. He opens the door, and his smile erases all the odd feelings as it washes over me, making me more at home than I ever have been. I walk inside and return his hug with my free hand.

"Merry Christmas, Morgan," he whispers in my ear. The sound of his voice and the warmth of his breath soothe me in the most primal of ways.

"Merry Christmas, Gunner," I say, as I pull away from him and take in the decorations all over his mansion. "Gunner, your house is beautiful. I didn't expect to see it decorated."

"Thanks. I never decorated until I started dating Missy. I did it for her and I sort of realized I liked it. It helps too that I hire people to do it."

"Oh, mercy, that explains a lot, but twinkle lights reflecting in your eyes still look good on you."

"Enough of this. What time do we have to leave? I have something to give you and obviously you have a gift for me," he says, sounding nervous and looking down at the large present under my arm.

"We have a few hours. He said six." It means Fred also has hours with Beth. "When we get to his parents' house, I want them to think I am friends with Fred. If by some miracle Fred and I come through our issues and have a real relationship someday I don't want them to know that it started before I was eighteen and while he was married."

"Believe me, it isn't too difficult to act that way," he says. I don't want to know the meaning of that sentence. "Come, let's sit down." He leads me into the family room, but I realize family room is a strange term for a 1500 square foot room that a single man has filled with more electronic equipment then a Tops store.

I look around the room and pause to reflect on my life as it is at this moment. I should feel out of place, yet I feel at home here. I find pure undiluted comfort for this spectacular man sitting before me.

"Your gift is bigger, so you should be first," he says before my brain can switch from admiring him to gift giving.

"Hey, that isn't fair. But okay, I am tired of carrying it around in this enormous house."

He takes the gift from my hand once he sits. "Please sit, Morgan," he says, coaching me as I stand frozen, staring into space.

"Gunner, thank you. I don't say it enough. You are the most amazing person I have ever met." I pause and move closer to him so I can hold his hands in mine. "I love how you make me better and stronger. I have never had a person care about me the way you do. It's pure and simple and I pray I never have to spend a day without it." I pause, my mouth feeling super dry. "I have been a tad bit more emotional than normal. Sorry to be such a girl today. Holidays make life mushier."

He smiles a smile that will always feel like a hug. "Morgan, you are not a girl, you are a woman." I smile back at him, tears welling in my eyes.

"This is too heavy for me, Gunner." I say this to stop my tears.

"Me too," he mumbles, as I lift his gift.

"This took me some time to do, since I spend all my free time in a Fred coma."

I hand him the gift and he tears the paper without ripping it. He holds the painting up. His expression says more than I expected. I'm enjoying watching him; how could I not? I am certain he is without a doubt the most attractive man I have seen, and the more I know him the better he looks. I admire Gunner's beauty and caress the necklace I got an hour ago from one of People Magazine's sexiest men, but Gunner holds a special part of my heart.

"Morgan, did you paint this?"

"Yes." I know he understands that the night he spent keeping me from falling apart while Fred was with Beth will always be a significant night in our lives. I don't know why that night was so hard for him. Maybe next year I will understand, because I plan on spending it with him. "I know I never divulge much about myself, well at least freely I don't, but if I am asked I tend to divulge too much. I contradict myself often. I love art, all media, but oil painting is my favorite."

I have never titled a piece before on the front of the canvas. My oil painting of Gunner's truck depicts the ocean and the stars; it does not have us in it. I was not comfortable painting us holding each other, but the words '5th Chamber' are written on the canvas.

"Do I get to know what this means?" he asks, before tracing the words with his graceful and long index finger.

"Yes." I exhale, then close and open my eyes in slow motion. "I wanted to write more, place it on the back, but I couldn't. I wasn't ready for it to be written. Odd since most of what we do is write." He nods and I know he gets me. "I too have felt a pull for you since the day I met you, and I still don't get it completely. I have never felt what I feel for you for anyone else. It's different than love, it isn't just friendship, it is family yet not family. I can't place you. I can't categorize you. You are in my soul. You are in my heart. I was thinking how my family and Fred are in my heart. Yet you are too, but there's no term for it."

He nods, wanting me to go on. "After that night we spent eating chocolate bars for dinner, my heart beat a little differently when you held me. It still beats a little off kilter, so I put my hand on my heart one night to feel it. It physically felt different to me when I was thinking of you. I dreamt up the thought that my love for you made my heart grow a fifth chamber. I didn't have to make room for you in my heart, because my heart made more of itself for you. You mean more to me than words can express, so I made up words to explain what you mean to me."

He is staring at me and I can't tell if he thinks I am insane or if he is touched. He gets up and walks across the room, puts the painting on the mantle and, with a rhythmic gait, comes back to sit with me. His eyes are burning into me. For the first time in a long time I become a little uncomfortable. Then he engulfs me in his arms and presses me to his firm tattooed body, and I am content again.

"Oh, Morgan. You are beyond important to me. Please promise me no matter what happens in our lives, we will always be something to each other. I feel closer to you than I have to any person on this earth, alive or dead. I want to express myself to you but I am scared of this uncharted territory. I agree we are indefinable."

We hold each other for too long and my foot falls asleep. The pins and needles sensation hurts a little. Gunner laughs at me when I get up and stomp my foot into the expensive Oriental rug too many times. "My turn," he whispers.

"Better not be anything more emotional, because I can't take anymore."

"Sorry. We have emotional down well. Why not continue it?"

"Because I will break."

"Morgan, you are far stronger than you give yourself credit for."

"Back at ya, Gunner."

"I love that you say my name all the time."

"I love your name."

"So. First, here." He hands me a small wrapped box. I open it to find a key chain with a single key attached to it. It says 'any'.

"The key opens the front door here. I will never change that lock. This is your home as well as mine, because I never felt at home here until you walked in the door that first time."

I can't find words that would be a fitting response, and he continues to use his words. "The 'any' stands for any 'any' word you ever need, and I will give it to you. Anything, anytime. You get it." He sounds embarrassed but he doesn't look embarrassed in the least.

"You are not just anyone now, are you?" He looks at me but doesn't answer.

"One more gift, then we should leave." I don't care if we are late anymore because I am frozen in this moment with him. As much I love and want to be with Fred, I want more for this to last forever. This simple pleasure of another human, without dilemmas. This is bliss. I touch the tear drop hanging from my neck again, and I know there is only one man who will rip my heart to shreds.

Gunner gets up and turns the elaborate stereo system on. He returns with the remote and I see it on his face that he wants to ask me to lie down with him. He is scared to cross a line, so I do what I want. I climb onto the couch and lie between him and the cushions, as I did almost two months ago.

Neither of says anything or moves. It is not right that this feels so perfect, but it would be so painful to say it is wrong. Gunner speaks first, in a whisper that captivates me. "So this is a little difficult for me. I have kept my past in the past, but since I met you I feel less afraid to deal with it. I know I don't reveal a lot, but I have been coming to terms with everything I brushed under the rug. You inspired me to embrace more of who I am or was and where I come from."

"Gunner, I don't know how to respond to that." He squeezes me tight.

"I composed a song for you. I wanted to put your name all over it, because I love when you say mine, but it felt wrong to do that. It will be on the new album, but no one knows it's about you. I decided to call it 610. Only you know the meaning." A tear runs down my face. I turn my head into his shirt and focus on breathing evenly because my heart and mind are fighting with each other.

"I pieced together old music with new music, sort of a duet. The two cellos are from an old recording of my parents. The violin music is from a new composition I wrote and played, inspired by you." He hits play. I am so emotional my ears could cry. I never knew he could play the violin, let alone compose classical music. There are no words to describe the beauty he has created. I lift my head to look at him after listening to the entire piece. He isn't as emotional as I am, but he isn't faring well either.

"When did you do that?" I ask, even though so much more is going through my head.

"I've been working on it as long as you took to do that painting." I put my head firmly in the center of his chest again so I can hear his heart. I ask him to hit play, again, and again, and again, until the tears flowing from my face rival the Colorado River.

"We should leave," he whispers.

"Yeah, and you need to change. I soaked your shirt."

"It will dry."

I hesitate to get up because I feel a type of weakness I have never felt before. Gunner hugs me tight once we are upright. I don't know what to say. Relieved, he speaks first. "Morgan, this is all so elevated. I don't know what to make of my feelings either. You are my best friend and that is what I want from you. I know this was a little heavy tonight, but we're lucky we can be ourselves around one another. I hope these emotions never hurt you."

"I don't think you will ever hurt me, Gunner. The love we share is as pure as it comes. How the hell that is possible I don't know, but we will make it last a lifetime, because I need you."

"I need you too. Let's go. My head is spinning."

"Mine too." We walk out the front door and I lock it with my key. Gunner watches me. "Just had to make sure it worked."

"Funny girl. You have it all, don't ya?"

"In your eyes I do."

"Let's take my truck."

We drive to Fred's parents' house with the music blasting. We both sing like we are the lead singers in the band. We are almost there when what I am about to do hits me. "Shit," I blurt out in the middle of singing "Pour Some Sugar on Me."

"What's wrong?"

"I forgot how nervous I was."

"Glad I helped you forget, but why be nervous? You have nothing to worry about, Morgan. Your personality is bigger than your fears."

"You are damn good with the lines, mister. Seriously, why are you still single?"

"I answered that question once before for you— a lifetime ago."

"Almost six months. A lot has happened since then, yet really nothing has happened."

We park on the street near the house. I look around as Gunner turns the truck off. The silence is welcoming. I must have a look on my face when Gunner says, "Fred's family is huge." There are cars down the entire street and the house is bright and full.

"Well, maybe I can find a place to hide in there. I don't see Fred's Jeep anywhere, do you?"

"Want to wait or go in?"

"You think I would pick go in?"

"No."

"Gunner?"

"Yeah?"

"Thanks isn't a grand enough word, but thanks. I don't know what else to say. You are so much more than I ever thought a person could be. Promise me you won't change. Someone will have to glue me back together when Fred rips me in two. I know it is going to be you who keeps me whole." I can't look at him, so I stare out the window.

"Morgan, I would do anything for you. I know you would do anything for me. We are special together, but what you have with Fred is exceptional. He better always get that. I hope you are wrong about him. If this tragic end you sense does happen it won't be for lack of trying on your part. I will have my best friends in pieces, and more than anything I never want to know what a completely broken Morgan looks like." My tear ducts are tapped out. "Morgan, he loves you. I don't always under- stand him – he is complex or maybe he is simple – but he loves you. Give him time to make it right. You are the best thing that ever happened to him. Give a little until he can see it."

"Gunner, thanks for the comfort. Time will tell if you are right." I want to say more but I can't handle more emotions tonight. "Come, let's do this. I feel brave now."

Two squealing girls who must be Fred's sisters assault Gunner as soon as we walk in the double front doors. He hugs them both at the same time; they are small compared to him. I am enjoying him tease them. I can't help think again what an amazing father he will make one day. I wish he would open himself up and date at least. I never wanted happiness for another person like I want it for him.

Gunner introduces me to Jackie and Vicki. Theirs voices carry over the chitchat around us as Vicki says, "We never met one of Gunner's girl- friends before."

"She is not my girlfriend," he corrects like a passive dad.

"But, Mom said that Beth said that she met your girlfriend, Morgan, in Hawaii, and then Fred said Morgan was coming, so Mom told us you were bringing your girlfriend."

"Oh boy, when was Beth here?" My blood heats up at the sound of her name.

"I don't know. I wasn't here. I don't like her so I hope she never comes when I am here," Jackie says. I relax a little.

"Morgan is my other best friend. She isn't my girlfriend, but you will love her as much as I do. Let's say hi to your parents." Jackie informs her mother the second we enter the kitchen that she was wrong about us. The twins talk so much, but I am grateful because I don't enjoy conversation with new people in a large group. I want Fred's parents to be a part of my life, but I don't know how to start my relationship with them.

Fred's family is easy to get to know. I spoke to both his parents briefly, but hosting a large Italian Christmas Eve dinner is a full time job. They are all outgoing, friendly. and extroverted. I see how different he is now.

I sympathize with both him and Gunner, because I fit together with my family like a simple four-piece puzzle.

We get some food and try to find a corner to ourselves, which isn't easy. There are fifty people here at least. "Sorry about that Beth shit, and the confusion about us. I wasn't expecting that," he whispers to me after we have been sitting on a window seat for a few minutes.

"Gunner you can't apologize for that. It's my fault and I should be apologizing, because I was the one who kissed you that day. Fred should be apologizing for anything Beth related, not you."

"Regardless, I'm still sorry. This whole situation isn't easy." Leaning in, he whispers, "But do me one favor. Never apologize again for kissing me that day. I forgave you for it and I am proud of you for being so damn bold. Brave looked pretty on you." He pulls his mouth away from my ear as Fred walks in. Our eyes meet across the sea of people. "Damn, I can hear your heart speed up. You have it bad for him."

"Yes, Gunner, I do. And it's going to be my downfall. I see it already, but I can't stop loving him."

"I hope he never hurts you, Morgan."

Fred says hi to some people as he works his way over to us. It seems an eternity before he is beside me. I want to be calm and reserved but the desire to jump into his arms is too strong. I can't hold back. My arms seem ten times longer as I fling then around him and press my body into his. Like a medicated patch, I absorb strength through his touch. "I missed you. Everything okay?" Since Gunner has given me the strength to see past his weakness with Beth, I decide confidence feels better than fear.

"Yes, no, you know, same shit. Sorry I'm late," he mumbles, letting go of me. The three of us squeeze onto the window seat, so now the limited seating is in my favor.

"It appears Beth told your mother about me and Gunner, about the kiss. It seems the household rumor is Gunner and I are dating. We corrected everyone."

"See, Morgan, family is worse than paparazzi," he says, squeezing my knee with a light smile that I can't read.

His sisters find us and start talking, their words like rapid fire. This has been a Christmas Eve to write about. "Morgan, where you from?"

Vicki is first to ask me something personal. I was hoping I could avoid personal questions all night.

"Jersey."

"Why were you in Hawaii?" Jackie asks.

"To celebrate your brother's birthday."

"Do you go to school or work?"

"Both."

"Where do you go to school?"

"Well, I hope to get a degree from Rutgers."

"What is your major?"

"I switch back and forth on my actual major, but I have to pick one soon. I am really boring. Let's talk about you guys. What are you getting for Christmas?" They talk like the young girls they are and it's a joy to listen to. "Oh, seventh grade was a lifetime ago, stay young," I tell them and Fred laughs a little too loudly at me. I give him a look.

"You are too much." He leans down to my ear. "I love you. I want to do dirty things to you."

He pulls his head back and looks into my eyes. Damn, he is so hot it hurts. I swallow and Fred leans down, working me up in all the good ways. "I mean it, my tongue is in an exploring mood." He pulls away again and I squeeze his hand behind my back as I gaze up at him. His eyes give me the feeling he is imagining his mouth on every inch of my body.

"Did Gunner show you around the house?" he asks, loud enough to be overheard.

"No," I whisper because my voice is hiding from this desire.

"Come." He pulls me up and takes my hand and leads me upstairs. I don't know how I don't fall. My legs can barely keep up with his long ones. We get upstairs and he pulls me into a bathroom and locks the door with a loud dramatic click. He says nothing because he is savagely kissing me with more passion than I ever felt out of him.

Fred reaches under my dress and rips my underwear down in one fast movement, as his mouth, like a wild fire, blazes into mine. I feel him moving roughly against me but I am so lost in his kiss I lose track of what he is doing. He lifts my legs around his hips, I discover him naked and I become even more excited.

He can read me perfectly as he kisses me hard enough that I can't moan through it. He is inside me so fast. He pushes every thought out the top of my head. I love my empty mind. Damn, he is making my heart pound into a new realm. Every thrust makes me feel more and more. I feel so much for him and having him possess my body intensely leaves me weak.

His hands push my dress down just enough so he can get his mouth on my exposed nipple. He bites me and it should hurt but it sends a sharp current of heat right to where he is deep inside me. My head bangs on the wall a little too roughly. It's loud and it hurts some. I forget it quickly as he pounds himself into me. "Fred. Please. Oh shit." I push my head back to his ear and I violently dig my nails into his biceps. "I can't tell how loud I am." The buildup is crazy intense. Pounding me with such need. I love to make love to him. I feel crazy but controlled when we do, but this totally out of control sex is to fucking die for. "Fred, harder." And damn, he does. One pounding thrust after another. "I need to come, Fred, now please, now." He holds me tight and bites my shoulder as I feel his body shudder against mine. And that is my undoing. His body slowly explodes inside me and I come around him with incredible force that leaves me shaking and wobbly. His arms grip me tighter to hold me up as I attempt to control my body.

"Damn, Fred, that was intense." He kisses me and pulls out of me. I grimace because I always hate losing that connection.

"Oh, Morgan. It is. You are intense. Don't be mad at me."

"Why would I be mad?"

"I don't want you to think I took you up here for the wrong reasons."

"I hope you did that because you love me and find sex as thrilling as I do."

"I don't want you to think I did it because I feel guilty about seeing her today. Or because I'm pissed everyone thinks you are with Gunner."

"I am not like that anymore, I told you. I am here for you regardless of what you are to Beth, and I am sorry about the Gunner problem. That is my fault. I shouldn't have kissed him that day, but you know Gunner and I are just friends, right?"

"Yes, Morgan, I do, but sometimes he looks at you when you aren't paying attention. It scares me. I don't know what to make of it because

I have known him for so long and I have never seen him behave like he does when he is with you."

"Fred, Gunner and I have a special relationship. We even talked about it today. I don't know quite what it is. It's better than friendship, but it's not love, not romantic love. He trusts me, and he opens up to me about his life. That is all it is. Please tell me again that you didn't bring me up here to prove to him that I'm yours, because I will be mad. I thought I showed you that over the last seven months."

"You did, you do. Morgan, men are idiots. Gunner slept with Beth when we were in high school before I dated her, but he knew I liked her. That is why I get this way. It's my bad. I know you wouldn't do that to me. You are different from her, from everyone. I would be a fool not to cherish you, always."

"I fear you are a fool, but I'll try not to be so cynical. And damn, why didn't you ever tell me he slept with her? Is that why he hates her so much?"

"He hates her because she makes me weak."

"Okay, we should have sex more often in bathrooms during holiday parties. It makes you rather chatty and open." I kiss him gently and check to make sure my dress is on right. "Let's leave before someone finds us."

"I love you. I love you so much, Morgan. Please help me stay strong." He falls against me and we hold each other.

* * *

We make it to my parents' house before midnight and it surprises me they waited up for us. They act normal when we walk in, but I still see the starstruck look on my mom's face when she sees Fred and Gunner. They command a room alone and together they own it.

Ryan is staying at Faith's house tonight so Fred is going to sleep in Ryan's room and Gunner will take the guest room. As weird as this still is, I have accepted it. My parents have too, so perhaps that is why it is easier for me. I hope by having them both here for the holiday it makes it seem like I am not with either of them. It isn't even about my age or Fred being married. Now it's about the fact that we have lied for so long.

I take Gunner down to the guest room and show him where everything is. My parents say good night and Fred goes up to Ryan's room.

Gunner is holding back from me suddenly, and it upsets me. I love that we are open and things are easy between us.

"You okay, Gunner?" I rub my hand up his back. He leans back into my hand, forcing it to press harder into him.

"I am more okay than I have ever been."

"Good. Thank you for coming here. It means a lot to me. I can't imagine not being with you for Christmas."

"Morgan, there is nowhere else I'd rather be." He turns around and hugs me tight, and I hold onto him like my life depends on it. I pull away and hold his arms while I look into his heartbreaking eyes. He is tearful but not crying.

"Gunner, you are very good to me. I treasure our time together. I want to be your friend, your family, anything you ever need, forever. I can't fathom life without you. Gunner, I love the amazing person you are. Merry Christmas."

"Merry Christmas to you too, Morgan. Let's sleep before I can't handle this properly."

"See you in the morning." I leave and don't look back. I can't see that look in his eyes ever again. I wish he could find someone to love him like he deserves to be loved. He could make her feel like she is queen of the world.

I head upstairs and see Fred on Ryan's bed; he's writing in a notebook. I walk in and sit next to him. I want to know what is on his mind, but for some strange reason, I don't read what he has written.

"Gunner okay?" he asks.

"Yeah, at least I think he is. Are holidays harder for him than the rest of the year?"

"I don't know. Maybe. I wish I knew, Morgan. He is my best friend but we don't really talk. He has told you more this year than he's ever told me. I don't blame him for picking you to open up to though."

"This is a tough relationship. Meeting your family wasn't easy. I wonder how different it would be if it was normal. I can't decide if it would be better or worse – different for sure. I'm going to get ready for bed. Give me ten minutes. My door will be open if you're feeling daring." I kiss him lightly and leave, not letting him speak again.

I swear, eleven minutes later I turn my light off as my door opens.

Fred locks it behind him. He is being quiet but it seems loud. He slowly climbs into bed and lies flush on top of me. My hands move up his sides and under his shirt. Light kisses up my neck and along my chin make me moan. I can't control myself; he makes me weak.

He slides down next to me and rolls me onto my side to face him. He leaves his hand on my hip. "Morgan?" He kisses me again.

"Huh?" I kiss him back.

"I should leave."

"No." I run my hand down his stomach and under his pajama bottoms. He is hard and there is no turning back now. "You need to keep me quiet. Can you do that?"

"Yes." And he does. I am so much more into him and how he makes me feel when I can't release the pressure verbally. He takes his time, teasing every inch of my skin. His mouth, his fingers, all move gently, but are determined. He makes love to me and it's almost too intense. I don't know what has changed. If we are growing closer or further apart. But I forget what I was thinking. With each slow, rhythmic thrust of his hips, he pushes me to a level I have never felt.

I start to shake before I start to come. I dig my nails into his back and he kisses me, trying to keep me silent. He thrusts himself deep into me one more time. As he starts to come he puts his hand tightly over my mouth. It scares me for a second; my eyes pop open to meet his burning eyes an inch above mine. My body releases the pressure instantly and I manage not to scream but to come with my eyes locked on his. There is no way to describe how intense we are. I shake and shiver. He wraps his body around me tightly.

"Don't leave me alone," I plead.

"Set the alarm, and I will stay for a few hours. I have to have you in my life, Morgan. We can't screw this up. I need you so bad that it kills me to imagine losing you."

"I love you. So was that the best Christmas sex you ever had?"

"I never had sex on Christmas Eve or Christmas Day, for that matter. Now we have done both."

"Well, perhaps Christmas is now my favorite holiday. Really though, you never had sex on Christmas?"

"Do you think I would lie to you?"

"No, just protect me when I ask such a dumb question."

"It wasn't a dumb question. Not only am I not lying, that was also the best sex I have ever had. I have never made love to someone like that, even you. I feel so connected to you, Morgan. There are so many reasons why it's wrong, yet it never felt anything but right."

"Your words make me weak and strong." I kiss him gently. "Let's sleep. You can't fill my head anymore with thoughts, or I will need to make love to you again to help fill the spaces in."

Chapter Thirty-One
New Orleans

WE ARE BACK at Fred's after spending a relaxing, easygoing Christmas Day with my family. Ryan and Faith were back by early afternoon, and dinner was wonderful, filled with enjoyable conversation. I was sad to leave, but once I was back in Fred's house alone with him, I forgot about those feelings.

"I have to get your present out of my car. Wait here." I leave him standing in the kitchen. I come back in and hand him a large heavy gift bag. "At least we still have a few hours of Christmas left." I smile and know he knows what is on my mind.

He leads me to the couch to open the bag. He smiles so big it makes it seem he has a million teeth. "Did you develop these yourself?"

"Yes. At school even." I gave him eight black and white eight by ten individually framed images of us touching each other. Very close up, no faces. Just his hand on my knee, my hand on his arm. They are simple and basic, but the simplicity is erotic. I always have my camera around but I have never shared my work with him.

"Wow, they are awesome! I never even saw you take them. Come, let me get a hammer to hang them."

"Now?"

"Why not?" I march upstairs after him and watch him measure them out and line them up four across in two rows, right above the bed. I am not certain if it's the photos of us above the bed or watching him use a hammer that ignites my insides.

I climb up on the bed with him and take the hammer from him. "It's still Christmas. Make love to me one more time."

Everything is improving, getting stronger, more solid, yet I lay wrapped in his limbs feeling that next Christmas I won't be with him. If he is still married to Beth after I turn eighteen, I wonder if I will put up with it any longer. I hate myself for these negative thoughts, but I can't shake them. I don't say them out loud anymore though. Maybe I am improving. How long can a person stay in this type of mental limbo?

The phone wakes me the next morning. I head to the shower instead of going to see who called. I come out of the bathroom as Fred walks into the bedroom with a silly look on his face.

"What's up? You look like you have a plan," I say, not looking away from him to even take my clothes out of the drawer.

"No, but I need one."

"Lay it on me. Who was on the phone?"

"Gunner."

"What does Gunner want that is making you look so cute."

"Oh, I'm cute again?"

"Yes, no subject changing," I say, as I get dressed. Slowly. Making him watch me change from wet and naked to fully clothed. He has stopped talking and I love when my body steals his words. "Please tell me what is making you cute."

He wraps me in his arms. "You are."

"Such a romantic. I love it."

"Gunner wants to go away for New Year's."

"What does that have to do with us?"

"We can go."

"Where? Can I even go?"

"Why couldn't you? To New Orleans."

"Should I tell my mom?"

"I don't know. What do you think?"

"I hate this lying, but she might not say yes. It's a little more than Gunner's house with Kelly. But I want to go. Let's do it."

"You sure?"

"When do we leave?"

"Friday for three nights."

"Who else is going?"

"Alex and Zach, and Zach's girlfriend."

"Zach has a girlfriend?"

"Yeah. I haven't met her yet, it's new."

"Wow, I won't be the only female. How weird. I wish Gunner would date. He needs to be loved."

"You are so damn sweet. I love you for everything you are. And for the things you aren't too."

"Oh, what aren't I?"

"Selfish, bitchy, mean, frigid. You are easy to love, Morgan. And really really not frigid."

A few minutes later I call my mom at work to see how everything is. She says Happy New Year and tells me not to get mixed up in any crazy parties. She says she will see me Tuesday after school. I'm confused about how she manages to do exactly what I need her to.

* * *

We take a large private jet that Gunner has once again arranged. I know he said his mother inherited money, but it had to have been a lot of money. We make it the Omni Hotel in the French Quarter by early afternoon. I fall instantly in love with this city, the smell, the sights, the sounds. Gunner has gotten everyone the largest rooms available, which seems unbelievable on such short notice, but I don't question it. Fred and I have a one-bedroom suite with a massive Jacuzzi tub and a view of the Mississippi. A narrow, small view but still a view.

"Let's check out this shower before we change for dinner." I grin, rolling my eyes up at him as seductively as I can. He never says no.

Eventually we are dressed and running late to meet everyone downstairs. Gunner has secured the private dining room off the Rib Room; I am truly excited to eat out with everyone. Dinner is enjoyable, except I was expected to sit next to Jennifer since she was the only other female. I tried making conversation, but I couldn't because she was painfully boring. Perhaps I prefer the company of men.

We drink too much, we eat too much, and we don't talk too much about me, so I consider the night relaxing. After dinner Fred and I go quickly back to our room. All the naughty words I whispered in his ear all night must have him ready to burst. He ushers me into the room quickly and shuts the door. I expect him to slam me into that door and get things started before the gun goes off, but instead he stuns me by simply standing before me. No part of his magnificent body is touching any part of mine.

"What's wrong?" I ask, because I thought I could read him better than this.

He moves his face closer to mine, making me shiver. His hands run firmly up my arms to my shoulders. Then to the back of my neck and he interlaces his finger there and puts his forehead against mine. "That's what is so weird."

"Huh?"

He leans down and kisses me, getting me to relax into him. His lips are soft and almost in slow motion his tongue licks across my lower lip. Instinctively I open my lips and that sensual tongue runs against mine. I moan deep enough to vibrate his hands on my neck.

"Morgan?"

"Huh?"

"You asked me a question."

"I forget."

He runs his hands down my back and takes the zipper on my dress down with them. He quickly slips his hand under my dress until it drops to my feet. He kisses me again, more passionately, leaving me standing in my underwear and heels.

"Morgan, you want to know what is wrong?" I slowly nod. "Nothing," he says on the sexiest exhale of all time. I look up at him. I stare into the eyes that own my soul, but I also find a way to get his belt off without breaking eye contact. I remove his pants and boxers. My movements rival a slow motion film. It takes us a long time to get the rest of our clothes off. We are way too wrapped up in each other. I have never felt this aroused, yet this controlled. I don't want this night to end.

Eventually, after my hands have unhurriedly caressed his taut skin, he removes my underwear and my heels. He kisses me longer, harder, and deeper. Everything that I love about what he does to me he does better tonight. He drops his forehead down to mine again. "Look at me." His deep whisper vibrates me to the core. I open my eyes and look up. Love, need, desire and pure bliss are all I can see. "You are too good for me. I don't know how to do this. I only know conflict, pain, and heart-ache. You aren't any of that. I love it, but I'm scared I can't make you happy. I love you so fucking much. I don't deserve someone like you. You deserve more."

"Fred, I deserve you. I want you. I need you. We need nothing more than to love each other and share this love intimately. Come to bed with me." I take his hand and walk to the bed with him an inch behind me. I kick my heels off then Fred gently turns me around to face him. I've never seen such love on another person's face and I can't believe I am on the receiving end of that look.

"Morgan, don't let me mess this up. I never loved this way, and it's too powerful sometimes."

He makes love to me with that love and power. We don't say another word. Our bodies do the talking for us. Just when I thought there was no way this could involve more feeling, it does.

I wake up and for a split second forget that we are not in New Jersey, but I don't forget that the hot, splendid body wrapped around me is Fred's. I glance at the clock to see it is only a little after nine. We slept a long time and didn't wake up and have sex again. I guess this below sea level air is wearing us out. Fred starts to wake up. I hate when I wake him. He is skilled at leaving the bed and not disturbing me. I say good morning and tell him exactly that. As always his response makes me weak. "I can't stand the thought of us being apart. My body doesn't allow it."

"But I have to pee bad. I drank too much wine last night."

"Go, bed wetting is not a turn on." He lifts the covers for me.

"Is watching me walk to the bathroom naked a turn on?" I am back in two minutes flat and once again assaulted by the pleasant rhythm of his hips as he makes love to me.

We are lying in bed, and my flesh is still humming. "Do you think Louisiana is beneficial to our sex life?" I ask, as I trace the tattoos on his arm.

"It sure hasn't hurt. I never had sex in Louisiana."

"Me either. How many states have you had sex in?"

"Let me think. You really want to talk about this?"

"Sure, what does it matter? It's in the past and you are my present."

"Okay, Ms. Maturity," he says, pausing to count. "Seven, now that I have Louisiana."

"You beat me, but not by as much as I thought you would. I guess I can try to even it up, but I might never be ahead unless I sleep with someone else, and I never want to do that."

We spend the majority of the day, that we are out of bed that is, at the Audubon Zoo. The weather is a bit cool, the zoo is not crowded, and the combo makes me feel normal. As much as I could spend the entire day locked in the bedroom with Fred, it does feel nice to get out in the world. We eat pizza on a picnic bench and take the ferry down the Mississippi back to the French Quarter, like typical tourists.

Gunner went to meet a friend from high school who recently moved here from New Zealand. I hope she turns out to be someone he can at least try to date. I want to go talk to him about it, but I don't even know what room he is in. Fred and I take the stairs up to the roof to sit by the pool before bed. The stars, the noise from the city, and the aroma from all the restaurants are pleasant to all the senses. I could sleep out here, it is so peaceful, but it is a little too chilly even with Fred's arms wrapped around me.

We get ready for bed like an old, tired, married couple, but instead we are a couple who had too much sex and walked around a zoo all day. When I come out of the shower he is sound asleep, so I decide to sit down and write in my journal. I have some decent thoughts and am stringing ideas together when I hear a light tap on the door. I walk quietly to get it and Gunner is standing there, head hung low, that unique look of sadness on his face.

I open the door for him to come in. "Should I wake Fred?"

"No, you up for taking a walk?"

"Sure, let me change."

I head back to the bedroom, change, and leave Fred a note. Gunner and I walk around the French Quarter for a long time in silence. We eventually get to a bench along the Riverwalk. I brought my jacket but it is not helping. I lay my head on Gunner's shoulder and he squeezes me tight. I wonder why he is with me and not the girl he came to see. I should ask him since Gunner isn't good at talking about himself. I part my lips to ask, when he speaks. It's creepy how he does that. "I can't talk about it yet."

"Okay." We sit in silence for a few minutes. I want to help him. I can only listen, but I hope it helps. "Gunner?"

"Yeah?"

"I won't push you. If you want to talk, I will always be here. I probably can't help but I can listen and sometimes when you let it out, you can hear it for yourself, and then help yourself."

He pulls me close to his side for a second before he gets up and reaches out his hand for me. "Let's go get warm. Maybe somewhere with alcohol."

"Shouldn't be hard to find that around here."

We walk back toward Canal Street and find a small bar, with only a few people and dim lights. Not a place I would probably walk into alone, but with Gunner I don't think twice. We sit at a table in the corner. I expect it to smell or be dirty, but it's pleasant and comforting. The warm wood and orange glow make it cozy and soothing. A waitress comes over and eyes Gunner up and down, but she doesn't seem to recognize him. He orders two shots and I get a Coke. She doesn't ask for I.D. I have a fake I.D., but I don't even have it with me. If I were to drink tonight, I would surely fall asleep.

She puts the shots down and Gunner shoots it before she even places the second one down. "I had a bad weekend," he says and bangs the shot glass down.

"I can tell."

"I wanted it to be a good weekend."

"No one ever wants a bad one."

He laughs. "I don't know how to feel good anymore. I hate being lonely."

I reach across the table and take his hand. "I don't want you to be lonely either. What happened when you saw Amber?"

"I thought maybe, finally, I could trust someone. She knew me before the fame and the tattoos. I was born with the money. It started off good today. I felt an attraction to her, which was a good start. I don't expect instant love, I just wanted a chance to feel something. Well, I was stupid enough to sleep with her. I was happy until she told me she is more into women now. She said she just wanted to tell people she slept with me."

I hug him. I cry for him because he won't cry. "I'm so sorry." He squeezes me tight but quickly pulls away and takes the second shot. I take his face in my hands and force him to look at me. "Well, Gunner, at least you got laid."

He laughs. It's the best sound I've heard all night. He laughs again. "You have a great poker face. I thought you had some big philosophical thing to say. You got me. Why couldn't you have a sister?"

"She would probably be nothing like me, or I would be jealous."

"She would have values like you, coming from your family at least." He doesn't acknowledge I said I would be jealous.

"You will find someone, Gunner. I know it. I don't know when, but when you do, she will be worth the wait." He doesn't look up at me as he normally would when we talk. "And she will be the luckiest girl in the world."

He still doesn't look up. "She won't be a girl, she will have to be the strongest woman ever to deal with me."

The bartender is either bored, crushing on Gunner, or just recognizes him. Probably number three and it's making me wish we had left already. "Why don't you give that patient man your autograph and let's get some beignets?"

"Really?"

"He recognizes you or wants a date, and he hasn't bothered us, and, well, my age. You owe him."

"I hate being recognized."

"I know, I would too. I will never be famous."

"Morgan, you will be, your songs are going to be out there. You even told me you want to be a writer."

"I can hide as a writer."

"You are very different. I will be right back." He gets up after leaving cash with a huge tip and heads to the bar. The bartender smiles a sweet smile that says he recognizes Gunner and is a bit star-struck. Gunner signs something on the bar before saying good night and comes back to me.

We walk slowly down to Café Du Monde. It is still chilly and I leave my hands in my pockets for warmth. At least that is what I tell myself. I would prefer to hold Gunner's hand. I know Fred would not be comfortable with that.

We sit down for coffee and beignets and I begin to warm up. We talk about pointless shit that is full of meaning. Gunner is a master conversationalist. "Hey, sleepy, let's get you back before Fred sends the cops out looking for you."

"He knows I'm with you. I left a quick note."

"I was suddenly worried he would wake up and wonder what happened to you. I don't remember you having time to write a note. It must have been short."

"I did it when I put my jeans on."

"So, what did it say?" he says, throwing me off. He is never this nosey.

"You want to know exactly what I wrote, or just know that I said I went for a walk with Gunner?"

"Well, since you look goofy, you should tell me exactly what you wrote."

"Okay. It said 'Fred, I went for a walk with Gunner, be back in a bit. Should we start with Vermont or Alaska? Love ya, Jellybean."

"Oh, mercy, why did I ask? I thought maybe a cute little snippet of how much you love him would cheer me up and give me hope that love isn't dead. All that did was leave me confused."

"I'm sure you could come close to figuring it out."

"You don't have to tell me," he says and I can tell he knows at the very least it has to do with sex.

"No, I am usually an open book with you, but guessing games can be fun," I say, as we walk back to the hotel in the rain. We aren't soaked but we are definitely chilled to the bone. Gunner, ever the gentleman, walks me to my room and says goodnight.

I start taking my wet clothes off as soon as I close the door behind me. I get in the shower, and the warm water caresses my cold tired skin and warms my soul. I turn the water off and turn around to see Fred leaning on the door jam, his eyes burning right through me. "Turn that back on. I was enjoying the show." I turn the water back on. I pick up the soap, about to give him one hell of a show. Suddenly he is too close to be watching anything but the pores on my face. He takes the soap from me and I patiently wait for him to use it on me, but instead he uses it on himself. "Oh, you are mean."

"It looked like you were done with your shower."

"I was, but I only came in to get warm. It is cold and raining out."

"It was colder in that bed alone."

"You were sound asleep and clueless that I was gone."

"That is true." He laughs. "I pick Vermont. The trip to Alaska would be long, and most of the sex would be on the plane," he says, raising his eyebrows and making me wish we were having sex on a plane right now.

"Next weekend too soon?"

"No." That is the last word we utter before he takes the soap and does naughty things with it that make me moan and beg. I have been up over twenty hours and I am still ready to do about anything as long as Fred does it with me. After we are both quite clean and extremely satisfied we crawl into bed.

"I need to sleep. What time are we supposed to leave for the party?"

"I don't know. Gunner is the one with the plans and you were the one with him all night, so you tell me."

"We didn't talk about tonight's plans."

"Really? You were with him all night, so what did you talk about?"

"Other stuff and his shitty love life. Nothing really. It takes hours to get one slice of info out of him. What he tells me stays with me. If he wants you to know he can tell you himself. He doesn't sleep like I do, so call him and see what we are doing later. I want to sleep."

"Okay, Jellybean. I love you, sleep well."

"Sorry I'm too tired to stay up with you."

"Stop, don't apologize, you and I have tonight. Sleep. I'll be back in a little while to wake you up."

"Thanks, you are the best."

"Wait, how should I wake you?" He gazes down at me and his smoldering eyes make me rethink this nap.

"Oh, I get to pick? How about you sing a sweet lullaby in my ear before you use that hot mouth on every inch of my body until every nerve is awake and vibrating. When you are done, you can feed me juicy shrimp, po boy."

"Always the detail oriented girl, aren't you?"

"I suppose. I know what I like... and I like knowing that you know what I like.... But right now I would like sleep."

It seems I have been asleep for five minutes when I feel Fred whispering in my ear and running his fingers down my naked body. I roll over to get away. "Oh no, you don't. It's four in the afternoon, Jellybean. You can't act like a rock star if you won't sing like one."

"Stop, I will wake up. You have food for me? I am starving."

"Do you want to eat your sandwich or me first?"

"Damn, you make me so hot." I wake up fast. I love the south.

I lay twisted up in his body when he repeats back to me exactly what Gunner said. "Alex has a friend who is having a party. He said it wouldn't be too crazy or full of groupies." I mumble okay while eating my cold sandwich.

Fred calls home again to check his messages while I eat, mostly to make sure my parents haven't called. He is making faces and I suddenly can't eat. "Shit," he sharply curses.

"What, my parents?"

"No, Beth. Fuck, he did give her the number."

"I can handle that over my parents," I say, not asking who 'he' is.

He chuckles. "Really? I can't."

I start to put on clothes and he watches me, baffled. I get my shoes, grab my purse, and walk over to him on the bed. "Call her, but I can't listen." I kiss his forehead and leave. I hear him say, "Where are you going?" but I don't turn around, and I sure don't answer.

I step into the hallway, shut the door, and take a deep breath. Since I still don't know what room Gunner is in, I head to see if Zach is around. It's that or walk the city alone. I knock and he answers quickly.

"Hey, Morgan."

"Hey, Zach." Damn this was a bad idea. I don't know him well enough.

"You okay? Wanna come in?"

"I don't know, and I don't know."

He laughs and smiles a sympathetic smile at me. He opens the door farther, and I walk in under his arm. His room is exactly the same as ours, except we don't have a playboy blond passed out on our couch. And we sure don't have a glass tray with remnants of cocaine on the table. Shit, I shouldn't have come down here.

"Sorry," Zach mumbles.

"You too?" I ask.

"Hell no, not my thing, never was, never will be."

"Good."

"You wanna get a drink? Alcohol I do like," he says.

"Me too, let's go downstairs."

We head downstairs to a very packed bar, New Year's Eve in New Orleans. With a smile that makes people melt, Zach gets us up to the bar efficiently. "What do you want?" he whispers in my ear.

"Dirty Martini, very dirty," I tell him because it fits my mood.

He gives me quite a look and orders our drinks. We are standing by the window for a few minutes when some people get up and we snap up those seats like lightning. Zach is fun, more youthful, as I should be.

I am devouring an olive, when Zach asks, "You want to talk or just drink."

"I want to talk and drink, but I don't want to talk about what is wrong yet."

"Sounds good to me. Let's see where the conversation takes us." He takes a big drink of his beer then speaks again. "I heard a few demos of your work with Gunner, and I like all of it. Going to be a blast recording them."

"Thanks. I didn't know you guys heard any of it."

"Just rough cuts. I like the ballads more than our rock songs. This may be my favorite album," he says and I just nod and drink. My drink is almost gone as is Zach's beer, so I don't feel too bad, but my head is pleasantly swimming. The bartender is quick on the refills and thankfully no one wants I.D. It would not be good if Zach saw that mine has the wrong name on it.

"Morgan, you gonna come out when we record your songs?"

"I doubt it."

"Why not? Got somewhere better to be?"

"No. You gonna keep dating her, even if she is strung out all the time?"

"She's history. I won't tell her how to live her life but I won't date someone who does drugs."

"Good. I am starting to really like you."

"So, attempt to change subject noted. If you have nowhere else to be, why not come to California?"

"No place I want to be, but a place I have to be, and maybe I will come at some point."

"I'm not drunk enough to not be able to follow you. Are you just too drunk to make sense?"

"No," I say, closing my eyes slowly because this conversation sucks.

"You can come out on weekends. Your school must have spring break."

"I do and I will probably come out that week."

"You think Fred's gonna dump you for Beth. Is that what this is about, because shit that bitch is nasty."

I laugh. "That isn't the problem. I'm not jealous or afraid of her. Afraid of how he is around her, yeah, a little. I have another issue bigger than Beth."

"Okay, but your code talk is pissing me off."

"You don't want to know the truth, Zach."

"Morgan?" he questions me calmly like he genuinely cares. I nod to tell him to continue. "You are so smart and normal. What the hell could possibly be the issue? We have all talked. Fred is lucky to have this perfect love with you. Not to freak you out but sometimes guys talk, and well damn, we all realize that women like you are extremely rare. You are different."

"Zach, one more drink and I will be a tearful stupid chick. I don't know where to start." He sits back and stares at me. Torn between wishing Fred would find me and telling Zach that I am seventeen, I take a huge sip of my drink. "One more drink and I will spill the beans."

He flags the bartender down and I chuckle.

"First, can you keep a secret?" I look at him for any sign he is lying.

"Yes, but I can't prove that to you."

"No, you can't." I take a giant gulp of my third drink. "You sure you want to know?"

"Yes," he says, folding his arms across his chest like he is protecting himself.

"This isn't something nice, or hot, or sexy, or cool. It's something horrible and wrong and bad."

"Morgan, stop. Nothing about you is horrible."

"See, I can't do everything I want, like fly to California. I have to get my parents' approval for most everything I do."

"Huh? Why, because they pay for your school? You can pay your own way once the album comes out."

I lean into him to whisper in his ear. "No, Because I'm seventeen."

Blank. So blank it almost hurts. He chugs his beer. "Shit, really? But who gives a fuck?"

I stare at him to see if he really wants to stick to that.

"Damn, I never saw that coming," he says after he finishes the beer off in one swallow.

"Gunner knows. He signed the contracts with my mom. Talk about a tough day."

"I bet. Damn though. I thought you were older than me."

"Nope, senior in high school. I won't be eighteen until June," I whisper. Out of nowhere I feel warm hands on my shoulder. Gunner and Fred are both staring at me like I was the bad little girl I should try being for a change.

"Zach, thanks for the drinks," I say and kiss him on the cheek.

"You have enough or are we going out still?" Fred asks, sounding damn annoyed.

"Your choice," I say, not looking at him.

We climb into a cab, while Zach goes to see if his date is alive. I get in the back with Fred, since Gunner went in the front even though I said I wanted it.

Fred leans over and whispers in my ear, but it sounds so loud. "I was worried. Why did you leave?"

"Really, me having a drink downstairs with your friend is the problem here?"

"No, it's not a problem. I was worried."

"If me having a drink worried you then please tell me how much should I worry about you talking to your wife. So stop now, because I did have enough to drink to make this ugly."

He stops. He stops everything. No talking, no touching, no nothing.

The party sucks. I had too much to drink already. It's only a little after eleven and Fred has been with Alex all night. He has completely ignored me like the child he sometimes is. I get up and walk over to Gunner. "I want to leave. Any chance you do too?"

"Yes, this is hell."

"Meet me at the door in two minutes." I walk over to Fred and Alex. Zach never showed up. I do hope he is just banging the hot girl one more

time and she isn't sick or dead even. "Gunner is taking me back to the
hotel. I am sad. That is all and you were an ass tonight. Even if I was
mean, you were the ass. I told Zach how old I am and I wanted you to
know. I want to sleep and for the first time ever, I don't care what you do."
I leave and I feel horrible. He has to know this Beth shit hurts like hell.

Gunner and I take a cab back to the hotel in silence, but he has his
hand on top of mine the entire cab ride. He walks me to my room and he
gives me the key to his room. "Sorry, I should have given you this when
we checked in. I didn't know he would call her, and I wish you had come
to me instead of Zach today."

"Thanks, Gunner, but Zach is cool. I told him the truth. I hate the
lies." He kisses my forehead. It's a little too much but it's also not enough.
I wish he could hold me again while I sleep. I love the security and comfort he gives me. "Thanks."

"Anything, Morgan. Anytime. I will always be there."

"Thanks.

He glances at his watch. "I don't have the dramatic flair you do, and
I won't apologize." He kisses me lightly on the lips. I almost didn't feel it.
"Happy New Year." He walks away. He just walks away. Good thing he
walked away because I am mad and drunk enough for the first time to
hurt Fred.

Trying to cry myself to sleep sucks, then twenty minutes later I hear
the door open. Fred must come right to bed because he is lying next to
me before I can decide if I want to be awake or pretend to be asleep. He
doesn't care apparently as he rolls me toward him. With both palms he
wipes the tears from my eyes, my cheeks, my neck, because everything
is soaked. He kisses me soft and lovingly. What more could I need? Lots,
unfortunately.

"Happy New Year, Jellybean. I'm totally sober and made it my reso-
lution to not make you cry. I'm done with Beth. Her threats won't be
answered anymore. I love you. Only you. I need you. Only you." He
kisses me with passion and I kiss him back this time.

"Unlike you, I am drunk."

He laughs. "I noticed. You are spunky when you are drunk."

"Well, now I'm drunk and mad and tired and less spunky."

"Let's sleep." He rolls away.

"You can't push your hard cock into my leg and tell me to sleep. Damn, do you not know me at all?"

He laughs but sounds sad when he says, "Sometimes I feel I know you better than I deserve to and sometimes I don't know you at all."

"Guess it's those moments I'm learning who I am that gets you confused."

"Shit, yeah, but you are too damn mature and smart to not get yourself. You know what you want, Morgan. I don't know if I am enough to give it to you."

I don't end this conversation by begging him to make love to me. Still, he does.

Satisfied once again physically by his body, I say, "I love New Orleans, so promise me you will hold your promise so this city isn't tainted for me."

"I will Morgan, I will."

I drift off to sleep with a man who may want more than he can cope with.

Chapter Thirty-Two

Come Again

WE LAND LATE on the first. Even with the emotional exhaustion, I find energy to note that private jets are awesome. Fred and I haven't talked about anything important since 1996 began, and our first night back we don't have sex either. These cold feelings I feel toward him hurt, but I can't help it. It is strange knowing I am exhibiting odd behavior, but I also can't find a means to alter it.

I get up a little after five to shower on Tuesday morning so I can get to school on time. Fred gets up when I do. "You can go back to sleep. I would if I were you." I don't intend to sound so callous but I seem to be unable to help it.

"I can't sleep anymore," he mumbles, sounding like he needs sleep more than ever.

He comes downstairs dressed to watch me pack my backpack.

"You okay?" I ask, because I truly care for him more than I can express.

"No."

"Fred, I have to leave," I say, hugging him. "I will call you after school."

"I want to come with you."

"To school?" I smirk and tickle him a little. The tension is killing me.

"No, please, to your house."

"Okay. It's only three nights though."

"I know, but I have to be with you. I will be in California soon and I need every second I can with you."

I drive us up the parkway in my mustang, and we barely talk. As I drive away from my house after I drop him off I realize my dad is still home. I guess Fred can handle himself, but still I worry.

School sucks this week, but coming home to Fred makes it a little easier. We eat dinner with my parents and even watch must-see TV on Thursday night. Fred and I rarely put the TV on at his house so this is feeling even more unusual to me.

On Friday afternoon Fred is about to start the car when Ryan pulls into the driveway. "I wasn't expecting you home," I yell to him through the open window.

"There is a massive storm coming this weekend, and since Faith dumped my sorry ass, I thought I would chill here before classes start up."

"Oh, Ryan, I'm sorry." Shit, this sucks for me. What if she gets revenge by saying something about us? "Hey, if you need anything let me know."

"I will," he says heading into the house.

Fred starts the Mustang and Ryan comes running back outside. "Hey, would it be okay if I came with you guys?"

I look at Fred and before I can give him a look he tells Ryan, "That would be cool."

"Why did you say that?" I say once Ryan is back inside getting his bag.

"I don't know. Seemed like a good idea. You need something I can't give you and having family around might help. I am afraid you will end us, I guess."

"Just because I'm sad and you hurt me doesn't mean I don't want to be with you. I love you, madly."

He takes my hand. "I love you just the way you are. Please don't ever change." Ryan comes back and we finally leave. At first the car is creepy silent, but eventually we all start talking and it starts to feel normal.

Gunner is at the island reading a magazine when we all come in the side door. He sees Ryan and gives me a sly and bizarre look. He hugs me almost passionately as Ryan runs upstairs to drop his bag off.

"Sorry, you looked like you needed a hug," Gunner says as he releases me.

"Thanks. Even if that isn't the real reason." I cock my head at him.

"You look tired."

"Tough year so far. Looking forward to some snow. Maybe a good snowball fight will knock some kid back into me."

"Oh-oh, watch it, snow is my favorite weapon."

"Damn, Gunner, thanks for finding a way to make me feel better." I hug him. Tight. He means so much to me. And to think he used to aggravate me something fierce. While our arms are wrapped around each other, Ryan comes back downstairs. Fred has been absorbed in his music at the piano, his safe place when he can't handle life. Gunner and I are used to that.

After dinner I do my homework while Ryan watches some movie with Fred and Gunner that I have zero interest in. When I'm finished I get really bored and antsy. Gunner comes over by me and says, "You almost done? We can work a little on that song we started on the plane."

"Yeah, okay, but…" I put my finger over my lips and move my eyes to Ryan.

"Oh," he mumbles and doesn't make me feel like I am being crazy wanting to keep things from my brother. Then I hear Fred ask Ryan to play pool and off they go, like best buds.

I love that Gunner never asks for more info and he reads me well enough to know I don't want to talk about it. We work on the song some, but my head isn't into it. I lean back with a huff.

"You okay?" he asks.

"Just worn out. Let's see what we can write before I go to sleep." Gunner pushes me to work since I am not feeling it and in the end we have a great start on a new song. He even has a melody to match it.

The chills you give me make me hot
Give a little, I'll take a lot
A love so fresh
I am lost to your flesh

Dancing at the party, dreaming of home
Or we could travel to Rome
A love so simple
It makes me want to kiss your dimple

Walking under the sun steals the pain
But I am longing to feel the rain

A love so perfect and majestic
I also love it when it's rustic

Up or down
Jeans or a gown
Black or white
Is all a delight

Swim at the shore I want nothing more
We can head to the mountain if we find it a bore
Hiking over rocks
Or hitting the hottest shops
We have a love so strong
It can't be wrong

Up or down
Jeans or a gown
Black or white
Is all a delight

Wine or beer
Have no fear
Grab a coaster, we are getting closer
To having it all
We can stand together as we fall

Playing in the snow
Making cookie dough
Sweating under the summer sun
Or wasting time drinking up some fun

Up or down
Jeans or a gown
Black or white
Is all a delight

My yawning becomes incessant when Gunner says, "Get comfy. Relax. Close your eyes." He soothes me as he strums his guitar.

Next thing, Fred is tapping my shoulder. I open my eyes and get my bearings. "Where are you sleeping?" His voice is the caress I crave most.

"With you."

He carries me to bed. He is undressing my exhausted body, but I see such love in his eyes, it starts to wake me up quickly. I sit up to watch him take my pants and underwear off. He sees me watching and he runs his fingertips up my leg.

"You tired?" he whispers.

"Not anymore."

"You sure you want to do this."

"Yes, why wouldn't I?"

"Because your brother is down the hall?"

"I will have to be quiet." I feel like I am back home now that we are sexual again. Wrapped in his embrace heals so many wounds. I love him with all my heart and all my soul. I need to find a way to get my heart and mind going in the same direction now.

I wake early the next morning. I hate running when it's cold out so I have taken to doing a lot of Yoga on the living room floor. Flat on my back, I open my eyes, to see Ryan and Gunner both staring at me. I had my headphones on so they scared the shit out of me. And damn they even laugh at me.

I ignore them and get myself some breakfast. Fred joins us and we end up watching the weather channel because this storm is looking to be one for the record books. We spend a lazy day doing puzzles and playing games that Gunner brought from his house. He also brought a ton of food and beer. I had dreamt of being snowed in with Fred the last few months; I didn't see it happening with Gunner and Ryan too.

Once again after writing with Gunner all afternoon my feet end up in his lap when I nap. I slowly open my eyes to find Ryan and Fred are silly drunk. Gunner and I laugh and ignore them and decide to watch a movie. We pick *Dances with Wolves* from his large collection. We somehow manage to watch it without falling asleep. Guess napping has its benefits. Gunner turns the TV off and says good night when I squeal. Then I squeal again even louder.

"What is wrong with you?" He looks at me like I have grown a horn.

"It's snowing. Come, let's go outside."

"Wait." He pulls my arm back. "Get your coat on."

"Grown-ups suck." I put my coat and boots on for Gunner. He does the same and follows me out the back of the house. Watching the snow fall and the ocean roar is an amazing sight. We stand frozen together admiring nature. I feel warm and secure in the cold contradictions, like the song we wrote. I even lean into Gunner. He wraps his arm around me.

"You cold?" he asks.

"No." We watch together in silence. Awesome silence.

Eventually we sit on the steps that lead down to the beach. "Morgan?"

"Yeah?" I answer, still mesmerized by the snow.

"Can I ask you something?"

"Anything. Anything goes both ways. I don't have as much to offer as you do."

"I fear you have more to offer, but how do you find such an amazing balance between kid and woman? Your lyrics go back and forth, you're so mature, but you squeal for snow. Damn, I never saw your face that lit up."

"I don't know, Gunner, I'm just me. I don't pretend to be anything and I don't hide who I am. Maybe I am a lot of different things, or maybe I am one thing, me."

"I hope you always have the strength and confidence you have now to stay that way. It is the most beautiful thing I have ever seen."

I say thank you but it sounds pathetic. I don't know what else to say. We sit outside until our cheeks are numb. Before I get to the bedroom door I catch Gunner with that look of pure sadness in his eyes that tugs at my heart like nothing else can. He walks alone into his bedroom. I wish I could make it disappear, but I am not the answer to his problems. I don't even know what his problems are.

I wake up early again, super excited for the snow, or perhaps having Gunner and Ryan in the house is with me and makes me get out of Fred's bed early. I get up with a massive bounce in my step. The snow is piling up fast and the pure beauty and cleanness of it brings me undiluted joy. I cook a breakfast feast with Gunner before a hung over Fred and Ryan come downstairs. It seems the Evans siblings have a genetic link to being in sync with Mr. Rhoades.

We eat and I tell the cutest boys I know that I challenge them to a massive snowball fight and afterward they will all get homemade apple pie. Snow turns me domestic. And horny, but I have to wait to satisfy the last craving. We are on our way outside when I take Fred to the side and tell him exactly how I feel. "No drinking tonight, okay?"

"Am I that bad drunk?"

"No, not at all. I get crazy horny for snow and I need you sober for all the things I want to do to you." He is staring at me like I said the craziest thing in the world. "What? Stop looking at me like that."

"The way you handle things always shocks me. You use words so differently and I love the way you deliver them too."

"Oh, I can deliver, no worries there."

"Stop, or I will take you right here against the house or in the snow even."

"Geez, do you think I would say no? Don't you know me at all by now?"

"I know you well, but I keep thinking it's a dream and you won't be mine to know one day."

"Oh, Fred." I jump into his arms. "I am yours. I love you. Only you, forever."

We are wrapped together when I hear Gunner laughing. Out of nowhere a snowball hits me in the back of the head. "No hugging in snow wars. Fred, you get the girl since you're hugging her. It's war." He hits Fred in the head this time.

We last an hour before we are soaked and frozen. No one can tell who won, since it was a blood bath of messy snowballs, but Ryan and Gunner sure did hit us a lot. We are walking back inside and Gunner stops me. "It was good to see something you don't excel at." I hit him in the forehead with a snowball. "Were you aiming for my mouth to shut me up?"

"So I can't throw."

"I know, I saw, it's cute. At least you try."

"Thanks, I have balls of steel and will try anything."

"See, that is what makes it no fun. You are fine with your few negative qualities. You are too mature for the rest of us."

Everyone goes upstairs before me. I take everything out to make the pie, but I am too wet and cold. So I go up and join Fred in the shower.

He seems shocked to see me, since my brother is in the house, sober and awake nonetheless. He cares very little about that once I have him firmly in my palm, stroking him until he is hard and moaning my name.

His body is firm and hot and I am getting worked up, when he turns around and slams me into the tile wall. Damn, I think it shook the whole house. "Fred, please, I need you. Fuck me hard."

"Damn, Morgan, how could I ever say no to you?" And he doesn't. I am turned on by my need for him. I come right before he does, shaking with insane pleasure. It takes all my will power to change and head downstairs to make the pie.

Downstairs, Gunner has the TV on and Ryan is coming out of the bathroom and no one says anything. Shit, I totally feel like I got caught. I choose to ignore it. My mom calls and tells me school is closed. She tells us to stay put and be safe and she is glad we are together. The rest of the day is fun, except for the uncomfortable feeling I suddenly have with my brother.

The next day being snowbound isn't that awesome. I am getting restless. I even go for a walk, but there is a lot of snow out there making it tough to get a run in. Lounged out in Fred's bed while writing with his guitar, Ryan comes in. I didn't hear him so when he sits down next to me I jump a little.

He puts his hand on my leg. "Morgan, you seem okay, but are you really okay?"

"Yes, why would you ask that?"

"I don't know. I don't want to intrude. You have taken care of yourself for as long as I remember. It's very confusing."

"What is confusing?"

"This." He looks around the room. "You fell asleep with Gunner on the couch the other night. I know you slept in here last night. I mean who the hell are you with? Mom talks a little. She said you and Fred are friends, but she sees such chemistry between you and Gunner she thinks something will happen with him. You are close to them both. It's very weird."

"Sorry, I know this isn't normal. I am close to them both. I don't have feelings for them both. I have slept in this bed with Fred since Memorial Day. We talk and work all night and it just happened and it didn't stop.

Gunner is a comfort to me. It's weird, I know. Don't look into it any further, but thanks for caring about me. Everything is more than fine."

"You were a little off Friday and it seemed Gunner helped and, well, I can't tell what is happening."

"It's been a long week, and Gunner does help. He gets me in a way no one can. Wait until you hear the music we wrote." Damn, I have to change this subject.

Thankfully he takes the change of subject and runs with it. Talking to Ryan was odd. I didn't actually lie, but I sure didn't tell him the truth. By Tuesday afternoon the roads are looking safe and school will be open on Wednesday. I hug both Gunner and Fred good-bye. Then I drive Ryan back home to Madison so he can get his car. What a freakin' weird life I have gotten myself into.

Chapter Thirty-Three
Never Say Goodbye

FRED SPENDS MOST weekdays throughout the winter far and away in sunny California. He planned it so he leaves on Mondays and comes back on Fridays. He has come home some Thursdays and worked in New York too. Even though it is business as usual, nothing is normal. Fred is slipping away from me. He is tired and overworked and over traveled. He says that's all it is, but I don't think it's more than that.

Fred and the guys are all back in Jersey for my winter break. They only work a few days, so I get a lot of chunks of time wrapped up and alone with Fred. I start to feel myself shifting back into a normal happy pattern.

The night before I go back to school and they return to California, Gunner is acting strange and seems to be trying to ask me something. I can't take him being weird, so I say, "What's up?"

"Huh?"

"You are acting weird. Did something happen?"

"No."

"You sure?"

"Positive." He turns to look at me. "Are you okay?" he whispers.

"Yes. Why would you think I wasn't?"

"You aren't normal. You look sad."

"Fred's not the same. It affects me, leaving me very lonely. I love him very much, but we don't talk or share time like we used to. It's different. Since New Year's. Maybe it's winter blues. It snows all the time and the snow is dirty and seems to never melt. School is almost over at least. Just a lot of change. I settled on Rutgers, and Fred is worth it, but it scares me.

Life is overwhelming me, but nothing is wrong. I will be fine, Gunner. I will get through it."

"You seem to have everything under control, but I'm always here for you, Morgan. Always. Call, fly out, tell me to come home, anything."

"I know. When I need you, you will know. It will be obvious."

We stop talking, but we don't get up; we also don't let go of each other's hands.

* * *

The smell of spring air puts a bounce in my step. I am looking forward to the middle of spring when I get to smell the lilacs again. The band will be working on some videos throughout the spring and summer, and the tour has been finalized. Starting in January they will spend five months in Europe, then summer and fall in the U.S. I can't help but think it won't matter that I am at Rutgers. Fred won't be here. I should have gone to California. I ignore my thoughts and focus on today.

Fred's first day back is wonderful. We cook, write, and make love. The uplifting thoughts of summer give me new life, even though I have to go back to school Monday. Fred is planning on coming back with me for Easter. I am feeling hopeful, but April 28th is always on my mind.

The day before Easter we are dying eggs with my parents; perhaps we all want to feel like children again. Ryan has gone off to drunk land, somewhere south, for Spring Break, now that he is twenty-one and single. He really seems to drink a lot since Faith broke up with him. Dad brings the mail in and hands me an envelope. The return address is the recording company. I open it and look over at Fred.

"Morgan, don't look so scared. It's your check for letting us record your songs."

I open the envelope and find a check made out to my mother and me for way too much. "Holy shit!" I say out loud with both parents watching.

"We recorded four songs of yours. You will get more when they are released."

"This is a lot of money. I guess college is covered."

My parents say nothing. They are too shocked to speak. I walk up to Fred and put my hands on his shoulder. I look at him so he knows I love him, and say, "Thank you. I never saw this life for myself and you have given me so much, taught me so much. I'm grateful for the miracle that you understand me and that you let me express myself. You are a remarkable person. This is too much for just the words thank you." I hug him tight.

He pulls me off him and grabs my face like he will kiss me, but I know he won't. My parents are watching us like the hottest new TV show. "Morgan, you did this yourself, and frankly Gunner was a bigger help than I ever was at teaching you, but I will accept your thanks. Maybe in the form of pie." I laugh and tickle him and get far away because what I want to do to him would not be something my parents should see.

Gunner joins us for Easter Dinner. It's the five of us and somehow it feels normal to me. I have been paid royally and my parents don't have to pay for college anymore. I don't think anything would make them say no. They are not the kind of people to make a decision based on money, but at this point because of the money I doubt they would stop me.

I spend Easter break between Mantoloking and Spring Lake. Alex and Zach have been around a lot since they came back from California, so we have been hanging at Gunner's. The heated pool and hot tub make it feel like summer is here already. The rest of April is normal, but the end of the month looms over me like the darkest cloud ever seen on earth.

On the 28th it will be one year since I met Frederick Rhoades, not an anniversary to celebrate. He wants to spend the weekend together as we always do. I said no. I won't spend his first anniversary to another woman with him. I told him if he wants to spend it with me he shouldn't have a wife in the first place. Why do I have to be in love with someone who can't be everything I deserve?

I come home from school on Friday and my phone is ringing. I know it is Fred, trying one more time to get me to come down, and I don't want to answer it, but I can't play that game. I pick up the phone. "Hey." I know I sound sad and I didn't even mean to.

"Hey." He sounds worse.

"Fred, please don't do this anymore. I am going into the city to spend the weekend with Kelly. You know I would rather be with you, but I love my friends, and I should spend time with them so they stay my friends."

"I know I need to let you be, but I miss you."

"Well, after the weekend if you miss me enough maybe you will file for a divorce." He is silent, which is not a good thing. "Hey, I have to leave, Brooke and I have a train to catch. I will call you later."

"I love you, Jellybean."

"Fred, I love you more than I thought I could love another person, but I can't do this right now. It is just too painful."

"Okay. Bye. Talk to you later."

"I will talk to you later. Bye." I hang up, full of dread.

Brooke and I make it into the city and to Kelly's dorm at NYU in record time. I have made a dinner reservation at a fancy restaurant, so I can spend a little of my money on the people who have always supported me.

At the restaurant, Brooke is a little shocked when she realizes how expensive it is. "Hey, I have been working, so I'm paying. I want you to know how much you mean to me even though I don't see you as much as I used too."

"Wow. I am shocked. You made money? I thought you were just hanging with those hot boys."

"Well, I do hang with them a lot, but I completely wrote one song that's coming out on the new album, and the lyrics for three others. I received my first check a few weeks ago."

"Seriously?" Brooks says, her eyes wide.

"Yes."

"How much?"

"Enough to pay for school."

Kelly just listens. I am certain she knows the gist of it from Steve. They are still dating and she is still planning on moving to California after graduation. I am sure her family doesn't know yet so I don't say anything. I love that Kelly and I have the type of friendship where we want the best for each other.

We enjoy an exhausting weekend of girl time. Shopping, eating, movies, and nails. Everything is fun, but this is never on the top of my to-do list. I prefer to be making something, music or love, or even pie.

Brooke and I are heading out early on Sunday since Kelly still has to study for finals. As we are leaving, the phone rings. "Hello." Kelly pauses for too long, but her face says nothing. "Hold on."

She looks up at me. My stomach hurts. "Morgan, it's Gunner." She reaches out the phone to me.

"Hello," I say, hanging on tight to the silence. I am not up for whatever he has to say. I watch Kelly take Brooke into the other room before he speaks.

"Sorry, Morgan, I didn't want to bother you. You never called Fred and well he didn't handle it too well."

"Gunner, I didn't want to hurt him. I just couldn't be with him today. I should have called. I am sorry for that, but I am not sorry for telling him he can't have us both."

"I know, Morgan, you are right, but I sent a car for you."

"Why, Gunner? I don't want to be there."

"He is popping pills and doing coke until he sees you again. At this rate he will be dead in a few hours." I am stunned, fucking stunned silent. Holy shit, this rock star lifestyle just hit me like a ton of bricks. I am so fucking numb I can't talk. "Morgan? You there?" I can't move either. "Morgan...answer me...please..."

"Yeah, car, you have the address?"

"The car is downstairs."

I hang up and take a huge breath. I will lie to my friends because I am getting good at doing it. So I walk into the other room and with control I didn't know I possessed I say, "I have to get down to the shore."

"Okay," they say in unison.

"Brooke, Gunner has a car for you too," I tell her.

Kelly walks out to the street with us, then she leaves Brooke and comes with me. "You okay?"

"Kelly, it's bad. Don't tell Steve, please. I won't tell you more so you don't have to lie."

"It will be fine." She hugs me before I get in the car. I am shedding a pool of tears that flood the back of this decked out limo. I see the bar. I pour myself a drink. I stare at it for over an hour, telling myself over and over that drinking this amber liquor is as bad as what Fred chose to do to cope. Maybe not as bad, but damn close.

I get to the house feeling sicker than I ever have and wishing I had chosen to drink the liquor. Gunner is in the street when we pull up. He waves to the driver as he comes to open my door. I crash into his arms as the driver gets my bag. "Gunner?" I ask him, but I don't know what the question is.

"Come, he doesn't know you are coming. You are going to scare the shit out of him."

"Wait, I have to catch my breath first. I feel used. Are you using me?"

"Yes, Morgan, I am. To save Fred."

"Can I have a minute, please? What will I say?"

"I don't know, Morgan. He did a lot of drugs the year we got out of school and this reminds me of that. I never knew what to do then either." I guess the look on my face says it all. "He never told you?" I shake my head side-to-side real slow cause I might vomit if I move it any faster. "Sorry, Beth too. It made me hate them both very much." He lifts me up off the ground now that I have fallen to my knees, too stunned to cry. "Come, let's do this together. Please."

"Yes, Gunner, I can do this. We can do this."

Stepping into Fred's house weakens me further. My home is abnormal, foreign, wrong. The house looks smaller, smells nasty, and the image before me is crushing my chest. If Gunner wasn't holding my hand I might turn to ash from the pain. Fred is at the coffee table with Alex and another man I don't know. Fred is snorting a line of coke with his left hand, a beer bottle in his right, when his bloodshot eyes find my dead ones.

I start to walk towards him, pulling Gunner with me. I am grateful he doesn't snort the coke, and he even puts the beer down. He stands up. The look on his face is enough to knock me over. He starts to walk towards me and I put my hand up. I close my eyes wishing I could erase what I see. I squeeze Gunner's hand so tight I feel his bones shift.

"I don't know what to say. There is nothing that could change this or make me not see it. Make me see you as the same person I fell in love with. I am going to turn around and walk away. And when you want to be the man I think you are, call me. I loved you so much, so very much, you had all of me. You broke me. You broke us."

I turn to leave and I drop Gunner's hand. It feels like a lifetime before I feel the fresh air on my face. I run, yet it feels like I am standing still. I make it to the street before I hear him. Gunner yells, "Morgan, wait." Even my name sounds different now that my world has collapsed around me. I hear it over and over trying to get away, but Gunner catches up to me. I collapse in the street. He catches me and we sink onto the blacktop. "If I had my damn sneakers on I could have gotten away."

"I know, I've seen you run. No running now, I have you." He stands up and gives me his hand to help me up. "Come with me to my house, please."

"Yes, thanks," I mutter, weak and tired. He starts to walk away, leaving me frozen in place. "Can you come pick me up? Even the driveway makes me sick."

Gunner's couch is a minor comfort. Ginger ale in hand, I just stare at him, numb. "When I'm ready to ask questions, will you answer them?" I ask.

"Yes, Morgan. I never thought in a million years I would feel this way, but I choose you over him. I will be loyal to you first. I love you both, but he royally fucked up. Morgan, anything you want to know or need to have, I will be here for you."

I sip the ginger ale for hours until Gunner drives me to my parents' house. We haven't even hit the parkway yet when I undo my seatbelt and lay my head in his lap. I don't understand how he is my greatest source of comfort, but he is, and I need every ounce of serenity I can squeeze from him.

Next thing I know the truck is stopped. I sit up and don't recognize where we are. "Sorry, I pulled over. I didn't want to wake you and I wanted to know what we should do when we get to your house."

"Shit, I don't know, Gunner. I never called, nothing. I have been irresponsible," I say, pushing my hair off my face, and he has the audacity to laugh. I punch him, not wanting to hurt him, in the stomach. "Don't laugh at me."

"Sorry, I shouldn't have done that. You are too responsible, Morgan. That is why I laughed."

"Fair enough. I am, but this is who I am and I don't plan on changing for anyone." He hugs me. "Gunner?"

"Yeah?"

"When did you hugging me become the most comforting thing?"

"Probably a couple hours ago, when I was mean enough to show you your biggest nightmare."

"You did the right thing. Even though I know it killed you too."

"It did."

"Okay, drive me home. Can you come in for a few minutes, say hi, maybe say we met up in the city?"

"Yes, I can do that for you, Morgan. Anything, remember?"

"Can you make Fred not turn to drugs?"

"I will try until I die."

* * *

The next night, alone and sad, I end up going to bed early. Reaching to turn off my light the phone rings, snapping me out of my blank state. I have told myself no matter how hurt and mad Fred makes me, I will not shut him out. I will help him because I love him. "Hello," I answer, feeling a sadness I didn't know I could feel.

"Hey," he pauses, sounding lifeless. The air between the phone lines hangs as lifeless as he sounds and I feel. I need him to open up first.

I know it's only minutes but it seems like an eternity when he says, "I'm so sorry. Is there any chance you will forgive me? Any at all or should I stop trying before I even start?" I wish he would just try because I am worth more to him than all the grains of sand on earth.

"Yes, but I don't know what it will take or how long either. I have never been in a situation like this before, but I know I want this pain to end as fast as it can.

"Can we talk more tomorrow?" he begs.

"Yes, but on the phone. I don't want you here yet. I will be at Gunner's for the weekend. We can spend time together but not the nights. Next weekend is Kelly's graduation so I will be at her party. After that let's see what happens."

"Yes, Morgan, whatever it takes. I fucked up. I will jump as high as you ask."

"I don't want that. I will never make a demand like that of you. I have to learn to trust you again." I sit silently feeling my heart beat out of whack and listening to his breathing. "I haven't stopped loving you."

"You are so level-headed, Morgan. Sometimes I wish you would stay mad at me and yell and scream. I will never stop loving you, Jellybean. Never."

"I feel very 'unlevel'. You need to learn to accept what you want in life for yourself. You have to do it for you. You can't have me or Gunner or Beth do it for you."

"I know, Morgan, you are always right. Your philosophical ways are one of the many traits I love so much."

"I love you too, and you can flatter me all day, but you picked cocaine over me. Don't say it wasn't that way because that is how I see it. Regardless of what you think, that is what I think. If you want me back, you have to see it that way."

"Okay." He sounds lifeless.

"I need to try to sleep. I will call you tomorrow. Night, Fred."

I hang up and try to sleep but my mind is racing. I never ever saw this coming; I never thought drugs would be a part of our lives.

We talk every day and eventually he tells me he only started using again when Alex came over Saturday night. He claims he did it because I never called, and I tell him that is a lame excuse. Thank goodness he agrees, but I hope he understands too.

Friday night after school I head to Gunner's. I cook dinner and once again Gunner listens to all my talk about Fred. I told Fred I would be willing to see him here tonight just for a little while. I don't want to be alone with him yet. The doorbell startles me. I try to settle my heart as I continue to dry the dinner dishes. Gunner has said he will hire full-time help if I am going to be around more. I tell him, "No way!" I don't want a stranger around, which is the exact reason he doesn't have help.

"Hi," Fred says timidly, as he comes toward me.

"Hi." I turn around and walk around the island. "Why did you ring the bell?"

"I don't know. I felt uncomfortable. You have so many rules for me and I don't want to mess up."

I walk over to him, drying my already dry hands on the dish towel for the millionth time. "Sorry, I didn't mean to make you feel that way. When you are the one who breaks the trust, you have a lot to do to show someone that you can be trusted again." I put the dish towel down and wrap my arms around his neck. "I don't want you to ever feel uncomfortable. I want you to always feel your best around me. But you hurt me more than I thought you could. That is the worst thing you could have done. It would be easier to have you be back with Beth, have you cheat on me, have you end this for no reason at all, but to pick drugs, that killed me. Did you do it because you wanted to hurt me?"

"No, I did it because I was so fucked up and Alex was standing there with it. I never thought twice."

"Well, next time you are tempted, please think a lot more than twice."

"I will."

I look deep into his eyes, which are pained as they were the day we met. I lean in and kiss him. Soft and gentle. I clearly have the upper hand. The problem is, I don't want it.

I stay home the weekend of Kelly's graduation. Her parents throw her one awesome party with Steve by her side. I would rather be with Fred. I love him and I can't just turn that off because he made a huge mistake. The third weekend in May I spend the days with Fred but the nights in Gunner's guest room.

It's like we are starting over and hoping our troubles make us stronger. I wish we could be what we were. I didn't want change. Well, besides Beth, I didn't want change. I tell Fred that I am jumping all in, opening my heart, and trusting him again. My love for him is stronger than his faults so I will continue to fight for us.

I ask if I can skip school the Friday before Memorial Day and my mom agrees, so I will drive to Fred's Thursday night and stay locked away with him until I have to go back to school Tuesday. I miss him so much that my plan is to never remove my hands from his hot body all weekend.

I walk in Thursday at dinnertime to find Fred, of all people, cooking. Miraculously, nothing smells burnt. I can't help but smile. He drops everything and almost runs over to me. He is standing before me just watching my face, like he is looking for answers. I can feel he wants to ask if he can kiss me even though I told him last night, "No more awkward moments."

I think he can see the thoughts in my head and he swoops down and kisses me. Soft turns hard. Hard turns passionate. Passionate turns wild. His mouth is so familiar to mine now. Absence makes the heart just need more. A lot more. I need more of him. I need all of him. He pulls away and stares at me again. His eyes are the way I prefer them – bright. "I love you," he says.

"Enough to cook for me, I see."

"I want to start over. A first date. Especially since we never dated."

"Well, I never cared about that."

He walks over to stir the pasta and comes back to me. I stand still taking in his beauty. "So tonight, dinner outside, we can talk until sunset, then I want to walk on the beach with you. After that I will hold you in our bed. All night, just hold you. The same as I did almost a year ago."

"Okay." My mouth feels glued shut from the love pouring out of him. I can only find the strength to stare at him.

"Tomorrow is another story."

"Oh." I laugh a little. "Will you fuck me until I can't walk tomorrow?" I ask, putting a piece of cheese in my mouth so I don't start laughing.

"If you want. I would never say no." He leans over and kisses me, while I am still chewing. "That cheese yummy?" he asks.

"It would be better with a taste of that wine you have there," I say, as he comes over toward me. He leans down and kisses me so I can taste his mouth fully, ingesting the most sexual mixture of cheese, wine, and Fred's mouth. "You are going to hold me all night, that's all. Shit, Fred, sex is coming out of every pore in your body."

"Yes, hold you. Tomorrow, like I was saying before you interrupted me, date number two."

"Intriguing. Do I get any hints?"

"Nope."

"Okay."

"That's all you say?" he says. frustration shooting from his lips.

"Yep, if I get all antsy it will give you too much pleasure knowing you are torturing me, so I won't show you how you torture me."

"Smart girl. Let's eat." He smirks and I come undone yet again.

I am feeling more and more normal as we eat dinner, perhaps it's just the wine. I don't know if I have forgiven Fred or convinced myself that I can, but for now this feels perfect again. After we take a long walk on the beach, I quickly find my home in him again.

As I step to open the door, Fred stops me. "Can we go to bed now?" he begs.

"I thought you said you were just holding me tonight?"

"I am. Let's sleep. I haven't slept in a month. I can't sleep without you. And I want to get up to see the sunrise again."

"Well, I have been up since six, and you know I can sleep. Come, I need to shower."

I come out of the shower and the pajamas that I wore the first time we spent the night together are on the bed. Also two huge arrangements of lilacs have appeared. Fred isn't around and I become tragically empty without him. I have allowed my mind and body to miss him again. And it hurts to miss him, but it hurts far less than it did to see him snorting cocaine.

I get dressed and I literally run into him at the top of the stairs, ice cream in hand. I burst into tears, like a hormonal teenager. How the hell is it that ice cream weakens me? Fred is torn between dropping everything to grab me and forcing me to walk back to the bed. I take the ice cream from him so he can carry my weak soul.

I believe I can do this. I can love him, fully. We eat the ice cream and claim we are going to sleep, but instead we talk and kiss for hours. I might have thought I time-traveled back a year, if I weren't so dramatically altered by love.

The alarm is blaring through the dark room. I don't want to move away from Fred, but honestly, I am ready to relive the start of this love. I slowly wake up and get him up so we can walk out to the beach.

I can see the life in his eyes and nothing ever looked so sexy. We don't talk. I love it that we both aren't morning people. Or at least we aren't people who talk in the morning. Fred wraps us up in a blanket as we watch the sunrise. His hands are all over me. I can't think straight, and I love it.

"If I let you keep this up, will you take me bed? Make love to me?" I don't turn to look at him even though I long too.

"No."

"Than stop, you are torturing me."

"Soon, I promise, soon. The torture goes both ways."

We watch the sunrise and he runs his fingertip up and down my arm, a soothing, loving touch. We sit for over an hour, no one moving when I turn to talk to him. "Thank you for this. I like the sensation of going back to the beginning."

"Me too. I wanted to tell you that morning last year that I was in love with you already, but I was scared I would scare you away."

"You wouldn't have scared me away. I was in love with you then and I am in love with you now." We join hands and walk back to the house.

Chapter Thirty-Four
Unpack Your Heart

"SHOULD I SHOWER? What should I wear? Give me some info, please," I beg as I hug him tight. I push my hands into his jeans to grab his sweet ass and press my boobs into him, hoping he caves.

"That won't work." He leans down and brushes his lips along mine. "Everything is already packed for you and I will be sure to get you clean." He smirks the smirk that makes me sexually weak.

I push up onto the balls of my feet to kiss him. "I am trusting you."

"You can trust me."

"Should I put clothes on or stay in my pajamas?"

"Clothes, but I prefer you naked. I will get us a breakfast. Be right back."

We are driving north into New York state when I try to control my yawning. It isn't even nine yet, but these sleepless nights are catching up to me fast. Fred catches my second yawn. "Coffee?"

"Yes, but I will have to pee and I don't know how long we are driving."

"I will pull over if you have to pee."

"On the side of the road?"

"No, a rest stop, silly. I am allowed out in public. It's not illegal."

"I know but I don't want you spotted with me still under age."

"Morgan, we are not doing anything wrong, and we aren't having sex on the NY Thruway either."

"I hope not, but I want you so bad I would."

"Okay, stop. Coffee and peeing I can handle. Sex talk I can't, yet."

A little before noon he pulls into a Hilton Hotel parking lot, near Albany. "So, sex off the highway is okay?"

"Come." He gets out of the car and opens my door. "Trust me."

"I do," I say, taking his hand.

Hand in hand we walk into the hotel. It may never feel normal being in public together. He checks in with a credit card that isn't his. I will have to ask whom it belongs to, but for now we have become Mr. and Mrs. DeLuca. He gets our keys and walks me to the elevator. He has a small bag with him. I assume anything I need is in there, but I hope I need nothing. Then it hit's me that DeLuca is his mom's maiden name and he must use it so he isn't recognized, but who the hell wouldn't recognize his gorgeous face?

He opens the door to a massive suite. It is a marvelous room, but it doesn't explain why we are in the middle of nowhere in upstate, New York. An arrangement of lilacs and sunflowers sits in the center of the table. My breath is stolen and my eyes drip. Fred takes two giants steps and he is in front of me, his hand holding my cheeks. "No tears. Pampering you and showing you how much I love you can't fix what I did, but I have to try." He kisses me. Passion ignites my body. I burn in a new way for this sexy man holding me. I crave him so bad I think I feel pain, the need, the physical contact, the simple sexual desire, it controls me. The swimming in pleasure sensation is the one I want most to dive into.

He brushes his hands down my sides and grabs the bottom of my tee shirt and I lift my arms so he can remove it. It hasn't even hit the floor and he has my bra undone and off me. "Damn you're fast today."

"I will slow down." The passion in his voice speaks to all of me.

"No, I need you very bad."

"Morgan?" I look up at him. "You have no idea how much I need you. In every way."

His kisses are hot, a perfect mix of pure skill and talent. My breasts are putty in his hands and I become insane from my arousal. He has managed to get me out of all my clothes yet I only get his shirt unbuttoned. He walks my naked body to the bed until my legs hit the edge.

His eyes focus on me as he takes his shirt off. My hands can't stay off his muscular body. He feels even more toned than the last time I touched him. I start to wonder if he has been working out more when he takes my nipple deep into his mouth, and the thought becomes a distant memory. The moisture, the heat, I can't do anything but moan, as he works my skin into a frenzy.

He continues until I will myself to fall onto the bed. I watch him undo his jeans and slip them off. His black boxer briefs accentuate him nicely. Almost looking as good as it when he's naked. His underwear should be off, but unfortunately he lies down next to me still in them. His mouth works its way up and down my body, making me wiggle so much I start to feel crazy. His hands are everywhere but where I long for them most.

"Fred, I need you."

"I need you too."

"Now."

"Slow and steady, baby."

"No, I will do it myself if you don't, it's been too long, I can't wait another second. I need to feel you inside me again. I need to be connected every way possible."

"Damn, Jellybean."

He gets up, pulls the covers down and slips into the cool sheets with me. "I need you, Fred. Now."

He supports himself above me, love pouring from his soul into me. Love, lust, and primal passion bounce off him and into me. He leans down to my ear and with a deep vibrating whisper, he says, "I will make love to you now, because I need to, but next time, I want to watch you touch yourself."

He pushes himself into me, and the slow pace makes it even more exciting. Every ripple pushing deeper. So hard. So damn erotic, hot breath in my ear, his arms locking our heads together, my hips crave it faster. The burning desire is building super-fast. He gives me what I need and moves harder and faster. I feel the build-up, but the release isn't happening.

I grind into him and bite his shoulder as he shifts his hips. I push harder with the sensation of him inside my body as my climax compares to nothing else on earth. I scream his name louder than I ever have, and my body continues to squeeze his. My body still has a few spasms left when I feel Fred shift again and I open my eyes to look at him. His face is scrunched like he is trying to find heaven. He pounds into me one more time, hard. His come is hot and welcoming. It feels longer than a month since I've felt our bodies experience this pleasure. It feels new yet so familiar.

We are lying in this fluffy bed, in this fancy room and I have no care in the world where we are, as long as we are together. I continue to wonder why the hell we drove this far to check into a random hotel. I open my mouth to ask, but he gets up out of bed. I decide just to watch him walk around naked.

He returns with a small wrapped box. Crawling back in bed he hands it to me. "Open it."

"You don't have to buy me things."

"I know and it makes me want to even more. You are a clever girl."

"Stop, that isn't true," I say, a little mad.

"I know, calm down. I know you don't think like that."

I unwrap it taking care not to rip the paper to find a ring box. No man who is married should be giving another woman a ring. I open it to discover a ring with three garnets. He takes it out and puts it on my right hand. It fits perfectly.

"I want to start over. Garnets are the birthstone for January, the first month of the year. We can work through each month. And, as it turns out, it is the state gemstone of New York." He smirks at me and leans down to kiss me.

"And? I feel an and?"

"And we now officially added New York to the states we have had sex in."

"Oh, you are bad. I was confused why we were here. Why not take me into the city?"

"Because we have more states to get to. I will order room service for lunch before we are off to Vermont."

"You are nuts," I say, shaking my head at him while falling deeper into love.

"If loving you makes me nuts, then I am."

Hours later we pull up in front of a quaint bed and breakfast. Fred, ever the gentleman, comes and opens my door. Once inside, a cute, older couple welcomes us with warm smiles and kind words. It feels even more welcoming because they have no clue who Fred is.

The woman grabs actual keys and takes us up the staircase to our room. It's super pink. The wallpaper is pink, the bedding is pink, but I know regardless of how the room looks, Fred will still look hot in it. She tells us dinner will be ready in the dining room at seven. Once she leaves I sit on the bed and watch him move about the room.

"What is going on in that gorgeous head?" he asks.

"Nothing."

"It's never nothing, Morgan." He walks over and pushes me down on to the bed and climbs on top of me. He looks at his watch. "We have almost an hour. Tell me what you are thinking so I can make love to you before and after dinner."

"You have zero patience. I was thinking how much I love how fun you are. Now please, get these clothes off me. Sitting in the vibrating Jeep has been glorious to my body, but I need you to finish the job."

Dinner as well as breakfast the next day were both delicious. Good thing we had sex before dinner; otherwise Vermont would have been a bust. We both ate too much and with all that driving, we fell asleep early.

We drive to an airfield in New Hampshire. Fred parks the Jeep and takes me by the hand to a private jet. We step on but there is no crew. "Hope you aren't flying!"

"Ha-ha, no. I told them not to be here until eleven. Gives us enough time to add New Hampshire." He pulls me into the back of the plane. It's a small area, but we fall onto a large soft bed.

Flushed and satisfied less than ten minute later, I say, "Sorry, I felt rushed. I was afraid we would get caught. Can we do that again in the air, a lot slower?" I whisper as my hands roll over his six-pack.

He chuckles and gets out of bed and throws me my clothes. "Yes. Get dressed. We have places to be, cute stuff." We meet the pilot and co-pilot and soon enough we are in the air and being served lunch. Maybe I could get used to this. We land a little after two in Savannah, Georgia. And for the sake of saving time, Fred says good-bye to the crew and we take advantage of the bed once again.

Savannah is a cute town that we see very little of on our drive out in a sparkling new Lotus. I always thought expensive cars were not on my radar, but now that I have driven a few I have become a certified car chick. We arrive in Hilton Head, South Carolina in no time at all and smoothly check into the hotel. Walking into yet another suite, I smell the fragrant smell of fresh flowers the second the door opens. All different types of purple flowers fill every surface and a beautiful purple dress lies on the bed.

Fred interrupts me and gets me to move with another jewelry box. I open it to find a large necklace with two rows of Amethyst's running almost the entire way around. It is beautiful and the same purple as the dress. "Would South Carolina and Amethyst go together?"

"Yes, but don't expect fifty states and fifty presents, just yet. I need to save some for the future."

I smile, elated, but I use that smile to cover the fear that there isn't a future. It's been thirteen months, and he has never brought up a single thought on divorcing Beth. I will be eighteen in four weeks and something tells me that isn't going to be my present this year either.

A candlelit dinner by the ocean, all dressed up, with the man I love, is as romantic as it sounds. Once we return to the room Fred takes his time getting me out of my dress. It is still a tie as to which is better: Those slow seductive moments when my brain is functioning enough to compute every pleasurable thing he does to me, or those fast brain numbing times when everything is on fire and I miss half of it.

Tonight we are slow and deeply erotic. He has every inch of me tingling and I pray a little it never ends. He is too talented with his body for it not to end because he always satisfies me. Laying in his arms, content, and full of energy, I say, "Shall we walk on the beach?"

"Yes."

"I love being near the ocean," I whisper almost just to myself.

Holding Fred's hand with my bare feet in the sand washes away any negative thoughts. We return to the room and head to bed early again. I am not sure if it's the traveling or the weight of the past month, but the sleep is welcome.

Kisses on my ribs wake me because they tickle, but nothing tickles after that. His kisses become deeper and wetter as he works down my leg and back up. He knows he has me squirming when he does the same to the other leg. I am close to begging, when finally, his mouth is not on my leg but between them. His tongue is expertly talented.

Perhaps it is stronger and more skilled from all the singing. I imagine a guitar player is talented with his fingers, and a drummer has perfect rhythm. No wonder groupies exist. Suddenly my mind is blank. His hands are holding my hips down so I can't squirm around and my head is under the pillow, it doesn't take long and I come, screaming his name into the pillow I might be ripping in half.

He climbs up me and sinks himself deep inside me before I can move the pillow off my head to see him. He moves it and leans down and kisses me. My hips fire back into him with relentless pounding. Damn, how can I be so turned on again? He feels harder and larger than normal inside me as my nails rake over his back. I move to feel him move inside me faster and out of nowhere a ripping orgasm takes me by surprise. I am still coming back to earth when Fred moans my name as he comes.

He rolls off and pulls me to him. He must have plans for us, so I start to get up. He pulls me back. "No, not yet."

"Do we have to get somewhere?"

"Yeah, but being with you is more important than keeping time." He holds me even tighter. "Morgan, that was mind blowing, but you know I don't like it when you hide under the pillow. I want to see your face, always."

"I know, but it was bright in here, and I was still half asleep."

"I feel like you are pretending it's someone else."

"What, really?" Wide awake, I say, "You can't be that insecure. You know that most women who would do that are picturing that it is you between their legs."

He laughs. "Well, you said before you met us that you thought Gunner was hot."

"I did say something like that. Gunner is beautiful. More beautiful inside than outside. I will find men besides you attractive, but it's you I love. Only you get to be with me physically and mentally. You are my fantasy and my reality."

"Maybe if you met Gunner first you would be with him. I get jealous and I know it's crazy but you two have such an easy going relationship. I am happy you make each other happy, and I trust you both implicitly. But I wonder if you could have even more with him than you have with me."

"Please stop, this hurts. You can't hold something I said before I knew any of you against me. I love Gunner, he is a wonderful friend, but that is all. I love you. Only you. I just wish you loved only me."

He doesn't say anything, which is best. I don't want another time away from home tainted with Beth. I get up and shower and dress for the day with a little bit of attitude.

"Come, let's leave. We can eat on the plane." He still sounds sad.

"Are we going home?" I am still thinking about his jealousy.

"No. We are flying back to New Hampshire to get the Jeep and we will drive home over the rest of the weekend," he says, realizing I prefer to know and not be surprised. We eat breakfast on the plane, but both our appetites are weak. After too much silence I undo my seat belt and climb in his lap. I rarely crave the need to feel small and safe, but right now I need him to hold me as he would hold a sad child. It is confusing when the person who brings you pain is also the one who can take it away.

By the time we land my mind is a bit more content, but damn emotions sure do make a person tired. I fall asleep in the Jeep then wake to see the ocean glisten on the coast of Maine. It's stunning. We sit in silence and watch the day. He takes my hand to hold and heal. He starts the Jeep and we head to a small hotel. He checks in and this time the young girl behind the desk knows who he is. She is staring at him like she is going to have a seizure. I want to laugh at her schoolgirl ways, when I realize she is older than me.

Our room is simple and cozy. Fred lies on the bed and I join him. "How long are we here for?" I ask.

"Just the afternoon. Do you want to leave sooner?"

"No, I was getting hungry."

"Let's eat." He goes to get up, but I hold him down. I kiss him slowly as he opens his mouth for my tongue. Between kisses, I find the strength to mumble, "After we eat…. I want you to make love to me, slow. I want to hold you above me, while I kiss you the whole time."

He moves over me and grinds himself into my stomach. "Damn, Morgan, I love everything about you so fucking much."

He kisses me more before he abruptly gets up to see what we can get for lunch. We eat pizza and drink Pepsi. What a great combo – comfort food heaven. Our conversation is easy again even though our hearts are both heavy. Fred turns the radio on and takes my hand to dance with me. He moves his body with the gift of rhythm he was born with. I love going along for the ride. Slowly, erotically, he dances me around the small room, as he takes each of my articles of clothing off.

As subdued as I am now, this will not last long. I get his shirt over his head and slowly unbutton his jeans. It's intoxicating taking his pants off and feeling how hard he is for me. I leave his boxers on, not ready mentally for everything yet. I lie on top of the comforter and like the rock star he is he takes my skimpy underwear off with his teeth. His hands run up and down my legs. I watch him, but he doesn't lie down with me. He takes my hands and pulls me off the bed, then pulls the covers back and climbs in before me.

I climb in with him. "Wait, you can't be in bed with me and have underwear on."

He takes them off and throws them. "This better, Jellybean?" For a second he looks more like the lead singer in a famous band. A bad boy with the drugs and tattoos and the wife.

"Yes," I say because the love I feel trumps the pain, for now.

His hands are light and stimulating, his tongue is firm and hot. He is my everything. "Fred, I need you, to be one with you." He runs his hand down my stomach and right between my legs. He doesn't hesitate a second and his finger dips easily inside me. "Oh, geez. Fred, shit." I am panting out of control. "I need you." His fingers are relentless.

"Shhh, I want to make you come. I want to make you come fast twice like we did that one night." That is exactly what he does.

"Fred, fuck, that was…. Shit, my brain is wordless. It felt out of this world awesome."

"Not as amazing as watching it, seeing you come undone, that's my heaven."

"Oh, I love that song."

He laughs soft and deep before he moves over my body. "Morgan, I love you undone. I love your obsession with music too, it is bigger than mine." He moves super slow over me and slips even slower into me. It feels different since I am swollen from desire and overuse. He moves so well inside me. It brings me nothing but pleasure. His arms are on the bed near my head, caging me in with his mouth on mine. My arms are digging into his biceps and my legs are wrapped around his firm thighs. We move with skill, like a well-oiled machine. Breaths increasing with each thrust and sweat glistening with each moan.

He moves his mouth off mine and kisses my ear. He is trying to slow down but I can tell he can't. "Damn, Morgan, it's too much."

"I know, I know, Fred, please come, come inside me. I need to feel you shake, need to feel how hot you are inside me."

"Oh, oh." He pushes into me twice and I feel his hot come hit me hard unlike I have ever felt it before. It is as if his orgasm causes mine. I come around him that second. Hard and tight. I feel him shake, as my orgasm must be crushing him. He shakes again and collapses on top of me. His weight is the best blanket I ever felt.

He pulls out of my body, then rolls over quickly, taking me with him. "I love you," he exhales and shivers.

"I love you too," I say, my head fitting perfectly on his shoulder.

Sometime later, I wake and then Fred wakes, startled. "It's almost five. Are we late for our next stop?" I ask.

"No, yes, but no. You are my only planned stop."

"You are such a romantic."

"No, I just found love."

"See, you are." He kisses me. "Let's leave before we have sex again and I can't walk."

"I am up for trying that."

I get up and get dressed. As much as I want to be with him again, I also want to move on. In the Jeep we share an entire bag of chips on the way to Boston. He checks us into a five-star hotel. The suite is almost the same size as my parents' entire house. "I wanted to take you out to eat, but since it's late would it be alright if we eat here, then get in that tub?" he asks, looking over his shoulder at the most astounding tub I have ever seen.

"Do you not know me well enough yet to know that is exactly what I would want?"

"I do, but you were enjoying being around other people this weekend. Being in the world together."

"That's true, but you know that I have and always will prefer being alone with you."

We eat a fancy dinner of steak and lobster, and a delicious bottle of champagne that costs more than my fancy jewelry. After we eat we take our tipsy bare asses to the huge Jacuzzi tub that overlooks the city of Boston. Relaxed and content, I stay between his legs, still. "This was a perfect weekend. You put a lot of thought and effort into it."

"Well, I had a lot of time on my hands. All I could think about was you, and I knew I needed something special to prove it to you."

"I don't need that. I need only you. I don't need to be spoiled, but I love everything you planned. It has been very creative.

"I know you don't need it. I needed it. Taking you all over the county has been super enjoyable. I want to make love to you all over this planet. Maybe we can be the first to have sex on Mars someday."

"Oh my, you are funny. And soft." I reach down and grab his flaccid penis.

"You wore me out."

I pump my hand up and down, slow and soft. He feels so smooth in water. I say nothing as I lie back and enjoy the feeling of him growing hard. I turn to face him and climb on top of him. His hands cup my cheeks before he looks into my eyes. "Oh, what you do to me."

I sleep like a log in Boston, but I wake up before Fred. I don't even roll over and his arms hold me against him. "Is it Monday? Memorial day? All this traveling has me a mess. How do you take being on the road?"

"I don't. I hate it, but I like the rush being on stage. The only thing better is being in a bed with you."

"See, always the romantic."

We leave Boston, and my heart hurts a little thinking this joy is ending, but when Fred says, "Ready to head home?" I realize I am past ready. I love that we call his house our home. At least I have one leg up on his wife. I never saw myself thinking that at any point in my life.

We head to a hotel in Connecticut for the afternoon, which is enjoyable, but we are tired. We managed to have sex in eight different states in four days. We also had sex in a plane, but I have still not joined the mile-high club. We make it home before eight. Fred holds the door for me and I stop to kiss him on my way inside. "Thank you, I had a wonderful weekend," I whisper.

"It was special, but I like home most."

"Me too. Take me to bed."

"You are insatiable. I thought women hit their sexual prime after thirty-five."

"I don't know, but maybe you will be lucky enough to find out someday."

"I doubt I'll be that lucky."

We head upstairs and for the first time it feels empty to me here. Fred must sense it because he is fast with his arms around me. "Bath or shower?"

"Shower."

Chapter Thirty-Five

The Violet Hour

SCHOOL IS ALMOST finished and I don't have a shred of sadness over it ending. When I ask my mom if I can skip school on Tuesday I feel a little foolish. She was cleaning up from dinner when I started the conversation. "Mom?"

"What, Honey?" She sounded odd since I was sounding odd.

"Can I go into the city with the band on Tuesday? They are doing an interview at Z100. I won't be on the air, but I want to watch."

"Yes, of course you can."

"Thanks."

"Morgan, relax. You missed five days of school this year. You are going to Rutgers and another check came in the mail. You are making a beautiful life for yourself."

"Thanks. Another check?"

"You have made a lot of money, and your father and I are proud of you. You will be eighteen soon and we won't have any say."

"You will always have a hold on me, because I love you so much." She hugs me tight and I feel a desire to tell her how much I love Fred, but I don't.

While doing my homework I always listen to the radio, but tonight it's a whole new world. I don't know if I should cry, scream, or jump up and down. Fred's voice is coming from my radio, and he is singing the song I wrote. I heard the recordings a hundred times, but no one told me the first single was my song. The song is typical of a CrossRhoades rock song, but it's mixed up with my words and melody and it blows my mind.

I find ballads easier to write but this one time I wrote words for them to rock to.

Gone is half my heart
Even if I had her from the start
Too little
Too late

We were fragile glass
Because I was an ass
Too little
Too late

You are stronger than me
Why can't you see
We could have been together
Now we are broken
Shattered in a single blast
Broken
Glass
You did the right thing
I couldn't fix it with a ring
Too little
Too late

I ache for our past
Wanted it to last
Too little
Too late

You are stronger than me
Why can't you see
We could be together

Now we are broken glass
Shattered in a single blast

Broken
Glass

Sorry will never work
I was a jerk
Too little
Too late

The blast was loud
I got lost in the cloud
Too little
Too late

You are stronger than me
Why can't you see
We could be together

Now we are broken glass
Shattered in a single blast
Broken
Glass

I throw myself across the bed and grab for the phone. Fred doesn't even say hello. "Guess you have the radio on?"

"Yeah, the... really? Why didn't you say something? I wish I was with you."

"Congrats, Jellybean. Everyone wanted your song first. It's gonna be a huge hit. The summer of 1996 is yours."

"I can't feel my face. I can't believe you did this for me. You must really love me."

"Well, first, yes, I love you more than you know, but you did this for yourself. Gunner did more for you than I did. I tell you that all the time."

"With music, I could make a list of the other amazing things you taught me."

"What the heck could they be?"

"Okay stop, I need to be high on this song. I need to hear it again."

"Keep changing stations. It's gonna get constant radio play."

"I need to tell my parents to listen to the radio and I have to call Kelly and Brooke. Fred, thank you so much. This is the gift of a lifetime. Can you call Gunner and tell him thanks and I will see him Friday? Dinner is on me."

"Call me before you go to sleep."

"You bet. Love ya."

After school on the tenth I arrive at Fred's and find him and Gunner eating dinner.

"You too are so cute together," I say to them, and they both sit mute.

Gunner comes over to me and gives me a sweet but firm hug. He pulls away and stares at me. "You know what today is?"

"Monday?"

"No, the date?"

"Um, June tenth right?"

"Yeah…"

"Oh, happy day I met you anniversary. I love that mind of yours, Gunner," I say. He hugs me again, then goes back to eating.

"I'm going to take a short nap, guys. Be down later."

Fred wakes me two hours later. I decide to go for a run to wake myself up. On my way back up Fred's street I see Gunner driving up in his truck.

"You look tired," he yells out the window.

"I am."

"Get in, I will drive you back. And I want to talk to you."

"Am I in trouble?" I giggle.

"No." I climb in the car and he drives back to Fred's. We are in the driveway when he finally starts to talk. "You okay?"

"Yes, I'm good."

"Okay."

"It's hard sometimes. But it's either this or nothing. I will know when I am ready for nothing."

"Okay."

"Thanks for caring."

"Always. Not to sound weird, but numbers are a thing I love. Well, we met on June tenth. We are dropping an album tomorrow, on the eleventh, with your awesome songs. Next year, the twelfth, can you make a little time for me that day?" he asks, a little sad.

"Gunner, I will make time for you every day of the year. But damn you are such a romantic, how the hell are you single?"

"I am super picky, beyond picky really."

"I should head inside. I need to shower and get to bed," I say, but I don't move. "Gunner?" He locks eyes with me before I continue. "I know I say thank you a lot, but I mean it. Thank you. You are an amazing friend and I am honored that you chose me to treat special." He hugs me tight, and I get out of the car and wave.

We are up early to get ready, and I feel odd. I don't have to do a damn thing but sit and watch, but still I pace the house. Gunner has a car service get him first. Alex and Zach went in separately.

The ride to NYC is long and quite boring. I take it for granted because this marvelous city is so close by. My parents brought us to the Zoo or Central Park often as kids, but there is so much I've never seen. Perhaps someday I could live here, but only if I were rich, Gunner rich.

"What is making those gears turn, Morgan?" Gunner asks.

"Oh, nothing interesting, just thinking how New York is appealing, but it doesn't appeal to me. Maybe if I was as rich as you I might enjoy living here."

"Well, that is a lot on your mind, and it is interesting. Stop saying your thoughts aren't interesting."

"Yes, Mr. Cross, thanks for the confidence lesson." I can't help but tickle him. But then Fred tickles me. "Damn, we don't look like mature people with a number one song."

"No, we don't but we don't need to be mature. We have fame and fortune," Fred says.

"I can't get any more immature."

"Stop. Twelve days, Jellybean, left to be a kid, but you are all woman." He kisses me. Gunner tickles him, forcing him to stop kissing me. The tickling stops when we arrive at the station. Two buff bodyguards meet us and bring us up to a holding room. There is a huge spread of breakfast food, but I couldn't eat now if even my biggest wish came true.

The guys walk into the studio and I watch from outside. The interview goes well and Fred comes out quite energetic. I think he needs to push himself to get through the public parts. Alex and Zach are naturals. Gunner is very quiet and I realize I never thought about what I expected him to act like.

We are talking to some people at the station and Fred puts his arm around me and sweetly kisses my head. It is such a nice and comforting gesture, but it is freaking me out. I say nothing, though it seems no one here thought twice about it.

We drive back to Mantoloking and even though we did nothing it has exhausted me. Fred orders a pizza and we eat before we snuggle in the hammock. "You okay, Jellybean?

"Just tired."

"Take a nap. Can I drive you to school in the morning?"

"That would be nice. Finals start Thursday. I can't wait until they are over."

"You will ace them like you do everything you touch."

"I don't know about that, but I will pass and graduate. We have to talk about graduation." I want to lean on his chest and look at him but I don't. "It's the day before my birthday. Will you come up to my parents' house for the weekend?"

"Geez, Jellybean, I wouldn't miss a second of it for anything."

"Well I want to miss it all. I'm so past high school."

"If you don't close those eyes now, I will take you upstairs to bed and make sure you don't get any rest."

"I will sleep."

"Morgan, don't be embarrassed. You do know that I know when you get your period, because you get so damn tired. I have dealt with enough PMS to swear off women. All I have to do is let you sleep."

"Enough period talk. I will nap now. And Fred? I do love that you know me very well."

Chapter Thirty-Six
Eighteen

SATURDAY MORNING, I wake up too early, nervous about graduation, but happy I will be legal tomorrow. The ceremony is more for my parents than myself. If it were up to me I would skip it. I have a tight red dress on under my maroon gown, and all this extra clothing is making me overheat.

Brooke rings the bell, and I walk out the front door, feeling as if I have no clue how to function normally. Fred says good-bye with a hug. I still wish he could come, but I am glad he can't because that would make me more nervous.

While lining up in the cafeteria, out of the blue, I feel a sense of euphoria wash over me. Maybe this sort of adrenaline keeps Fred going on stage. I can't wait to get this over and done. Maybe feeling nervous makes the feeling when it's over even better. I guess I will know soon.

When I walk across the stage to get my diploma my heart skips a beat. In the shadows near a closed door, I see Fred and Gunner. It warms my heart beyond belief that they snuck in. Diploma in hand, mortar board flung and released, I exhale stale breath and inhale freedom.

Looking for my family in the sea of people around me, I run into Brooke's parents first and they congratulate me. I leave Brooke when I see my family with Gunner and Fred. I feel a sudden need to protect them. The girls in my class alone could trample them to death. Fred wraps me in a huge hug, then Gunner does the same.

"It can't be safe for you guys to be out here. Let's head home," I say, starting to walk away.

"Okay," Fred says. "Gunner, you ride back with Morgan's parents." Gunner nods. We run like we are being chased. Fred throws me the keys and I catch them like I was on the softball team. I hear someone yell my name but I don't look back. I start the engine and put the sexy beast in gear, back out, and drive down Ridgedale Avenue like it is the Autobahn. I have been on this street a million times but this time I have rose-colored glasses on. Nothing looks the same. I will be eighteen in a few hours and school is over and done. Freedom is what I was granted today. I should be scared, but excitement is my top emotion.

We are back for a while before everyone else gets there so Fred and I make out as if we were still in high school. Once they get back we eat dinner and play monopoly. My mother baked me my favorite chocolate cake, with chocolate frosting from scratch. The perfect way to spend my graduation from high school and my graduation from being underage.

We are going to Fred's tomorrow, so we will celebrate my birthday with my family tonight. My parents gave me an elegant pearl necklace and some new clothes for summer. Next Fred hands me a wrapped box. "Just open it," he says, making me believe I must look freaked out.

I open it fast. "A phone," I say, surprised. "Wow. Do you have one?"

"Got one when I got yours. The car phone is history. Gunner won't get one, because he said he isn't ready for it." He punches Gunner's shoulder.

I giggle. "Yeah, I buy that. What's my phone number?" He shows me how to use it and the first number we ring is the house phone. My dad answers and I must admit it is a cool gift. I hug him a little too tight and too long, but what the hell, it doesn't matter anymore.

Fred is sleeping in Ryan's room again tonight, but he comes to my room with me on our way upstairs to bed. He turns the lights off and puts the radio on low and lies down on my bed, fully clothed. Which is my least favorite way to see him on a bed.

"Lie here with me, Jellybean." He pats the bed. I lie down on my left side so I can look into his baby blues. He cocks his head and his mouth meets mine for a gentle kiss. "One last kiss for seventeen-year-old Morgan." He looks at his watch and counts down from ten.

He leans over this time, his face just above mine, his eyes looking as hot as I feel. "Now your first kiss as an adult." This kiss is worthy of the word adult. His mouth possesses mine and mine molds to his like we have been doing this for decades.

* * *

We leave my parents' house on Sunday morning. My mom was never this emotional the other times I left. I choose not to ask her about it. I drive the Lamborghini and Gunner drives the Mustang. We are all heading to Gunner's house first. Fred tells me Gunner wants to talk to me, and I won't say no to that. I hesitate to hand Fred the Lamborghini keys when we get to Gunner's. "Next year I will buy you your own." He kisses me and pulls the keys from my grip.

"Stop, that's crazy talk."

"I'll miss you, but you are good for him. I will see you when you get home. I love you, Jellybean. You always amaze me."

I kiss him back, because I need him. I never needed someone to this extent. I watch him leave and I am still waving when Gunner comes up behind me and makes me jump.

"Sorry," he says. His voice wobbles, making me wonder why he is nervous.

"I was in a daze. Sorry I jumped. What's up?"

"Did Fred tell you I wanted to talk to you?"

"He did."

"Do you have time?"

"I have lots of time, being that you have been a most excellent teacher, and there is a band crazy enough to record my songs. Well, it turns out that gives me a lot of free time. I have about two months before school, so will it be a long conversation?"

"Oh, Morgan. You have a way with words. Let's go inside." He takes my hand in his and guides me up the stairs.

Gunner's house still stuns me every time I enter it. The size, the décor, and the 'I don't know what the hell feeling' I get in here. It's not something that I can name, but it feels like a home to me.

"You want a drink?" he asks, after letting go of my hand and walking towards the kitchen.

"Water would be fine," I say, as I follow him.

We are standing in the kitchen, both of us doing nothing. I am never uncomfortable around Gunner these days, but right now he is uncomfortable. I clasp his left hand in mine and look into his eyes. He smiles a typical Gunner grin.

"Gunner, please say something. You look uncomfortable and sad. You know you can say anything to me, right?"

"That is why I want to talk to you." His eyes close and don't open. I watch him, wondering what is going through his head. He opens his eyes like his lids are made of uranium. "I never trusted anyone the way I trust you. The guys are cool, but they are guys. They love me, but they don't get some of the shit, ya know?"

"Yes, Gunner, I know all about how men don't get all the shit."

He pauses, chuckles and then says, "This might seem weird, but will you sit upstairs with me while we talk?"

"Why is that weird?"

"In my bedroom, the place I find peace, I want that with you right now. But it's weird to take my best friend's girl to my bedroom."

"First, it's not weird. If we did something besides talk, that would be weird. Gunner, you have held me while I slept. If something was gonna happen it would have happened already, don't ya think?"

He doesn't answer me. He takes my hand and leads me upstairs.

My painting is above the sofa we sit on. "You put it in here?"

"Yes, this room is my soul. And Morgan, you are a part of my soul now. A part of me loves you unlike any love I have ever felt. Our friendship is a step above unique. You have brought me a new level of comfort. Knowing you this past year has given me hope. Hope is priceless. Don't laugh or worse, please don't think less of me."

"Gunner, I would never laugh at your feelings, and nothing could make me think less of you. I know the real you, and I love you, and your friendship too."

A tear runs down his face. I wipe it away. He gets up and walks to the closet to a get a box. He takes the biggest breath I have ever seen someone take. I should ask if he is okay again but how many times can I do that?

"I thought high and low about what to give you for graduation and your big birthday, and nothing I came up with was special enough. You aren't the type of person who wants material items. I do have three gifts for you, and only one is an item."

"Three?" I say, shocked.

"Well, one is more for me in the end, but you will appreciate it because of the person you are. One is on me, but because of you." I smirk at that one. "And the other is a small token."

"Okay, what first? It's beginning to feel like Christmas."

"I love your smile. I hope Fred always makes you happy, because you are such a happy person." He pauses and the next breath isn't quite as dramatic. "This is tough for me. I thought about what you would want most for your birthday, and it felt selfish of me to think this, but I realized it is what you would want because nothing about you is selfish."

"I understand that, but you are not selfish either, so now I am beyond curious."

"I trust you, and because I trust you, I feel ready. I need you by my side. I can't do this alone." He is on the edge of tears and it's breaking my heart in a way I didn't know my heart could break. I move up against him and put my left arm around his back, I rub his shoulder.

"Gunner, I will always be by your side, I will always be here for you. No matter what."

"I do know," he says softly but firmly as he turns to face me again.

"When my parents died, my dad's sister came to New Zealand. She stayed with me, planned the funerals, and did her best to help me. She helped me look for my mom's family but we didn't find anyone. My Aunt Emily was my only living relative. She told me she was my legal guardian and I had to come to live with her in New Jersey. I already assumed that, but I was shocked still. I wanted to torch the house, to rid myself of the pain. I didn't want anything to do with my parents or their house.

I packed my clothes, my guitar, and left on a plane with her. I didn't take a single picture with me. I started to regret that after a few years and I told my aunt. She was sick already when she told me where everything was boxed up. I took it from her house when she died, but I never touched it. I grabbed the box labeled pictures. I thought it would be the best one to start with."

"Sounds perfect." I sit waiting for him to speak when I hear a foreign sound. "What is that?" Before he can speak I realize it's my phone. "Hello?" It is Fred. He tells me he is horny and asks how much longer I will be. I want to yell at him but that wouldn't be fair. "A little while. How about I call when I leave?"

He says, "Fine," without attitude and I hang up.

"See, this cell phone is no good. It will be interrupting important conversations." I toss the phone back in my bag and turn my full attention to Gunner. "You are not selfish for wanting to share this with me for my birthday. It's actually perfect. When I blew my candles out I wished for you to find peace in your life. I break every time I see that look on your face that says you know you are missing something. Maybe this will help you. And I will be right by your side, every step."

"Fred is a lucky fuck, isn't he? Morgan, I'm lucky he found you under that lilac tree because if he didn't I wouldn't be here with you. You give me strength. I can't explain it. You are priceless to me. You can see my soul, and you can protect it too. I want to say thank you, but those words are not big enough for what you give me. You make me more."

"Geez, Gunner, you slay with your words. I never tried to be anything to you but a friend. I will be your friend forever. Anything goes both ways."

"Yes, it does. Morgan, you wasted a birthday wish on my happiness?"

"Last year I wished for Fred to get a divorce, and well we both know how that wish panned out." Gunner pauses as if he wants to say something, but there is nothing left to say.

He takes the box and opens it. He pulls a photo envelope out and hands it to me while he puts the box down. "Let's do this nice and slow. Maybe every June we open another box together."

"Whatever you are comfortable with, I will be here every time you call. Maybe the cell phone will be a good thing."

"Thank you too for always making me laugh. I don't thank you for that enough, and sometimes we are too serious. Let's do this or you will be eighty before we get done."

"And you would be ninety-one." I say.

We look through the pictures, one at a time, like he is also seeing them for the first time. The first picture shows him when he was ten. It was summer in New Zealand, right before his eleventh birthday. He is a lot skinnier, but it's still Gunner. He looks the same. Until we come to a picture of him in a bathing suit.

"Wow, look at you, not a single tattoo," I say, rolling my finger over the image.

"I don't even remember what that was like."

"Did you always want to be covered in tattoos?"

"No." He flips through the pictures, telling me who everyone is. "Fred took me for the first tattoo." He lifts his sleeve on his left arm, two drum sticks and the date 10/30/83. "This looked small and uncool alone, so I put the Auckland skyline underneath it. It became a habit I loved. Every part of it. The physical pain would erase the pain in my mind, and the image would give me pleasure every time I saw it. It became a way to express ideas and emotions that were important to me. And now I can't imagine ever not having all of them."

"Wow, I should have written that down."

"It's late. Your man probably called because he is horny. I should let you go."

"Fred is fine. I'm here for you and I love spending time with you."

"I know, but I had enough for one day."

"Will you be okay alone and will you come by later?"

"Yes and yes. But first more gifts."

He goes over to the dresser and gets a small, wrapped box. "For you, Happy Birthday."

I open the box to find the word Twix carved in wood, on a keychain like my other one. "Oh, Gunner," I say, wondering what the key is for.

"Our secret, a special night in my heart, even though yours was breaking, because you let me in to help hold it together." I get misty eyes and throw myself at him. I need to steal some strength from him.

"What's the key for?"

We hug for too long before he answers. "The key is to the safe where I have everything personal and private. You are the only person I ever wanted to share my past with, so I want you to be the one with the key to my past, literally."

"Wow, I don't know what to say to that. It's been an emotional night. Can I handle the last one?"

"No." He releases me so he can unbutton the top of his shirt. I watch as if on the edge of my seat. In between other tattoos over his heart, it says 610 in fancy detailed script not written like a date. Under that in a more beautiful font is the word ANY, with a line of dots. I move my hand to touch him, his inhale so sharp it could pierce his heart.

"Does it hurt still?" I ask, as my finger ghosts over his skin.

"No," he answers, so softly I almost can't hear him.

My eyes move up to his to find his eyes blank, so blank it scares me. He takes my hand off his chest and he kisses the pads of my fingers. His eyes close and he lowers my hands. "Do you understand it?"

"Yes, but I wanted to hear you say it."

"Morgan, damn." His breath catches.

"Please. Then I will leave to be with Fred."

"Good plan." He grabs me and pulls my head to his chest before he leans down to whisper, "It's the day I met the most incredible person on earth. A reminder that I would do anything, anytime, anywhere, any-how... any any... whatever it would take for her to be happy."

My face is a wet mess and so is his shirt. He continues to hold me until my stomach interrupts us. I pull my head away and look up into his sad glowing eyes. "I guess stomachs are as bad as cell phones. If we are so good to each other, Gunner, why do we cry so much?"

"I don't know. Maybe we can figure it out together."

He walks me out to the car. I call Fred and tell him I am coming home. "See ya later," Gunner says, trying to sound less at war with his feelings.

"Thank you, Gunner, for everything, for sharing with me, for trusting and loving me enough to do it. It was a perfect day, even though it was emotional."

"It was. Now leave before Fred never talks to me again."

"You know that would never happen." I put my window up and drive away. I cry the whole way back. I cry for what Gunner lost, for what I gained. I just cry.

Still feeling incredibly emotional, I pull into the driveway and find Fred sitting on the steps. It makes me feel like he doesn't trust me when I know he misses me. I fear how lost he becomes when we are apart; he has become more and more dependent on me daily.

I walk up to him and wiggle myself onto his lap. "You okay?" I ask, as I kiss his cheek.

"Yeah, Jellybean. I missed you. I'm jealous of what you have with Gunner. I know that isn't right to say, but I am."

"Fred..." He silences me with a passionate kiss.

"I don't want to talk about it. It's your birthday. I want to make it an amazing and fun day. Come inside. I have something for you."

"Why do you spoil me?"

"Because I love you." He leads me to the front entryway, then through the new studio. He stands before a closet door. I look up at him with massive confusion. "You make funny faces sometimes. I love them. There is never a dull moment with you, Morgan. I am a lucky man."

"You do things to make me make funny faces, and that was all so beautiful I don't know how to respond."

He squeezes my hand tight and looks like he can't find the words he wants to use. "I should have done this sooner. Sometimes I don't think until it's too late. Well, I guess this isn't too late but I could have done it sooner."

"What are you talking about?"

"A birthday gift." He opens the door and the room is pitch black. He switches on the light. He has transformed a small area off the studio into a darkroom. I walk inside and touch the equipment. Everything is new and top notch.

"You did this for me?" I ask.

"I know you love photography and you won't have the school darkroom anymore and you have no art classes on your schedule for the fall. That makes me sad."

"It makes me sad too. I don't want be a business major. I have time to change it at least." I walk closer to him. "You know I can take dirty pictures of you now and develop them and no one will have a clue."

"Morgan, everything you do makes me crazy horny. Fuck, how do you turn me on so fast?"

"I have to do that so you stay at this elevated level with me. I can't be horny all alone."

"Well, we will both have to wait to be satisfied."

"Huh, why?" I say, moving away from him a little. He never turns me down.

"I have plans for us. Come, you can take dirty pictures of me tomorrow."

"Where are we going?" I beg.

"You know I won't tell."

"I told Gunner to come over later. You have to call him and tell him we won't be here."

"He knows. Come, silly."

Once again I have no info from Fred. He says I can shower and change when we get there, and I wasn't even home thirty minutes. I wanted to play in my new darkroom, in a few different ways, instead we are in a limo heading north on the parkway. He won't tell me anything and he only packed a very small bag for us both. I slide across the long leather seat and climb in his lap. "Please give me a clue."

"Nope."

"At least tell me you will feed me."

"I will feed you. Soon." We ride in silence again. I love the silence, especially when my body is pressed into his.

"You like to take me into the city on my birthday," I say when I see the signs.

"Yes." He kisses my lips once. "Morgan, I love you so much, all the minutes spent with you are the only minutes that matter." He kisses me and it's like his saliva is made of the most coveted drug on earth because I am beyond high.

The limo drops us off in front of the Waldorf Astoria Hotel. Fred leads me right to the elevator as he takes a key card out of his pocket. "What are we doing?"

"Shush, let me lead."

It is difficult not to ask, but the pleasure of the unknown is growing on me. He has never disappointed me before so I choose to hold his hand and let him take me on this journey. The elevator ride is long, and the hallway is silent. I am inside a snow globe waiting for someone to tip it and make the action happen. He opens a door at the end of the hall and ushers me into a majestic hotel suite. Everything is light and airy, the sun is pouring in the windows, but the brightest light comes from Fred's eyes. He locks them on me and I drown in the bluest of blues as he engulfs me into a mammoth hug.

"Let's take a quick shower."

"I don't have clothes to change into."

"Play along with me, Jellybean." We shower and he won't let me touch him because we need to be somewhere, but somewhere can't be better than here.

I come out of the bathroom after drying my hair and find Fred dressed in the tightest jeans he owns and my favorite, a tight black tee shirt. He hands me a small black dress and high heeled black leather boots.

"Whoa, this is a little too little. Are we going to a club?" I say.

"Just change, Jellybean."

"Do I get undergarments?"

"Maybe, but I do love when you go without." Then he hands me a skimpy red lace bra and matching thong. "I can't wait to take these off you. My. Finally. Legal. Lover."

I take the clothes from him and want to correct him. Lover is not my only term; mistress also applies. I drop my robe like a trained stripper. I pick up the bra and slip it on as drawn out as I can without laughing. I adjust each boob a little too much, then turn around and bend a little too much to get my underwear on, loving that he is watching me. A loud knock on the main door makes me jump and almost fall over.

"Calm down, I won't let anyone see you."

"For your eyes only?"

"Yes. But I might show you off a little." He leaves to get the food. I throw the dress on without a show and head back to the bathroom to finish my make-up. This outfit requires more. I put the dryer down and look up to see his eyes locked on mine. His are full of sex.

He feeds me a piece of cheese on a cracker. "I want you more than I ever have, but let's have a bite of food. We have a long night ahead of us."

I walk into the main room and grab some grapes. I take the bunch and head to the window. I look out upon Times Square and the intriguing bustle of people. I turn around and lean back as seductively as I can, eating one grape at a time and using my tongue to excess. Fred watches me, and deep down I hope he has a change of heart and just takes me to bed.

"What are you doing? You don't have ants in your pants for info."

"Just playing it cool. Hoping it leads me to having you in my pants."

"Fuck, Jellybean." He slams into me. The cool window at my almost bare back feels exquisite, and my front is heating up fast.

"Grab something and let's eat on our way down." He moves away without another word, leaving me shocked, but I follow after him as I continue to eat the grapes.

"Wait, do I need my purse?" I yell in the hall behind him as he flies to the elevator.

"I have everything you need."

He takes my hand as we enter the elevator. "You okay, hot stuff?" I ask as I turn my half naked body toward him.

"I'm so okay, I just want to give you a night out, but I also can't think of anything but being in bed with you. It's conflicting. I fucking love you more than I have ever loved anything. Even music. It scares the shit out of me."

He pushes me gently into the back of the elevator as his tongue roughly explores my mouth. I hear the ding and see the doors open but he doesn't look away. He says, "Sorry, I thought music was all I needed until I met you. I would give up music for you."

I want him to say more but instead he pulls me from the elevator and practically flings us both into a taxi. This whirlwind makes me feel like I haven't taken a solid breath in hours. As odd as I feel I also know I love the out of control moments he grants me. In the taxi my head is abuzz with words to throw at him, but my heart is loving him too much to speak, because I know he loves silence.

We walk into a club. Through the front door. It's early for New Yorkers to be partying, but the place is jammed. Before I take in my surroundings we are whisked up the stairs. The club music has a great beat, but it also makes me feel like I am moving faster than I am. We get to the top of the stairs and Fred pauses in front of me.

He leans down and kisses me full on with undeniable passion. I want to question his bravery but I just look up at him. He whispers in my ear, "Happy Birthday, Jellybean." He kisses me one more time, then grabs my hand and pulls me along the edge of the railing overlooking the bar and dance floor.

We walk into a closed off area, and like a magic wand was waved my eyes find Gunner in the mess. Then I see everyone else. Ryan, Brooke,

Kelly, Zach and Alex and a few faces I don't recognize. My mouth is hanging open in utter shock. Brooke runs over and throws herself at me as she screams, "Happy Birthday." Kelly comes next, calmer with her words, and hands me a beer.

I never imagined spending my eighteenth Birthday with Fred in a club in the city, dancing the night away with my closest friends. Ryan, Zach and Alex all brought dates. It amazes me how suddenly I don't care who sees me and Fred together. At first I hide upstairs more than I should and when I first go down to dance I go with the girls.

After way too many shots on top of a few beers, I am dancing way too close and personal with Fred. It is scary and the most exhilarating thing we have shared today. To be sexual and close in public is such a bizarre treat.

Turns out it wasn't just a bouncer who brought us upstairs, but instead Fred had hired a personal body guard for the night. It made him free to be all over me in public. Perhaps we need to hire him full-time.

* * *

The room is dark except for the clock and a sliver of light coming in from the curtains. I try to roll over but my head and body seem to be made of cement. I close my eyes and fade out again. I want this pain to end so I try to sleep more.

"Morgan." It sounds like Fred is a million miles away. I long to answer him, but my mouth and head can't work together to get the job done. An eternity later he speaks again. "Morgan, open up. You need water."

I try to sit up but my body aches. "Fred, why did I drink so much?"

"We all did, but you may have danced your muscles into a ball. You were a little party animal."

"You were too." I finally get to a seated position.

"Here, drink this." I take the water and sip it like it is poison.

"I can't tell if the alcohol or dancing hurts more." We lie in bed and sip ginger ale and water for hours. Neither of us can help the other out too much.

"Morgan?"

"Yeah?"

"You good staying here again tonight?"

"Yeah." And we sleep again.

The sun has set. I feel hungry like a switch was flicked. "Fred. You up?" I hoarsely whisper toward his face.

"I don't know," he answers, rolling over to me.

"I think I am hungry. I want a shower."

"Okay."

"I might need help."

"Okay." I wish I could read the clock to know how long it takes to get us both showered. I sit on the bed in a robe, soaking wet, when Fred asks me what I want to eat. I feel too sick to even think of food.

We sit numb again. No one moves or talks. "I might never drink again," I utter.

"I bet you will. How about some soup?"

"I will try. And get soda, one with caffeine."

We manage to put some food in us and we lie in bed half naked and half dead. My hands run up and down his arm because even in this state of mind I still can't keep myself from touching him. "Fred?"

"Yeah?" he says drawn out.

"Is this what drugs are like or are they different?" I can't tell if I said it out loud or not, but when I feel him move sharply I realize I said it out loud.

"You know I don't want to talk about that. I am weak, Morgan. You are not. Please don't ever do any kind of drug."

"I won't, but I am curious." He doesn't answer me. "Fred, why can't we talk about it?"

"I don't want to. And I don't want to with you." He kisses me, but I don't know how to answer him. Thankfully he keeps talking. "I don't like drugs; my weakness feeds off them. They were a means to be completely absent minded. And the side effects are small so far, except the desire to do more."

We sit in silence.

"I wish you didn't have that past, or that desire."

"I know, I do too."

Chapter Thirty-Seven
Iceland

THE ALBUM HAS been released, the videos are shot, Broken Glass hit number one on the twenty-fifth, and I turned eighteen. The sky's the limit, right? Not? The summer of ninety-six is the same as the summer of ninety-five. We do nothing but hang around the shore house. I love Fred, sex is still indescribably satisfying, time with him is perfection, but I have cabin fever. Or maybe I am just pissed he doesn't mention his intentions toward his wife. I bet my life it is the wife situation that has left me with this sour taste.

My mom calls me one afternoon when we are listening to music and stretched out in the hammock. She tells me another check came in the mail and she sounds funny. "Mom, what's wrong? I will come home and deposit it."

"Okay."

"The checks will come every month if any of the songs I wrote even make ten cents."

"Well, this isn't ten cents."

"That's because my song is number one right now."

"Yes, it is, and I hear it every day and can't get enough."

"That is so sweet."

"So is this check."

"You know money isn't important to me. I will deposit it when I come home."

"You should do something else with it."

"Like what?" I ask, confused.

"First, hire a financial planner. You could possibly buy a house or something to live in at school instead of the dorms."

"A house?"

"Or a townhouse."

"I will come home to talk about it."

"Okay, honey. Call me and let me know your plans. I love you."

"Love you too."

I hang up and tell Fred and Gunner about that conversation. They are both genuinely happy for me. They don't get that I couldn't have this without them. I love that they are both so giving and loving. Fred tells me he will help me house hunt, but he seems upset about me living elsewhere. We talk about it and he doesn't seem to understand I can't commute every day, but he knows I will be here every second I can.

A few weeks later I ask Ryan to look at houses with me, since Gunner is away and Fred's mood hasn't changed. We spend some time with the realtor before she takes us to look at some places around campus. The sixth place we look at is a three-bedroom three-bath townhouse. I can afford it and I love it.

Ryan and I are upstairs when I say, "This is the one."

"Morgan, it's huge and expensive. Mom said you made a lot of money, but this much?"

"Will you live here with me? It would be too lonely if it were just me."

"Yeah, I would love to. Can I afford the rent? Can Mom and Dad afford the rent?" We laugh.

"Rent free for you."

I love when I feel light and carefree like I do once I put in an offer on my first home. I return to Fred's and he is still not feeling the same. He is down and depressed and it's killing me. I should tell him I put an offer in but I can't do it, fearing I will hurt him more. How can he expect me not to live near school? Damn, I even gave up the school I wanted for him, and he gave up nothing for me, and now he is upset. I have two choices: show him how I feel or give him a little more time and hope he gets it on his own and comes through for me.

I climb on his lap. "Let's do something."

"What do you have in mind?" He smiles and it starts to warm me up.

"Let's go somewhere."

"Where?"

"It doesn't matter. I'm eighteen. I have a passport, money, and I have you. You are the most important one."

"Out of state, an island, a country. What are you thinking?"

"I wasn't thinking. Where can you go?"

"Anywhere."

"I mean where can we go and not be seen."

"Anywhere."

"No we can't, Fred. People spot you easily. Cities would be tough, an island might work, Europe is dangerous, too many fans. How about a remote island or Iceland or Siberia?"

"I would love to see Iceland."

"I hear it's gorgeous."

"Let's do it."

Fred called a travel agent and had everything arranged for us. We are going for his birthday. It was the only time we could get the best suite in the best hotel. I wanted to leave sooner but this is the perfect plan.

Everything is set for school and I will close on my townhouse a week before we leave for Iceland. I left it up to Ryan to have it painted and buy furniture for everything but my room, as I had already ordered it. Ryan had no problem taking on the task, with my money in hand, and I had no problem handing it over.

I never imagined in my wildest dreams my songs would be heard and loved by millions. I was starting to see how this type of fame could make one's head grow, as this opportunity has humbled me so. I may always be stunned by the success of my words.

The summer flies by. Before I know it, Fred and I are landing at the Reykjavik airport in Iceland. It's Friday, August sixteenth, and tomorrow Fred will be twenty-nine. We will be celebrating alone. Last year we had a huge party at Gunner's and a visit from Beth; this one seems to be the polar opposite. It's exciting to be somewhere new with someone I love. Fred has been extra quiet the last few days, and even though nothing bad has happened, nothing has moved forward. Walking into the hotel I notice Fred is lighter, almost normal. More like the man I fell in love with, less like the man he has been the last few months.

The hotel room is exquisite. It has enormous, dark, rich furniture and

views as far as the eye can see. I always feel grimy after flying a commercial airliner. I have become spoiled by Gunner's extra funds. "I need to
shower," I tell Fred. He smiles that sexy smile at me, one I haven't seen
much of lately.

"Okay."

"Will you join me?"

"Yes." And boy does the smile grow, as does my heart. I love him. I
hurt that he has been so sad and depressed. I wish I could make all his bad
days bright again.

The bathroom is as big as Fred's bathroom, which says a lot since this
is a hotel. The tile in the shower looks more like glass, and it's blue and
green and reminds me of the lamps in Fred's bedroom. Our bedroom. I
turn the water on and turn back to Fred. I watch him lift his shirt over his
head in one quick move. I follow with my eyes as he drops it to the floor.
He walks over to me, slinking like a cat. I enjoy being his prey. He stops
in front of me, his eyes blazing, hot, and full of love. I haven't seen his
eyes this full since last year.

Wow, he is hot when he is whole. I suddenly can't breathe. I need his
mouth for air. Like a mind reader, he crushes his lips into mine. I whim-
per for the man I am in love with. His tongue slips into my mouth as his
hands unbutton my jeans. My hands fly to his neck and my nails run up
into his hair and back down his wide back as my jeans fall to the floor. I
want my top off but I don't want to separate from his mouth. I slide my
tongue slow and deep past his and glide it out over the roof of his mouth
as I unbutton his jeans and slide my hand into his boxers.

"Fred, I've missed you."

I grab him in my hand as he pushes the rest of his clothes off onto the
floor. "Missed me?"

"Miss the real you, miss the man who is kissing me right now."

He says nothing as he opens the shower door. I rip my top off and as I
step backwards into the shower as he slowly takes my bra off and roughly
takes half my breast in his mouth as the hot water covers my body. A
moan escapes from deep inside me, a place that has been asleep for way
too long.

His mouth trails up my chest and neck and to my ear. His breath
is warm and shallow. Needy. We are so needy. Needing what we had.

Finding something lost. He tugs my earlobe with his teeth. "Morgan, I need you, I need you so bad." My entire body ignites with need. Need to please him, need to be pleased.

"Fred, touch me. Now. I need you too. I need you to love me. Inside and out."

He lifts his head off my body and looks me in the face. "Morgan, open your eyes, look at me." His voice is deep and it makes me vibrate. I open my eyes and look up into his. Dark, sultry, hungry, and all mine. I own his eyes. They see only me, only us. His finger points at my nose and starts to move down my cheek, forcing my eyes to close as I follow it. "I want you to watch me touch you."

I watch. It is slow. My eyes never exerted this much energy, but I watch his finger glide easily down my body. Between my breasts. Down my belly until he circles my belly button and goes left to my right hip. I want him to move down. I burn for him. Instead he moves it to my other hip and back up to my tattoo with the date of his birth etched into my skin.

"So beautiful, my Morgan."

His finger goes back to the center of my belly. He inches it down lower and lower. I watch his finger gracefully glide over my burning flesh. Each inch making my chest pound harder. I can't remember the last time I felt this perfect, this loved and this aroused. His finger is on a collision course with what I want it to crash into when he runs it down my thigh instead. I should punch him for torturing me, but I will always covet this weakened sensation. So mesmerized by him as I watch his finger move back up my thigh.

Slow, painfully slow, he moves his finger over me. So soft, no pressure, his fingers slide against me where I've needed it for the last ten minutes and I feel my knees give out. Then gloriously slow his fingers slip inside me.

"Morgan, you make me better and damn do you turn me on. You are everything to me."

I can't talk, the burn from his finger circling inside and outside me has me sexually paralyzed. I am his to play with, as he desires. My nails dig into his shoulders as he pushes another finger inside me.

"Fred, please, please, more, more." His fingers are fast now and his mouth finds mine and he pushes me against the back wall of the shower.

"Morgan, shit, come for me, please, now, come around my fingers. I need to feel you first."

His words make this even better. I move my head back only to bash into the tile. He reaches behind me and grabs my ass and runs his hand down to my thigh and as he lifts it around his hip, I come from the shift of my hips. My orgasm crashes down around his fingers out of nowhere, but it doesn't end. My body spasms around him over and over. My body is turning to Jell-O when I mumble to him, "Don't let me fall."

"I will always hold you up, Jellybean." He kisses my mouth, deep, as my orgasm ends and I gain the ability to see again.

"Fred, that was…." He cuts me off, kissing me harder.

"I need you in bed, baby." He moves his arm back without taking his mouth off me and turns the water off. I realize that we did nothing to clean ourselves but I forget that thought as the cold air outside the shower hits me and wakes me up a little too much. Fred grabs a towel and wraps it around me, then picks me up and carries me like a new bride.

Warm, naked, and buried under a fluffy heavy crisp white comforter, Fred is on top of me. I long for his weight above me, but he is trying hard to hold back. I run both hands down his chest and belly. His breath catches in his throat before I get to where we both want my hands to be. I take him and hold him, one hand wrapped around him. Touching him, my greatest source of pleasure.

"I need you so bad. Oh, Morgan, what you do to me." He kisses me. We have passed a point today. A point of no return. Either this moves forward or it ends and in the moment we are only moving forward. It feels right to move somewhere and not be stagnant. I say a silent prayer that it's all forward progression, as he slowly slips himself inside me. I love the feeling when he first enters my body. The simple connection, the body mind connection we share is more pleasurable than anything else on earth. He moves with rhythmic slow motion that leaves me spinning with love, then I move my hips to match him.

Caged in by his body, pinned in pleasure, and wrapped in his safe strong arms, his tongue deep in my mouth, tangled up in every way. Every movement brings us more than the one before. He starts to move faster and I am not ready. Content and wrapped in love I could stay here for hours, but he is ready to explode.

"Morgan, I can't hold back, oh baby, it's too good."

"Fred…." I can't form words as he moves his arms down around my lower back and angles my hips up. He knows exactly what will happen. He hits me deep inside and I scream. We go from content slow lovemaking to painful arousal. He thrusts deep, so deep inside me.

"Come for me, Jellybean, come on me, now, please, please, I'm going to explode. Fuck baby, this is heaven." And my body pauses. The largest pause ever. Everything is silent. On the top of Mt. Everest about to fall. Fred pushes his hips into me and screams my name through clenched teeth and quickly I fall behind him. I fall from the highest mountain. I fall around him. Hard and tight. It feels like forever before I land on earth, a slow journey back down, returning to the man I will always love.

I am liquid. My body has never felt this relaxed, I can't feel anything. I open my eyes and Fred is staring down at me. He is still hard and deep inside me. He moves his arm from behind my back as my hips fall to the bed as he pulls out of me. I hate losing the connection and after the way I feel now it's even more significant than the hundreds of other times.

It is long past dinnertime and the sun is still bright in the sky. For night owls, the far north is a great place to be, but I need darkness to sleep off this high. Or this fear of never feeling this high again. The thought of losing him always lingers on my mind. Maybe I should believe this is forever and he will be mine somehow, someday, somewhere, maybe Iceland.

I start to fall asleep, wrapped in him and this bed of perfection when he runs his hand down my arm. "You hungry?"

"Yeah, but I don't want to move. I wish this feeling could last forever."

"I know, Morgan, I never felt anything like this. It is stronger than the first time I fell in love with you. I've never loved you more than I do right now."

I lean up and kiss his moist lips. "I want to always love you as I love you today." He leans down and kisses me as our hands travel all over each other.

"Morgan, I am going to do it, as soon as we get home," he whispers.

"Do what?" I mumble half asleep.

"File for divorce," he says and I hear it loud and clear. I freeze, numb and utterly void of the ability to speak.

"I want you. I never loved like I love you. You are everything. I can't live without you. I will call the lawyer Monday. Sorry I was so slow. I should have done it last year. I am not the man you think I am, but I want to try now to be that man."

"Fred, you are everything I think you are. Please don't do it because I bought the townhouse. I need to be near school some of the time. Do it only because you don't love her."

"I never loved her, not real love, not right love, it was a sick love. Morgan, you are the most mature person I know, yet you have an innocence. Your eyes see me differently. I will spend the rest of my life trying to be what you see."

He kisses me. Firm and strong and renewed. We are one again. We can win something in this scary life. We can come out on top together. I fall asleep on his chest after I watch the light fade outside.

Fred shifts under me and I wake up. I use the bathroom and come back to bed beyond hungry. I climb in next to Fred's hot body and he stirs. He stretches, saying, "Damn, I'm hungry."

"Me too, we haven't eaten since the plane." I look at the clock. "It's three, is there twenty-four-hour room service?"

"Yes."

"Good. I thought having the sun set so late here would lead to a normal lifestyle. Funny, isn't it? Thinking something about us could be normal."

"Morgan, you are funny, and sexy, and damn soft. Your skin is crazy smooth." His hand runs up my stomach and cups my breast. "Shit, I can't stop touching you." His hand runs back down my stomach. "And your stomach is concave. I need to feed you." He jumps out of bed and finds the room service menu.

We are lying in bed waiting for our food when I remember that I didn't give Fred his birthday present. I hop up and walk to my suitcase to get the small box. "It's a little gift with huge meaning. Happy Birthday."

"You could wrap shit up for me and I would open it, as long as you always run across the room naked."

"Really, that's all you need in life, me running around naked?"

"Yeah."

He opens the box. Inside is a red glass heart, too light to be a paperweight. There is an M etched into the top. "I wanted to give you my heart. All of it. It's fragile and I trust you to care for it, because since I met you it hasn't been just mine to watch after."

His face is sad and his eyes are wet, but I can't read his reaction. "Why do you trust me?"

"Because I love you."

There is a loud knock on the door. Fred puts it away, carefully, and gets the door.

I lie in bed naked as Fred deals with getting the food. Having a hotel suite is the best way to travel. We eat in bed, I am naked, I hate that he is clothed. Breakfast never tasted so good. Pancakes and sausage are the perfect my-boyfriend-is-finally-getting-divorced food.

The rest of the week goes by way too fast. I can't tell if we are in a vacation bubble or if Fred and I have crossed over to a new side. Iceland is breathtaking, beautiful, but cold. More of a cool spring than summer. I can't complain though because we spend lots of time in hot tubs and under blankets.

He tells me Monday morning that he spoke to his lawyer, who will contact a divorce attorney for him. The divorce lawyer calls back later in the day and I hear Fred telling him to start the filing and he will be seeing him in a week in his office. Sometimes there are no winners, just, hopefully, better times ahead.

We eat dinner out, every night in a different restaurant, just in case. No one has recognized Fred, so maybe it is working. We are leaving tomorrow so I think we are in the clear. For our last dinner, Fred has found a cozy little restaurant. It has to be the most romantic place I have ever seen. A picture of this place should be in the dictionary under cozy and romantic. We sit and order our food and a bottle of champagne. Conversation is light and enjoyable. I feel extraordinary. I have never felt such peace and happiness.

After we finish off a rich piece of chocolate cake, Fred takes out a small present. He goes mute. My heart starts to pound so loud, I can hear it in my ears. He looks at me, the love written all over his face. I start to relax but my heart doesn't.

"I bought this for you in April. I wanted to be able to give it to you then, but I messed that up. In May when we went away, I wanted to take you to Arkansas to give it to you, but I could see you weren't ready."

"Why Arkansas?"

"I will tell you later. I know I haven't been 100% the last few months. I tried. I really tried."

"I know you did."

"This week has been perfect. I have felt perfect. You always see the best in people. Always accept them for everything they are. I bring this box everywhere with me, waiting to give it to you. When the time is right. Tonight might not be right, but it's the closest it will be before the divorce is final. After that I hope we have what we have today, but without my baggage."

"Fred, you are scaring me a little." I know I make a funny scrunched face.

"No, no, don't be scared. Here, open it."

He hands me the box and I open it, but I keep my eyes on his looking for answers. The waitress hasn't returned with our check and I imagine he has told her not to somehow. I lift the lid and pull the chain out of the box. The chain is simple; what hangs from it is not. A large round diamond ring with a band of diamonds is dangling in the air as I hold it up. I look up to meet Fred's eyes. Somehow my heart has gone erratic and I can't find air.

"I wanted to do it right, wait until everything was normal, ask you to be my wife, but I never do anything right. I want you to have this now. I can't wait any longer. I don't want to put it on your finger yet and I don't want an answer from you until this is right. Will you wear it around your neck?"

"With honor," I whisper as he reaches around me to put the necklace on me, I can't tell if his face is sad or happy. "I love you. I know you are everything I think you are. You are amazing, you are strong, and you will be the greatest love of my life. We are all weak sometimes. I will wait for you to be strong, so we can always be a we."

He kisses me. He moves his mouth off of me and grabs my head in his hands. I open my eyes to look at him. "I love you, Jellybean. You are too perfect for me, but I will try to be everything you deserve. I will love you forever." He kisses me again.

"Let's pay the bill and leave," I say, wanting nothing more than to be alone with him.

"Already paid. Come to bed with me."

If ever I could say I felt weightless, it would be on the way back to our room. Fred opens the door and I walk in ahead of him. The room is filled with lilacs and sunflowers. The bedroom is sprinkled with rose petals. Champagne is opened and waiting. It feels and looks like a honeymoon suite. "I guess you were hopeful I wasn't going to freak out and that I was accepting of this grand gesture of yours?"

"Umm, how about I give you my grand gesture." His eyes radiate love and lust. "The Arkansas state gem is the diamond."

"Oh," slips from my lips as he carries me to bed.

He brings me complete satisfaction in the most tantalizing of ways. I lie content in this bed, with this man, in this new and different country. I can't sleep. I don't want a second of this night to be wasted on sleep. Fred must sense my restlessness. He is running his fingers up and down my arm and holding me tight. "You okay, Jellybean?"

"I'm restless. I don't want to sleep. I don't want this to end. I finally feel completely safe again. I don't want to sleep the rest of this feeling away."

He gets up and goes in the other room. I hear him getting utensils before he climbs back into bed with me and hands me the pint of ice cream. I smile. He knows all the ways to make me purr. "You are thoughtful and romantic."

"No, I'm not, just for you, because I love you so much, and because you are easy to please. Loving you is all I have to do."

"Yes, yes it is."

We eat our ice cream, naked in bed. What more could anyone ever need?

The plane lands in New Jersey, and my emotions are as stormy as the weather here. I know I am in a funk and I shouldn't be. I rub my fingers over the ring under my shirt and smile up at Fred. Seeing him smile back at me makes my mood improve in the perfect way. We exit the plane as fast as we can, but I wish Fred had his sunglasses on.

We have an exact location to meet the driver so we can be in the car fast. It is no longer abnormal to plan an exit or entrance when I am with him. We are walking into the underground parking garage at Newark airport, when someone recognizes Fred. She can't be older than me. She screams, "Rick. Holy shit, it's Rick Rhoades." I want to run but that will make it more obvious. We walk a little faster to the car and get there without another issue, but someone did get behind us with a camera. I see the flash several times before we get in the car and lock the door.

"Damn, that was weird. How do you take it?"

"I don't. This part I do hate."

Lucky for us no one storms the car. The driver puts the bags in and off we go. We make it back to Mantoloking in one piece but it is almost midnight and we are both exhausted. I fall asleep wrapped up in Fred. So glad that the feeling we found in Iceland has translated back home.

We spend a lazy Sunday afternoon at his house before I call my parents to tell them I will be at the townhouse for the night. Hopefully Ryan hasn't partied too much and trashed it. We enjoy the beach air. I make pasta and the whole band joins us. It is the perfect end to a great week. The end of summer always makes me sad, but since we will party at Gunner's next week I technically don't have to say good-bye yet to this amazing season.

Fred follows me back to school Sunday night. He is falling back into a funk already and it affects me more than I want it to. I can't block his emotions from infiltrating mine. He has only come to my townhouse twice. The day I closed on it when my face was up close and personal with my kitchen countertops, and when I moved boxes from my parents' house. He came across to me as very unhappy about me buying a house almost an hour from him, but I only plan on sleeping here on Tuesday and Thursday nights, so he should learn to deal with it.

The house is quiet when we walk in. We head upstairs to my room and I see Ryan's light is on. I yell to him as we get to the top of the stairs. I don't want to knock. I mean how weird would it be if he had a girl in his room. I guess since I have sex constantly I tend to think that way. Ryan comes out of his room, alone and dressed.

"Hey, stranger, where have you been? Hi, Fred." He walks over to shake Fred's hand.

"Iceland." I walk into my room and put my laundry basket of clean clothes from Fred's house down on my bed. Fred follows me and Ryan sticks his head in the doorway.

"Wow. Iceland. That's awesome! Was it gorgeous?"

I smile at him. "Ryan, everything about it was breathtaking, but now it is even harder to get ready for school." I say those words as I fondle my necklace.

"You will be fine. Let me know if you need anything though. I will leave you to get yourself together for tomorrow."

"Thanks." He leaves and Fred throws himself on my bed, a king-size thick white wood four-poster bed. Everything is white and a touch of blue. I needed to feel like I was near the ocean.

"Can I stay here tonight?"

"Of course, you don't have to ask."

"Well, your brother is across the hall."

"I slept with you before when he was across the hall. That shit is in the past. I know I haven't laid it out for everyone, but I am also not hiding it."

"I have to leave early tomorrow for the meeting with the lawyer."

"Okay," I say with a smirk. "I will wake you up the best way I know how."

* * *

The sun is just breaking through my bedroom window when I kiss Fred good-bye. He woke me up exactly how one should always wake up on a Monday. Forget something borrowed, something blue, and the old and the new. I prefer the something hard, something fast, something exciting and orgasmic.

He kisses me good-bye while I am still tired and coming down from the paradise he put me in. "I love you, Jellybean. Have a good first day of college. Can't wait to have you back home." He kisses me and leaves. I want to protest and make him stay, but I also want to push him away. I want him to eliminate the demon in our lives that is his wife.

I survive my first day of college. My classes are not what I expected. I sort of hide on the sidelines or perhaps I don't fit in here. It's too soon to tell if it's the school, being a marketing major, the people, or me. I am not looking for a friend, but it sucks not to have one. I never thought returning to Mantoloking would be the highest thought in my head.

I head to the townhouse to get my books for tomorrow, then turn around and hop into my car. I need to see Fred. I didn't realize how out of place I would feel here. The drive is quick and easy. I told him I would be there around six for dinner. I thought I would stay around campus longer, but I couldn't wait to get out of there.

I walk into Fred's house and it is a little too quiet. It gives me chills. I have never come to the house when he wasn't here. He or Gunner is always around, and someone is playing an instrument or the stereo is on. I yell Fred's name. I feel out of place in the place I call home. I can't wait to talk to him about the lawyer today. I don't really want to talk about it, but I want to comfort him. As much as I know he loves me, I know it will be difficult for him to see her. He doesn't have a pre-nuptial agreement, so he has to deal with every asset now, and I know that will be tough. He is an emotional man even if he won't admit it.

I walk upstairs yelling his name; each thump of my foot is followed by silence. My heartbeat becomes more erratic with each step. Our bedroom is empty, but the bathroom door is shut. I knock. "Fred?" Silence. I turn the knob. It's unlocked. I open the door and the world as I know it ends instantly.

Chapter Thirty-Eight
Bloodstream

August 26, 1996

I RUN TO HIM, dropping to my knees. I grab his face and shake him. He is out cold, but he is alive. "Fred, Fred, wake up. Open your eyes." Nothing. I get up to get the phone. I stop dead in my tracks when I see the needle and the heroin on the counter. "Shit." I shake uncontrollably when I pull my cell phone out of my bag.

Gunner answers on the first ring. "Hello?" His voice is as weak as my heart and as frantic as my soul.

"Gunner, it's Fred. He isn't awake. He shot heroin."

He slams the phone and hangs up. I turn mine off and with my shaking hands I grab Fred's face again. I throw cold water on him. I scream. I scream his name. I scream no. I just freakin' scream. My entire body is functioning on adrenaline because according to my mind I am closer to death than he is. My cell rings and makes me jump. I answer it but I can't feel my tongue to say hello.

"Morgan, please tell me he is still breathing," Gunner says.

"Yes, but shallow. I tried everything to wake him," I manage to say through tears.

"I will be there in ten minutes."

"Please, can I call 9-1-1? Gunner, please."

"I'll call. You know CPR?"

"Yes."

"If he stops breathing, do it, until the ambulance gets there."

"Be careful, I can't handle you getting hurt. But hurry."

I hang up and lean my head down to Fred's mouth. His exhale brushes my cheek. His breaths seem to be further apart when I finally hear the door slam, then Gunner's pounding footsteps on the stairs. All the noises are so loud compared to the silence in this bathroom. "Oh, fuck, is he breathing?" he says as he slams the door open.

"I don't know how much longer he has. Go look for the ambulance. Turn the lights on. We need help." Gunner goes downstairs, ten seconds later I feel nothing. I sob one last time before I turn my emotions off to save him. I shake him. I lay him flat and tilt his head, breathing my weak air into him. I press his chest, over and over a little too hard, I am weak and full of hyper nerves. The thunder on the stairs is such a relief. Gunner rips me off Fred and gets me in a tight hold as the paramedics take over.

They have him in the ambulance lightning fast as they pump air into his lifeless body. Gunner lets me go so we can follow them outside, side by side. The ambulance is ready when the EMT yells to me, "You getting in? Hurry."

"No. Gunner, you go. I can't."

"Morgan?" he yells as he walks to the ambulance. "Are you sure?"

"Yes, I will call Beth. What hospital?"

"Ocean," the EMT yells, as the doors slam and my world goes with them.

I walk inside, my legs turned to lead. It hurts to walk. I crave pain. I suddenly require pain to feel alive. I never knew what this feeling was like. I want to scar myself to release the pain. In a flash I understand the pain Gunner felt that sent him to the tattoo shop.

My mind is overwhelmed with questions. Why? Why? Why? is the one playing over and over.

I get my bag and pull Beth's number out of my wallet. I don't know why I carry it around. I liked having it with me after that first time he left me to see her.

I pick up the phone; the dial tone in my ear is numbing. I take a large breath and dial. Three rings later, I die a little, when her nasty mouth says, "Rick, why the hell you calling? You got the point across."

"Beth, it's not Fred," I say, flat, devoid of emotion.

"Oh," she snaps. "Who is this?"

"Morgan."

"Gunner's girlfriend?"

"Did something happen today? Did you see Rick?" Damn that is difficult to say. But if he isn't technically dead he is dead to me. So who cares what I call him now.

"The bastard was going to file for divorce. Even had a damn appointment with the lawyer, but I told him no, no fucking way. I want it all. I will take him for everything and I will make his life hell. I know he is screwing around on me but damn I will take him down, steal everything he loves away. I will find that little bitch he is screwing and show the media what a scumbag he is."

"Well, he doesn't have anyone else in his life, I can promise you that. He made his life hell for himself. I found him unconscious a few minutes ago. He stopped breathing. I had to do CPR until the ambulance arrived. Gunner went with him to Ocean Medical. You are a cold-hearted bitch and he deserves so much more than you, but if you are going to be his wife, you should get over there."

I hang up before I can hear another word from her putrid mouth. I sit frozen. What the hell do I do now? I sit numb and sad and fucking pissed. I want to trash the house or run away.

I walk upstairs. It feels like it takes an hour to force myself to the landing, then as fast as possible I pack everything I want to keep. The rest I throw away. Most of it ends up in the bin at the end of the driveway. Tomorrow I will have to get rid of the car, but right now I have no other option except to drive it to Gunner's. I don't even look back or say goodbye to my home.

I walk up to the front door and for the first time ever I use my key. It's been eight months and two days since he gave it to me and I need it more than I ever needed anything. I put my clothes away in the guest room closest to Gunner's bedroom.

Once all my things are tucked away extra neatly, as if I developed OCD today, I pace the house. Lost. I am lost. I pace his mansion as if it is a million miles long, lost in my mind to the pain I endured today. I learn one cannot walk away from agony.

I wish Gunner would call. I thought he would call the house or my cell by now. I check my cell phone again; he hasn't called. Nothing. I walk upstairs to Gunner's room, stop in the doorway and fall to my knees, my body overwhelmed with tears. The adrenaline is running out, leaving me weaker than I have ever been. Finally, my cell phone rings. My voice is weak when I answer. "Hello." I push the phone into my ear.

"Morgan, he's good. Breathing on his own, but it was touch and go. I thought he was going to die. You should come down. Should I come get you?" He talks fast, unlike words I ever heard from the calm relaxed Gunner I am used too.

"No, no, I never want to see him again. Never."

"Morgan, you don't mean that."

"No, I do. Beth can have him. I'm not strong enough."

My cell battery dies in my hand. I throw it to the floor as if it is the thing in my life that shot up heroin today. I walk into Gunner's bathroom. I take my clothes off and put them in the trashcan. I never want to see them again. I take a quick, scalding hot shower. Still numb, I walk back into Gunner's room. I find a pair of his boxers and a t-shirt in his dresser. I slip them on and crawl in his bed.

I must have fallen asleep because a loud slamming door makes my heart pound. Gunner is yelling my name. "Upstairs," I croak as loud as my tired throat can yell. He comes running into the bedroom. As I sit up he sits down and grabs me tight.

"I couldn't find you." He almost cries as he crushes me against his cold body.

"You told me I was always welcome here. I had the key. I should have gone into a guest bed but I need to feel close to you."

"Morgan, I wouldn't want you anywhere but here. Sorry to scare you. I thought you would stay at Fred's."

"No, I told you no, no more. Never. I moved out. I put all my clothes in your guest room. I don't want to explain it to Ryan. Can you sell my car for me tomorrow? Get me a new one. And I want a new cell phone too. I need help. I need you." I rattle every thought I've had for the past few hours off in ten seconds.

"Morgan. Anything, always. I would do anything for you. I'm so sorry this happened." He pauses and lowers his head. "It's not the first time," he says sadly.

"I figured, given the questions you asked. I knew you had been through it before. I hoped it wasn't with Fred."

"I know, I know. Me too. Let's sleep. We can talk tomorrow."

"Can I stay in here?" I ask, because I know I can't be alone.

"Yes, anything you need."

"Will you stay with me?"

"Yes, yes, anything, Morgan, anything." He gets up fast and takes his jeans off and has on a t-shirt and boxers, like me, as he climbs into his bed. "Can I hold you so you can sleep?" he mumbles while engulfing me in the biggest hug ever.

"Please."

* * *

I wake up and for one second before I remember what happened, I stare at Gunner's ceiling and realize I am far from feeling much of anything. I put my arm over my head, hoping if I can't see I can't feel. It doesn't work.

"You up?" I hear Gunner whisper.

"Unfortunately." I open my eyes and roll over to look at him. He is sitting in his bed with me, reading.

"You didn't have to stay in bed for me."

"I wanted to. I called the hospital and spoke to Beth. He is doing good. She is taking him to rehab in Arizona tomorrow. He is fighting her, saying it was a one-time thing. It probably was, but she is bitchy enough to get him there and it sure can't hurt."

"Okay."

"Do you want to see him before he leaves?"

"No. What are you reading?"

He lifts the book for me to see. *A Son of the Circus,* by John Irving.

"I haven't read it. Any good?"

"I'm enjoying it."

"I thought that huge library was just for looks. I didn't picture you reading over here."

"Oh, what did you picture me doing over here?"

"I don't know. Nothing. Writing maybe."

"I do that a lot too." In an instant I start weeping like a hurt toddler. Gunner puts his book down and pulls me to him.

"Gunner?" I mumble into his shirt.

"What?"

"Do you find comfort with me too or do you just do it to help me?"

"Really, Morgan? You know better. You know no one has ever caressed my soul as you do. You are the only person who has ever brought me comfort."

"I'm messed up, Gunner. I'm so scared."

"I know. I am too. We have to take it one day at a time. You can count on me, Morgan, to always be here."

"I know."

"Let's try to eat something. Then I will go to the hospital. What time do you have class?"

"I have to leave by one thirty."

"Will you be coming back here tonight?"

"My last class doesn't end until nine. I will try to stay there tonight but I have to accept my new place as home."

"Anytime you need to come back, do it, okay?"

"Don't worry, I will be back. You are a part of my soul now too, Gunner. I don't have to stop being your friend just because Fred is a stu-pid fuck."

"Say it again?"

"What?"

"Stupid fuck. I want to hear you curse and be angry. You never curse or say fuck, that's for sure. You are too good."

I laugh. "Thanks for making me laugh. Fred is a stupid fuck." I get up and walk to use the bathroom. I stop in the doorway. "Gunner?"

"Yeah?"

"I am not as good as you think." I shut the door before he can respond.

After my afternoon class, I pick up a sandwich for dinner before head-ing to my three-hour-long philosophy class. It is going to be a long night. I feel sad when class ends; sitting numb inside my head wasn't as bad as I expected. I pull up at the townhouse and Ryan is sitting on the steps with my ex-boyfriend's older brother. This sucks. I get out of Gunner's truck and walk up to them.

"What are you driving?" Ryan says, drooling over Gunner's mas-sive pickup.

"It's Gunner's. I might get one for myself. It sure makes a person feel tougher than they actually are."

"Really, a pickup?" I hear Gunner say, coming up behind me.

"What are you doing here?" I turn and look at him, quite surprised but unable to control my bright smile.

"Just came to see how philosophy went."

"It was very philosophic."

"Gunner, this is Kevin Bailey, Kevin, Gunner Cross."

Kevin shakes his hand. "Yeah, I know. Wow, awesome to meet you."

"Come inside?" I say to Gunner. He follows as I head to the fridge. "Want anything?"

"Water is fine." I grab two waters then he follows me upstairs to my bedroom. I throw by bag on the floor and myself on the bed.

"How are you holding up?" he asks as he lies down next to me.

"Not great, but moving forward."

"Good. So that guy out there, what is he to you? You always try to hide that you know us crazy famous people."

"I know, I'm sorry about that. The underage shit messed with me a lot. Damn, what a joke. I once thought that was one of my biggest problems. Kevin is my ex's older brother. I needed a little rush of good shit, ya know. A little fuck the world."

"I get that. I really get that."

"You leaving soon or staying a while?"

"Got nowhere else to be."

"I am going to shower. Be right back."

I come out of the shower and Gunner is sitting in my bed reading again. He is the most amazing friend I could ever ask for. I never knew a guy who didn't try to get something from a girl and be so attentive. "You are too good to be true, you know that?" I slip a t-shirt on over my towel. Then my underwear and shorts up under my towel. If Gunner has a hidden agenda this will give me some insight. He hasn't said anything. I throw my towel in the laundry basket and climb into my bed next to him.

He still says nothing. I think he is pretending to read, so I continue talking. "Thank you. Whatever the reason you are good to me, I just want you to know how much it means to me. Thank you for always holding me up, Gunner. I didn't know people like you existed. I love you so much for how you care about me. I never felt this protected."

"Morgan, I would do anything for you. What do you want? Anything that will help you through this, just ask."

"I want you to stay with me. Keep me company."

"Easiest thing in the world to do. There is nowhere else I would rather be."

* * *

After class on Wednesday, I head down to Gunner's. I pull into his driveway and my car is gone. It breaks my heart a little, but I have committed to moving forward without Fred and I must go through each step. I can't skip over it.

I head inside and Gunner is outside with Zach. They are so much better with this hell than me. Zach gets up and hugs me, then asks how I am, and I see the sadness and stress on his face.

"Want a drink?" Gunner asks me.

"Not yet, but I have been thinking about it."

"Okay."

"I don't know if I should have alcohol, I mean. He made me so mad and I can't fix it with a drink, but I fucking deserve a drink, right?"

"Yeah," Zach says as he gets up. He brings me a beer. "It will help. You are not going to become an alcoholic. Relax, you do deserve it. Pretty bad week."

"Ya don't say."

"So Gunner said you were brave and knowledgeable the other night."

"Yeah, so?"

"Sorry, he told me how you knew what was happening and knew CPR. Sounds like you have been there before."

"No. Sure you guys have seen a lot more shit than me." We sit in silence. This is awkward so I drink my beer. Gunner is watching me like I will break. "I had a friend, she had a drug problem, freshman year. All I could do was be there if she needed help. I read a lot about different drugs, what they do to you. How to help with an overdose. That kind of shit.

"She was caught with some guys, strung out. She was arrested because they were selling. Her parents sent her away to school after that. They blamed me. I never spoke to her again. I wanted to help and no one would let me. I put myself in some bad situations and no one cared. I should have told my parents but I felt they wouldn't trust me after that, or worse they may have assumed I was doing drugs too. It was bad. I was only fourteen. Basically, I have no tolerance for this shit. I don't want to hear again that I should see him. This is my choice and if I regret it one day it's all on me.

"He was going to leave her finally. He gave me a ring, but he couldn't handle it. I don't want to ever be a burden to anyone. I want it behind me." I talk too fast, but they both let me ramble. I take the necklace off my neck with the ring on it. "Could you put this somewhere safe for me? I will return it one day when I can face him. Thanks for getting rid of the car. I am sorry I did this to you, to your band, sorry I caused this trouble. I need to be alone for a little while." I walk upstairs, my body telling me I am walking the entire Great Wall of China. I take a change of clothes from the guest room, but I shower in Gunner's bedroom. After I shower, I climb into Gunner's bed. I lie here numb, as the sun sets and another day has ended. When the room is dark, I lose it, sobbing uncontrollably.

Minutes after the flood rivers start to drown me, Gunner comes in to hold me. He lets me cry and doesn't try to make me talk about it.

"Sorry to be such a mess. I was mean to you guys too."

"Geez, you were not mean. Morgan, this isn't your fault. You are the best thing that ever happened to him. I wish you would decide to fight for him. I wish you would fight to get him away from Beth, but I accept what you want too. I understand it well. I would do exactly what you are doing. I just wish you wanted to fight more for him."

I say nothing. I just can't be with him. I know I can't. I don't want that life anymore. I let Gunner hold me as I wish for sleep. "You hungry?" he whispers in my ear.

"I don't know. I haven't been able to feel much."

"Let's try to eat, maybe watch a movie. Zach is funny when he is drunk too. We could just watch him."

"Okay."

* * *

Gunner is in the shower when I wake up. I head to the kitchen and find Zach looking tired and sick. I pour myself coffee and consider trying to eat something, but I sit next to Zach instead. "How are you feeling this morning?" I ask him.

"Better than I deserve. You?"

"Better every day, I suppose."

"Morgan, you do know this isn't your fault, right?"

"Maybe, but I was a part of it on some level, and that can't be changed. I should have left and never started anything with him. I mean what sixteen-year-old dates a man she met hours after he got married? It's fucking sick."

"Married?" He chokes on his coffee.

"Yep. Fred married Beth in Vegas last year. I met him later that night. I thought it was fate. I would say I wish it never happened. But then I wouldn't know you and Gunner. And Gunner is a part of me now. I wouldn't trade what I have with him for anything."

"What do you have with him?" He looks at me with a weird expression.

"What do you mean? He is an amazing friend," I say with solid conviction.

"I found it a little odd that you went to bed with him last night."

"I know, it is odd, but he makes me feel safe. He is always there to help me, hold me, love me. Maybe it's wrong, but in this hell, he is my heaven."

"I didn't think you were the kind to work your way through a band, but it was weird seeing you in there. I was drunk, but still it didn't look right. I see the way you two are together. It is different. It is like you are the only person he lets in and he has been in need of a good friend for a long time."

"Me too."

Gunner walks in. I can tell he was listening but I don't call him out on it. "What time do you have to be at school?"

"I had one class today but it's been cancelled. Tomorrow I have to be back by eleven."

"Okay, your new wheels will be here in the morning. I didn't cancel the party. Should I?"

"No, I will be here. I might not be fun to be with, so maybe I will stay upstairs. Kelly will be here and I need to see her." I don't know how I will survive the party or telling Kelly about Fred. I keep reminding myself that with each step it will get better. Even if each lift of my foot feels like it's stuck in cold wet sand. I need to find a way to fill in all the space where my brain starts to control me. The spaces that Fred used to fill are now ripped open.

I will always love Fred. I will always love the beach. Lilacs will be bittersweet every time I smell one. I carry the weight of every lilac he gave me as if it turned to sand. Unfortunately, I know with absolute certainty that lilacs cannot grow in the sand. The environment is too unstable.

Acknowledgments

Thank you to my parents and grandparents for giving me the ability to see the world the way I do. They shaped me into the person I am by allowing me to be myself.

To my husband and children for helping me find time to write this book. Also for the times they didn't. It was those times that made the desire to get back to work even stronger.

I would like to acknowledge everyone who answered my questions big and small to help me finish *Lilac Sand*. My family and friends who endured reading it prior to the book being edited, especially Allison Irwin. A friendship formed by our mutual love of books and book boyfriends. I will always be glad she was the first person to read *Lilac Sand*. Her countless hours of reviewing my words are priceless.

A world of thanks to my editor, Elizabeth Bruno. Her patience and ability to teach me so much in such a short time have been invaluable. Also the many editors that I requested a sample edit from. The knowledge I acquired in finalizing this novel was an education in itself. I am grateful that everyone I contacted in this field has been so insightful and helpful. It has made this journey simply thrilling.

I would also like to thank everyone who has the talent to make music. Music is involved in about half my daily emotions and without it I would never have been able to create these characters or this story. Each chapter title of this book is a song title because I needed to add some of the music I listened to while writing it. Those who inspired me most include, Matt Nathanson, The Civil Wars, Chase Rice, Richard Marx, The Veronicas, and Bon Jovi.

Thanks to my cats, Jambalaya, Lefty, and Linguini, for being the perfect companions while an introvert writes.

About the Author

Tara Jenkinson Cignarella lives in New Jersey with her husband, daughter, and son. A graduate of the Freeman School of Business at Tulane University she recently found a passion for words. *Lilac Sand* is her first novel.

Made in the USA
San Bernardino, CA
12 January 2017